THE PHOBIA OF RENEGADE X

CHELSEA M. CAMPBELL

1st edition published by Golden City Publishing, 2017

Copyright © 2017 Chelsea M. Campbell
www.chelseamcampbell.com

All rights reserved. No part of this publication may be reproduced, stored in a retrieval system, or transmitted, in any form or by any means, electronic, mechanical, photocopying, or otherwise, without the prior permission of the publisher and copyright owner.

ISBN: 978-0-9898807-8-7

Books by Chelsea M. Campbell

Renegade X
The Rise of Renegade X
The Trials of Renegade X
The Haunting of Renegade X
The Betrayal of Renegade X
The Torment of Renegade X
The Phobia of Renegade X

Dragonbound
Fire & Chasm
Starlight
Growing Up Dead
Harper Madigan: Junior High Private Eye

DEDICATION

TO THE YOUTUBERS, MUSICIANS, COMEDIANS, HOSTS OF LATE-NIGHT TV, SITCOM WRITERS, NOVELISTS, AND MAKERS OF BBC RADIO DRAMAS WHOSE WORKS HAVE HELPED ME THROUGH THE HARD TIMES AND MADE THE GOOD TIMES EVEN BETTER.

THE PHOBIA OF RENEGADE X

CHAPTER 1

"**R**iley got the go-ahead to stop wearing his walking cast," Sarah says on the phone. "You know what that means." She sounds way too excited about that.

I lean against the kitchen counter. "Yeah, but I *really* don't need to hear about your sex life."

"That's not what I meant." She hesitates. "Not that you can't still have sex with a cast on."

"Wow, Sarah. What did I *just* say?"

"I have to hear about your sex life all the time. And I didn't mean that we… It's none of your business."

And I'd like to keep it that way. "I won't be able to use the elevator with him at school anymore, but other than that, I don't see how this affects me." Except that I do. Or, at least, I know how Sarah wants it to.

"We're going on superhero missions again, Damien. Or should I say Renegade? We're going to have to come up with a code name for Riley. I've been thinking about it for months, but I haven't found the right one yet. What do you think about the Invisible Tangent?"

"Sarah, I don't—"

"I know, I know. His superpower probably shouldn't be in his name—it's too obvious."

"I just think—"

"It should probably be something that goes with our names, though. So everyone knows we're a team. But I guess it's not something we have to come up with right now. And I haven't even told Riley my ideas yet, so—"

"*Sarah.* Will you let me finish?"

"Renegade X, the Cosine Kid, and…?"

I pace back and forth in front of the fridge, trying to figure out the best way to say this. "Riley might not want to go on a mission, like, the moment he gets his cast off."

There's a pause, then, "Why? You mean, like, because he's still doing physical therapy? Because his doctor said he's progressing nicely and should be able to do normal activities again."

The TV's on in the living room, set to the news. The rest of the family's watching as the city takes down a few statues from the Heroes' Walk in Golden City Park. They must have gotten to Helen's—my stepmom's—because someone turns the TV up. The news reporter calls it a "solemn day for heroism" and says that "this marks the end of an era."

I wince a little at that, because I may have had something to do with it. Maybe a lot to do with it.

"Sarah… he had to have his leg screwed back together."

"I just told you, the doctor said everything looks good. He's going to be fine."

"Yeah, but…" But the ceiling caved in on him, and he almost died, and she's not the one who found him like that or who heard him screaming. Who still hears it. My heart races at the memory, and little zaps of lightning run up my back as I start to relive it. "It was kind of big, what happened. There were heroes *shooting* at him." Because of me. Because he's my friend, and they knew that. And if me and Amelia hadn't found him, they would have come back and finished him off.

"Don't worry," Sarah says. "I'm planning something light for this first mission. There won't be anyone shooting at us. Well, maybe one person, but that's it."

"I think we should wait."

"We've waited long enough. With me going on hiatus and then Riley breaking his leg, it's been almost eight months since we went on patrols. And that was without Riley. This is the first time the three of us have gotten to work together."

"He might not be ready. So don't be disappointed if—"

"*He* might not be, or *you* might not be?"

"That's not what I said."

"Riley's the one who got hurt, and he's fine."

I stay quiet, considering that. She's right—compared to his injuries, I barely got scratched. But I don't know if *fine* is the word I'd use to describe either of us.

"You guys have had two and a half months to get ready while his leg healed," Sarah goes on, "and you haven't even gotten to do anything for school." She means because both of us ended up having to do the paperwork-only alternative assignment. "It'll be good to get back into fieldwork."

"I..." I want to believe that. I want to believe that *so badly*. "Yeah, you're right, Sarah. Of course it will."

"And we won't be doing fieldwork right this second."

"Okay. Good."

"Because it's only Tuesday and our mission isn't until Saturday evening."

"Great." That's, like, so much time. I don't know what I was even worried about.

My half sister Amelia storms into the kitchen. She glares at me as she shoves a popcorn packet into the microwave.

"It'll be fine," Sarah says. "You'll— Heraldo, no! Get down from there! Damien? I have to go—Heraldo gets antsy if he doesn't get his walk on time, and we should have left fifteen minutes ago. And don't worry— everything's going to be great."

She hangs up.

Amelia's watching me, her nostrils flaring in and out. "I hope you're happy. Mom's been in the Heroes' Walk my *whole life*."

I slip my phone into my pocket, even though part of me kind of wants to pretend Sarah's still on the line, so I can ignore what Amelia just said. "I didn't want this to happen."

"But it's your fault."

Not directly, but I was a spokesperson for the Truth, my grandpa's villain organization, and I did help stand up for villain rights. To the point that now everyone's questioning the League's past deeds—or at least what's left of the League, since it's not exactly up to its former glory—and how they've treated villains.

"It's your fault," Amelia says again, studying my face, "but you don't care. You didn't even watch the news with us."

"Why would I want to do that?" So they could all gawk at me and shake their heads, like I caused this on purpose? "I don't get why *you guys* watched it."

"Mom earned that statue. And now they just took it away, like everything she did doesn't matter anymore."

"I don't know what you want me to say. I can't change what happened, and it's not like I went down there and pushed her statue over myself or anything."

Her popcorn starts popping. It sounds like tiny explosions. "That's not how they did it. They saved it, so they could put it in a museum."

I shrug. "Then it's still around. I don't see the problem."

She gapes at me. "Being in the Heroes' Walk is a huge honor. Mom still deserves to be there!"

"Why? Because she killed villains?!" I don't mean to sound angry when I say that. It just slips out.

"Only the really bad ones."

That was Helen's job. She assassinated villains for the League. And yeah, some of them probably deserved it, but that doesn't mean the League should have gotten to decide that.

I clench my fists. "If a villain killed heroes—but, you know, only the 'really bad ones'—you wouldn't think taking down their statue was so tragic."

"Um, it's called the *Heroes'* Walk for a reason. Villains can't have statues in it."

"That's kind of my point."

"And there *aren't* really bad heroes."

I stare at her. "Amelia, how can you say that? You were *there*, at that gala. You saw what those heroes did. You *know* what they did to Riley!"

The popping in the microwave slows way down, but she doesn't tell it to stop like you're supposed to. Instead, she gives me this defiant look. "Those heroes were bad, but they weren't *really* bad. They were just confused. And they weren't anything like the villains my mom had to deal with."

"Deal with?!"

She rolls her eyes, like I'm the one being unreasonable. "She risked her life to make the world a better place. That hasn't changed, so her statue being in the Heroes' Walk shouldn't have changed, either."

"I never said it should have."

"But it's, like, the most devastating thing that's happened to our family, and you don't even care."

I raise my eyebrows at her. I'm pretty sure me coming to live with them was more devastating. Or when the whole city hated Gordon because of me. "It's not a big deal."

"Yes, it is!" Amelia shouts. She practically tears open the microwave door, almost hitting me with it, and snatches out her bag of popcorn.

Someone clears their throat, and we both look up.

Helen's standing at the entrance to the kitchen. Her face is kind of blotchy and her eyes maybe look wet, but it's hard to tell. "Everything okay in here?"

I didn't notice her come in, so I don't know how long she's been standing there. How much did she hear? Dread twists in my stomach, even though I didn't say anything that wasn't true.

Amelia takes a deep breath. "Everything's fine. I was just getting the popcorn."

"We're watching a movie," Helen tells me. "If you want to—"

"He *doesn't*," Amelia says, grabbing a giant bowl out of the cupboard. "He didn't care about watching the news with us—he doesn't care about watching a movie."

Helen gives me a questioning look, like she doesn't believe that.

But Amelia's made it clear that I'm the last person she wants around right now. Helen must not have heard what I said about her, or she'd probably feel the same way. And for all I know, the rest of the family was offended by my absence, too.

And even if they weren't? They're all upset about this statue thing, and I'm not. It's my fault it happened, and it doesn't even mean anything to me. Not like it does to them.

I don't belong here right now. I get that, even without Amelia glaring at me.

And even though Helen can probably tell that I'm making this up, I force a smile and say, "Can't—I already have plans. I'm going over to Riley's."

CHAPTER 2

I bring my stuff to stay the night, even though it's a Tuesday and I didn't even tell Riley I was coming over. But I don't need to.

Zach answers the door. He's Riley's brother and a year younger than us. He'll be starting at Heroesworth in the fall. He's also Amelia's boyfriend, thanks to my excellent matchmaking skills. Not that they have any idea I set them up, but still.

He grins when he sees me, then motions for me to come in. "Riley doesn't have to wear his cast anymore."

"So I heard."

Their mom pokes her head out of the kitchen. "Is that Damien? Has he had dinner?" Then, to me, "Have you had dinner?"

Their house smells like spaghetti, and my stomach rumbles a little, even though technically I did have dinner. I just didn't eat very much of it, what with everyone else at the table acting like someone was about to die—and maybe like I was the executioner—and me not wanting to be there any longer than I had to.

"I'll make you a plate," she says, before I even have a chance to answer.

I don't argue with her.

"I heard about your mom's statue," Zach says.

"My stepmom, you mean."

"Amelia texted me the whole time. She said you didn't watch it with them."

I shrug.

"It wasn't really your fault, though." He glances back and forth, like he's afraid Amelia might somehow be lurking nearby and hear him. "You didn't do anything wrong."

I want to argue with him, because I'm pretty sure I did *a lot* of things wrong, but he looks so sincere about it, and... Honestly? It feels good to have someone on my side, even if I think he's being naive. "Thanks, Zach."

Their mom brings out a plate of spaghetti for me, and we all sit down at the dining table, even though I'm the only one eating.

"Zach, go tell your brother Damien's here," their mom says.

Zach turns in his chair toward the hallway and shouts, "Riley, Damien's here!"

"I know!" Riley calls back. He joins us a few moments later. "Hey," he says, acknowledging me as he sits down.

I nod at his leg, which is indeed cast-free now. "Congrats," I tell him while slurping spaghetti into my mouth.

"Thanks. I still have a few more weeks of physical therapy, but the doctor said everything looks good and that my life can basically get back to normal."

Normal, right. Whatever that means.

Their mom's watching me, concern creasing her forehead. "Damien, how are you holding up?"

For a second, I think she means because of what happened at the gala, back when Riley broke his leg and everything kind of fell apart. But then I realize she's talking about Helen's statue. Not that those topics aren't unrelated. "It's like Zach said, it wasn't my fault."

"It must be tough right now, though. For your family."

I think about how red Helen's face was earlier, how much it looked like she'd been crying, or like she'd been trying really hard not to. Amelia's been pissed at me for a couple weeks now, ever since she found out this statue thing was happening. Gordon was quiet about it. In the days leading up to this, and tonight all through dinner, before the news was on, he was just *quiet*. He didn't get mad at me. He didn't blame me, like Amelia did. But he didn't tell me it was alright, either. And as for Alex and Jess, well... Alex is nine and plenty old enough to understand what happened and to hate me for it, though I don't *think* he does, and Jess is only three and could care less about the Heroes' Walk, so at least there's that.

"Helen's statue's been in the Heroes' Walk for eighteen years," I say, "so, yeah, that's been kind of tough for them."

"And for you?"

I try and pick up the one last noodle on my plate, but it

keeps slipping off my fork. "It was just a statue."

Riley frowns at that. "X, you know that's not true."

"Okay, fine. It was a statue she got *for killing villains.*" Specifically for killing my girlfriend's grandfather. I mean, he's one of the villains who actually deserved it—even Kat's family thinks he was bad news—but murdering my future grandfather-in-law still hits a little close to home. Especially since it's made Helen more than a little prejudiced against Kat, though she's come around and at least lets her in the house now. "She 'took care of' villains that the League decided needed to be put down, the city built her a freaking *statue* for it, and now that they've realized murdering villains isn't something to be honored for, they took it down? Big deal. Except they didn't even take it down, they just moved it, so everyone can still go to a museum and see what a shining example of heroism she is. And maybe it's my fault that the city's re-evaluating Helen's past deeds, but it's not my fault that she killed villains before I was even born."

Their mom blinks at me.

Zach swallows.

"See?" Riley says. "It's not just a statue."

Their mom pats my hand as she gets up from the table and shoots me a warm-but-still-kind-of-concerned smile. "You make sure your dad knows you're staying over, okay? Or if you want me to call him—"

"No, it's okay. I texted him on the way here." When it was already too late for him to try and convince me to stay. Because I didn't want to be convinced, and because I didn't want to know for sure that he wouldn't try. Maybe the family really is better off without me there tonight, reminding them of everything that's gone wrong lately. And that might not be a secret or anything, but *knowing* that Gordon thinks so, too? That my own dad doesn't even want me around right now? I don't really want to think about it. So I texted him when I was well on my way here, saying I was spending the night at Riley's and not to worry about me.

He texted back and said, *Okay. See you tomorrow.*

That's it.

"Well," Riley's mom says, "you know you're welcome here anytime."

"Thanks, Mrs. Perkins."

"I mean it. Now, you boys don't stay up too late. You've got school tomorrow."

X·X·X

"Okay," Zach says, "now you get to move your werewolf three spaces and take"—he pauses to glance at the game manual—"two elf coins and one... dollop of slime?" He makes a face, then roots around in the box. "That must be these."

I take the two cardboard coins from him and the plastic chunk that's apparently supposed to be slime. It looks kind of like a chocolate chip, only green and translucent.

All three of us are sitting on the floor of Zach's room, with the board spread out between us. The game's called *Fantastic—the Fantasy Epic You Can Play at Home*, and Zach got it used a few weeks ago. He said it's only supposed to take an hour or two to play, but I swear it took him almost that long just to set it up.

Riley yawns. "That's the end of your turn. And I don't need a code name."

I was telling him what Sarah said earlier, about trying to come up with a name for him. "Yes, you do, Perkins. You can't not have a name." I hand him the dice so he can take his turn.

"Wait," Zach says, frowning at the rule book. "If you have any slime dollops at the end of your turn, then you have to roll a die, and if it's higher than three, then you have to give the person to your right the chance to buy it from you, for ten elf coins."

"What? Why would anyone want to buy my slime?"

"It's right here, see?" He tries to hand me the rule book, but I don't take it. Mostly because I don't care what the reason is, but also because the book is, like, eighty pages long with really tiny print, and I don't want to bother.

"Perkins, do you even have ten elf coins?"

Riley squints at his tiny pile of them. "I have four. And I don't want to buy your slime either way, so I'll just roll. Okay, Zach? *And*," he adds as he shakes the dice in his hand before tossing them on the board, "I didn't mean I'm not going to use a code name. I meant I already have one."

"You rolled two fives," Zach says, consulting the rule book again. "That means you get to take one free weapon card from the pile, but you can't play it until the end of your turn."

Riley picks up a card that has a picture of a sword on it,

along with some numbers and symbols in the corner.

"You don't have a code name," I tell him.

"I haven't told Sarah yet, so I don't know if she'll approve it. I mean, it's just an idea I had. I was still thinking it over, so—"

"Just get on with it."

"Secant."

"What?"

Riley clears his throat. "Secant. You know, like, *see can't?* Because I can turn invisible?"

I blink at him. "I hate you."

He grins. "You think Sarah will like it?"

"I think Sarah's going to kill you for thinking of it first. But yeah, she'll like it."

"It's still your turn," Zach tells him. "You rolled a ten, but you didn't move your goblin yet. You should be over here"—he moves Riley's character for him—"and then you get a blue card, which says you eat a bad gingerbread house, so you have to roll to see how much damage you take. Oh, wait, *unless* you have a star talisman card, to ward against witches, or six slimes you can trade in to counteract the food poisoning. That must be what the slimes are for. But you don't have any of that stuff, so... Roll one of the dice."

It's been less than ten minutes of actual playing, but I already hate this game. I share a look with Riley, who I'm pretty sure feels the same way. I'm also pretty sure that neither of us has the heart to tell Zach yet.

"I got a three," Riley says.

"Then you get these." Zach hands him what looks like

three red plastic pebbles. "Damage tokens. And now you decide if you want to attack anybody else, since you have that sword card."

"Pass. Your turn, Zach."

Zach rolls the dice.

"So," Riley says to me, "did Sarah mention when she thought the three of us might start going on missions?"

"Saturday."

"Saturday...?"

"As in, *this* Saturday."

Riley's eyes go wide. "But I only just got the okay to stop wearing my cast. That's not much time. Did you tell her we have our superpower tests on Friday?"

"No, because that's going to take, like, five seconds. All you have to do is turn invisible, and I just have to use my lightning. We do that all the time."

Zach sighs. "You guys are so lucky."

I raise my eyebrows at him. "Why? Because we have to take a test?"

"No. Because you get to do fieldwork."

"Not at school we don't. Not anymore." Not until next year, anyway.

"You still got to, and now you're doing stuff outside of school." He moves his character a few spaces across the board and takes a green card from the pile. "It just seems so cool."

Me and Riley exchange another look.

Zach seems to catch that he's said something wrong. He looks back and forth between us. "I mean, not *cool*. But exciting? I know you got hurt, but you're better now, and because of you guys, nobody died at the gala. It was heroic, and all I did was warn some people about it. Amelia did most of the talking, *and* she ended up helping you guys." His shoulders deflate. "I just want to be *doing* something. Something that matters."

"Warning people did matter," Riley tells him.

"And," I add, "I'm the reason people almost died there. So, cleaning up my own mess—no, having to get my friends help me clean up my own mess and putting them in danger—doesn't count as doing something." And it certainly wasn't heroic.

Zach still seems unconvinced. "I can't wait to start at Heroesworth. That's all. And maybe, after I have some experience, maybe..." He stares down at the board, not looking at either of us. "Maybe I can join your group?"

"Zach," Riley says, half scolding him for even asking.

Zach glances up at me real quick, then away again.

I open my mouth to say something, but nothing comes out. It's not that I don't want him to join our group. I'm just not sure I actually want there to be a group, what with the idea of going out on missions again sounding like the worst idea in the world right now. Plus, if Zach joins, then Amelia's going to want to join, and that is *not* happening.

"Okay," Zach says after a while, sounding totally defeated. "I get it."

"It's a long way in the future," I tell him. "And it's complicated."

"I know you already have someone who can turn invisible, but I could still be useful." He clenches his fists.

"Zach," Riley says, "this isn't a job interview. And like Damien said, it's a long way off. Who knows what's going to happen?"

"I do," Zach mutters. "I'm not going to get to join, because you guys just see me as your stupid little brother."

Riley scowls at him. "Finish your turn. It's getting late."

Zach looks hurt by that, and like he has something to say to it, but whatever it is, he swallows it down. "The card I got says I run into a band of elves in the woods." He rolls one of the dice. "I take six damage." He reaches into the box, but only comes back with three damage tokens. "Man, the rest of these are missing."

"You have more," Riley says.

Zach glares at him. "I *know* that. I have extras," he tells me, "in case of emergencies like this one. They're on my dresser. You're closest," he adds, when I don't get up right away.

"What? Perkins can't get them?" I look over at Riley. "Is your leg broken or something?"

Riley rolls his eyes at me. "I am *not* going to miss that."

I get up to get the extra damage tokens, but only because I feel bad about not telling Zach he could join our group. He's not just Riley's little brother—he's my friend—but telling him that would sound stupid. And kind of patronizing. Even if it's the truth.

And maybe I really don't want him to join. It's bad enough that Riley and Sarah are going to be in danger—I don't need to add Zach to that list.

The top of his dresser's covered in junk. There are a couple of board games stacked on one side—that are shoved so far over they look like they're about to fall off—and there are a bunch of mini-figurines tangled up in a pile of string, some loose change, a battered fantasy novel with three bookmarks sticking out of it, a couple markers, his ticket stub from *Heroes on Ice*, and a pink sweet-sixteen bracelet that was a party favor at Amelia's birthday.

"I don't see any damage tokens."

"Oh, right. Top drawer. They kept falling off and spilling all over, so I put them there for safekeeping."

I expect his top drawer to be socks—and hopefully not underwear—but it's actually just more junk. Better organized junk, but still. There's more gaming supplies, including a baggie full of damage tokens. Right next to—

"Actually, wait," Zach says, suddenly jumping up and sounding super nervous, "maybe I should—"

Right next to a box of *condoms*.

Zach must notice the way my shoulders go stiff, because he doesn't finish that sentence.

My blood runs cold, and I feel really sick. "What the hell, Zach?!"

Riley wrinkles his eyebrows. "What's going on?"

My hand shakes as I hold up the box to show him. I glare at Zach. "You and my *sister*?!"

"Whoa," Riley says.

Zach swallows. "We haven't done anything!" He glances at Riley, then at me. "I mean, not yet."

"Not yet? Not *yet*?!"

"Hey," Riley warns, scowling at me. "You want to keep it down? We don't need Mom coming in here and seeing those."

I shove the box back in the drawer and slam it closed, despite what Riley just said about staying quiet.

"Amelia doesn't even know I got them," Zach whispers. "They're for just in case."

"Just in case you want to have sex with my sister?!" I run a hand through my hair. "I can't believe this."

Riley gets up from the floor and sits down on the bed. "Come on, X. It's not that bad."

"Yeah," Zach says. "You have sex with Kat. And Riley has sex with Sarah."

"*Zach.*" Riley's face turns red.

"Well, you do. And Amelia's my girlfriend. I really like her, and we've been going out for over six months."

"Great. You should get a certificate of achievement." I say that through clenched teeth. Little sparks of lightning run up my spine. It's making the hair on the back of my neck stand on end. "But you and Amelia? Doing *that*?" I shudder, pushing the image out of my head. "Not happening."

"But… But… You don't get to decide that." Zach looks to his brother for help. "Tell him he doesn't get to decide that."

Riley sighs. "He doesn't, but… I don't know, Zach. You're kind of young."

Zach screws up his eyebrows. "I'll be sixteen in two weeks! You guys were both sixteen."

True, but it wasn't, like, the day I turned sixteen. "It's not about how old you are," I tell him. "You're *not* sleeping with her."

He sucks in a deep breath. "Why?"

Um, for all the obvious reasons? Like that I don't want him to? "You're not ready. *Amelia's* not ready."

"You don't know that. And you don't get to say what we're—"

"She's my little sister!"

Zach stares at me, hurt flashing across his face. "And I'm just Riley's little brother, right?"

"I didn't mean it like that."

"Yes, you did. That's how you guys think of me. You never trust me with anything important, you don't want me to join your group, and... and it's obvious that you guys didn't want to play this game with me. But you did it anyway, to humor me, like I'm some baby or something."

"Come on, Zach," Riley says. "Don't be like that."

"Like what? Like someone who tells the truth? If you guys had said you didn't like the game, we could have played something else, or just hung out. I wouldn't have cared. But instead, you treat me like a little kid. But I'm only a year younger than you guys. I'm starting at Heroesworth next year. I almost have my driver's license, I already have my superpower, and in two weeks, I'll have an *H* on my thumb."

"None of that makes me okay with you sleeping with her."

"We haven't done anything! I don't know if we even *are* going to do anything. But... I thought I was your friend."

"You are." At least, as long as he keeps his hands off of Amelia.

"Then why am I not good enough?"

"I didn't... It's not about that."

He folds his arms, hunching his shoulders. "I don't need your permission. I didn't ask for it. I didn't even ask for your opinion!"

"Yeah, and I didn't ask to find a box of condoms that you plan to use with my *sister*. You can't expect me to be okay with that."

"This is *my* room. It's getting late, and I think you should go."

"You what?"

"Zach, wait," Riley says. "Don't you think you're—"

"That means *both* of you." Zach holds open his door. He looks pissed, but also like he might be about to cry. "I thought you guys liked hanging out with me. I thought we were friends. But you don't see me as anything more than a little kid, and if that's how it is, then I guess I was wrong about us being friends. So just go already."

CHAPTER 3

"So," Kat says on the phone Wednesday night, "Prom's only a couple weeks away." She means the one at Heroesworth, since the one at Vilmore is only for seniors. "What are we wearing?" I can hear the smile in her voice.

"Um." I'm in my room, lying on my bed. I sit up. "It's Prom, so I'll be in a tux, and I assume you'll be in a dress."

"Come on, you know what I mean. We wore our bathing suits to Homecoming."

"Right." And look how that turned out. "I thought we'd keep it low key."

There's a pause. "You're serious?"

"Kat, I blew up the roof at Homecoming. I got expelled. Do you really want a repeat performance?"

"That didn't have anything to do with what we were *wearing*. Sarah was crazy—*she's* the one who freaked out and tried to kill us. So. There's nothing to worry about this time."

Except that I don't want everyone staring at me. It was fun at Homecoming. It doesn't feel fun now. "Riley and Sarah will be dressed normal. Maybe I just want to blend in."

"You? *You* just want to blend in? If I'm talking to a pod person, I want you to know that you're not doing a very good job of impersonating Damien."

"Ha ha. I'm not a pod person."

"That's just what a pod person would say. The theme is *A Night to Remember.* That's practically screaming for us to do something memorable."

"How do you know what the theme is?" I didn't even know that.

"Sarah told me." She says that grudgingly, like she doesn't want to admit she was talking to Sarah. They're not exactly friends, though at least Kat doesn't completely hate her now. "She mentioned doing a group dinner before the dance."

"Like, a double date?"

"More like a triple date. Amelia and Zach will be there, too."

Great. "You know, Kat, maybe we should just skip dinner."

"What? Why?"

"Because..."

"I know I've had my differences with Sarah, and she's not exactly my favorite person, but I think I can get through *dinner*."

"It's not that. But me and Zach, we sort of—"

A knock on my door interrupts me.

"Hold on," I tell Kat.

The floorboards creak beneath me as I make my way over to the door. I've lived in the attic for eight months now, and I *still* feel like the floor's going to fall out from under me every time I take a step. It doesn't feel as bad as when I first moved to the attic, but living up here and having to face the rickety stairs every day isn't exactly doing anything to help my fear of heights, like Gordon seemed to think it would.

I open the door to find Amelia.

She wrinkles her nose at me. "What did you say to Zach?"

"Nothing. Why? What did *he* say?"

"He was supposed to come over tomorrow afternoon, but then he asked if you were going to be home. I said probably, and he said then he wasn't coming over. So, what did you say to him?" She folds her arms. "And don't say *nothing*, because I know you did."

"We had a disagreement."

"About what?"

"It doesn't matter."

"Yes, it does. My boyfriend won't come over to my house now, because of you. It's like you're *trying* to ruin my life."

"Well, you know, Amelia, they say to play to your strengths, and ruining your life is the one thing I'm really good at."

She glares at me. "First Mom's statue, and then you tell my boyfriend he can't come over anymore?"

"I never said that."

"I thought you guys were friends, and now—" Her phone rings. She checks the screen, sighs, and says, "I have to take this," before wandering off to her room.

I shut my door.

"What's going on?" Kat asks when I get back to my bed and pick up my phone. "Are you fighting with *Zach*?"

"Not exactly." I pace across the room, sticking to the path with the floorboards that creak the least.

"Damien, you love Zach."

"I don't— I do not love Zach."

"Yes, you do. You guys never even disagree on anything, and now he won't come over? What the hell happened?"

"You want to know what happened?" I glance over my shoulder at the wall to Amelia's room, as if I'll be able to tell whether or not she can hear me. I keep my voice low. "I found condoms. Zach has condoms in his *room*."

"Wow. That's... Okay, that's kind of a surprise, but, I mean, so do you."

"I know that, but I'm not planning to use them with my *sister*." I hesitate, hearing how that sounds. "You know what I mean."

"Damien, you set them up. What did you think was going to happen?"

"I wasn't thinking that far ahead. And it's Amelia—I figured they'd break up way before this." What with her sparkling personality and all.

"Well, whether it was with him or someone else, it was going to happen eventually."

"It hasn't happened yet. She doesn't even know he has

them."

"Then why do you sound like the crazy parent in an after-school special?"

"Because. It's weird to think of them like that. They're supposed to stay innocent."

She snorts. "Yeah, right. Listen, Damien, I have to go soon, but I wanted to ask you something first. You remember my friend June? You met her at my dorm a couple months ago."

"Yeah, of course I remember." Kat had a bunch of friends over, and we all played Monopoly, and then June told me about how her mom had been abducted and tortured by the League. She said her mom cried when she saw me in that broadcast for the Truth, and she thanked me for speaking out for villain rights.

"She started a villain rights group here at Vilmore. Because of you. What you did really inspired her." Kat pauses, waiting for me to say something to that.

"Oh."

"Damien, this was really hard for her. You know what happened to her mom, right? June doesn't talk about it much, or at least she didn't. Now she's telling everybody what happened, so other people like her won't feel so alone. It's not just about villain rights—it's kind of a support group for everyone who's gone through something like she and her mom did. It's a big deal, and she wouldn't have done it if it wasn't for you."

"Okay." I know I'm supposed to feel happy about that. I'm supposed to feel like I've done a good thing, inspiring June to help people. But I don't feel anything. "Good for her?"

Kat sighs. "June wants you to come speak at one of their meetings. It would really mean a lot to her."

I swallow. "Kat, I... I don't do that anymore."

"It wouldn't be for the Truth. This has nothing to do with them. It's just about villain rights, and you still believe in that, right?"

"Yeah, of course."

"Then I don't see the problem."

"I don't want to speak. I mean, not in public." That sounds like just about the worst thing right now. Second only to going on missions again.

"It's not really that public," Kat says. "June said her group has about twenty people in it, but if you're going to speak, she thinks more like fifty will show up."

It's not that many. I mean, I've done stuff way more public than that. But even though it's only fifty people, it feels like it would be the whole world watching. Because it would be. Someone would have their phone out, recording the whole thing. Probably more than one person. There'd be another video of me online, telling everyone what I think. Cold dread creeps up my spine and fills my stomach. "Kat, I... I can't."

"What? What do you mean, you can't? They meet every week. You can figure out a time that works for you."

"You know that's not it."

"Damien."

"I told the world my opinion, when I was a spokesperson for the Truth. And look how that turned out."

"Uh, yeah, villains are finally being heard."

"The whole city's messed up because of me. A *lot* of people almost died. Helen's statue got taken out of the Heroes' Walk. The League kind of fell apart, and... Okay, I was never pro League or anything." I pretty much hated them, even before I found out how they really treat villains. "And they're the ones who lied to everyone and did all those bad things. I just helped bring it all to light. But... all this upheaval still feels like my fault. Everyone hates me for it. And Gordon's not in the League anymore, because of me. And Riley got seriously hurt. He's my best friend, and the League almost killed him. He wanted to join up with them his whole life, but one glimpse of him with me..." I trail off.

Kat's quiet for a second, taking all that in. Then she says, "That doesn't mean you didn't do the right thing."

I shake my head, even though she can't see me through the phone. When I speak, my voice is tight. "I don't know anymore. How could it have been the right thing if all those bad things happened because of it?"

"Bad things were already happening—people just didn't know about them. Now at least things have a chance to change."

I don't say anything to that.

"Damien, I'm worried about you. You're fighting with *Zach*, and you just want to blend in at Prom? And you don't want to speak to a private group about villain rights? Even if what you did caused some upheaval and people are upset about it, June's group isn't. *They're* not hating on you—they think you're awesome."

"Is it so bad if I just want to lay low for a change? I don't always have to be in the spotlight. And maybe June's group thinks I'm awesome, but that doesn't mean that they *should*. I lied to everyone. I didn't mean to, and I didn't know I was doing it. But Grandpa told me what to say, and I said it, and I *believed* in it. Because of that, people listened to me, and they really shouldn't have, because it almost got them killed. Maybe standing up for villain rights and making my opinions public was technically the 'right' thing to do, but it feels like it just ruined everything for everyone I care about, and it put a lot of people in danger. So, tell June I'm sorry, but I'm done with that."

"But, Damien—"

"I'm sorry, Kat." I really am. "But I just can't do it."

CHAPTER 4

"We're thinking of that Italian place on Fifth," Riley says, "but so is everyone else, so we have to make a reservation." He's talking about where we're going to eat dinner before Prom.

It's Friday morning, before class. There's a table set up in the lunchroom, where they're handing out schedules for the first-year superpower tests we're taking today. Me and Riley are waiting in line, except nobody wants to stand near me, so there's a gap before and after us. "I don't know, Perkins. Spaghetti sauce and formal wear don't exactly mix."

"Sarah told me that Kat told her that you told Kat that you're not sure if you're coming. So, are you?"

"Am I what?" I lean out past the line for a second, to see how far we have. There are about a dozen people still ahead of us.

"Are you and Kat coming to dinner? Because I need to know if the reservation should be for two people or four."

"Not six?"

"Zach and Amelia are going with some of her friends. He's still pissed at us. Well, mostly at you."

I'm not exactly Amelia's favorite person right now, either. "We'll be there. And... make the reservation for six. Just in case."

"All right, I— Wait." He narrows his eyes at me. "What are you going to wear?"

"Not swim trunks, if that's what you're thinking." I roll my eyes at him. The line moves forward a little.

"Okay, good, because—"

"I thought I'd just go with, like, a fig leaf this time."

"*What?* X, you can't show up naked."

"Uh, yeah, I know. What do you think the fig leaf's for? And, yes, I *will* be dressed like that for dinner."

He's gaping at me, studying my face. "You're not serious."

"I'm still having trouble getting the fig leaf to stay in place, but that's okay, because Kat's going to be wearing practically the same thing, so I think it's safe to say that everyone will be focused on her, not me. So if my leaf slips..."

"X." His face goes pale. "You... you can't do that! It's against school rules, and the restaurant won't even let you in, so—"

"Relax, Perkins. I was joking. I'll be wearing a tux."

"You will?"

"Yeah, don't worry—you can be seen in public with me." Just not without getting his picture taken and ending up on half a dozen websites, but that's nothing new.

"Good." He exhales, then frowns. "But… why?"

"Why what? Why am I going to be *wearing clothes* to Prom?" We move up in line again. It's almost our turn.

"You know what I mean."

"No, I don't. I don't see what the problem is with me wearing a tux. Because, for one thing, I look hot in one. And, for another, it's what everybody else will be wearing."

"Yeah, but that's what I mean. That doesn't really sound like you."

"You *want* me to show up naked?"

He scowls. "You can still wear clothes without coming dressed like everybody else."

"Did Kat tell you to say that?"

He shakes his head. "I haven't talked to her."

The line moves up again. It's Riley's turn. He goes up to the table where a second-year student is handing out the schedules and tells her his name. After he's done, I do the same thing.

"Damien Locke."

The girl at the table obviously recognizes who I am, because instead of flipping through her stack of files, she glances up real quick, her eyes wide. Then she looks back down, trying to pretend nothing happened. "Here," she says, her voice shaking a little as she hands me my schedule slip.

Except she's so nervous, she accidentally gives me two of them. I give the second one back without looking at it. "This isn't mine."

"It has your name on it." She hands it back to me, then

calls for the next person to step up.

Riley's waiting for me off to the side. "My test's at ten fifteen. When's yours?"

I don't answer him. I'm too busy staring in horror at the schedule slips. Because they really do both have my name on them. One's for my lightning test, scheduled for this morning, and one's for *flying*, scheduled for this afternoon.

I feel sick.

"What's wrong?" Riley asks.

"It's nothing. They made a mistake."

He peers over my shoulder. "That doesn't look like a mistake."

"Well, it is." It has to be. "I don't fly."

"X…"

"Don't say it."

"If you don't pass your superpower test, you don't move on to second year."

I hold up the slip for lightning. "I *will* pass my superpower test."

"But… both of them?" He looks worried.

Almost as worried as I feel. "I'm not taking both of them. I told you, it's a mistake."

He opens his mouth to say something, then hesitates.

"Don't worry, Perkins. I'm sure it's nothing."

"We're doing fieldwork again next year. We're supposed to work together."

"I *know*. Stop talking like I'm not going to be there."

"You have two powers. It makes sense that they'd want to test both."

"But I only use one of them. And nobody else has to

take two tests."

The first bell rings, signaling that we have five minutes to get to class. Neither of us moves.

"I don't think it works like that," Riley says.

"Who cares if I can fly or not? My lightning's the one that matters." After all, I've never accidentally blown anything up with my flying power. "I'm going to go to the office and get this straightened out."

Riley tilts his head, like he thinks I'm fooling myself. "You have to be here next year, X."

"I know. I will be. This flying test thing is just a mistake. You'll see."

X·X·X

It's not a mistake.

At least, that's what the woman in the office said when I asked her to double-check for me. Twice. She must not have realized who I was at first, because she seemed concerned that there really had been a mistake, since no one has two powers. But then after she looked me up, she said, "Oh, you're *that* student," and told me I had to pass both tests if I didn't want to repeat my first year at Heroesworth.

Which I do not.

Especially not if Riley's moving on to second year, which of course he is, because all he had to do was turn invisible. And if I thought I was going to be left behind before when everyone else graduates, I *really* will be if I get stuck repeating a year. Which is pretty much the only reason I show up for my flying test.

I try to tell myself on the way there that maybe it won't be so bad. I can get off the ground—I've done it several times now. Maybe all they'll want is to see that I *can* fly, if I really need to. That's totally different than having to actually be skilled. I already passed my lightning test earlier, and... okay, it wasn't, like, super simple or anything, but lightning's way more complicated than flying. Maybe there's a chance I can do this.

But when I get there, it's so much worse than I thought.

For one thing, there's another student still taking his test, and he's obviously really good at it. He's flying through freaking *hoops* that are hanging from the ceiling in the gym, and doing all sorts of twists and turns that make the test look like some elaborate dance routine. I don't know if that just means he's on the flying team—the way Amelia describes it, it's like synchronized swimming, only in the air—or if I'm supposed to do that, too. Either way? Not happening. And I've only ever flown straight up and down before. It's kind of a big deal that I can do it on command at all, but having to fly through hoops?

And that's not even the worst part. Besides this being, like, the worst act to have to follow, I also recognize the guy administering the test. I recognize him from the family Christmas party Gordon dragged me to, because he's Gordon's older brother, Ted. Technically, that makes him my uncle, but it feels weird to think of him like that when he pretty much hates my guts. He told Gordon he didn't want me at the Christmas party—that no one did—and then there was sort of an eggnog incident involving one of his douchey sons. I mean, Amelia was the one who threw eggnog on Nolan, not me, but I was also *this close* to getting into a fistfight with him, so it's not like I wasn't involved. Though, for the record, I'm not the one who started it.

But Ted's made it clear that he thinks I'm complete devil spawn and shouldn't be allowed anywhere near him or his precious kids. And here he is, the guy the school's brought in to give me my stupid flying test, which I already know I can't pass but that will determine my entire future.

He hasn't noticed me yet. I should just walk out of here before he—

Ted looks over and scowls at me, then motions for me to come closer.

Okay. This is happening. I can do this. All I have to do is suddenly not be afraid of heights and have spent months practicing flying. That's *all*. I just have to be so good at it that even my uncle who wishes I was never born will see that I deserve to pass. Yep.

The guy currently taking the test spins through the last hoop and then somersaults in the air before making a perfect landing on the floor, like one of those gymnasts at the Olympics.

Ted smiles at him. "Great job, Sam!"

Sam grins. "Did I pass?"

Ted laughs and claps him on the shoulder. "The Golden City Annual Flying Competition's next month. I'll be there with several of my top flying students. You should consider signing up. I can hear it now—*Will Sam Baskin come down to the winner's circle?"*

"You really think I'm good enough?" Sam's eyes go wide, and he even gasps a little as he says that, as if him being good at this is news.

I stop myself from rolling my eyes. Okay, I don't stop myself, but I make sure Sam's not actually looking when I do.

"I think you've got some real skills. You should do this professionally."

You know who should *not* do this professionally? Or, like, *ever*?

Sam says something like, "Gosh, me, really?" a couple more times before finally leaving the gym, all beaming and starry eyed, and then Ted looks over at me like I'm the scum of the earth. "Damien."

"Ted."

"It's Mr. Tines." He holds up his clipboard. "Should I just fail you now, or are you going to pretend you can do this?"

"I can fly."

He raises an eyebrow.

"I *can*." Just not very well.

"It's a basic test. Touch the ceiling, fly through the hoops in a zigzag pattern, and then do a controlled landing. Don't touch the hoops, or I take off points."

So basic. I look up at the ceiling. The hoops are all at different heights and angles, and they're all so far *up*. Just thinking about going up there makes my stomach drop and my legs get shaky.

Ted clenches his jaw. "Don't think you're getting

special treatment, just because you're Gordon's son."

Is he serious? "You mean, you wanting to fail me the second I walked in here doesn't count as special treatment?"

He glares at me. "You're used to skating by in the world because of who your father is—"

I laugh.

"—but that's not happening here. This is a hero test, and we both know a villain like you can't pass it."

I hate that he's right. I mean, the reason I can't do this has nothing to do with being a villain. But... I don't even know why I showed up here. What the hell was I thinking?

Ted taps his clipboard. "Any time now."

I feel locked in place. I can't move. And even if I could? There's no way I'm humiliating myself in front of Ted. He doesn't get to see how freaked out I get just from lifting off the ground. That's reserved for friends and... well, for family who actually *care*.

"So, that's an *F*?" He sounds too hopeful about that. And not at all surprised.

I slip my phone out of my pocket and hold it to my ear, pretending to have a call. "Mom? Slow down. What happened? Oh, my God. Are you— No, it's nothing I can't miss. I'll be there as soon as I can." My hand shakes as I put my phone back in my pocket, which wasn't on purpose, but I think it really helps sell the situation. "I have to go. Family emergency."

Ted shakes his head, dismissive. "Your phone didn't ring."

"I had it on vibrate."

"You didn't even hang up."

"She hung up first. I didn't need to."

"A family emergency."

"Yep."

"You're really doing this?"

"I can't control when emergencies happen."

He writes something on his clipboard. "You'll have to do a make-up test, or you'll still fail first year. You haven't gotten out of anything."

"I'm not trying to get out of anything. My mom is—" I swallow. "Look, I have to go, okay?"

"You have to check out at the office. And someone has to actually come pick you up."

I start to leave. I have to get out of here.

"Damien?" Ted says. "One more thing." He waits until I look over at him. "You're ruining my brother's life."

CHAPTER 5

Mom texts me when she gets to Heroesworth to pick me up, but when I get outside, I see my grandparents' car waiting for me. Grandpa's in the driver's seat.

Great.

He opens the passenger door. "Get in."

I just stand there. "Mom texted me."

"I know—I told her to."

"So that was… what? Another lie?"

"I just want to talk, but I didn't think you'd come out if you knew it was me."

I adjust my backpack, pulling it higher onto my shoulders. "I can walk home."

"You can't avoid me forever. Get in the car."

"Fine." I get in, but I make sure to slam the door.

He checks for cars before pulling out into the street. "I deserve that. The attitude, you not wanting to see me…"

"You think?"

"But this has to end. We've got to be able to talk to each other."

I fold my arms and slouch down in my seat. "I don't owe you anything. Not after what you did to me. So if you've got something to say, then say it already. And you can drop me off at the park. There's no way you're coming to my house."

"The night of the gala, you told me you didn't want to lose me. Well, I don't want to lose you, either. But that was two months ago. Your grandmother said I had to give you your space, so that's what I did. But there's space, and then there's never speaking again. Maybe that's what you want, but that's not okay with me."

I glance over at him. "It's not. I mean, it's not what I want, either. But, Grandpa, you lied to me. You used me. And you made me lie to other people." I clench my fists and press them into the seat. "You didn't kill anyone at that gala, but you still did all that other stuff, and you're still the leader of the Truth. That means you're torturing superheroes, and doing who knows what else. I don't know how to trust you anymore."

He's quiet for a second. Then he says, "I'm trying to make things right."

"What does that mean?"

"It means I shouldn't have let the Truth come between me and my grandson."

"It's a little late for that."

"We're not torturing heroes anymore. Not unless it's someone we know for sure has done the same to us."

I raise my eyebrows at him. "Am I supposed to be

impressed? That you're only torturing *some* people?"

"I'm trying, all right? You don't know how hard it is to lead a revolution, and doing it without bloodshed..."

"The League made excuses, too. For why they had to torture villains." For why they're still doing it. They might not be grabbing random villains off the street anymore—not since the city put its foot down—but they still have the authority to arrest criminals, and I'd hate to be a villain in League custody.

Grandpa pulls up to the park and finds a space. "The Truth isn't the League. No matter what you might think."

"I get that people are going to get hurt, but you hurt *me*. You put everyone I care about in danger. If I hadn't been at that gala, if you hadn't been going to attack..." I rub my face with my hands. "My best friend almost died."

"Damien, I never meant for that to happen."

"No, that's right, you didn't. Because if you'd had your way, there wouldn't be an *almost* in that sentence. He'd be dead. My other friends would be, too, and my family. Maybe you didn't know my friends would be there, but you knew my dad would be. The whole city knew that."

"The plan wasn't to kill anyone."

"But that's not how it would have played out."

He doesn't argue with that. We both know it's true. "If I could take it back—"

"You can't." I unbuckle my seat belt and open my door to get out. "And maybe I don't want to lose you, but I can't just forgive you, either."

"What I did... It's in the past. I can't change it, but I can promise it won't happen again."

I look him in the eye, not sure if I should believe that. He sounds like he means it, but he *always* sounds like he means it. And maybe he really does, at least right now. He might change his mind tomorrow. "Too bad your promises don't mean anything." I get out of the car.

"Damien, wait—"

But I don't wait. I slam the door and walk away.

CHAPTER 6

"I was the best one," Amelia says at dinner, stuffing a complimentary roll into her mouth. She chews it for, like, only half a second before continuing. "I mean, there were only two other people with the same power as me, but they just did easy stuff, like teleporting a pen. But I summoned up a chair. One of the heavy wooden ones from the library."

She means she was showing off, but instead of calling her on it, Helen and Gordon give her warm smiles, like that's a great story.

The whole family's at a restaurant downtown, celebrating me and Amelia passing our superpower tests. Gordon must not have heard that I left school early, or that I was supposed to take a flying test—I guess he and Ted aren't that close—because as soon as he got home from work, he said we were going out to celebrate. He and Helen exchanged knowing looks, like they'd been planning this surprise. They didn't even ask if we passed our tests, they just assumed, and I didn't have the heart to tell them what happened. Though, to be fair, technically they're celebrating me passing my lightning test, which I did. They just don't know it won't be enough for me to pass first year.

"Mrs. Cunningham—she's the one who was giving the test—was super impressed with me," Amelia says. "I could tell."

I poke at my baked potato with my fork, mashing the scoops of butter and sour cream into it. "But you weren't *in* the library."

"So?"

"So, you couldn't see the chair you took. What if someone was sitting on it?"

A look of horror washes over Amelia's face. Her mouth hangs open a little, and her eyes dart over to Helen. "I didn't think about that!"

"It's okay, honey," Helen says. "I doubt anyone was sitting on it. And if they were, I'm sure they didn't get hurt."

"Yeah," Alex says, "you probably would have gotten in trouble if they did."

Amelia considers that, not looking very reassured.

Gordon drops a hand onto my shoulder, startling me. "What about you? How'd your test go?"

I look over at Jess, who's happily eating individual kernels of corn with her fingers, with no obligations or expectations, and kind of wish we could switch places. "I zapped things."

"Come on, son. There had to be more to it than that."

"Not really. There were moving targets. I had to zap the ones that looked like bad guys and avoid the ones that looked like old ladies. Which I think was kind of discriminatory, especially since all the 'bad guys' had *V*s on their chests. And who says old ladies can't be criminals? But I passed."

"Well, that's great." Gordon sounds like he means it. "I know the year's not over, but you've only got a couple months left, and I'm just so proud of both of you. And, Damien, I know this has been a tough year for you. There were times when I wasn't sure if you were going to..." He clears his throat. "You could have decided Heroesworth wasn't for you, and I would have understood. But you stuck with it, and you didn't let anything keep you from succeeding."

"Dad, you remember I got expelled, right?"

"I know that. But you negotiated your way back in."

"I also ran away to live with Grandma and Grandpa and missed two weeks of school."

Gordon's smile falters a little. "Yes, that's true, but the point is, you came back. You're working hard to make up for what you missed. It would have been so much easier to give up, but you didn't."

"He's right," Helen says. "You had more challenges to deal with than everyone else. It can't be easy, being the only half villain in a hero school, especially after what happened with the Truth." She glances over at Amelia, then back at me. "I know the other students have been..." She searches for the right words.

I help her out. "Complete and total jerks?"

She nods. "I can't even imagine how difficult it's been for you, but you stayed in school, your grades are improving, and you're almost done with your first year." Helen reaches across the table and puts a hand on my wrist for a second, looking me in the eyes. "I don't know how to express how proud we all are of you."

Guilt squirms in my stomach. I wish they'd given me a chance to tell them the truth before they whisked us off to dinner. But then again, maybe it's better this way. Everyone's actually happy, and it's not like Amelia didn't pass her test, but if I'd told them what happened, they might have changed their minds about coming here.

I'll tell them later, after we get home.

Amelia squints at me, then at Helen and Gordon. "What about me?"

Helen smooths her hand over Amelia's head. "We're proud of you, too."

"This is just like what happened before. He's a screwup, so even though I'm doing way better than him, he gets all the attention."

"That's not true."

"You're *both* getting all the attention," Alex mutters.

Everyone ignores him, except Jess, who flings a kernel of her corn at him. I'm not sure if it's to shut him up or meant as some kind of consolation prize, but I kind of love her for it either way.

"Nobody ever cares about how good I'm doing," Amelia whines. "It's not fair."

Helen and Gordon exchange a conspiratorial grin.

Whatever's going on, I'm pretty sure I don't like it.

Amelia notices them being weird, too. "*What?*"

"We got you something," Gordon says.

"Both of you," Helen corrects him.

Gordon smiles at me. "You wouldn't let me get you anything big for your birthday, so..." He reaches into his pocket and pulls out a set of car keys.

I press my hands against the table. "Dad... This isn't—"

"It's for both of you."

Amelia blinks at him. "You got me a car?!"

"To share," Helen says. She takes the key ring from Gordon and pries one of the keys off, then hands one to each of us.

"You got me a car, but I have to share it with *him*?" Amelia makes a face. "Are you punishing me for something?"

"You both have your licenses now," Gordon says. "It's used. We couldn't afford two of them, but there's no reason why you can't both use it."

"Is it here? Can we go look at it?!"

Gordon laughs. "It's at home. I parked it a little ways down the street, so it would be a surprise."

I stare at the key in my hand. "And this is because I passed my superpower test?"

"Not just for that. It's for everything. Like I said, I know it's been a—"

"I'm dropping out of school."

Gordon sputters, not finishing that sentence. "Damien, you're... You're *what*?!"

"I passed my lightning test, but the school wants me to pass a flying test, too. We all know I can't do that. It's impossible, and I don't see the point of humiliating myself, or of repeating first year all over again. Not when the same thing's just going to happen next year. And let's face it, I don't even know what I'm doing at a school like Heroesworth. So, thanks, but no thanks." I set my key on the table and slide it toward Amelia. Then I get up, even though I haven't finished my dinner yet. "If anybody needs me, I'll be in the car, re-evaluating my life choices."

X·X·X

I'm sitting in the back seat, texting Kat, when Gordon comes out to check on me.

"I didn't leave so you'd come after me," I tell him, glancing up from my phone. "I'm not Amelia."

He slides into the back with me anyway. "We have to talk about this."

"Not right now we don't. You're supposed to be eating dinner. You should at least get to celebrate having one kid who's going to graduate."

A text from Kat pops up on my screen. *A car?! What color?*

It doesn't matter, I type back. *It's all Amelia's. I'm not keeping it.* But then curiosity gets the better of me. "What color is it?"

"What color is what?"

"The car." I hold up my phone. "Kat wants to know."

"It's green. Listen, Damien…"

"You said you'd understand if I quit school. Well, I'm quitting school."

"I said I *would have* understood. But now? You worked so hard to be there. I just don't get why you'd throw that away."

"Of course you don't. Flying's easy for you. Imagine if you had to pass a lightning test."

"That's not the same thing. I don't have lightning power—*you* can fly."

I shrug. "Not the way I'd need to to pass the test. Ted was the administrator. Did you know that?"

"I know he's done it in the past. He's a professional flying coach."

"Well, he hates me. You should have seen the look he gave me today. And then he told me I was ruining your life."

Gordon runs a hand through his hair. "It's not true. He shouldn't have said that."

"I couldn't do it. I mean, I knew there was no way I was going to get through the freaking obstacle course he had set up on the ceiling. But I couldn't even try. Not in front of him—not in front of someone who so obviously *wanted* me to fail."

"Now, Damien, I'm sure Ted didn't..." But he can't even finish that sentence. We both know Ted's not exactly my biggest fan.

"I got out of there. I didn't even fail the test—I just left." Well, I faked a family emergency first, but whatever.

"There are make-up tests."

"That's not my point. Besides, it's more than just the test. Fieldwork was the only part of school I actually liked, and I don't even get to do that anymore. I know I'd get to next year, if I made it that far, but the thing is, I'm not sure I even *want* to. It's a relief not to be doing fieldwork. And if I don't like the one thing that made going there feel like the right choice, despite how hard it was, then... what the hell am I doing?"

Gordon's quiet for a second. "Do you really think you'd be okay with just quitting?"

"No, probably not. But I don't know if staying feels right, either." I wait for him to tell me I'm being stupid and that there's no way he's letting me quit school. I almost actually want him to.

But instead he says, "You and Amelia both deserve the car, whether you stay at Heroesworth or not. I'm still proud of you." He presses the key into my hand.

"Dad, what should I do?"

"You should come back inside and eat dinner with us."

"No, I mean about Heroesworth."

"That's up to you, Damien. You're the only one who really knows what's right for you, and you're the one who has to live with the consequences. Now, let's go, before our food gets cold."

Which is basically no help at all.

CHAPTER 7

Saturday night, I'm in my Renegade X costume, sneaking downstairs to go meet up with Riley and Sarah. It's past midnight, and I'm not really expecting anyone to be up—except for Amelia, but I know she's in her room, talking on the phone with Zach—so I'm a little startled when Helen comes out of the kitchen. She has her bathrobe on over her pajamas, like she couldn't sleep.

"Going somewhere?" She folds her arms and raises her eyebrows at me. "It's awfully late."

Not really. It's not like I have school tomorrow or anything. "I was just going for a walk."

"Uh-huh. In your superhero costume?"

Gordon and Helen disapprove of our extra-curricular superheroing. Or at least Gordon does. I'm not actually sure what Helen thinks, though judging by the way she's tilting her head at me, she's not too crazy about it. And I know I should be annoyed that she's busting me and not letting me leave, but mostly I just feel relieved.

"Everything else was in the laundry."

She sits down on the couch and pats the spot next to her. "Talk to me."

"Um." Busting me is one thing, but can't she just let me go back to my room now? I'll text Riley and Sarah, tell them I can't make it and that they can't do it without me—and that Riley should be off the hook—and then I'll see if Kat's still up. We've been watching bad movies together over the phone. Up next on our list is *Attack of the Killer Robot Zombie Slaves,* which looks particularly terrible. I've really been looking forward to it.

Helen sighs. "Damien, sit down."

I sit. I wonder if she'd notice if I got out my phone and started texting Riley. Just to tell him I'm not going to make it, what with him and Sarah waiting for me and all. "Is this about the car? Or about me dropping out of school? Because you didn't see the look in Ted's eyes when—"

"This is about my statue."

"Oh." I swallow. A guilty feeling squirms in my stomach. "I never meant for it to get taken down. For any of them to." I never meant for a lot of things.

"You're not in trouble."

"Riiiight." So why am I getting a lecture?

She frowns at me. "I don't blame you for what happened. And I just wanted to say..." She glances over her shoulder, toward her bedroom door, like she doesn't want anyone to hear this. Not even Gordon. She keeps her voice low. "I'm not upset about the statue."

"That's what you wanted to say?"

"No, I... The truth is, Damien, I'm kind of relieved."

"Seriously?"

"I did terrible things to earn that statue. I know I saved lives by taking out Bart the Blacksmith, but I still killed him. And others. And they were all sanctioned by the League, and I was always following orders, but..." She looks down at her hands. "I'm the one who committed those acts, and I'm the one who has to live with them. I don't regret any of it. I always did what I believed was right, and I'm proud of that. But celebrating the fact that I've killed people has never sat well with me."

She looks over, like she's expecting me to give her a medal for how awful she feels about killing villains. "Yeah, right."

"What?"

"Come on. I've heard how you talk about Bart the Blacksmith—how you talk about *Kat* because of him. And yeah, he was pretty bad, and you probably did the world a favor by murdering him"—she flinches at that—"but don't pretend you're upset about it."

"It's complicated. More complicated than just being upset or not. Yes, I'm glad I killed him, I'm happy to have made the sacrifices that I did so my friends could get away and so he couldn't hurt anyone else, but that doesn't mean I ever deserved a statue for it." She exhales. "I don't think I've ever said that out loud before."

"But you're telling *me*? Why? So I can forgive you on behalf of all villains?"

"I don't want forgiveness, from you or from anyone else. I'm just trying to say that I understand what it's like to have to make the hard choices. Especially out in the field."

"Okay."

"I know why you're quitting school, and it's not because of that flying test."

"So this is a stay-in-school lecture?"

"It's not a lecture. And no, it's not about staying in school. Gordon's never had to…" She glances over at their bedroom door again. "He's never had to make those kinds of decisions in the field. He chased a few bad guys around when he first joined the League, but they weren't life-or-death situations. So what I'm trying to say is, he might not understand what's going on with you, but I get it. Ever since that gala—"

"No one died. It wasn't life or death." I don't look at her when I say that.

"A lot of people *could have* died. Including the people close to you."

"But they didn't. And Riley's better now. His leg is, I mean. The gala was months ago, and everyone's okay."

"Not everyone."

"I… I'm fine."

"But you're dropping out of school. A place you worked really hard to be."

"I'm dropping out because of the flying test. And I don't know if I'm dropping out. Not yet."

"And I want you to know that if you do decide to, I understand."

"You… what?"

She pats my knee. "I don't regret the things I've done,

but there are some days—maybe a lot of days—when I wish I'd never joined the League. I wish I'd never gotten involved with Special Ops. I made the world a better place, but I made myself worse, and… I know you're not planning to join the League. You never were, and after everything that's happened, I don't see how anyone could expect you to. But you're still on a path, and if you decide that you don't like where it leads and that you want to change directions, I get that."

"Oh."

"I've never told Gordon any of this. How I feel—felt—about that statue, or about my time in the League. But I'm telling you because you have to make whatever decision is right for you, and if he doesn't agree with that decision, I just want you to know that I'm here for you. That I get it."

"You think I should drop out?"

"I didn't say that."

"But you think this path I'm headed on is going to ruin me."

"What happened at the gala hit you pretty hard. Anyone can see that. And you're always going to have friends and family on both sides of this—hero and villain. Someone you care about is always going to get hurt."

"So I shouldn't even bother trying to protect them?"

"You should protect yourself."

I lean back into the couch cushion, taking that in. "That's pretty much the worst advice I've ever heard."

She laughs a little, then sighs. "I wouldn't have listened, either, when I was your age. But maybe that's a good thing. If kids listened to their elders, the world would be full of people who never try. Just promise me you'll think it over. And that you'll be careful on your mission tonight."

"On my mission? I thought I was busted."

"For what? Leaving the house on a Saturday night? Besides, you haven't done any fieldwork since the gala. It's good to see you getting back to something you love." She says that wistfully, like she still misses it, too, despite the spiel she just gave me.

And if I don't love it anymore? If I'm dreading going out there tonight, and every part of me is screaming that this is a bad idea? *What then?*

I almost ask her, because I think she might actually get it. But she might also tell me that feeling like this means I'm doomed, and that I really am on the wrong path and should just give up now, and I don't think I can take hearing that. Especially not from someone who's been through way worse and who might actually be right.

So I don't say anything about it. I just tell her I'll be careful, and then I get out of there.

CHAPTER 8

I meet Sarah and Riley at the train station downtown. Sarah's staring at her phone, and Riley's leaning against the balcony railing, watching trains come in on the lower level. Or at least I assume that's what he's watching, since I'm not about to go check it out for myself, what with not having a death wish or anything.

Sarah notices me first. She nudges Riley, then comes over and makes a face. "Why are you wearing that?"

She means my Renegade X costume. "Because this is a superhero mission?" Last time I showed up not in costume, she gave me crap for it, even though it didn't actually matter.

"I told you to come dressed in plain clothes. We're supposed to be inconspicuous." She gestures to herself, then behind her to Riley. They both have on jeans and T-shirts, though Sarah also has tinfoil wrapped around a lock of her hair, which isn't exactly what I'd call *inconspicuous*.

I look down at my costume. It's all green and black spandex. "People recognize me all the time even when I'm dressed normal. How am I supposed to be inconspicuous? And anyway, we're downtown. Maybe no one will notice." It's not that crowded in here, what with it being almost one in the morning, and nobody's even looking at us. Well, there might be a couple people looking, like the guy pretending to read the newspaper who keeps glancing over at me when he thinks I won't notice, or the woman sitting on a bench not that far from us who's doing pretty much the same thing, except that she's pretending to look at her phone instead of at the newspaper. But she also looks really bored, especially when she twirls the end of her ponytail around her finger and snaps the gum she's chewing, so she might not really be watching us.

"It's almost time," Riley says, joining us and checking his phone. "His train should be pulling in."

"The bad guy's a thief," Sarah tells me. "We're getting back a ring he stole from his wife. Well, ex-wife, as of last Friday. It was her grandmother's ring, and she really wants it back. He should have it on him."

I wrinkle my forehead. "Sarah, how do you know all this?"

"His ex-wife told me. I answered an ad. She almost wouldn't give us the job, because, as she put it, we're 'just kids,' but I told her we had a long track record of taking down bad guys. And getting lost jewelry back. I may have fudged that last part a little bit, but I really wanted her to say yes."

I exchange a look with Riley. "A long track record of

taking down bad guys? We've never even worked together before. All three of us, I mean. And—"

"We can handle it," Sarah says. "Riley's going to—"

"Secant," he corrects her.

"Right. Secant's going to turn invisible, steal the ring, and all we have to do is be ready, just in case." She pats her purse, which no doubt has some kind of homemade weapon in it.

"In case of what?"

"In case something goes wrong, which it won't. The target's never even going to know we were here. But if he does find out, well, his ex-wife said he can get pretty violent. That's why she's not going after him herself."

"And *we're* confronting him? *Here?* With all these people around?"

Sarah rolls her eyes at me. "It's not that many people. And if things get dangerous, just use your lightning. Once you're all lit up, everyone will run screaming. Problem solved."

"Yeah, I'm not doing that." I hope. I turn to Riley. "And you're okay with this, Perkins?"

He opens his mouth, hesitating, then shrugs. "I'll be invisible. And you guys will be backing me up, right?"

"Of course."

"So there's no reason not to do it." He doesn't sound too convinced about that.

I don't blame him. I can think of a lot of reasons not to do this.

"Everything will be fine," Sarah says. "The only one in danger here is the target, and he's not even going to know about it. We'll get the ring, get the reward money—"

"Reward money?"

"Fifty dollars, each. I made the lowest bid."

"So she didn't hire us because of our long track record of taking down bad guys?"

Sarah ignores that. "We'll get the reward money, and we'll feel good about ourselves for a job well done. And then when I tell people we have a history of retrieving stolen jewelry, it'll actually be true."

"You mean," Riley says, "there are going to be more of these?"

"Lots more." Sarah grins at him. "This is just the beginning. I've been waiting forever for the three of us to get to work together, and now that we are, we're going to do a lot of good. Help a lot of people. That's what Golden City needs right now. The League doesn't mean what it used to, and it's up to people like us to step up and make a difference."

"And collect reward money," I add.

She scowls. "It's not about the money. I would have said we'd do it for free if I thought she'd still take us seriously. And if I didn't need a new hard drive. But we're going to show everyone that just because they can't trust the League right now, that doesn't mean there aren't people out there that they *can* still rely on. And the three of us are going to be a force to be reckoned with. No bad guys are going to be able to stop us. We're—"

"Sarah," Riley says, jerking his head toward the platform to our left, "isn't that our target over there?"

"Oh, crap. You're right. He's getting away. Okay, let's

go. You guys know what to do. And remember, Renegade—stay inconspicuous."

X·X·X

Nobody looks twice at me in my costume, but it only takes about two seconds for someone official-looking to stop Sarah and ask her what she's doing. Maybe it's the way she's so obviously stalking someone, or the way she keeps putting a hand to the gun in her purse—and okay, I don't know for sure that it's a gun, but I've known Sarah plenty long enough to know it's *some* kind of weapon—but she kind of looks like a terrorist.

So much for being inconspicuous.

The train-station security guard who stops her says he just wants to ask her a few questions. She glances meaningfully at me, then over at the bad guy, before letting herself be lead off. I guess to make sure I know I'm supposed to stay here and be Riley's backup. As if I didn't already know that, and as if I would volunteer to be hauled off by security. It wouldn't take long for them to figure out who I was, or for them to call my dad, or for this to all end up in the news tomorrow. Which really wouldn't help our track record.

Not that I want us to have a track record, or to be doing this at all, but it's a little late for that.

The bad guy stops to check something on his phone.

I wonder where Riley is and if he saw what happened to Sarah. He's invisible, hanging out somewhere near our target, but I have no idea how close he is, or if he's trying to pickpocket the ring right now. Or maybe he's too busy freaking out about his girlfriend getting hauled in for questioning. Okay, not *hauled*. They were pretty civil, probably because a sixteen-year-old girl with tinfoil in her hair looks more crazy than criminal.

There's another train coming in on the platform closest to us. It shakes the walls, rattling the fancy chandelier hanging from the ceiling. Pieces of glass bang together, and if I didn't already know that the chandelier had been here for years, I'd think it was about to come down.

Riley must think it's *actually* about to come down, because he turns visible and gapes up at it in horror.

And suddenly I'm reliving that night at the gala again. I wasn't even *there* when the ceiling caved in on him, but I remember what it was like to find him. Flickering in and out of visibility, delirious with pain. And the way he screamed when me and Amelia had to move him.

My stomach twists. I push the memory away.

Riley only stays visible for a second, but it's enough for the bad guy to notice him. Not just to notice him, but to register that he was trying to sneak up on him. He grabs Riley with both hands, dragging him toward him. "What do you think you're doing?!"

Riley stays visible, panic washing over him. He opens his mouth a little, but no words come out.

Sparks run up my spine. This wasn't supposed to happen.

"Come on! Who sent you? Was it Frank?"

Riley still doesn't say anything, frozen in place.

"Answer me!" The bad guy suddenly hauls him up onto

the balcony railing, holding him partway over the edge. "Whoever you're working for, kid, they're going to regret this."

"Perkins!" My throat goes dry. Lightning crackles across my arms.

Every instinct I have is telling me to zap this guy, but if I do, he'll let go. He'll *drop* Riley.

So instead I run toward them—toward the balcony and the ledge and the open space. I reach out a hand, trying to grab Riley before it's too late, but I'm not fast enough. The bad guy shoves him over the edge.

He *shoves* him. And I see it in Riley's eyes, the flash of realization that he's going to fall.

It's nothing like the gala, and yet it feels the same. I couldn't save Riley then, so I have to save him now. I don't hesitate when I get to the railing—I *leap* over it. Because I can fly. Because in theory I can grab him and slow his fall, even if I can't stop it.

But I don't grab him. Riley's already falling, and I can't reach him. Not without flying toward the ground. There's this moment where I know I could save him if I just sped downward. But I hesitate. I don't do it. I *can't*. And then it's too late, and I'm watching Riley slam into the floor.

CHAPTER 9

I'm sitting in the driver's seat of the new-old car the next afternoon. Amelia's already taken over. She's put sparkly stickers of flowers and unicorns on the dashboard and set all the radio stations. And I had to move the driver's seat back before I could even get in, since it was so close to the steering wheel. I'm not going anywhere, I could have just got in the passenger side and not bothered, but I did it anyway.

The car smells weird. Kind of musty, but also like some kind of cleaner.

My phone chimes with a new text. I don't check it. I already know it's from Kat. She's texted me a couple times, asking how our mission went yesterday. I'll call her later. I should call her now, but then I'd have to admit out loud how badly I screwed up, and I'm not ready for that yet.

I mean, it could have gone worse.

Riley could have gotten hurt, instead of just getting the

wind knocked out of him. It took him a while to get back up, but when he did, he said he was okay. Nothing was broken, though he was obviously freaked out, and I saw him wincing when he put weight on his newly healed leg.

And Sarah could have gotten arrested, but she explained to the train-station security guards that she was part of a hero group and on a mission. She said that all she was guilty of doing was trying to uphold justice and that she hadn't done anything wrong. And the weapon she had in her purse looked like a hair straightener—well, a hair straightener that a garage sale threw up on—so the security guards decided to let her off with a warning. I'm not sure what they were warning her not to do—don't stalk criminals at the train station?—but she wasn't actually in trouble.

But I don't think I'll ever forget the terrified look on her face when she saw Riley on the ground, with me crouched next to him, trying to make sure he was okay. Or how quickly her look of terror changed to accusation. I was supposed to be backing him up, and it was obvious that I hadn't.

Riley said it wasn't my fault. He's the one who turned visible and botched the mission in the first place.

But I shouldn't have let him fall.

The passenger door opens, and Amelia gets in, her nose scrunching in accusation. "What are you doing in here?"

"They said it was for both of us."

"And you said you didn't want it."

"I changed my mind."

She glares at me. "You didn't have to move the seat

around. I had it right where I wanted it."

"Uh, yeah, I did. You're too short."

"No, you're just too *tall*. And you better not have changed the radio stations. And if I see even one sticker out of place, I'll—"

"You'll what?"

"We're supposed to *share* Tom. That means you don't touch my stickers."

"Who the hell is Tom?" The only Tom I know is Kat's dad, and I *know* she doesn't mean him.

She pats the dashboard. "This is Tom. My—I mean, *our* —car."

I make a face. "You named it Tom?"

"I named *him* Tom."

"You couldn't have thought of something more interesting?"

"I don't want interesting. I want reliable. Tom sounds reliable. And if we're going to share him..." She pauses to take a deep breath, like having to talk to me about this at all is a huge inconvenience for her. "We need to lay down some ground rules."

"Later, Amelia. I'm not in the mood."

She clears her throat, ignoring me. "First of all, *I'm* the only one who's had her license long enough to drive with someone else in the car. So if you want to ride with me to school, I'll be driving. And you'll have to sit in the back, because I told Melissa and Hil that I'd pick them up."

"Shouldn't I be in the front, so neither one of them has to sit by me?"

"Then *I'd* have to sit by you. And second, you can't...

you know. In here. With Kat."

I raise an eyebrow. "I can't what?"

She doesn't look at me when she says it. "Have sex."

"We weren't planning on it."

"But that's the rule. No sex in the car." She glances over at me real quick, then away again, like she's afraid I'm going to argue with her and she'll have to keep talking about this.

"Okay. *No one* has sex in here." I want to add, *That includes you*, but I can't bring myself to say it.

"And I'm taking the car to Prom."

"It's going to be hard finding a tux in Tom's size."

"You know what I mean. I'm taking Zach. And you can get a ride with Riley and Sarah, or with Kat. Plus, like I said, you can't drive anybody, so—"

"Yeah, fine. I get it. You need the car on Prom night, and Zach doesn't want to be in the same space as me."

"We're going to dinner with my friends, so it wouldn't even make sense for you to ride with us." She hesitates. "He's still mad at you."

"No, *I'm* still mad at *him*." I twist in my seat a little, so I can stare out the window.

"He won't tell me what the fight was about, but he said you were being a jerk, which I can totally believe."

"Stay out of it, Amelia."

"Well, you're a jerk to me *all the time*. But you're usually nice to Zach. Then again, Riley's your best friend, and you—"

I whirl around to face her. "*Shut up.*"

She sniffs. "You weren't there for him last night. You

let him get hurt."

"You don't know what you're talking about."

"It's true, isn't it?"

"Did... Did Riley say that?"

"He told Zach what happened, and Zach told me. And Zach said it was typical of you, only caring about yourself."

My blood runs cold, and my stomach suddenly feels like there's a rock in it. "That's not... Riley didn't get hurt."

"You let him fall. You could have saved him, but you didn't." She shrugs, as if it's no big deal, just a fact.

Rage twists inside me, mixed with guilt and dread. "You weren't there, and neither was Zach."

"His leg's *still healing,* and you—"

"You think I didn't want to save him?! You think I'm so horrible that I'd watch my best friend get hurt again *just because*?!"

She shrinks back in her seat. "You don't have to yell."

"I jumped over a freaking banister! *Me!* You know what that... you know how hard that would be for me! So don't tell me I wasn't there for him." I run my hands through my hair and slouch down. "Don't tell me what happened when you weren't even there."

"Okay, but it's just obvious you're not being a good friend to anyone right now."

"Amelia. Just... *don't.*"

"Why are you and Zach fighting? And don't tell me it's none of my business, because it affects me, too."

"It doesn't matter."

"If it doesn't matter, then why are you guys not even talking?"

"It's like you said. I was a jerk to him."

"If you know that, then you should apologize."

"It's complicated."

She makes a frustrated sound. "No, it isn't. He's your friend."

"My friend who apparently thinks I'd let Riley get hurt." Even if he's still mad, how can he think that about me?

"Whatever happened between you two, it really upset him. And as glad as I am that he's finally come to his senses and stopped being on your side about everything, you guys not talking is just weird."

"Okay, Amelia. I'll talk to him. But I can't promise anything."

"Just promise you won't be a jerk this time. I'm sure everything will go fine. And," she adds, motioning for me to move, "get out of the car."

"What?"

"I want to go to the mall. To get more stickers, and maybe some fuzzy pink dice for the windshield."

"What if I wanted to hang something in the windshield? It's my car, too, you know."

"You can have the trunk. To decorate, I mean. But just the inside."

"How generous of you."

"I suppose you could put *one* sticker inside the glove box. But I have to approve it first. And you really should be talking to Zach before you worry about decorating, because, no offense or anything, but you need all the friends you can get."

X·X·X

"I told her it wasn't your fault," Riley whispers on Monday. We're in the library, doing our alternative assignment for Advanced Heroism, which is basically a giant binder full of annoying worksheets. Riley's almost halfway through with his, while I'm barely a third of the way through mine, despite having started a few weeks before him.

"Yeah, but I saw how Sarah looked at me," I whisper back. We're not supposed to talk in here, but it's the middle of third period, so it's not like there's anyone else around. "I know she's mad."

"Well..." He pauses, lifting his pen from the short-answer question he was working on.

"Don't sugarcoat it, Perkins. Don't you dare say she's just disappointed."

"Okay. But she is. In both of us—not just you. She'll get over it, though."

"Let me guess, she doesn't want to be anywhere near me at Prom, and me and Kat are going alone."

"She didn't say that."

"Yet." I sigh and put my chin in my hands, resting my elbows on the table. "I really screwed up."

"Come on, X. It was me. I'm the one who got caught. And all because of that stupid chandelier." He slides his hands over his face. "God, I thought... I thought the *ceiling* was coming down. How dumb was that?" He tries to laugh it off, but it comes out half-hearted.

"Not dumb. The ceiling really did cave in on you."

"That was months ago."

"Only two and a half. And don't say you should be over it, because *I'm* not over it, and it didn't even happen to me."

He nods, staring down at the table. "I still screwed up."

"We both screwed up. We shouldn't have even been there."

"Try telling Sarah that. Can you believe she's already talking about doing that again?"

"It's Sarah, so, yeah. I used to like fieldwork."

"No, you used to *love* fieldwork." He pauses, then adds, "So did I."

"I knew that I wasn't… that we weren't… I knew we shouldn't have gone on a mission yet, but I let Sarah talk me into it."

"Me, too. And I know she just wants to feel like things are back to normal, but…"

"But us doing more fieldwork right now is pretty much the worst idea ever?"

"I just wish I didn't have to disappoint her."

That makes two of us. "Part of me was hoping that Sarah was right. That we'd been out of the game long enough, and getting back into it would, I don't know, make everything okay. I'd see that I still loved fieldwork, and that… This might sound stupid, but going on missions made me feel like I wasn't just some useless screwup."

"Hey. Come on. You're not *just* a screwup."

I glare at him.

He grins. "You know what I mean."

"Being good at fieldwork and going out on missions used to make me feel like I was more than that. Like the world actually needed me or something."

"Yeah, me, too. And like... like even when things got really tough, it was still worth it, because it *meant* something. But now..." He shrugs. "All I can think is why does it have to be us? Haven't we done enough? There are plenty of other heroes out there who didn't break their legs or get left for dead by someone they thought was their friend. I mean, my dad *died* saving a bunch of strangers. Was that worth it?"

"Depends on who you ask."

"He helped those people, and they got to live, and their families didn't have to feel the pain of having them ripped away. But *me*?" Riley clenches his fists. "I'm his son. I shouldn't have had to... Why is it heroic that he cared more about a bunch of strangers than he did about me and Zach? Or about my mom?"

He's shaking a little, though I can't tell if it's from anger or sadness.

"Perkins, it's—"

"Don't say it's okay, X, because it's not."

"I won't. I wasn't going to. But your dad didn't know he was going to die that day."

"But he knew it was dangerous. He knew there was a chance that he wouldn't come back. He still picked them over us, and I don't ever want to be like that. And I think about that night at the gala, and I think what if you hadn't found me? What if I'd died, and Mom and Zach had had to go through that all over again? Because of me." He squeezes his eyes shut, taking a deep breath.

"It wasn't the same situation. You went to a freaking *awards ceremony*. You didn't know it was going to be dangerous, and you weren't sacrificing yourself for a bunch of strangers. You were trying to help *me*."

"I know, X. And I don't regret that. But I still put myself in danger, and if I'd died, I'm not the one who would have had to live with it."

He means Zach and his mom, but I think it pretty much would have destroyed me if one of my friends had died that night, especially because they were helping me. "Dangerous situations come with the territory."

He doesn't say anything to that, and I wonder if he's thinking the same thing I am, that maybe we don't belong here anymore. I consider telling him how I might drop out of school, because there's no way I can pass that flying test, and without fieldwork, what's even the point? But I don't have the guts to say it out loud.

"It's not like we have to decide right now," Riley says, and we both know what decision he means. "We're not even doing fieldwork again until next fall. That's four months from now. We'll tell Sarah we're just not ready, and we'll wait and see what happens."

I feel a sense of relief as soon as he says it. Four months off from having to deal with this. And maybe in four months, things will be different. I mean, I'll know whether or not I'm repeating first year. But even ignoring that, maybe it's enough time that I won't feel this tight ball of dread in my stomach every time I imagine going on a mission again. Maybe I'll know whether or not I'm on the right path.

"Okay," I tell Riley. "We'll wait, and we'll—"

The door to the library opens, and we both turn to look as Amelia comes in. She spots us and marches right over. She's got this really smug look on her face, like she knows some secret that I don't.

"What are you doing here?" I ask. "I told you this morning, I didn't see where you lip gloss rolled to in the car. It's probably under the seat."

"I *know* that." She folds her arms. "I didn't say you knew where it was, I said your arm is longer than mine and I needed you to try and reach it."

"And you felt the need to get a hall pass and come in here and tell me that?"

"That's not why I'm here. Mrs. Deeds sent me." A grin spreads across Amelia's face, like she's about to tell us the best news of our lives. "She said that now that Riley's cast is off, it doesn't make sense for him to do the alternative assignment. And she's decided that, since he needs a partner, you can have a second chance."

I look at Riley, not liking this, then back over at Amelia. "What are you saying?"

"I'm *saying* that you guys are starting our new unit with us tomorrow. You can stop doing this stupid alternative assignment, because you're back to doing fieldwork, just like you wanted."

CHAPTER 10

"I need to see your sticker collection when you come home this weekend," I tell Kat on the phone later that night. I'm lying upside down on my bed, with my feet pressed against the slanting wall.

"Is that a euphemism? Because if you want to have sex, you could just say so."

"I think that goes without saying. But no, I actually mean your sticker collection. I'm going to borrow some."

"Borrow? As in, not stick them to anything?"

"Well..." I clear my throat. "I might be going to stick them to Tom."

"What? Since when are you and my dad on a first-name basis, and since when are you putting stickers on him?"

"*Ha.* Not your dad, the new car. Amelia named him, obviously. And she so generously said I could put one sticker in the glove box."

"So, you're going to cover him in stickers, right?"

"Or use one very carefully chosen sticker. One Amelia

will never live down once her friends see it. I might need something custom for that, though. How's your printer?"

"Out of ink. And you're going to have to raid someone else's sticker collection, because mine aren't for sticking."

"What's the point of stickers if they're not for sticking? Who do you love more? Me or your—"

The sounds of arguing downstairs interrupt me. Gordon and Helen *never* fight. But they're fighting now, or at least arguing really loudly, which amounts to the same thing.

They're arguing because I accidentally let it slip over dinner that Helen wasn't actually upset about her statue getting taken down, on account of having misgivings about her work with the League. She trusted me with that, and I didn't even make it a whole *two days* before blurting it out in front of everyone. But Amelia was giving me crap about the statue again, since the news announced it's officially in a museum now, and I just wanted her to shut up. And before I could stop myself, before I could, like, think it through, the words were out of my mouth.

To be honest, I didn't realize it was going to be this big of a deal. But I knew Helen didn't want Gordon to know. And as soon as I said it, this weird silence settled over the table, and it was obvious that I'd really screwed up. Again.

"You never told me any of this," Gordon shouts, "but you tell my son?!"

I sit up, a sick feeling settling in my stomach.

"Damien?" Kat says. "Are you still there?"

"Yeah, I'm here."

"I love you more than my stickers, but you're still not getting them."

"Maybe I could come stay with you this weekend. After the Prom, I mean."

"I'm serious about our printer being out of ink."

I laugh. "I could spend the night."

"Really?" She sounds excited about that, then hesitant. "But you'd just have to go back in the morning."

"No, I'll—"

From downstairs, I hear Gordon's voice again, shouting, "How could you keep how you really felt from me?!"

And then Helen, who isn't as audible as him, "Because I knew you wouldn't understand!"

I wince. "I'll stay Sunday night, too. We'll spend the whole weekend together."

"That sounds amazing. But, Damien, what about school? What about your homework?"

"I'll bring my homework, if I have any." I'm pretty sure I'll have some, which I will conveniently forget to bring. There's no way I'm ruining my weekend getaway with homework. "And I'll leave really early on Monday."

"That's what you said the last time you stayed over on a school night."

"And I only missed first period. Nothing happened." Other than a surprise group project that I'm pretty sure the teacher only assigned because I wasn't there. "And even if it had? Totally worth it."

She sighs. It's a longing kind of sigh, like she's already thinking about how awesome this weekend is going to be. "We've all been going to that waffle place on Sundays. I can finally bring you. You're sure you're not going to get in trouble for this? Because if—"

"Nope. No trouble. I'm all yours for, like, thirty-six hours."

"Okay. Wow."

I kind of want to ask her if I can just come over right now. Maybe live in her dorm with her forever, where the biggest decisions I'd have to make about my life are what flavor of waffle to get. But even if I was actually going to do that, leaving the house would involve going downstairs, where Gordon and Helen are, which is something I'm definitely not doing right now. So I guess I'm stuck here.

Amelia's door opens. I'm thinking maybe she's actually braver than me for once, but then a couple seconds later, *my* door opens, and Amelia ducks inside as fast as she can, like she just ran through a war zone instead of a couple feet of hallway.

I glare at her. "What the hell are you doing? I could have been naked."

"I could hear that you were on the phone."

"I could still have been naked. I could have been having phone sex."

"Oh, could you?" Kat says.

Amelia makes a face. "You didn't *sound* like you were having phone sex."

"And you know what that sounds like?" I shake my head at her. And for the record, no, me and Kat have never had phone sex. But I'd like to think that if we did, Amelia wouldn't just barge in.

Amelia rolls her eyes at me. "You were obviously just talking. And you're in your pajamas, which are stupid, by the way—"

"*Hey*. They are not." My pajamas have Superstar, my favorite band, on them. I briefly considered getting Crimson Flash pajamas, since I thought it might annoy Gordon, but I wasn't 100% on that. Plus, then I'd have to actually wear Crimson Flash pajamas, which sounded pretty horrible.

"Superstar doesn't even exist anymore." She says that in her snottiest voice. "They broke up."

"They didn't break up—they're just on *hiatus*."

"Well, they're stupid. And I was talking to Zach, but his mom made him go to bed, and I thought Mom and Dad would be done fighting by now, but they're not, and they *never* fight, and…" Her chin wobbles a little, and she sucks in a deep breath, obviously trying to fight off tears.

I sigh. "Kat? I have to go."

"Okay. I'll call you tomorrow. And, Damien…" She swallows. "I really miss you."

"I miss you, too."

Amelia makes a disgusted sound.

I ignore her. "I love you, Kat."

"I love you, too."

We hang up.

"You're so gross," Amelia says.

"What? You'd rather we were having phone sex?"

Amelia opens her mouth, but then there's more yelling from downstairs.

"He's seventeen years old!" Gordon shouts.

Helen says something, but it's too muffled to make out.

Then Gordon again. "He's *my* son! I was handling it!"

My hands clench, gripping my comforter. I wish I could teleport to pretty much anywhere but here right now. "Okay, Amelia. Let's get this over with."

She just stares at me, not saying anything, still trying not to cry.

"You came here to yell at me, right? So just do it." Not that I want to get yelled at, even by Amelia, and even if I deserve it. But if it's going to happen, it might as well happen quickly.

A couple tears slip down her cheeks. "I didn't... I didn't come here to yell at you."

I find that really hard to believe. "Come on. It's my fault that they're..." I wave my hand at the floor. "I spilled Helen's secret. I started this. And in case you didn't notice? A lot of their argument is about me. So let me have it."

"How could my mom not care about her statue? How could she have lied to me my whole life?"

"I don't think that was—"

"And why did she tell *you*? Of all people."

"Look, Amelia, I don't know. You should ask her."

"But you're the one she told." She rubs at her eyes, then comes over to the bed and sits down, even though I didn't invite her. "If she was going to tell me, she would have already."

I press my hands between my knees. "The only reason she said anything to me is because I'm messed up. She thought it would help."

Amelia gives me a really skeptical look. "Did it?"

"I'm not sure yet. I'll let you know."

"That still doesn't explain why she lied to me my whole life."

"She had to kill people, when she was working for the League. That must have been hard enough without having to tell everyone she wasn't sure she'd done the right thing. Going along with what she was supposed to feel was probably just easier. A lot easier."

"She still told you and not me. You're not even her kid."

"Yeah, well, I'm sure she regrets it now." What with me blabbing her secret to everyone. She told me all that to help me, and this is how I repaid her.

"No one ever trusts me with anything. It's like I don't even matter."

"That's not true." I glance over at her. "If you hadn't been with me the night of the gala, Riley would have died."

She looks down at the floorboards. "You would have saved him."

"No, I wouldn't. I wouldn't have even been there to find him, and I couldn't have freed him from the rubble, so... You were the only other person who was there. You heard him screaming, and you—" I put my hands to my face. I hate talking about this. My heart races, and I just want to disappear. "How can you be okay about it? How can you just... move on?"

She stares at me, looking a little freaked by my reaction. "I don't know."

"It doesn't bother you?"

"Sometimes. But I knew you'd figure it out. I knew

you'd help him."

"*I* didn't know that, so how could you?"

She shrugs. "I figured that whatever happened, you'd make it okay. You're good at fieldwork, and you're my brother, and you always know what to do."

I laugh. "That's funny, because it feels like the opposite."

"But you *did*. You got us out of there. All of us, including Riley."

I nod. "I don't know how to make this okay, though."

"Maybe you don't need to. Just listen," she says. "One time I really thought I was going to win the spelling bee. This was in second grade. Or was it third grade? No, I think it was second. Anyway, I really wanted to win, and I was the best in the class. It was so obvious."

"Is this going anywhere?"

She waves that away. "I didn't even need to practice, but I did anyway. Then, on the day of the big bee, I felt kind of off in the morning, but I didn't really think anything of it. Okay, I knew maybe I was getting sick, but I didn't want to miss the contest. And, well, on my first turn at the microphone, I ended up barfing all over. On stage, in front of everyone."

"Wow. What a great story. That's *so* the same thing as finding your best friend trapped under some rubble because superheroes were trying to kill him. How did you ever get over it?"

"*Shut up.* You didn't let me finish. So, I was really embarrassed. Like, really, *really* embarrassed for the rest of the school year. I had nightmares about it every night for over a month. I couldn't even be part of the school play because seeing the stage just made it all come flooding back."

"I thought Riley was going to *die*. I don't know if anything's ever going to be the same. But you threw up during a spelling bee."

"*Yes*. I'm trying to say that even though it was traumatizing, it got better. Eventually, I stopped having nightmares, and it didn't even bother me that much when the other kids called me Spew. It hurt at first, but, like, after a while it was kind of funny. And I even did the play the next year. I got cast as an extra, so I didn't have a lot of stage time, but the important thing is that it didn't bother me. I was really nervous, but I faced my fear, and it turned out okay."

"I don't think it's going to be that easy." Not for me. Not for this.

"But it might get better. Someday."

I start to argue with her again, because I'm not sure I believe that, but I stop myself. "Thanks, Amelia."

"And if it doesn't get better, there are plenty of normal jobs you can do. Like working at the gas station or maybe at one of the superhero diners. Probably not the one where they named something after you, because that would just be sad, but maybe one of the other ones. Or—"

"*Okay*, I get it."

"I'm just saying that you have options. The world is, like, your oyster or something."

"I *said* I get it."

She holds her hands up, as if she wasn't doing

anything. She seems like she's about to say something else, but then my phone chimes.

I assume it's going to be Kat, telling me again how excited she is for this weekend, but instead it's Riley. And it's not even for me.

Zach says he texted Amelia, but she's not responding.

I type back, *I thought your mom told him to go to bed? And what, he can't even text me himself? His girlfriend didn't text him back for two whole minutes—ANYTHING could have happened to her. This could be an emergency.*

Is it an emergency?

No, she's right here.

"Wait, are you talking about me?" Amelia asks, after leaning over to see my screen.

I jerk the phone out of her view. "Your boyfriend's trying to text you."

Her face lights up, and she holds out her hand for the phone. But only for, like, a split second, and then she just uses her power to teleport it to her and starts typing.

"Before you declare your undying love for him," I tell her, "you should know two things. One, that's *Riley*, because Zach's still not talking to me. And two, it's awfully brave of you to touch my phone, considering how much phone sex it's been a part of."

She immediately drops it, her mouth falling open in disgust. My phone clatters on the floor, and I pick it up.

"Gross." Amelia's holding her hands up, like she's afraid to touch anything now, and makes a face. "And I can't even go wash my hands because Mom and Dad are still…" She pauses to listen for the yelling downstairs, but it's quiet. She exhales in relief. "I'm going to run downstairs real quick and wash my hands. Tell Riley to tell Zach I'll be *right there.*"

Then she takes off for the door, unable to get out of my room fast enough.

CHAPTER 11

I knock on Zach's bedroom door the next day after school. He must think it's Riley, because he actually starts to open it, then sees that it's me and shuts it in my face.

From his room across the hall, Riley gives me a look, like *I told you it wouldn't be that easy.*

I knock again. "Come on, Zach."

He doesn't open the door this time, though he does shout at me from the other side of it. "I have nothing to say to you!" Which seems unlikely, judging from how pissed off he sounds.

"I came here to apologize!"

"Yeah, right!"

"I mean it! And— Will you just come out here?"

Zach opens the door, but only just barely, and he makes a big point of glaring at me.

I take a deep breath. "I'm sorry. Okay? And, I mean, you know me, so you know how rarely I say things like that."

He stares at me.

I guess he can't take the hint. "You should be honored."

"Sorry for what?"

"Exactly. Let's just forget that stupid fight ever happened."

"*No.* I meant which part are you sorry for?"

"Um." I glance over my shoulder at Riley, but he just holds up his hands in a not-getting-involved gesture. "I don't want you to be mad at me. It's weird."

"That's not the same as being sorry for what you did."

"Okay, I'm sorry I freaked out."

He just stares at me again, like I said the wrong thing.

"I'm sorry I freaked out… *and* that I was a jerk to you."

"That's kind of the same thing."

"What do you want me to say?"

His eyes widen. He looks hurt, and I think he might slam the door in my face again. "I shouldn't have to tell you what to apologize for. Not if you really mean it. But since you need so much help, you could start by apologizing for thinking you have any say in me and Amelia's sex life—"

"Whoa, Zach. Don't *say* things like that."

"—or for treating me like a little kid, or for acting like I'm not good enough for her. And if I'm not good enough for her, or to join your group, then I'm not…" He swallows. "Then I'm not good enough to be your friend, right?"

"Zach."

He shakes his head. "Just tell me the truth."

I motion toward his room, and he takes a step back, letting me in. He closes the door, but I keep my voice hushed anyway, in case Riley can still hear us. "Did you really tell Amelia that I didn't save your brother?"

He looks away, his face going red. "You didn't."

"Yeah, but you said I *could have* and I didn't. That's completely different. And no, I didn't save him, and I know his leg is still healing, and if anything had happened to him—*again*—I would never have forgiven myself, and..." My throat's getting tight, and I'm clenching my fists. I force them to relax. "You weren't there, Zach."

"I know." His voice comes out small. He's staring at the floor, looking ashamed. "I shouldn't have said that. I was just mad."

"I tried to save him."

"You jumped over a banister. That's probably the most badass thing you've ever done. Well, *one* of them, at least."

"You really didn't mean it?" Because I can't take Zach thinking I'd just let Riley get hurt.

"I... Maybe a little. But only because I was so mad at you, and because I was worried about Riley." He says all that without looking at me.

It's not quite the answer I wanted, but it's close enough. "I'm sorry I don't want you sleeping with my sister."

He inhales sharply and glances up at me, then away again.

"It's not about you. I like you, Zach. You're my friend, for reals, and not just because you're Riley's brother."

"You don't get to control what we do."

And yet, I'm the one that set them up in the first place. Amelia would probably be boyfriend-free if not for my meddling, and Zach wouldn't be trying to sleep with her.

"I thought you liked that we were together," Zach says.

"I do."

"It's hypocritical of you to be mad at me for having… you know. *Protection*."

Okay, I really wish I wasn't having this conversation right now. I sit down on his bed.

"And it's just for in case. We haven't even talked about it."

"Yet."

"And you and Kat—"

"I know, okay? I know it's hypocritical. But that doesn't mean I'm okay with it." It felt right for me and Kat. And I get that I can't actually know what's right for Zach and Amelia, or at least I get it in theory, but… "Do you love her?"

I didn't know those words were even going to come out of my mouth. Apparently neither did Zach, because he gets this look on his face like he might throw up, and then he flops down into his computer chair.

"I… I really like her."

"That's not the same thing."

"I *might*."

"You would know."

"How? How would I know?"

"You just would." It's a crap answer, but it's also the truth.

"You don't have to love someone to have…" He clears

this throat. "I mean, you know, it's... You're being hypocritical again."

"No, I'm not. I love Kat, and I sure as hell loved her before we started having sex."

Zach flinches on the word. "But you went out with her before. You guys were getting back together, so you already loved her, right? That shouldn't count."

I give him a look.

"I just mean," he adds, "that you probably would have slept with her anyway. You guys just also happened to be in love."

I open my mouth to protest, but then I stop. *Would* I have slept with Kat if I didn't love her? Was it just convenient that we happened to be in love when we started doing it? I don't think so—I don't *want* to think so—but I can't say for sure.

I slide my hands across my knees, smoothing out my jeans. There's one thing I do know. "Me and Kat were in love when it happened, and that matters to me. A lot."

Zach takes that in. "Just because it was right for you to be in love doesn't mean it has to be that way for us. And just because we're not in love yet doesn't mean we won't be."

"Maybe."

"It *doesn't*. But... I'll think about what you said, okay?"

"You will?"

He shrugs. "I don't want us to be fighting, so if it's that important to you, I'll think about it. I care about Amelia a lot, though, even if I don't know if I'm in love with her yet."

"Okay."

"Are you still mad at me?"

"I thought *you* were mad at *me*. I mean," I add, "I was mad, too. But I think we're okay." I'm not sure I like his "I'll think about it" answer, but I guess it'll have to do for now. "So, you guys like Italian, right?"

"What?"

"Your brother made reservations at some Italian place. For Saturday. He made it for six people, so you and Amelia can still come with us."

"Oh. We made other plans."

"Yeah, but that was before, when you were pissed at me. But now that you're not, you guys can come with us, where you belong."

"But we made plans with Amelia's friends."

"I'll talk to her. You know you'll have more fun coming with us."

He doesn't say anything.

"Zach, come on. You want to come with us, right?"

"We made other plans, okay? We're going with Amelia's friends."

Yeah, so maybe things aren't that all right between us. "Fine, Zach. If that's what you want."

He swivels in his chair a little, so he's not pointed at me. "Yeah, it is. Me and Amelia have plans, and not everything is your decision."

CHAPTER 12

"What do you think they're doing up there?" I wave my hand at the ceiling toward Amelia's room. Where she and Zach currently are. Alone.

It's Wednesday afternoon. Riley's sitting across from me at the dining table. "You guys *just* made up, like, yesterday," he says.

"Sort of." Enough that Zach felt comfortable coming over to the house again, at least. "But that doesn't mean that I'm okay with knowing that they might be... you know."

Sarah's sitting at the head of the table, between me and Riley, with her binder open in front of her, since theoretically we're all doing our homework. "I doubt you have anything to worry about."

"Yeah," Riley says. "They're just watching a movie."

Me and Sarah both give him incredulous looks.

"Well, they could be."

"What I meant," Sarah says, "is that they're probably

not going to do it for the first time with us right downstairs."

I exhale in relief. "You think? I mean, that's what I was thinking, but—"

"And they're probably waiting for Prom night. It's only a few days away."

"*Sarah.*" I gape at her.

"It's a common rite of passage. And you don't have to look at me like that. It's not like I invented it."

"I'm looking at you like you're not helping."

"Can we talk about something else?" Riley says.

"Your brother knows I could kill him, right? I could actually kill him." I hold up my hands and let lightning spark a little.

"Let it go already."

"I can't believe you're okay with it."

"I didn't say I was okay with it. But that doesn't mean I want to spend all afternoon discussing my little brother's sex life."

"Alleged, theoretical sex life that hopefully doesn't exist."

"Right, but it's going to happen eventually. For both of them. So I guess it might as well be together."

"Wow, great, Perkins. I'm so glad to hear that romance is still alive and well in the world."

Sarah adjusts her glasses. "I think what he meant was that it might as well be Amelia, because that way if she gets pregnant and they get married, at least you two will be brother-in-laws."

We both stare at her.

"I just mean it could be worse."

"That's... There are so many things wrong with that, Sarah, I don't even know where to start."

"New topic," Riley says.

Sarah nods. "It's time we got down to business."

I raise my eyebrows at her. "You don't mean actually doing homework, do you?"

"I've got the perfect mission lined up for us. Now, I know our last one didn't go so great."

"*That's* an understatement," I mutter.

"But I'm willing to forgive and forget so we can move on."

I exchange a worried look with Riley.

"You guys were out of practice," Sarah says, "and we'd never all worked together before. Of course there's going to be a little turbulence, especially in the beginning. But our next mission will be better. I hope neither of you has plans for next Tuesday night. I know it's a weekday, but crime doesn't always happen when it's convenient. I mean, I don't know if it's happening Tuesday night, either, but that's when I know for sure no other superhero teams will be patrolling the museum. Well, from one to three a.m. I hacked the League's database, and it turns out the team that normally has that slot has been reassigned for the night, so the museum will be vulnerable. And if I could find out this information, somebody else could, too, including criminals. Now, we won't have access to the inside of the building or to any security footage, so we'll just have to be extra vigilant along the perimeter, and... What?" She glances back and forth between me and Riley.

Probably because I was mouthing, *She's your girlfriend—you tell her*, and he was frantically shaking his head.

"What?" Sarah says again.

I clear my throat and jerk my chin toward Riley.

He swallows. "Um, Sarah, I... I don't know if we're, um, if we're ready for that kind of—"

"It's perfectly safe. Well, probably, unless bad guys show up, but there's only a low to moderate chance of that, and it's all at the ground level. It won't be like last time."

"Yeah, but we... It wasn't just... We don't..." Riley trails off.

I take over. "Sarah, we're not doing it."

She frowns. "What do you mean?"

"I mean we're not doing fieldwork right now."

"Yes, you are. You're investigating that stolen painting for school. Riley told me."

Well, that's what we're *supposed* to be doing, anyway. We have yet to actually start on it, but I guess that's beside the point right now. "I know, but that's only because we have to. But other than that, we decided we're not doing fieldwork."

Sarah blinks at me. "But you're *superheroes*. Well, Riley is, and you're getting there. Either way, it's what you guys do. It's what *we* do."

I spread my hands out on the table. "Maybe that's how it was, but it's not anymore. I'm sorry, Sarah."

Her mouth slips open a little. "I... Okay. Okay. If it has to just be me and Secant for a while, then—"

"Sarah." Riley's voice is just a whisper.

"It can be just the two of us. Just because Renegade's backing out doesn't mean you have to."

He shakes his head. "We shouldn't have even been there last weekend."

"But..."

"We're not ready."

"*He's* not, you mean."

Wow. *He* is in the room.

"Sarah, *I'm* not ready. I just got my cast off."

"So? Your leg is healed. And Damien didn't really even get hurt."

Riley stares down at the table. "It's not that simple."

"You guys are fine. You're just scared and a little rusty. And the only thing that's going to fix that is getting back on the horse and going on more missions."

Riley slides his hands over his face. "I don't know, Sarah. I think... I think that last mission just made it worse."

"And you think doing nothing is supposed to help?"

"You don't understand."

"No, I don't. You two are telling me you finally have the chance to be yourselves again, and now you don't even want to do it. And I'm supposed to understand that?"

"I don't expect you to understand. I wish you did, but..." He looks up at her. "I just need time."

"For what?"

"To figure things out. To see if this really is who I still am." He stares down at the table when he says that part.

"It *is*," Sarah says. "It's who both of you are."

"And if it's not?"

"I know you guys, and this is who you are—who you still are—even if you don't realize it yet."

"But—"

"It *is*," she repeats. And even if she didn't pick up her pen and start flipping through her binder, like she's going to actually do her homework now, it would still be clear from her tone that the conversation is over.

CHAPTER 13

"So," Amelia says on the way to school on Thursday, "where are you really going this weekend?"

She could have asked me this earlier, but she waits until Melissa and Hilary—I mean, "Hil"—are in the car.

"Because," Amelia goes on, not even giving me a chance to answer, "I *know* you're not staying at Riley's like you told Dad."

Melissa and Hil both look properly scandalized by that, and Melissa even turns around in her seat to gape at me.

"No, what I *said* was that I'm going to be having amazing sex all weekend. If he assumed that meant I'm going to Riley's, well, that's his problem."

Melissa gasps and quickly turns around to face the front again. Hil laughs nervously, like she's not sure if I was joking or not.

Amelia scowls in the rear-view mirror. "That's *not* what you told him. And I know you're going to Kat's. That's his girlfriend," she adds, in case the others didn't already know that, though I'm sure they could guess. "It's so obvious."

"If you already know I'm going to Kat's, then why did you ask?"

She goes on like I didn't say anything. "He stays over at her dorm all the time, and my parents pretend like they don't even notice."

I glance up at the mirror. "They *don't* notice." At least, I hope not. And if they do... I'm sure I would have heard about it by now.

"He gets to do whatever he wants, but Mom said I have to be home from Prom by eleven. It's so unfair."

Melissa's mouth falls open. "*Eleven?* Seriously?"

"Well," Amelia says, "Dad was going to make it ten, but Mom said that was ridiculous. Eleven's not much better, though."

Hil sighs. "My mom said I could stay out till one, but everybody else I know has to be home before then, so it's kind of pointless."

"My mom actually called Zach's mom to find out when he was supposed to be home. Can you believe that? They didn't give me a curfew for Homecoming."

Of course they didn't. Back then, Zach was just some random date. Well, sort of. Now he's her boyfriend and has condoms in his room. Er, not that they know about that last part.

"What?" Amelia says.

It takes me a second to realize she's talking to me. "What?"

"That's what I said."

"Yeah, but... *what* what?"

"You had a look on your face. I saw it in the mirror. Like you know something I don't."

"I was just thinking that after what happened at Homecoming, they probably don't want you staying out late."

"Why? Because *you* might blow up the school again?"

Melissa nods in agreement, and Hil just shakes her head at me.

"I can't believe they're even letting you go to Prom," Amelia says. "And you don't even have a curfew. *And* they actually had the nerve to say that if me and Zach were going with you and your friends instead of mine that I could stay out until midnight."

"Because they know how responsible and trustworthy I am." Or maybe more like how responsible and trustworthy Riley is.

She scoffs. "More than me? I don't think so. And I told them no way. We already have plans with my friends, and we're not ditching them just to get to be out a little longer."

Hil leans forward, in between the front seats. "It's because Zach's your boyfriend now. My sister had this problem last year when she was going out with Ethan. They went to a dance as friends, and my parents didn't even tell her when to be home. Then a couple months later when they were together, they wouldn't even let her stay past nine *at a birthday party*."

"Speaking of birthdays," Melissa says, "isn't Zach's

coming up? Did you ever figure out what you were, you know, *getting him*?" She says that like what Amelia was thinking of getting him involved a lap dance or something.

Amelia's face turns red. "*You guys.*"

Melissa grins. "What?"

"Melissa," Hil says out the side of her mouth, jerking her chin toward me.

Which is obviously code for "don't talk about Amelia's possible sex life in front of her brother." I think it might also be code for "today would have been a really good day to have gotten a ride from Riley."

"What?" Melissa says again. "You were just talking about him and his girlfriend, so—"

"That's different," Amelia snaps. "And anyway, we're here." She pulls into a parking space at school. Then she tells Melissa and Hil to go in without her.

They get out of the car and say they'll see her in a little bit, leaving us alone.

There's a really awkward silence. I'm considering pretending I don't notice it and just getting out and going to school like normal when Amelia turns around to face me. "Damien, can I talk to you about something?"

"No."

"But—"

"I'm really busy, Amelia. I have to get to school."

"No, you don't. We've still got ten minutes. It's about me and Zach, and—"

"I don't want to hear about it, okay? Like, seriously." And I really, really don't want to be here right now.

"But I have to hear about you and Kat *all the time.*"

"I know, I know. It's hypocritical. But this is..." I make a face. "It's none of my business."

"It's just that Prom's this Saturday, and it really seems like the right time."

"What do you think 'It's none of my business' means? I don't want to hear about it."

"But none of my friends have really... It's kind of a big deal, and I don't have anyone else to talk to about it."

Erg. "It *is* a big deal, but I'm your brother. It's too weird." And I already got in trouble from Zach for giving him my opinion. I'm staying out of it.

"Oh." She sounds kind of dejected. "But, I mean, do you think it's a good birthday present? Do you think... do you think he'll be happy?"

"Amelia, seriously. I don't want to be having this conversation."

"But you're a boy, *and* you know Zach, even if you guys were fighting recently. I just want to know..." She sucks in a deep breath. "I think things are going really well, but I don't want to freak him out."

I raise my eyebrows at her. "Trust me, Amelia. You're not going to freak him out. He'll be into it."

"I was thinking about waiting until his birthday next week, but his mom and his friends will be there, and it might be kind of hard to find any time alone, you know? Plus, Prom is more romantic."

Wow. "Yeah, I get it. You don't have to spell it out. Geez."

"Okay, but do you think—"

"I think you really don't need me for this."

"But, I mean, I'm really nervous."

"Oh, look at the time. We only have eight minutes to get to class."

"Were you nervous? The first time you...? Because I know, in the movies, people are always—"

"It's not like in the movies. It's probably going to be really awkward. I mean, at least at first."

"Oh. But were you nervous? Because you're never nervous about *anything*."

I laugh.

"Well, not stuff like this," she adds.

"I don't know. Maybe a little bit? But in a good kind of way. And can we *please* drop this?"

"But I'm *really* nervous."

"Then don't do it."

"But I'm really nervous about everything, so maybe that doesn't mean anything."

"Look, Amelia, it's not about how nervous you are. But it's not something you can take back. So, I mean, if you think you'll regret it—"

"I won't." She sounds pretty sure about that.

"Oh. Okay."

"But I think I'd really regret it if I didn't do it." She grins at me. "So, thanks."

"You're not welcome. We never had this conversation. It didn't happen."

"Well, even if it didn't happen, it still really helped."

The woman who works at the Golden City Museum scowls at me and Riley when we tell her we're from Heroesworth, doing an investigation for school. She looks each of us over, sort of sneers, and says, "No, you're not."
Which really isn't what we expected.

I glance over at Riley. He glances over at me.

"It's true, though," I tell the woman. "We're supposed to figure out who stole that painting."

She scoffs. "We've already had someone in here about that."

"The police?" Riley asks. "Because we're not with them. We go to Heroesworth."

"We can prove it," I tell her. "Show her your thumb."

Riley starts to hold up his hand, but the woman stops him. "No need. I know who you are. Well, who *you* are." She looks right at me for that.

"Then you know that we *do* go to Heroesworth."

"I know you got expelled."

I roll my eyes. "That was months ago."

"Well, I don't keep up with the tabloids." She sniffs.

"We have I.D.," Riley says. "From school."

"Fake ones, no doubt. And we've already had a couple students from Heroesworth in here, doing the same investigation."

"What?"

She gets this self-satisfied look on her face, like she just caught us in a lie. "That's right. They were just here. I don't know what you're trying to gain from this, but you picked the wrong day to try and scam me."

Riley's mouth hangs open a little. "But we really are

from Heroesworth. I don't know who else was here, but—"

"Maybe your teacher gave you the wrong assignment," she tells him, in a voice that says she doesn't believe that we're from Heroesworth, like, *at all*. "Now, I need you to leave the museum before I have to call for security." She signals for another staff member to come over.

"But we really are—"

"Come on," I say, grabbing Riley's arm. "She's not going to listen to us."

We head out of the exhibit, into the hallway.

Riley glances back inside. "That was weird."

"Maybe Mrs. Deeds screwed up. Maybe she really did give us the same assignment as somebody else."

"That's a pretty big mistake." He looks at me like that couldn't be possible.

"So she screwed us over on purpose. She hates me."

"But she doesn't hate *me*."

Well, that's true. "Look at it this way, Perkins. There's no point in us wasting time on an investigation that might have wrongfully been assigned to us. And that we're obviously not going to get anywhere on." At least, not until that lady's shift is over. "So we should probably just go home."

"Go home? We just got here."

"I'm not hearing any better ideas. We'll talk to Mrs. Deeds tomorrow and figure out what happened." Maybe it'll turn out that there weren't enough assignments to go around, and we'll get to sit out the rest of the semester after all.

"I don't think it was a mistake."

"Yeah, well, I don't know what else is—"

"Oh, *great*," someone behind me says. Someone whose voice I definitely recognize. And hate.

Followed by a voice I do *not* hate. "Damien?!"

Me and Riley both turn to look.

Kat's standing there with a surprised smile on her face. Next to her is Tristan, her fieldwork partner, looking way less happy to see us. Tristan's the idiot who first started calling her 'Katie,' and he's also the douche who wouldn't stop flirting with her at the beginning of the school year, even though he knew she was with me, which pretty much made me want to kill him. I kind of almost did at Homecoming—the one at Vilmore, not the one where I blew up the gym—or at least I came really close to punching him in the face, which should still count for something. I mean, he's moved on, now that he knows Kat really isn't interested, but neither one of us is exactly thrilled to see each other.

"Kat?!" I can't believe it's her. She moves toward me, and I put my arms around her and hug her really tight. It's been weeks since the last time we saw each other in person. She kind of melts into me, wrapping her arms around me, too, and buries her face in my neck.

Tristan clears his throat. Then again, a little louder, when we don't move.

Kat takes a step back. "I didn't think I was going to see you until this weekend."

Her hair seems a little longer than when I last saw her. I mean, maybe she just shapeshifted it to look that way. Because there's no way I haven't seen my own girlfriend in so long that her hair is noticeably longer. Just a little bit. Just enough so that I can't tell if it's real or I'm imagining it. Because it's only been a few weeks.

Or maybe more like a month.

The thought hits me hard and makes my chest ache. And then I'm just standing there, staring at her, thinking about how much I've missed her.

Tristan clears his throat again, like we didn't hear him the first couple times.

"We're here for our fieldwork assignment," I tell Kat. "I was just about to go distract that lady while Perkins here turned invisible and looked for evidence."

Riley makes a garbled sound in his throat. "You said we were going home! You said—"

"I mean, we probably won't find anything, because the police have already been here. But we should at least try, and maybe I'll be able to sweet talk some info out of her." I glance over at the museum lady again. She still has a sour look on her face, or maybe that's just her natural expression.

"The one who threatened to call security on us, you mean?" Riley sounds pretty skeptical.

"Oh, that lady?" Kat says. "We talked to her earlier. She was really nice."

Tristan nods.

"Of course, we told her we were from Heroesworth." Kat grins and holds up her thumb, which she's shapeshifted to have an *H*.

I gape at her. "*Kat.*"

"What?"

Riley scowls. "You stole our assignment."

"No, I—" She stops herself, considering that for a second. Then she gasps. "You're investigating the missing painting?"

"Yep." Not that Kat knew that, but still. I shake my head at her. "She wouldn't talk to us because someone else from Heroesworth had already been here."

Kat's face falls. "Oh, my God, Damien. I didn't know. I just thought it would be—"

Tristan busts up laughing.

Kat glares at him. "It's not funny."

The museum lady whips her head in our direction, like she can't stand the sound of laughter. We all move farther into the hall, so she'll think we're leaving. All of us except Tristan, since he's too busy laughing. Kat has to grab his sleeve to make him move.

"I just thought," Kat says, keeping her voice low, even though I don't think anyone who matters can hear us, "that she'd be more cooperative if she thought we were from Heroesworth. I couldn't tell her we were from Vilmore."

Riley wrinkles his forehead. "You're investigating a theft?" He glances over at me, like I have the answer. "But I thought—"

"You thought villains only stole stuff?" Tristan says, not laughing anymore.

Riley shrugs. "I didn't think you solved crimes. That's all."

"Right." Tristan looks him over and scoffs. Then he mutters, "*Letterist,*" under his breath.

I take a step forward, getting between him and Riley. "What was that?"

"You heard me."

"*Hey.*" Kat gives both of us a warning look. "We're trying to figure out who stole the painting so we can steal it for someone else."

"You're posing as Heroesworth students. So you can steal something." Riley says that like it leaves a bad taste in his mouth. Like he's disappointed in her.

"See?" Tristan snaps. "Letterist."

"Well, we are, though," Kat says.

"And if you call him that again," I tell Tristan, "I'll assume it's because you *want* me to fry you."

"Nobody's frying anybody." Kat holds up her hands. "Especially not in the middle of a *museum.*"

Tristan snorts. "Yeah, you break it, you bought it."

Kat grits her teeth and looks like she wants to strangle him, but otherwise ignores him. "I took notes during our interview. You can see what she said."

"Thanks, Kat."

"What?!" Tristan's face turns red with anger, or maybe it's because his power involves being a human flamethrower.

"It's our fault they couldn't interview her," Kat says. "It's only fair that we share what we found out."

"We're not sharing notes with them, Katie. Your traitor boyfriend and his stupid hero partner can figure it out on their own."

"Excuse me?" I say to him.

"I'm just calling it like I see it. First you're a hero,

sucking up to the whole city with that cheesy video about your dad, then you're a villain, working for the Truth. You acted like that was real, like you actually cared. Now you're... what? A hero again?" He makes a disgusted face.

Electricity prickles the back of my neck and runs along my skin. "You don't know what you're talking about."

"Yeah, I do, 'cause if you were really a villain, if you were *really* on our side, you'd go to Vilmore, not Heroesworth. And you wouldn't be defending your letterist friend, like you're not even one of us."

"He's *not*—" I turn to look at Riley, but he's not there. He's not in the hallway. And even though I know it doesn't mean anything—it doesn't necessarily mean something bad's happened—a wave of cold fear suddenly clenches my stomach. "Perkins?"

"Oh, I guess he's a coward, too. He couldn't even own up to what he—"

"*Shut up.*" Lightning surges in my hands, and panic makes my heart beat too fast.

"I'm sure he's fine." Kat starts to put a hand on my arm, not noticing the electricity, but I step out of reach so she doesn't get zapped. "He probably just went to the bathroom or something."

"He wouldn't just disappear."

"Damien? He can turn *invisible*. So, yeah, he would."

"Dude," Tristan says, staring at me like I just told them I escaped from an asylum or something. "Chill the hell out."

Electricity crackles. My thoughts race. What if that lady did call security? What if she didn't just call security, but the League? She might have done that. She probably thought we were villains, just pretending to be heroes. She could have called them, and they could have come here with rayguns, and... I don't know what they could have done without us noticing, and I know I'm freaking out for probably no reason right now, but none of that makes me feel any better.

"You have Riley's number, right, Kat?" I can't use my phone. Not without frying it.

"Yeah." She gets hers out and starts dialing.

Tristan's still got that look on his face, like he can't figure out if I'm crazy or if he's completely missing something.

There's a few seconds of tense silence. I listen for a phone ringing. I don't hear anything.

Then Riley's voice, right beside me, says, "What's going on?"

I startle and almost lose control of my lightning. Just a few months ago, I probably would've accidentally blown up part of the wall, which, with my luck, would have had some priceless artifact on the other side. "What the hell, Perkins?!"

We all stare at him.

"What? What's wrong?"

"I thought you were— Where were you?"

He jerks his thumb toward the painting exhibit. "You guys were busy arguing, so I went to check out the scene of the crime again. In invisible mode, I mean. I figured it couldn't hurt."

"And you couldn't have answered your phone?!"

"I turned it off. What? We're in a museum. That's what you're *supposed* to do."

"Right. Yeah." My voice isn't as steady as I'd like it to be.

Riley squints at me. Then understanding dawns on him. "I'm okay, X."

I nod. I don't look at anybody.

It was stupid to have freaked out like that.

"Well, this has been fun," Tristan says, checking his phone, "but we have to go. Our train's leaving in ten minutes."

"Crap." Kat bites her lip, looking torn between wanting to stay longer and knowing she has to leave.

I put my arms around her. "I'll see you on Saturday."

"Yeah. And I'll send you a picture of my notes."

Tristan makes an annoyed sound, but we ignore him.

Kat kisses me, and I kiss her back. I don't want to let go of her.

"Nine minutes, Katie," Tristan whines. "And we still have to get to the station—we don't have time for this."

I hug her again before she can leave.

Saying good-bye to her is always so much easier on the phone. Not that it's easy, exactly, but it doesn't hurt like this does.

"Two more days," she whispers, and then she rushes off after Tristan, who's already hurrying down the hall.

"So, you want to know what I found?" Riley asks, once they're gone.

"I don't really want to see any of the exhibits, if that's what you mean."

"No, at the crime scene."

"I thought the police already went over it?"

"They did. And I didn't see anything when we were there the first time, either. But when I went back in invisible mode, there was something written on the wall."

"Like, in invisible ink?"

He rolls his eyes at me. "I don't know how they did it, but whoever stole that painting left a secret message."

I didn't know that was even possible. "What did it say?"

"It said, *This is Frank's business—stay out of it.*"

"Who the hell is Frank?"

"I don't know, but that's what that guy at the train station said, too. He asked if Frank sent me."

I remember that. "What kind of a villain name is Frank?"

"Maybe he's not a villain, just a criminal."

"It's still weird. And it doesn't give us much to go on."

"No, not really," Riley says. "But I guess it's a start."

CHAPTER 14

"You're really wearing a tux?" Riley asks, raising his eyebrows when me and Kat get to the restaurant Saturday evening.

"I told you I was."

"Yeah, but…"

"Geez, Perkins. I wear swim trunks, you have a problem with it. I wear a tux—which you're also wearing, I might add—and you have a problem with it. I just can't win."

The table is one of those round booths, so that if someone in the middle has to go to the bathroom, everyone on one side has to get out first. I slide in next to him, and Kat sits next to me. Sarah's on Riley's other side, opposite Kat.

Kat nods at Sarah. "I like your dress."

It's a deep purple evening gown that only comes up over one shoulder. Sarah shrugs and scowls down at the table, not saying anything.

"Um, okaaay," Kat mutters.

Kat's dress is a shimmery pink. She told me earlier when she came to pick me up that all it needed was one of those cone hats and she could be a fairytale princess. I told her that was a great idea for Halloween. Then she said she'd do it, but only if I wore a similarly themed costume, and I said I didn't think pink was really my color. Then she punched my arm and said I just got myself demoted to her court jester and that I would definitely have to wear tights.

"You look great, Kat," I tell her, partly to fill the silence, but also because it's true.

"Thanks."

"Yeah," Riley says.

Sarah sort of sucks in her breath and looks at him like he just said something way worse and totally inappropriate.

I squint at them. "Did something happen?"

"Like you don't know," Sarah says.

"I have no idea what you're talking about."

"I'm talking about your mission on Thursday. Riley told me everything."

He sighs. "Come on, Sarah. It wasn't like—"

He shuts up as a waiter comes over to our table, refilling water glasses and asking if he can take our orders. Me and Kat glance through the menu real quick while Riley and Sarah both order lasagna. Kat gets chicken Parmesan, and I order spaghetti.

"Marvelous choices," the waiter says before hurrying off, taking our menus with him.

We all sit in silence.

"It wasn't like that, Sarah," Riley finally says.

I exchange a confused look with Kat.

"You lied to me," Sarah tells him. "*Both* of you. That really hurts."

I unroll my napkin, dumping my silverware out on the table, even though our food won't be here for a while. "Uh, you want to tell me what you're talking about?"

"You two told me you weren't doing fieldwork right now. That's what you said."

"And we're not. Except for our mission for school, but you already knew that." I don't see how she gets lying out of that.

"You wouldn't work with me, but now you're working with Kat?"

Kat shakes her head. "They're not working with me. We don't even go to the same *school*."

"See, Sarah?" Riley says. "We're not working with her."

"But you have the same assignment, and she gave you guys a copy of her notes."

And I told Kat about the cryptic message Riley saw on the wall, but now really doesn't seem like a good time to bring that up.

"So?" Kat scowls at her.

"So, that's working together. That's…" Sarah spreads out her hands. "It's not fair. I've been waiting eight months to get to work with them, and they tell me they can't, but then working with you is no problem?"

One side of Kat's face twitches. "Are you kidding me right now?"

"You guys said you didn't want to do fieldwork, and I was stupid enough to believe you, when really you just didn't want to do fieldwork with *me*." Sarah sounds pretty upset. Like she actually might start crying or something.

"Sarah…" Riley tries to take her hand, but she pulls away from him. "We didn't lie to you. And we didn't not want to work with you. Right, X?"

"Right. It's not you, Sarah. It's…" It's a lot of things. "It doesn't have anything to do with you. And it's not like we planned to run into Kat. I mean," I add, off the murderous look that Kat gives me, "we didn't have a problem with running into Kat. We were really happy about it. I know I was. And she's just sharing her notes with us. It's not a big deal."

"I can't believe this," Kat says. "Don't give in to her."

"What? I'm not—"

"And so what if you guys were working with me? I'm not saying they were, Sarah—don't worry, you're still getting your way—but *so freaking what* if they were? You've had to wait eight months to work with them? *I* was supposed to be partners with Damien." She jerks a thumb to her chest. "Me. His *girlfriend*. We were supposed to be villains together. But then you came along—"

"He got an X," Sarah says. "It wasn't my fault."

Kat grits her teeth. "You're his sidekick. You got to work with him plenty before, and you know you will again. And yeah, your boyfriend will join you guys, too. Even though you're the one who pushed them into going on a mission again before they were ready, put them in danger, and then *blamed* Damien for it. What happened at that train station was on you."

"You weren't— You weren't there."

"Neither were you. Not when it mattered. But despite all the danger you've put them in, they're both going to go back to working with you. We all know they are, because that's just how this works. You get what you want, and I don't."

"Kat." I put a hand on her arm.

"Don't defend her, Damien. She has nothing to complain about. And she doesn't get to whine about you guys running into me on one measly assignment. *I* was the one who was supposed to get to work with you. I know it's never going to happen. I've had over a year to get used to that, but..." She shakes her head, then looks at Sarah. "Maybe you can't work with them right now, but at least you're all on the same path. You and your boyfriend don't live in different cities, headed in completely different directions. You don't have to worry about what that means for you in the future. You get to see your boyfriend *all the time*. And, as if that's not enough, you get to see mine, too. So don't tell me what's fair or not. Because you have everything. You have *everything*, and I just— I just don't."

X·X·X

I follow Kat out to her car. She gets behind the steering wheel, and I get in the passenger side.

She puts her face in her hands and sucks in a deep breath. "Well, I guess I was wrong about being able to get through dinner. But, for the record, she started it."

"It's okay, Kat."

"No, it's not. I shouldn't have let her get to me. But *come on*. All that stuff she was saying? It just hit too close to home."

"I didn't know you felt that way."

"I know, I thought I was past blowing up at her. But sometimes..." She squeezes the steering wheel.

"No, I mean all that stuff you said about us living in different cities."

"Well, we do."

"I know."

A group of people dressed for Prom walks past the car, toward the restaurant. All six of them slow way down and stare at me as they move past, and one guy even snaps a picture of us with his phone. He tries to do it discreetly, like we won't notice.

I glare at them, making eye contact, and they move on.

"I know we live in different cities, Kat. But I just thought..."

"What?"

"I don't know. That it didn't bother you the way it did me?"

She laughs. "Are you serious? Do you have any idea how much I miss you? Like, *all the time*?"

Of course it bothers her. I knew that, and now I feel really stupid for doubting it. "But you have all your friends. And movie night. And waffle breakfasts."

"And a butt ton of homework."

"Yeah, that."

"None of that is you, though. And you have Riley, and Zach, and... Sarah, I guess."

"Yeah, well, I don't know if you've noticed this, but they're not you, either."

She smiles a little. "I thought it bothered *me* more than you. The not seeing each other. I always end up crying when you leave, or when I have to go back."

"You can't help it if your boyfriend is just that amazing. I wouldn't want to spend that much time away from me, either."

"Shut up. I'm being serious."

"I know." I swallow. "The truth is, Kat, it totally kills me every time I have to say good-bye to you, too. Spending the whole weekend with you is going to make Monday so much worse."

"Just think about next year, about how hard it will be to be apart after we spend the summer together."

It was bad enough this year, when I didn't actually know what it would be like. But next year? I can't even picture it. "I should have gone with you on that ski trip last winter. It was stupid not to."

"You went to your mom's wedding."

"And you were right—it just made me miserable."

"But you would have regretted not going. And I'm not going anywhere this summer."

"I don't care what you do this summer, as long as I get to be there. I won't miss it this time. And we're not headed in different directions."

"Oh, really? Because you're a hero and I'm a villain."

"Yeah, but I'm not a very good hero. That's almost like

being a villain. And anyway, I might be dropping out of school soon."

She must think I'm joking, because she ignores that last comment. "You're the one who's always saying you don't know what your future will be."

"True. But the one thing I do know is that it'll have you in it."

"It better."

"You're the one who's going places. You'll have some amazing career as a villain, and I'll just be... here. Hoping you don't leave me behind."

"You're famous, Damien."

"More like *infamous*. And not that much."

"Really? Because people we don't even know keep staring at you, and I'm pretty sure someone tried to take a picture just a minute ago."

"So?"

She holds in a breath, then lets it out all at once. "I worry that you'll forget about me. That we spend so much time apart that one of these days you'll forget why you ever even liked me. You don't need to be *going* anywhere, because you're kind of already there. You already do amazing things, and sometimes I feel like I'm the one who can't keep up. And maybe some people don't like you, but there are a lot of girls who would—"

"That's not going to happen."

"Us being together is really hard. And..." Her voice goes tight. "What if someday you decide that it's too much?"

"It's not too much. *Kat.*" I put my hands on her wrists. I

look her in the eyes. "It's not. I don't want things to be easy, and I don't want anybody else. I just want to be with you."

"Okay. I... Okay." A look of relief washes over her.

"Do *you* want it to be easy?"

"What? *No.* Of course not, Damien."

"Good. Because I... I love you, Kat. All the time. Not just when it's convenient. And being with me is pretty much never convenient, so I can only assume you feel the same way."

She grins, though her eyes are a little watery. "You assume right. And not seeing you all the time doesn't change how I feel about you."

"It's only another year."

She squeezes my hand. "I know."

"A really long year, but still."

"*Damien.*"

"Well, it's true. But that's all. Just one. And if you want to drop out of school and get married and join the circus or start up a detective agency or something, I'm available."

"Thanks. I might take you up on that detective agency thing."

"I mean it, Kat. I'd do anything for you. You know that, right?"

CHAPTER 15

We go back inside the restaurant and have dinner with Riley and Sarah.

Even though Kat leans over in the car and whispers seductively in my ear about just forgetting all this and going back to her place.

And reminds me that it's been over a month.

And slides her hand up my leg and kisses my neck.

Okay, so maybe we make out a little bit first before going back in. At least until a camera flashes and I hear some people laughing.

Another group of Prom-goers is meandering past the car, stopping to watch us like this is a free show.

Me and Kat pull apart. Her face is flushed, and she stares down at her knees in embarrassment.

And I think about how there was a time, not that long ago, when I wouldn't have let random onlookers stop us like that. I would have just kissed her more. Especially if there were cameras.

But it's not fun when they don't want to look away. When instead of being horrified, they actually *want* to watch us. It's gross, and it kind of really creeps me out.

So we stop and go back inside and have dinner.

I mean, Riley and Sarah are my closest friends besides Kat, so we weren't *really* going to just leave to go have sex at her dorm. Plus, it's a forty-five minute drive. My house is way closer.

After dinner, we all head over to the dance.

Apparently *A Night to Remember* means a night-sky theme, plus lots of red roses everywhere, and some fake pillars with gauzy material draped between them.

"I'm just asking when you might have time to work on it," Sarah says, getting out a small notepad and pen from her purse.

Kat makes a frustrated sound. "I already told you, *no*."

Sarah shakes her head, like that answer's unacceptable. "I know from what Damien's said that you have a really busy schedule that doesn't allow for a lot of 'alone time.'"

Kat glares at me.

"But I can come meet you on campus."

"Okay, first of all? You are *never* coming to Vilmore again. Not after what happened last time."

She means when Sarah went crazy and tried to wipe out a whole generation of supervillains. Not that she was exactly herself when she did that, but I can still see how Sarah and Vilmore would be a bad idea.

Sarah opens her mouth to say something to that, but Kat cuts her off.

"And *second* of all, I already told you, you're not

working with us."

"We can meet somewhere halfway. Or talk on the phone. I just think that this mission would go more smoothly if all four of us were involved."

Kat stares at her in disbelief.

"I can help," Sarah adds.

"You're not part of this. You don't even go to their school—"

"Neither do you."

"—and you don't go to mine. And I'm not working with them. *And* I already have a partner."

"He can come, too. I don't mind."

"Uh, no, he can't," I tell her. "Because I *do* mind."

"So do I," Riley says. "Tristan's a total douche. And we're not even working with them."

Sarah purses her lips, giving us all a look that says she doesn't quite buy that. "I really think I could help. And you guys have to do this mission either way, whether I'm involved or not, so—"

"Not happening," Kat tells her.

"But—"

"So, who wants punch?" I ask, getting between them.

Sarah narrows her eyes at me. "Don't try to change the subject."

"I'm not. I just thought punch was part of the whole Prom experience."

"Hey," Zach says as he and Amelia come up to join us.

Speaking of the whole *Prom experience*. They're both grinning, and kind of sweaty, though I think that's just from being in a room with a couple hundred people in it.

And maybe from dancing. At least, I hope it is. But Amelia's hair still looks perfectly in place, despite being in lots of curls stacked up on top of her head, and Zach's tux doesn't look rumpled or anything, so they *probably* haven't defiled each other. Yet.

"Hey," Riley says, nodding at his brother.

Kat smiles at Amelia. "Cute dress."

"Huh? Oh, thanks." Amelia glances down at the black velvet dress she's wearing and laughs nervously, even though no one said anything funny. She unhooks her arm from around Zach's to wipe her palms on her thighs.

So, they definitely didn't do it, then, or else she wouldn't be so nervous. Right?

"How's your night so far?" Riley asks.

Zach wrinkles his nose. "Dinner was kind of gross. The place we went to only served fish. I can still smell it."

"Melissa didn't know that when she made reservations, though," Amelia says. "And she's allergic. So after dinner, I called up a bunch of snacks from home." She holds out her hand, mimicking using her power. "Everyone was *really* glad I was there."

I raise an eyebrow at her. "Even though they could only have food you've touched before?"

"Ha ha. I only touched the packaging, because I helped Mom put all the groceries away."

"Uh-huh."

"I did. And I saved Melissa from starving to death."

"At least you didn't get spaghetti stains on your dress," Kat tells her.

"Aw, man," Zach says. "You got the spaghetti? It's *so*

good there."

Kat points at me. "*Damien* got the spaghetti, and then *Damien* flung his noodles all over me."

"Is that what the kids are calling it these days?" I grin at her.

She smacks my arm. "Stains, Damien. My dress has *stains*."

"Two very tiny stains that you can't even see because they totally blend in." Orange and pink aren't *that* different. Sort of. In the grand scheme of things.

"You mean those ones? Right there?" Zach squints and points at Kat's waist.

Kat gives me a look.

I hold up my hands in innocence. "I still say it's hardly noticeable. Zach must have really good vision or something. And I'd like to point out, for the record, that it was only *one* noodle, not *noodles*, plural. And it was Riley's fault for elbowing me."

"For the last time, I wasn't elbowing you," Riley says, sounding really put out about it. "I was putting on my coat so I wouldn't get lasagna on my clothes."

"You still elbowed me."

"But not on purpose."

"The real question," Zach says, "is do any of you have leftovers? Because I'm kind of starving."

Amelia's nostrils flare, like his hunger is a personal affront. "But I saved the day. With snacks."

"I know," Zach tells her. "Think how much more starving I'd be if you hadn't."

"I've got some of the noodles from my chicken

Parmesan left," Kat says.

"Noodles with *sauce*, Kat." I shake my head at her. "That's practically spaghetti. In fact, I think that *is* spaghetti."

"I know where you're going with this, Damien, but we all saw you lose half your plate to the floor."

"And yet, only one noodle landed in your lap. That sounds kind of suspicious to me."

She rolls her eyes. "Anyway, Zach, it's in the car. There's not a lot, but you can have it."

"Really?!" His whole face lights up.

"Yeah, I'll go get it."

"Oh!" Sarah raises her hand, even though we're not in class. "I'll go with you."

Kat's mouth drops open, but she can't seem to think of a reason why Sarah should stay here.

I'm about to volunteer to go with her instead when Amelia grabs my arm and pulls me a little ways from the group.

"*So.* It's Prom night. This is it." Her voice is really high-pitched, and she's talking kind of fast.

"And what part of me not wanting to be involved in this in any way whatsoever didn't you understand?"

She goes on, like I didn't say anything. "How do I look?"

I make a face. "Like my sister?"

She scowls. "Well, Zach already told me I look gorgeous tonight."

"Then why did you ask?"

"Because." She bites her lip. "I thought maybe he just

said it. Because that's what you're supposed to say to your date on Prom night, right?"

I sigh. "I'm sure he meant it. And Kat said you look cute."

"No, she said my dress was cute. It's not the same. Besides, tonight's a big night. I want to look more than just cute."

"Yep, wow, look at the time. I left Riley all alone over there, so—"

"He's talking to Zach." She peers past me real quick to confirm it. Then she takes a deep breath. "I'm so nervous. About, you know, *that thing we talked about*." She gives me a knowing look, as if I could have possibly forgotten.

I consider faking a bout of food poisoning. Pretending to be sick right now wouldn't exactly be hard.

Amelia's wringing her hands together and shifting her weight from foot to foot. "I've been waiting *all night*, and I just feel like... like I'm going to explode, you know?"

"Um."

"I just need to get it over with. Then I can relax and enjoy the rest of the dance."

"Please stop. Just stop talking."

"And go for it? I know, I know. I just need to take Zach somewhere a little more private and get it done."

"I said I— Wait, what?"

"Wish me luck!" She grins at me and hurries back over to Zach and Riley.

I follow, not sure what the hell is happening right now.

Amelia grabs Zach's arm. "Hey."

"Hey," he says, smiling back at her. "What's going on?"

"Nothing. I mean, something. I mean... I just need to see you *over there* for a minute." She indicates somewhere further in the crowd, away from us.

Zach shrugs and wanders off with her.

Riley wrinkles his eyebrows. "What was that about?"

"You don't want to know."

"Okay. If you—"

"My sister's going to go have her way with your brother."

"What?" He looks at me, then in the direction Amelia and Zach just went. "Wait, seriously?"

"That's what she said."

He gapes at me. "Here? At the dance?!" Actually, he looks a little sick.

"Maybe? That's what it *sounded* like."

"X, that's... That couldn't be what she... And you just let them?!"

"Geez, Perkins, now who's freaking out? What happened to you being cool with it? What happened to it not being our business?"

"I never said I was cool with it. And I... I know it's not our business, but... *Here?* There's no way you heard that right."

Kat and Sarah come back. Kat's got a little paper box of leftovers in one hand. She holds it up. "Where's Zach?"

"He's right over there," Riley says, gesturing to a spot in the crowd not that far from us. Meaning it's *way* too close for comfort.

I make a face. "I don't want to know."

Riley scowls at me. "Oh, my God, X, they're not having

sex on the freaking dance floor!"

Kat's eyes go wide.

"Rite of passage," Sarah mutters. "What did I tell you?"

I look over. And yeah, Riley's right—I mean, of course he is, because no matter how crazy Amelia sounded, she wouldn't really do *that*. At least, I don't think. But anyway, she and Zach are standing a little ways apart, obviously talking about something.

It looks kind of serious.

Maybe kind of really serious.

And then Amelia's face crumples. Zach reaches out to her, but she turns and runs, tears already streaking down her face.

X·X·X

"Amelia?" I call, poking my head into the girls' bathroom.

There are three girls in front of the mirror, fixing their makeup and talking, though they all go quiet and stare at me when I open the door.

Which makes it easier to hear Amelia sniffling in one of the stalls. Not that she's exactly being quiet about it.

One of the girls rolls her eyes at the noise, and they all exchange a look. Then one of them says, "Uh, this is the *girls'* bathroom?" as if I hadn't noticed.

As if I don't feel completely out of place. I'm actually kind of thinking I should have sent Kat or Sarah in here instead, but it's a little late for that now.

I ignore the death glares the girls are giving me and come in anyway. One of them sucks in her breath, and then all three of them grab their stuff and run off.

"Amelia?"

"Go away!" she wails.

"Are you..." I stop myself from asking her if she's okay, since obviously she's not. "You want to tell me what the hell happened?"

"*Nothing.*"

Yep, *nothing* is why she's hiding in the bathroom, crying. "I'm not going anywhere until you tell me!"

"It's none of your business!"

Seriously? Why couldn't it have been none of my business ten minutes ago? "Just come out here!"

"No!"

"Is it— Did Zach do something?"

Amelia sobs harder.

"Whatever he said, whatever he did to you—"

"He didn't do anything!" She swings the door open and glares at me. Her face is red and puffy. "*You're* the one who did something!"

"Me?" I wasn't even there.

She points a finger at me. "You're the one who gave me bad advice!"

"I didn't—"

"You're the one who told me to tell Zach I love him!"

"Whoa. You told him you *love* him?" I should probably make an effort not to sound so horrified about that, but I can't help it.

"You told me to." She takes a deep breath, then puts her hands to her face as she sobs again.

"I think I'd remember that."

"In the car the other day. I asked you about it, and you said—you said Zach would be *into it*. That's what you said."

Crap. "*That's* what you were talking about?"

"Of course it is! What did you think I was talking about?"

"I thought..." I clear my throat. "I thought you were talking about, you know, having sex with him." Not telling him she loves him, which I could have told her was a dumb idea. Er, not that I would have put it like that exactly, but I could have steered her away from it.

Amelia puts a hand to her mouth. "Oh. My. God. *That's* what you thought I was talking about?!"

"Yeah, well, what was I supposed to think?"

"Not *that*!" A mixture of emotions twists up her face. Though it's not so much a mixture of emotions as it is varying degrees of disgust. "So when you said you were nervous the first time, you thought I meant...?"

I nod.

"Ew ew ew! I didn't want to know about that! You're my *brother*." She shudders.

On the bright side, at least she seems more squicked out now than sad. That's an improvement, right? "Great, well, I'm glad we cleared that up."

"And I don't know why you'd assume I was talking about sex, because I'm only sixteen."

"I was sixteen."

"Yeah, but you're... *you know*."

I raise an eyebrow at her.

"You're a boy. And you're *you*. And I'm not going to

have sex until I'm at least seventeen, but probably not until I'm out of school, and only with someone I've been with for at least a year."

"Wow. That's a lot of rules."

"I just want to be prepared. I don't want anything to go wrong."

Somehow I don't think she and Zach share the same meaning of *prepared*. "If you say so."

"And we also have to be in love, so I guess that means it's *not* going to be with Zach."

"You want to tell me what happened?"

"I told him I loved him, and he didn't say it back. He didn't say *anything* at first. He was just looking at me like... like he didn't even know me. And then he told me he'd been thinking about it lately, about whether or not he loved me, and I thought he was going to say he did. Because why else would he say that?"

I scratch my ear and try not to look guilty. "Yeah... Why else?"

"Well, he didn't. He said he's been giving it a lot of thought lately, and he *doesn't* love me. He just likes me. A lot. He had the nerve to add that *a lot* part at the end, like that makes it any better!" Her mouth squishes up, and she breaks into sobs again.

And I kind of really, really wish I wasn't here right now. And that I hadn't had that whole conversation with Zach about whether or not he loves her. Not that I can tell Amelia that. Like, ever.

"Who does that?" Amelia squeaks. "Who *thinks* about whether or not they love someone and then says that they don't, right to their face?"

"That's... I mean, I..."

"I can't believe I was stupid enough to think anyone would ever love me back. It's my fault. I was so stupid, and now I ruined *everything*."

I put a tentative hand on her back.

She takes it as an invitation to lean into me and full on sob into my shoulder.

"It wasn't your fault, Amelia. And if you want me to, I don't know, kill him or something—"

"I just want to go home."

"Yeah, sure. I'll drive you."

She takes a step back and sniffles. "But you haven't had your license long enough to drive with someone else in the car."

"Seriously? That's what you're worried about?"

"Well, it's true."

I roll my eyes at her. "That doesn't matter right now, and even if it did, I'm pretty sure it doesn't apply to family members. Come on." I get out my phone to text Kat. She can meet us at the house, and we can go to her dorm from there.

Amelia doesn't move.

"Amelia?"

She opens her mouth, then hesitates. Then, so quietly I almost don't hear, she says, "Why am I unlovable?"

"Hey. You're not."

"But why doesn't Zach love me? Why can't he just..."

"I don't know."

She nods, too choked up to talk for a second. Then she

says, "There's this movie I always watch when I'm sad—"

"I'm familiar with it." Familiar with its soundtrack blasting through the attic wall, anyway.

"Will you watch it with me? When we get home?"

I hesitate. Just a little too long.

"Never mind." She hugs her arms around herself. "It was a stupid idea."

"It's not stupid."

"It's just that I don't really want to be alone." She sniffs. "But you probably have plans. With Kat. Because you love her and she actually loves you back. You guys are so"—a sob interrupts her—"so lucky."

"I'll watch the movie with you, Amelia."

"But—"

"It's okay. I can... I can see Kat tomorrow." I hope. If she's still speaking to me after I have to cancel our big weekend together. I mean, she will be—she'll understand—but I wouldn't blame her if she also wanted to kill me.

"But tonight is Prom, and you shouldn't have to miss anything."

"Yeah, well, it's my choice. And I haven't blown a hole in anything yet, so maybe it's better to quit while I'm ahead."

CHAPTER 16

Kat's the best. Not only because she understands when I tell her Amelia's having a breakdown and I can't just abandon her, but because she insists on coming with us. I tell her she doesn't have to—watching sad movies with Amelia all night probably isn't anyone's idea of a good time—but she just gives me this look, like don't even try and stop her.

Which is, all in all, pretty cool of her. And also way hot. A trait I will most likely not be able to, uh, fully appreciate tonight, what with this change of plans. But still.

Amelia protests a little bit when I tell her Kat's coming, too. She says she doesn't want someone like Kat watching her cry all night. I ask her what she means by *someone like Kat*, and she says someone who has their life together, particularly their love life. And then I remind her that I'm with Kat, and therefore I must have my love life together, too. And then Amelia tells me that I don't count because not only am I her brother, but I'm also pretty much a total screwup, so me seeing her cry is completely different.

But then Kat meets us at our car before heading over to hers, hugs Amelia like she means it—and like she doesn't care about getting snot and makeup smeared on her dress—and tells her it will be okay. Then Amelia says maybe it'll be alright if Kat hangs out with us after all.

Go figure.

Half an hour later, all three of us are sitting on Amelia's bed, after changing out of our Prom clothes.

"But I don't understand," Amelia says. "Why would he have been thinking about whether or not he loved me if he didn't actually love me?"

Kat chews her lip, thinking that over. She's got on my old pajamas—the Christmas ones that say *Do not open until X-mas!*—since she wasn't exactly planning on changing clothes until she got back to her dorm and didn't bring anything. "Boys are dumb."

"Really, Kat?" I ask her. "That's the best you can do? *Boys are dumb?*"

"Well, they are." She thinks again for a second. "Maybe he does love you but is too afraid to admit it."

Amelia perks up a little. "Do you think?"

I shake my head. "Nope."

"*Damien.*" Kat gives me a look. "You don't know."

I kind of do, though. Not that I can tell her that in front of Amelia. "I just mean that, uh, Zach's pretty honest."

"He is." Amelia sniffs, her eyes tearing up again. "He always tells me what he really thinks."

"Uh-huh."

"He *does*. And he's really cute, and sweet, and funny. So, basically the exact opposite of you."

"You know, if I leave, I'm taking Kat with me."

"I'm just saying that he was the perfect boyfriend, and now it's over. Because when one person says they love the other person—on *Prom* night—and the other person specifically says that they *don't* love that person back, then..." She pulls her knees up and buries her face, her shoulders shaking as she cries.

"Amelia..."

"I don't understand what went wrong. I thought we were happy. I thought everything was going great. But I guess it was going greater for me than it was for him. Now everything we ever did together feels like a lie."

"You couldn't have known how he'd react," Kat says. "Or what he was thinking."

"But I was his girlfriend. I was supposed to know stuff like that."

"For what it's worth? You guys looked really happy together tonight. *Both* of you," she adds. "I never would have guessed that he'd say something like that."

"I should have listened to you," Amelia wails. She's looking at me when she says it.

"What? When?" She can't mean that conversation in the car, when I kind of sort of told her to have sex with him.

"*Before*. Back before me and Zach even started going out. You said I shouldn't date him because he was your friend. And if I'd just listened to you—"

"Come on, Amelia. I was joking."

"No, you weren't."

Well, I sort of was. I only told her that so she *would* go out with him. "You and Zach were good together."

"But if I'd listened to you, then I never would have gone out with him, and then I wouldn't have to feel like *this*. Like the whole world is ending, and I don't even know what I did wrong."

"You didn't do anything."

"But I wasn't good enough. Because if I was, he would have loved me back."

"It doesn't work like that."

Amelia nods, though she's still crying, and I'm not sure she believes me. "I'm going to go to the bathroom real quick, and then we can start the movie." She gets up, sniffling, and looks at me and Kat. "Don't do anything on my bed."

"Wow," I tell her. "We're not animals." And how long does she really expect to be in the bathroom?

She narrows her eyes at me, letting me know she doesn't trust me, then leaves.

"This is really bad," Kat whispers, even though we're alone now and no one can hear us.

"I know."

"I thought... Okay, I didn't think they were going to get married or anything, but I thought things were going alright."

"They were." Until I got involved. "Kat, I have to tell you something. I..." I scratch my ear, staring down at Amelia's pink bedspread. "I might have, um, accidentally broken them up."

"You what?"

"What happened tonight was my fault. Amelia never would have told Zach she loved him if I hadn't accidentally encouraged her. I mean, to be fair, I thought she was talking about having sex with him. Which I'm not saying I approved of, either, but I was trying to stay out of it."

"Okay, but once she had the idea in her head, do you really think you could have talked her out of it?"

"No, not really." Even if I had realized what our conversation was actually about and told Amelia that confessing her love for Zach was insane, she probably would have gone through with it just to prove me wrong.

"So, it wasn't your fault."

"Yeah, sure, if that was all I did."

"You did something else?" She shifts her weight on the bed, moving so she can get a better look at my face. "Like what?"

"I sort of had a talk with Zach. I was just trying to apologize for being pissed that he had condoms in his room, that he planned to use with my sister. So, like, I was trying to do a good thing."

"But?"

"I kind of accused him of not loving her."

"*Damien.*" Kat looks horrified. She glances over at the door, to double check that Amelia isn't coming in.

"I know! And, I mean, it wasn't really an accusation. But I brought it up. I actually *asked him* if he loved her. I made him think about it. And if he hadn't been thinking about it so much, then maybe when she sprung it on him at the dance, he wouldn't have broken her heart or whatever."

"Yeah, but if he really doesn't love her..."

"I know, but he might have thought that he did, in the moment. I mean, as much as Amelia thinks she loves him, which I don't even know if she really does. Maybe she just likes the idea of it. Because, like, she had no idea he was thinking about sleeping with her, and he had no idea she had all these crazy rules about waiting until she's seventeen and having to have gone out for a year first and stuff."

"She could really love him," Kat says, glancing at the door again.

"Maybe. And if she really loves him and he doesn't love her back, then I guess it's better that they know that." I spread my hands out on the bed. "But I'm not convinced that they wouldn't have both been blissfully clueless together if I hadn't opened my big mouth about it."

"Damien?"

"Yeah?"

"You really screwed up."

"Gee, thanks, Kat."

"You have to fix this."

"Sure, let me just get into my time machine and stop myself from opening Zach's dresser drawer."

"You know what I mean. And I don't blame you for freaking out about the condoms thing."

"But it screwed things up. Between me and Zach. And if that hadn't happened, then I wouldn't have needed to apologize—I mean, I *chose* to apologize, out of the goodness of my heart, not because I owed it to him or anything—and then I wouldn't have told him how much it mattered to me that I was in love with you before we started sleeping together."

She grins. "You said that?"

"Yeah, well, I was being honest. But I still should have stayed out of it."

Kat opens her mouth to say something else, but then we hear the floorboards in the hallway creaking, and she stays quiet as Amelia comes in.

"What?" Amelia says, squinting at us. Her face is still red, but she seems to have gotten rid of all her snot. At least for now. "Were you guys—"

"We didn't do anything on your bed. Geez." I scowl at her.

"*No*, I was going to ask if you guys were *talking* about me. Because obviously you were." She flares her nostrils, then stomps over to the bed and sits down, making a big deal out of smoothing out the covers first. "What did he say about me?" she asks Kat.

"Leave her out of it—Kat would never betray me like that. And what I was saying was that if Zach's too stupid to love you back, then he doesn't deserve you."

"Really?" Amelia blinks at me.

"I'm paraphrasing. But it was something like that."

Amelia tries to catch Kat's eye, but Kat conveniently sees something interesting on the wall and can't be bothered. "Do you think Mom and Dad would let me take the rest of the semester off from school?"

I laugh. "No. And Zach doesn't even go to your school."

"No, but all my friends who were at the dance do. Plus, a broken heart takes a long time to fix."

"How would you know?" Kat asks.

"TV. And movies. And Tiffany's sister whose boyfriend cheated on her when he went to college. It took her, like, a year to start dating again."

"Fair enough."

"And I know you're a screwup," she says to me—well, *obviously* to me—"but if they're letting you completely drop out, then I don't see why I can't take a couple months off. Maybe I'll feel better enough to go back by summer and I can make it up then."

Kat wrinkles her forehead, trying to make sense of that. "What did you say?"

"I know it'll probably take longer than that to get over him," Amelia says, totally missing what Kat's confused about, "but I don't want to graduate late, so I'll just have to power through somehow."

"No, what did you say about Damien *dropping out of school*?"

"Huh? Oh. Well, he's—"

"I'm not." I laugh, but it comes out sounding way nervous and kind of crazy. "I didn't tell you about it because it's not happening. I mean, I'm only thinking about it."

Amelia snorts. "Yeah, right. He's at least going to have to repeat first year, because of the flying test. Then he'll either be a dropout, or I'll be in a higher grade than him." She's smiling a little at that, then catches herself. "Um, not that that's a good thing."

"Yeah, well, I'm sure as hell *not* repeating first year."

"So you're dropping out?" Kat gapes at me.

"It's not his fault," Amelia says, helpfully for once. "He has to pass a flying test."

Kat swallows. "You can fly. Damien, you can fly. You know that, right?"

I don't look at her. "Not like this. There are hoops on the ceiling."

Amelia nods. "It's true. I peeked in the gym and saw them. There's, like, no way he can pass."

I glare at her.

Kat's voice comes out kind of squeaky. "Why didn't you tell me?"

"Because. I'm still trying to figure it out, and I didn't want you to worry."

"Do all your friends know? Does everyone know except me?"

"You're doing really well in school, Kat. I didn't want you to think I was a loser."

"Damien, you're *not*."

Amelia tilts a hand back and forth in the air. "Well..."

"You're not a loser, and you can figure out a way to pass the test. You always figure something out." She sounds like she's trying to convince herself as much as me. Maybe more than me.

"Did I mention my uncle Ted's the one who's administering the test?"

"The one from the Christmas party?" She winces.

"Yep. And he hates my guts. And even if I could fly through hoops on the ceiling, which is already a pretty big *if* for me, he'd probably still fail me."

Kat's face is turning kind of pink. She looks like she's about to cry. "So you're just giving up? That doesn't sound like you."

"Passing that flying test doesn't really sound like me, either."

"Is this why you said you weren't going anywhere?"

"It's part of it, but I didn't mean—"

"You can't give up on this, Damien."

"Kat. Come on."

She clenches her fists. "No. Giving up on this feels like… it feels like giving up on *us*."

"I would never do that." My throat goes tight, and I kind of wish Amelia wasn't sitting here, witnessing all this. "It's just Heroesworth."

"It's not. You know it's not. I'm going to be somebody, Damien, but so are you. And you don't just give up on things. Not when they really matter."

"I know. But me, passing that flying test? In front of my uncle? It's…" I hate myself for saying this, because she's right, I don't give up on things. But it's also the truth. "It's impossible."

"Nothing is impossible."

"But some things are so hard, so completely unattainable, that they might as well be."

"You said you'd do anything for me."

I slip my hand into hers. "I know what I said. But it would take a miracle for me to pass this."

"I'm not asking you to perform a miracle," she says, squeezing my hand. "I'm just asking you not to give up."

CHAPTER 17

"And then," Xavier says, in that stupid screechy voice of his, "after I got to ride all the rides, we went to the zoo, and they let me ride a zebra, because I'm so special and amazing."

I glare at Mom. I'm over at their house, having dinner Monday evening. "You went to Super World?"

Mom forces a smile. "Anything for my little sweetiekins."

"And then you went to the zoo, and he rode a *zebra*?"

"It was so fun!" Xavier shrieks, right in my ear.

I scoot my chair a little farther away from him. "I can't believe this."

He gives me this smug smile. "It was only for me and Mommy. But maybe if you're really nice to me, I'll let you come to my next birthday."

It wasn't really his birthday. Even though Xavier looks like he's about twelve now—which is way too old to be calling her *Mommy*—he's really only eight months old, thanks to Mom's crazy growth formula. "Mom, seriously. I can't believe you're still doing this."

"Mommy *loves* me. She says I can do whatever I want for my parties."

"Am I still making sure my special little angel has a good time on his birthdays? Of course I'm still doing that, Damien. What do you expect?"

"He shouldn't have even had any birthdays yet, and I can't believe you're still pumping all these fake memories into him." I look over at Taylor, Xavier's dad and my stepfather. "And I can't believe you're okay with this."

Taylor takes a deep breath. "Well, it's not as if I—"

"Daddy's happy for me," Xavier says, interrupting him. "Everyone just wants me to have a really special day."

"Uh-huh."

"And don't say this happened for your birthday, too, because Mommy already told me it didn't."

He means because some of the fake memories Mom fed him happened to match up *exactly* with one of my birthday parties from when I was a kid. Because I guess she couldn't be bothered to make up something new. And maybe she thought I wouldn't find out, since it's not like I make a point of ever choosing to hang out with Xavier or anything, but really I think she just didn't care.

"I can definitely say it didn't happen to me," I tell him. I'm not a big fan of amusement-park rides, what with most of them not staying on solid ground. "But it didn't happen to you, either."

"Yes, it did!"

"The zoo doesn't let people ride zebras." And, okay,

they *could have* gone to Super World, but it's kind of expensive, and taking Xavier there sounds like a nightmare. Mom wouldn't go through all that when she could just slip some headphones on him and hypnotize him into thinking it happened, or however it works. And if it had been real—if she really did take him to Super World—there's no way she'd still be up for going to the zoo afterward.

"They let *me* ride one, though. They made an exception. That's why it's special."

There's also no way anyone in their right mind would let Xavier touch, let alone ride, a zoo animal. I look at Mom. "Don't you think this is going to, like, mess up his brain or something?"

"*Damien.*" Mom grits her teeth. "Your brother had a good time on his birthday. Please don't try and ruin that for us."

"It wasn't even his birthday!"

"Everyone had a good time. There was no harm done."

"That you know of. What about long-term effects?"

"The long-term effects are that my little sweetiekins has nothing to worry about."

"Mom. That's not... That doesn't even make sense."

"He has a point, Marianna," Taylor says. "I've been meaning to talk to you about—"

"It's fine," Mom snaps. "There's nothing wrong with Xavier." She pats him on the head. "Or with you, dear."

Taylor raises his eyebrows. "I suppose I should take that as a compliment?"

She laughs. "Not with *you*. I meant Damien."

"*Me?*"

"Yes. There's nothing wrong with you. Well, other than the obvious, but that had nothing to do with me." She holds up her hands in a not-my-problem gesture. "But clearly you had no long-term effects."

My blood suddenly runs cold. "Uh, Mom, no long-term effects from *what*?"

Xavier gives me a nasty grin, even though I'm pretty sure he doesn't know what she means, either, just that I'm unhappy about it.

"Well, sweetie, I knew that I... That is, I knew who your father was—"

"I should hope so."

"—and about his ability. And I was worried that there was a teeny, tiny chance you might inherit it. Which I was right to worry about, since you did."

"You mean, because I can fly?"

She nods, shuddering a little at even the idea. "That's exactly what I mean. And I didn't want— Well, I didn't want it to happen at all, but I couldn't control that. So I simply made sure that if you did inherit his awful power, you'd never want to use it. You see, dear, I was afraid that you'd take after him too much and leave me one day to join the enemy." She says that wistfully, her voice full of regret, as if she's not the one who kicked me out.

"You made me not want to fly." My hands are shaking. I feel like I'm going to be sick. "You mean you made me afraid of heights."

"Mm-hm." She takes a sip of her wine, all casual, as if this isn't a big deal. "I didn't have the exact same setup I have for Xavier—the technology just wasn't there yet—but I had an earlier version of it."

"You... You *what*?!"

She sighs. "It was a long time ago. There's no need to get so worked up."

"Get so worked up?! No need to?! *You*—" Lightning crackles across my skin. All my hair stands on end. "You messed me up on purpose?"

Xavier snickers. He doesn't realize she's doing the same thing to him, only worse.

"I didn't *mess you up*. I ensured your future. I was only looking out for you. And as you can see, you've had no long-term effects other than the intended one. So." She grins, looking pretty pleased with herself. "I think we can all agree I know what I'm doing here."

"Um, no. No, we cannot. What the hell were you thinking?!"

"I've already explained that part. And will you please get your lightning under control? We wouldn't want my little sweetiekins to get zapped, now, would we?" She pokes Xavier in the side, pretending to zap him, and he giggles. "Or the furniture," she adds.

I'm going to throw up. Or I'm going to blow up the house. I take a deep breath.

"Don't be so dramatic," Mom says. "I could have made you afraid of heights by dropping you a bunch of times, but instead I chose this more sophisticated route. I mean, I couldn't let you grow up and actually *fly*, so it had to happen one way or another."

I stare at her.

She clucks her tongue. "Being a mother is such a thankless job."

"Gee, Mom, thanks for not dropping me on my head when I was a baby."

"Oh, not on your head. Don't be ridiculous. I would never have hurt you, sweetie. But I didn't know what might happen, with you being half hero. What if you'd gotten a *V* but ended up able to fly? It would have been better if you never discovered that and thought you had no power at all."

"But I have an *X*. And I *can* fly."

Disgust twitches across her face. "Something you never would have discovered on your own. But I did my best. Actually, I'd kind of forgotten about it."

"You forgot about it?!"

"Well, you broke the device when you were four. Riding your bike in the house." She actually clucks her tongue at me.

Okay, I'm supposed to be over her purposely giving me a phobia about heights and messing up my life, but she's not even over me riding my bike in the house over a decade ago?

"I didn't think about it again until Xavier came around and I knew I needed a way to…" She looks over at him. "A way to make sure my little angel miracle grew up big and strong."

Ugh. "Mentally unstable, you mean."

She glares at me. "When I had him, I remembered that old device, and I looked up the company to see if they had a newer model. And of course they did, and it's worked out really well."

"You made me afraid of heights." I feel numb.

"*Yes*. And it was for your own good, so stop looking at me like that."

"Marianna," Taylor says, "I think Damien just needs a chance to absorb this information. It's kind of a lot."

"He was afraid of heights before and he's still afraid of them now—it doesn't change anything. And the point here is that the device did exactly what it was supposed to, just like I said."

Another surge of electricity runs up my spine and across my skin. "I'm going to flunk out of school because of you!"

"Hero school," she says. "Which you shouldn't have even been going to in the first place. And if they don't want you because you can't fly, well, then I'd say that's mission accomplished."

X·X·X

"Hello?" Riley sounds really groggy when he answers the phone.

Probably because it's 2 a.m on a Monday. Well, Tuesday, technically. "*Finally*. You only let it ring, like, twenty times." I drum my fingers on my bed, even though it doesn't really make any sound.

"I was asleep. It's..." He pauses to check the time. "It's after two in the morning, X. Did something happen? Are you okay? Is—"

"Everyone's okay." Except me. "It's nothing like that."

"Oh." He sounds relieved. Then kind of pissed. "So what *are* you calling for?"

"Actually, you know what? Never mind. It wasn't important."

"You woke me up in the middle of the night!"

"I didn't realize what time it was, that's all. Go back to sleep, Perkins. I'll see you tomorrow."

He's quiet for a second. Then he says, "What did you really call about?"

"I'm going to pass that flying test."

Silence.

"Did you hear me? I said I'm going to pass that flying test."

"Look, X, I want you to be there next year, but tampering with your records isn't the way to do it. Someone will notice, and you'll get kicked out."

"Who said anything about tampering with my records?"

"Um." He yawns. "I just assumed. Because… Okay, don't take this the wrong way, but how else are you going to pass it?"

"I'm going to fly." My voice sounds too high and a little shaky when I say that, which doesn't exactly make it convincing.

"You're going to fly."

"You don't have to sound so skeptical."

"You said it was impossible. You said there were hoops on the ceiling and that your uncle was dead set on failing you. So, yeah, I'm skeptical."

"I *have* to make it work. I have to do this. So I'm going to." Because if I don't, then Mom and this stupid fear she put in my head both win, and that's not okay.

"You're going to fly through hoops?"

"I have to, don't I?"

He yawns again. "You can't really... I don't want to say you can't fly, because obviously you can, but not, you know, like *that*."

"You want me to fail this test? You want me to not be there next year?"

"I didn't say that. But, X, I mean... When's the make-up test?"

"In two weeks."

"So you're telling me that you can barely get off the ground, but in *two weeks'* time, you're going to somehow be able to fly through hoops on the ceiling?"

He forgot the part about how I also have to do it well enough to impress Ted, who hates my guts and will probably fail me no matter what I do. I swallow. "Yep."

"*How?*"

"I don't know. Training, I guess?"

"Training. You guess."

"I'll figure something out, okay? But I'm passing that test. I'm *not* letting my stupid fear of heights keep me from being there next year."

"It's not stupid, X. You can't help what you're afraid of."

No, but apparently Mom can. "I don't care. It's... I can't let it get in the way this time."

"X."

"I *can't*."

"I know I was upset when you found out about the test.

I know I said you have to be there next year, but if you're doing this because of me... You don't have to, okay?"

"This has been, like, the longest year of my life. There's no way in hell I'm repeating it. And I'm not flunking out, or quitting, or letting my stupid letterist uncle think I can't do it."

Riley's quiet for a second, and when he speaks again, his voice is kind of hushed. "Is this about what happened at the train station? During our mission?"

"No." It's mostly not, anyway.

"Because it was my fault I got caught. It was my fault that I fell. I don't blame you."

"Perkins, it's not about that. And it wasn't your fault."

"Yeah, it was. I was afraid. I freaked out."

"Me, too. But that's not why I'm calling."

"So, what happened? Because you did *not* lose track of time."

"It's nothing. I mean, I was over at my mom's house, and... It's kind of a long story."

"So?"

"So, it's two in the morning."

"Oh, *now* you care about that?"

"I'll tell you tomorrow."

"You sure? Because I'm already up, and whatever it was, it obviously really bothered you."

"Yeah, I'm sure." I yawn. "You can go back to sleep. I just needed you to know that I'm going to pass that test."

"If you say so."

"I do. I *am*. So if you were worried that I'm not going to be there next year, don't be."

"Okay."

"I mean it, Perkins." I'm not going to let my fear of heights beat me this time. And I'm not going to fail that flying test.

Even if I have absolutely no idea how.

CHAPTER 18

Grandpa slams his hand down on the kitchen table, causing some of my lemonade to slop over the top of my glass. "Absolutely not."

I pick up my lemonade—Grandma made it fresh this morning, and it's *really* good—and take a drink, in case he does something else to spill even more of it. "It's for school."

"You know what I think of that damn school. And here they are again, putting you in danger."

He means because me and Riley are supposed to find that painting, which means finding Frank. We looked online, but we couldn't find anything about him. Not really, anyway. There were some mentions of a criminal named Frank, but only up until about ten years ago, and then it's like he disappeared. None of it was very helpful, and I'm not even sure it was about the same Frank we're looking for. There were a few more recent forum posts where people mentioned him possibly coming back or asked if anyone had ever actually seen this new Frank, but there weren't any responses. Well, there were a few, but they'd all been deleted.

Which is maybe kind of ominous, but it could also just be a coincidence. And either way, it means we didn't actually have anything to go on. Hence me coming to see Grandpa.

"Kat has pretty much the same assignment," I tell him. "So it's not just a Heroesworth thing." Plus, Riley's working on this, too, and as much as I could believe the school would give me an assignment they hoped I wouldn't come back from, there's no way they'd do that to him.

"I thought you came here to see me," Grandpa mutters.

"I did."

"I mean to patch things up." He stares down at his hands.

I can't tell if he's actually upset or just trying to make me feel bad. It's not something I would have questioned before the gala, before he lied to me and almost got everyone I care about killed. A few months ago, I would have taken his actions at face value. But now? I want to believe he misses me and feels bad about what he did. I want to believe that I can trust him and that he'll never do anything like that again. But *want* and *can* are two totally different things.

"There's nothing to *patch up*," I tell him. "You betrayed me."

"So you're only here because you think I have information."

"No, I'm here because I *know* you do. Frank's a criminal. You know about criminals. There's no way you haven't heard anything."

"Only bits, here and there. Only enough to know you shouldn't go anywhere near him. It's too dangerous."

"Why? Because I go to hero school?"

Grandpa looks me over, not answering right away. "Because you're seventeen. And no matter what's happened between us, you're still my grandson."

"You owe me."

"Oh, yeah? So because you blame me for putting you and your friends in danger at the gala—"

"*Blame* you? It was your fault!"

"Because of that, you want me to give you information that will put you and them in even more danger?"

"This is different."

"Because you think you'll win?" He scoffs and shakes his head. "I won't be there to save you this time."

As if that's even what happened. Lightning twitches up and down my back, but I keep it under control. I don't want him to see how much he's pissing me off. "Going into danger on our terms isn't the same thing as being thrown into it on yours." I take another sip of my lemonade, trying not to let my hand shake. "And what you owe me is the truth."

"Alright, here's some truth for you." He leans forward and looks me in the eyes. "You don't want to mess with Frank. Even if I don't know a lot about him, I know that much. Now, you might not like how I run things, but at least I've got rules. They might not be the League's rules, or the city's, but they exist, and every good criminal follows them. I've got people to look out for, and people that I have to answer to if something goes wrong. But Frank? He doesn't play by anyone's rules. He does what he wants, no matter the consequences. He kills people, Damien. Anyone who gets in his way is fair game. Doesn't matter if they're hero, villain, or regular citizen. Even a kid like you—he wouldn't hesitate."

"Okay."

"Okay? I tell you that if you go after this guy you're going to get yourself killed, and all you can say is *okay*? Maybe you're not listening. He doesn't make ties with anyone. If you get in trouble with him, I can't pull any strings to get you out of it."

"I don't want you to do that for me. I can take care of myself."

"No one's ever seen Frank and lived."

I don't need to see him, technically. All I need is proof that he took that painting. And since I don't think he'd pose for a picture with stolen goods for us, completing this mission doesn't need to involve ever being in the same room with him. Ideally, anyway. "I'm doing this whether you help me or not."

"I'm sorry, Damien. Sorry for the ways I've let you down, but not for this. I can't send my grandson after someone like Frank, knowing what might happen to you."

I swallow. He sounds like he means it. "You going to chain me to the radiator again?"

"Damn it, kid. Maybe this doesn't scare you, but it scares the hell out of me. And I'm not sending some stupidly fearless teenager after a hardened criminal who would kill you as soon as you set eyes on him."

"Stupidly fearless?" I grip the edge of the table. My hands are definitely shaking now. *"Stupidly fearless?!"*

Grandpa leans back in his chair and looks down at me. "That's right. I warned you how dangerous the gala would be, and, as you said, I even chained you to the radiator to keep you out of it. I did everything I could to keep you safe—"

"Except, like, *not* threaten my friends and family."

"—and it still didn't do any good. You showed up at that gala and almost got yourself killed."

"I had to. Grandpa, I *had to*. You were going to kill everyone I care about!" Lightning sparks along my arms, but I don't bother trying to hide it now. "Why can't you understand that?"

"I do understand it. But I never meant for you to be in danger like that, and as soon as I told you about it, you went running toward it the first chance you got. I can't watch you do that again with this. You're young, and right now, you think you're invincible."

"Grandpa, I don't—"

"Just hear me out. You think you can't be hurt—or that you won't be—and that everything will work out somehow, no matter how impossible. You think bad things only happen to other people."

"Grandpa—"

"You can't imagine not making it. You don't know what it would be like to get yourself into a life-or-death situation and find you come up short. You think you'll never be defeated, or that you'll—"

"Stop telling me what I think!" I shout that at him, even though he's only a couple feet away. I fling my arm out in frustration, accidentally knocking over my lemonade. We both stare at the liquid spilling over the table, shocked. I know I should get up and get a towel, but I have to say this first. "Ever since that gala, I've been nothing but afraid. Riley—my best friend—got hurt, because of me. He almost died. And even though I saved him, and even though I helped save everyone who was there that night, I can't shake the feeling that I still failed somehow. Like maybe I did okay in that moment, but it was just a fluke, and next time... next time I really will let everyone down."

"Damien—"

"*No.* I'm not invincible, okay? I *know* that! And I know I can be hurt, both physically and..." I clear my throat. "Everything changed after what happened at the gala. I used to love fieldwork, and now it's the last thing that I want to do." I wrap my arms around myself and stare down at the table. At the lemonade dripping onto the floor. "The people I care about could have died that night. And even though it was your fault, I'm not completely innocent. I helped you build up the Truth. I made people believe in it. And those superheroes would never have been shooting at him if I... If they hadn't seen him with me."

"It wasn't your fault," Grandpa says.

"It doesn't matter whose fault it was. It still messed me up. And Riley. And this mission, finding that painting, isn't something either of us wants to do."

"You don't have to go through with it. You can work something out with that school, and if you can't, you let *me* talk to them."

I shake my head. "I can't give up on this. I wish I still loved fieldwork, but I'm just terrified of it, all the freaking time. And I *hate* that. Maybe that means I'm not meant to do this, that I should just give it up, but it's part of who I am. Or, at least, who I was. And if I walk away from it, then it's like walking away from myself." I look up at him. "I can't do that. I won't. And maybe it won't work out, and I'll let everybody down, or maybe I'll succeed in this mission and still feel like I hate fieldwork. But at least then I'll know. I'll know that I'm really not who I used to be before the gala, and… and maybe then I can move on."

"I'm sorry I caused all of that, Damien."

"Some of it would have happened anyway."

"But not like this. And not now, when you're so young."

"I'm not stupidly fearless."

"No, you're not. I almost wish you were."

"I'm finding that painting, with or without your help."

He gets up from the table to go grab a towel from the kitchen. When he comes back, he tosses it on the spill—which really doesn't do much to clean it up—and says, "I don't like this. I want to make that clear right now. But maybe there's something to what you said, about facing danger on your terms. And I think you might be right."

"About what?"

He sighs. "About me owing you this."

CHAPTER 19

I go over to Riley's house after I leave Grandpa's. Zach lets me in. I haven't seen him since Prom. At first, he looks relieved to see me, but then his expression turns worried. His eyes flick up to mine, then back down. His shoulders lift as he takes a deep breath, but he doesn't actually say anything.

Guilt twists in my stomach. I should have come over sooner, or at least called. "Hey, Zach."

"Hey." He moves to let me in.

Riley must be in his room or something, because I don't see him. "Where's—"

"Riley's here. I'll get him."

"Wait, Zach, I—"

"Riley!" he shouts in the direction of the hallway. "Damien's here!"

"I know!" Riley shouts back from his room. His door is open, and I'm pretty sure he heard me come in. "I'll be there in a minute! I'm on the phone with Sarah!"

"Tell her it's rude to keep a guest waiting!" I shout at him.

"She says that's ridiculous because you practically live here!"

"Not lately," Zach mutters. I don't know if he meant to say it out loud, because his eyes go wide in surprise, and he glances over at me.

It would be stupid to ask him how he's been, right? Because, for one thing, it's only been a few days since I last saw him—not, like, a year. And for another, it's not as if I don't already know. I told Riley about Amelia locking herself in her room and crying her eyes out all weekend, and he told me Zach pretty much did the same thing, except without the rom-com marathon. Though even without Riley's secret intel, it's pretty obvious that Zach's not, like, having the best day ever or anything.

"I'm sorry," I tell him.

"For what?"

"For not coming by as much."

"Oh." He sounds almost disappointed.

"And... for you guys breaking up."

He winces. "She won't talk to me. I tried to call—a bunch of times—but she wouldn't answer."

I was there when she hit *ignore* on some of those. "She's just upset."

He takes a shaky breath, then nods. "I didn't mean for this to happen. I didn't—I don't *want* to be broken up."

I know I told Kat I was going to try and fix this, but I don't know what to say to that. "Zach..."

"She hates me now."

"No, she doesn't." Not really.

"I just wish I could talk to her."

"She'll come around eventually."

"But do you think she'll take me back?" He gives me a really desperate, hopeful look.

I glance down at my shoes. "I don't know."

"Oh. Okay." His voice sounds tight, like he might be about to cry. He swallows.

I consider barging into Riley's room, despite him being on the phone. I mean, it wouldn't really even be barging, since his door is open. And not just partially open, but all the way open. His conversation with Sarah couldn't be *that* private.

Though if it is, I'll be scarred for life and never be able to look either of them in the face again. But judging from the way Zach's shoulders are starting to tremble, it might be worth the risk.

Oh, no. Now he's putting his hands to his face. He's sucking in a deep breath, and... Okay, now he's actually crying.

And I've missed my window to run away from this situation without seeming completely heartless. I mean, I'm *not* heartless. I care about Zach. But I'm guessing that crying in front of me over breaking up with my sister wasn't on his list of things to do today.

"Hey. Um. Zach." Fine words of comfort if ever there were any.

He sinks down onto the couch and cries harder. His voice is squeaky and barely audible when he says, "Leave me alone."

I probably should. All I've done so far is mess things up. But I can't just walk away, so I sit down next to him. "It's my fault. If I hadn't gotten involved, then you two would still be together."

"But you're not the one who said that to Amelia. *I* did. She told me she loved me, and I said... I said..." He chokes up, unable to finish that sentence.

"I know what you said. But you wouldn't have even been thinking about whether or not you loved her if I hadn't said anything to you. So." I put my hands on my knees, steeling myself for this. "I'm really sorry. For messing things up between you."

He shakes his head. "It wasn't you."

It kind of was, though. "I'm sorry I messed things up between *us*, then."

"You mean because you started that fight, or you mean because now that me and Amelia aren't... aren't together anymore, then you and me can't be friends?"

"What? No. I meant that first one. The fight thing. *Not* that I'm saying I started it, because I didn't. It just happened. It was the inevitable outcome of me finding out that—" I get a hold of myself. Now probably isn't the best time to remind Zach that not all that long ago he was thinking about sleeping with Amelia because she was his girlfriend and they were happy together and stuff. And there's maybe also a teeny tiny chance that I really did start that fight between us, even if I think I kept pretty calm, all things considered. Okay, maybe *calm* isn't the right word, but I could have freaked out even more than I did, so that's something. "Just because you and Amelia broke up, it doesn't mean that *we* did. I'm still your friend, Zach."

"You... you are?"

"Of course I am."

"Don't just say that because you feel sorry for me. I know Amelia's your sister, and you have to be on her side."

"Being friends with you doesn't make me not on her side."

Riley joins us in the living room. His face falls when he sees that Zach's crying, but he doesn't seem that surprised by it. "Hey," he says, sitting down on Zach's other side. There's not really enough room, so we both have to scoot over.

"I'm okay," Zach tells him, even though it's obviously a lie.

"Yeah, but you don't have to be," Riley says. "It's okay if you're not."

Zach ignores him, looking over at me. "You thought Amelia was going to get hurt. That's why you were so upset before, in my room. I get that now."

"Zach, I wasn't—"

"And if you were that mad at me just because you thought she *might* get hurt, then you must really hate me now that she did. So you don't have to say that we're still friends if we're not. You don't have to pretend." He covers his eyes again as another sob shakes him.

Me and Riley exchange a worried look.

"It wasn't just Amelia, okay? I was worried about *both* of you getting hurt. And now you did, and... It was stupid.

How I reacted, I mean. And I know that what happened at Prom wasn't on purpose. You didn't even do anything wrong—you were just being honest with her."

"I didn't know that meant we had to break up. I thought that even if I didn't love her yet, that it could still happen. And I don't even know if what I said was true, because if I only *cared about her a lot*, then why do I feel like this?"

I look over at Riley, waiting for him to say something. He just showed up, and he hasn't had to answer any uncomfortable questions yet, so I figure it's his turn.

Zach looks over at him, too.

Riley realizes we're staring at him. "What? What are you guys looking at me for?"

"You're his brother. Impart your wisdom or something."

"*Me?* You're the one who's been through this before."

Erg. Fine. "Listen, Zach, whether you love her or not, this is still going to hurt. And in retrospect, maybe you wish you'd said something different to her on Prom night. Because saying you loved her even if you didn't probably seems way easier than feeling like this right now. But if you don't love her, then you did the right thing."

"And if I do love her?"

Then he really screwed up. But there's no way I'm telling him that. "You'll figure things out."

"But what if I don't? Or what if I do, but she hates me now, and I can't ever make her not hate me? What if I ruined everything?"

"Even if you did, it won't feel this bad forever. And...

and even if Amelia never comes around, you've still got me."

"Both of us," Riley says.

Zach looks almost hopeful for a second, but then he shakes his head. "She's your sister, though. If she decides she hates me forever, then—"

"It won't change anything."

He hesitates, like he's almost afraid to ask. "You really mean that?"

"Yeah, I do. You're my friend, Zach. And Amelia might be my sister, but you're like a brother to me. And no matter what happens between you and her, I'm not going anywhere."

X·X·X

Riley mashes the buttons on his controller to fight off the zombie horde that's attacking us in the video game we're playing. Zach was playing with us for a while, but his heart obviously wasn't in it, and eventually he retreated to his room. "So," Riley says, "did your grandpa tell you anything?"

"He said— Watch out!" I press the button to swing my ax at the zombie that's trying to attack him. "He said nobody knows who Frank is."

"What? How can nobody know who someone is?"

"Well, he's not on Facebook."

"But someone has to have"—he pauses while he fights off a zombie that managed to grab his character and is trying to eat his face off—"met him before."

"Grandpa said nobody ever sees him and lives to tell about it."

"Great, and we're supposed to find him?"

"Just the painting."

He snorts. "Oh, right. Just that. No problem. That's— Crap!" A whole group of zombies closes in on us, so we're trapped in a dead-end alleyway.

I can only remember one combo, and I can't seem to make it work. Then my ax breaks, and there isn't anything else to pick up and fight with, so I start mashing all the punching and kicking buttons.

We both lean forward in real life as we attack, as if that will help somehow. Once we defeat the group of zombies and escape the alley, we both exhale in relief.

"Anyway," I tell Riley, "Frank is seriously off the grid, according to Grandpa. And not someone we want to go up against."

"We can't fail this class, X. I'm still on probation for my scholarship, and you're... well, you know."

"*Thanks*, Perkins."

"You know what I mean. You missed two weeks of school this semester, and I know your grades haven't completely recovered from it. And Mrs. Deeds would love any excuse to fail you. And what's the point of you passing that flying test if you're going to still get held back? Fieldwork classes are required, so—"

"I get it." I pick up a crowbar off the ground and smash a zombie with it. "Wait, you actually believe I'm going to pass the flying test?"

"You said you— X! Behind you!"

"I know! I see it! I'm just not used to this weapon." I end up dropping the crowbar and punching the zombie instead. Which doesn't make a lot of sense, since the game makes a big point of the zombies bleeding all over every time they get hit. It sounds like a good way to contract zombie-ism, if you ask me.

Riley uses a sword to slice another zombie headed my way. "You said you were going to pass."

"And I thought you didn't believe me."

"Well... that's beside the point. You have to be there next year, and that means not flunking a required class."

"We're not going to flunk. Grandpa told me the time and location of Frank's next robbery."

"He what?" Riley turns to look at me.

"Watch out!"

He focuses on the screen again and attacks more zombies. His sword breaks. "How does he know?"

"Frank put a message out and hired some guys to do it. I figure all we have to do is be there when the robbery goes down and follow them to see where they put the stolen goods."

"Oh, is that all?"

"Shut up. It's a good plan."

"I don't know, X. It involves, what, just watching them steal stuff and not stopping them?" His eyebrows come together, worried.

"Yeah, but... I don't know how else to find that painting. And we'll know where they put the stuff they take, so the gallery will get it back."

"I don't"—he pauses to fend off an attack—"I don't like

this."

"You want the truth? Or you want me to tell you something inspirational?"

He considers it. "The truth."

I shrug. "I don't like it, either."

"I changed my mind. I want inspirational."

"The thing is— Is that where we're supposed to go?" I'm talking about the game. The sun suddenly went down, and there's creepy fog everywhere with some ominous streetlights leading us off the road and onto some path through the forest.

"Yeah, we made it through town. This is the farthest I've been. Me and Zach played on Saturday, but then we had to stop and get ready for Prom."

"Okay, creepy forest path it is. And anyway, the thing is, we don't have a choice."

"That's not inspirational."

"Because fieldwork is supposed to be who we are. And we owe it to ourselves to find out if that's still true."

"By confronting some guy who doesn't exist but who will probably kill us? Hey, did you see something move?"

"The bushes twitched." And everything's gone really quiet, except for the occasional creaking sound. "It's just trying to scare us."

"Well, it's working. I should have saved my sword for later. I thought I'd find something else."

"We're not confronting Frank. We're following some hired goons to, like, a storage facility. Probably."

"What if they take everything to his house?"

"Then he'd have to kill them. Why would anyone ever

work for him if he just kills them? That seems like bad business. And we'll be, like, skulking. The whole point is for them to not know we're there."

"But if they catch us—"

"They won't."

"We could ask Mrs. Deeds for a new assignment. We could tell her this one's too dangerous."

I scoff. "She already thinks I don't deserve to be there. I can't let her think she's right." And more importantly, I can't let myself think that. "And we've never backed down before."

"True, and I kind of like that about us, but I also like being alive. Plus, that was before the gala, and… Ugh, this place is so creepy." The forest path we're on keeps getting bloodier and bloodier, even though we still haven't seen anyone, and now there's a red mist in the air along with the fog. The ground starts rumbling. It sounds far off, but like it's getting closer.

"Perkins, you know why we have to do this."

"Yeah, I do. But I still don't like it."

"We'll be careful. And if I have to zap someone to save our lives, we'll say you were looking the other way this time."

He laughs, but only a little. "And if we find out that we're not who we thought we were?"

"Then we'll know. And other than completely ruining our lives, what's the worst that could happen?"

I say that right as the rumbling in the game stops and a giant worm bursts up from the ground beneath our characters and swallows them whole.

CHAPTER 20

"Dad, can I ask you something?" Me and Gordon are in the car later that night, on our way home after running to the store. Well, after running to two stores, since the first one was sold out of the brand of chips Amelia *has* to have.

"Sure, son. Oh, hey, you know where we are?" His face lights up.

I glance out the window, but I don't see anything out of the ordinary. "Leaving the grocery store?"

"We're near the Super Freeze. It's an ice cream place—"

"I know what a Super Freeze is."

"Right, well, it's a little out of our way, but..." He stops at a red light and glances over at me. "They can put anything into a milkshake there. Candy, pie, cake. I know you'll love it. My father and I used to go there together. Usually only on special occasions, like on my first day of Heroesworth. And when I made the flying team. And when I made captain—"

"Uh, Dad? It's not my first day of school. And I haven't done any of that other stuff."

He laughs. "It doesn't have to be a special occasion. Besides, I haven't been there in *years*."

"Your dad's a complete and total douche, and he really, really hates me."

Gordon squirms behind the wheel. "Damien, that's not... Your grandfather doesn't..."

"Yes, he does. But the feeling's mutual, so whatever. My point is, I don't know why you'd have good memories of spending time with him."

"He was never like that with me. You only saw one side of him, of everyone in my family. They're not normally like that."

"To you, maybe."

"I know. And I was really disappointed with them at the Christmas party."

"Disappointed?"

"Disgusted," he says, quietly, like he's ashamed to admit it even with no one else around.

"Your dad would probably hate the fact that you want to carry on your traditions with me."

He smiles a little. "He probably would. But this isn't about him."

"Really? Because you're totally within your rights if you want to, like, send him selfies of us enjoying ice cream together at his favorite place."

Gordon laughs. "We went there because it was *my* favorite place. And I just want to share it with you. And have ice cream with pieces of banana cream pie in it."

"They have that?"

"They certainly do."

"Okay, let's go."

"We're already on our way." It starts sprinkling outside. He turns on the windshield wipers, but it's not raining hard enough, and every other swipe makes a sound that's half squeak, half screech. "So, what was it you wanted to ask me?"

"Nothing." The word comes out automatically, before I can think about it. "I mean, it wasn't important."

"Okay, well, if you—"

"I need you to teach me how to fly." I blurt all that out all at once, despite what I just said about it not being important. Then I sink down in my seat and stare out the window, not wanting to see his reaction.

"*Damien*. That's... that's wonderful!"

Oh, great. "It's not a big deal."

"Not a big deal? I've been going over this in my mind ever since you told me about that flying test. Of course I've wanted to teach you for a lot longer than that, but you made it clear you had no interest in using your flying power. I hoped that might change, on account of the test, but I didn't want to push you. Not after what happened last time."

"Geez. If I'd known you were going to be this excited about it, I wouldn't have asked you while you were driving. You want to pull over or something?"

"Damien, I'm fine. This is good news."

For him, maybe.

"We're going to need to get going right away for you to

pass your test. We can start tomorrow. Or tonight. How about as soon as we get home?"

My chest gets a little tight. I really thought I'd have more time. I mean, *tonight*? Is he serious? "I can't. Homework."

"Well, tomorrow, then. Hey, I think we can squeeze in a lesson before school. And you know what? You're going to be flying down those stairs before you know it. Think how much time that'll save you in the mornings."

Flying down the stairs. And he says it like it's no big deal, like even if it won't happen tomorrow—because, you know, that would be a miracle—by the next day it should be no problem. I feel like I'm going to be sick. I put my hands over my eyes and take a deep breath.

"Don't worry," Gordon says. "Your training won't involve any tall buildings this time."

"Does that mean it's going to involve *short* buildings?" How about no buildings? Or stairs? Or leaving the ground?

"We'll start off easy. Ceiling circles, stair swooping, skyscraper races—"

"What the hell are skyscraper races?"

He grins. "We race each other to the top of a skyscraper. Me and my brothers used to play that one all the time. But we can work our way up to it, start with something smaller."

"I think you and me played race to the *bottom* of a skyscraper."

His smile fades. "If there are other exercises you'd rather do—"

"It's fine." It's not fine. But I don't know any other exercises—I don't even know these ones—and I said I was going to do this. I'm not getting left behind, and I'm not letting Mom completely mess me up. All I have to do is pass the test, and then I never have to fly again. What's a few skyscraper races and stair swoopings?

Okay, even imagining it makes me feel like the floor is falling out from under me. I don't know why I thought I could do this. I can't even get through a conversation about it without freaking out.

Gordon's hand on my shoulder makes me jump. He frowns. "We're here. You want to go inside or go through the drive-thru?"

"Whatever you want. I don't— I'm not hungry."

"Oh." He sounds hurt by that. "Maybe we should just go home, after all. It was silly."

"No, you should get your ice cream. You said you haven't had it in years."

"That wasn't really the point." He looks over at me, all serious. "Maybe this was a bad idea."

"Give mine to Amelia. Or Alex—Amelia will make you listen to her spiel on why she's never dating anyone again."

"That's not what I meant."

"You're being really hard on yourself about this whole ice cream thing."

"Damien. I was trying to say that maybe... Maybe I shouldn't be the one to teach you how to fly."

"Wait, *what*?!" I sit up in my seat. "But it's, like, your lifelong dream. And I *need* you to. And— Did I do something wrong?"

"No. You didn't do anything, but I don't think I should teach you. You obviously don't want me to."

"I just asked you to, didn't I?"

"And then you got weird about it." His eyes meet mine, pleading with me, though I don't know what for. "You have a problem with heights."

"So I've noticed."

"Whereas flying's always come easily to me."

"Good for you?" Is he trying to rub it in?

"No, that's... I've never taught anyone before, and..." He shakes his head. "Listen, Damien, it's taken us a long time to get where we are. I don't want to ruin that."

"You won't."

He gives me a stern look. "A few minutes ago, you seemed fine. Then we started talking about flying, and I watched you become more and more panicked."

"You were supposed to be watching the road."

"I was, but anyone could see how uncomfortable you were. Maybe a year ago, I wouldn't have noticed. Or I would have, but I would have pretended it was alright, because I wanted it to be. But it's not."

"You can't do this. I *need* you to teach me. Nothing's going to get ruined—that's ridiculous."

He runs a hand through his hair. "I wish I could believe that, but you still haven't forgiven me for what happened last time."

When he pushed me off the tallest building in Golden City, he means. "What? I... I mean, it's not like you'd do that again. You even said, no tall buildings."

"No, I won't do that again."

"You didn't know I was afraid of heights."

"But it's no excuse. I should have seen that you weren't ready. But I wouldn't listen to you, and now you're still not over it."

"It's hard to forget something like that, that's all."

"I'm not the right person to teach you how to fly."

I stare at him. And as much as I was dreading his flying lessons, the thought of him *not* teaching me, of just abandoning me like this, is terrifying. "You can't do that! I'll fail first year. Is that really what you want?"

"Of course not." He squeezes his eyes shut and presses his palms to his forehead. "But even more than that, I don't want you to end up hating me."

CHAPTER 21

I'm sitting at the kitchen table, eating breakfast the next morning, but I hardly taste anything. I think I got maybe four hours of sleep last night, tops. My mind just kept spinning, going over and over again how Gordon's *not* going to teach me how to fly, and how that was really my only plan, and how I have no idea what I'm going to do now.

Fail Heroesworth, probably, and then watch all my friends graduate without me and go on to get really cool jobs that I'm not qualified for. Not that I can think of any heroes who have what I'd call *cool jobs*, but I'm sure Kat will have one. And then I'll just be her loser boyfriend who couldn't cut it as a villain *or* a hero, despite how much I made fun of them, and who'll probably end up working at one of those superhero-themed diners, but only because my dad's the Crimson Flash and everyone knows I'm his screwup son and there's a chance customers might want to take pictures with me. And who knows how long that will last? Probably only until the novelty wears off, and then I'll be completely unqualified for *anything.*

And maybe it doesn't matter anyway because *maybe* I don't even want to be doing fieldwork. And graduating from Heroesworth doesn't necessarily mean I'll have any kind of future, either, because I'm not joining the League or any other stupid hero groups. But I don't want to be left behind. So I think what that really means is that I need to convince Riley to drop out.

It won't be easy, because he's pretty set on the whole *not failing* thing, but getting him to drop out still sounds easier than me magically learning how to fly. Then I just have to convince Kat and Sarah not to do anything with their lives, either. I mean, Sarah could graduate high school in her sleep, so I don't see much point in her dropping out. But does she really *need* to go to college? And Kat—

"Hello?" Alex says, waving a hand in front of my face. "Earth to Damien. Did you hear me?"

I blink. "What?"

"Do you want my last pancake?"

"Nah, I'm good."

"Well, I'm not eating it," Amelia says, even though no one asked her. "I'm too heartbroken to eat. I'm probably going to waste away."

"You had, like, five pancakes."

"*Four.* More like three and a half."

"That's not exactly wasting away."

"What were you thinking about so hard?" Alex asks me.

"Sabotaging my friends' futures." No big deal.

He looks like he doesn't know whether to laugh or not.

Amelia clears her throat. "So. You went over to Riley's yesterday, right?"

"Amelia."

"What? You did, didn't you?"

"If you want to know about Zach, then just talk to him."

"I *don't* want to know about Zach. I left a sweatshirt at his house, that's all."

I hold up my hand, miming her using her power to call it up.

Her face goes a little pink, and she stares down at the table. "Fine. But all I want to know is—"

She shuts up as Helen comes in from the living room. Jess follows and comes over to the table. She sizes up the situation, sees that Amelia's in the chair closest to mine, and tells her, "*Move.*"

"*Jess*," Helen scolds. "What did we talk about?"

"*Please*," Jess adds in her most grudging voice, not sounding at all like she means it.

"You heard the lady," I tell Amelia.

She ignores me. "Jess, I'm still eating."

"So, still not wasting away, then."

"And there are other chairs."

Jess looks over at Alex, who grabs onto the edges of his chair, refusing to budge, even though I'm pretty sure Amelia didn't mean she should take his.

"Come here," Amelia says. "You can sit in my lap."

Jess ignores her and just stands next to me instead, hooking her arms around mine.

Then Gordon comes in. Helen stops making Alex's lunch, her eyes darting over to Gordon, then to me.

Great, so he told her I actually asked him to teach me to fly—a moment I'm not super proud of—and that he turned me down. I guess I should be happy that they're conspiring against me instead of fighting because of me, but still. Why stop there? Why think my humiliation is even remotely private? Why not just tell the whole family while he's at it?

"Damien, there you are," Gordon says, beaming at me like I don't have less than two weeks to figure out how to keep my life from falling apart. "I'll pick up some brochures today for those flying schools I was telling you about last night." He means after he told me he wasn't going to teach me. His brilliant backup plan is to just have somebody else do it. "We can look at them together after school."

Seriously? I already told him I didn't want to do that, and I don't know why he'd think I'd want to talk about it in front of everyone. I gape at him like *What is wrong with you?* but he doesn't seem to notice, since he keeps going.

"I know you're not the, uh, average flight student, but I'm sure there are programs that can handle your situation."

"My *situation*." Lightning prickles beneath my skin, but I force myself to keep it under control, since Jess still has my arm.

"I'll explain things to Ted and ask for some recommendations. He's in the business, so I'm sure he knows where we can start looking for specialty programs."

I stand up as lightning sparks across my skin, yanking my arm out of Jess's grasp before she gets zapped. She stumbles back a step, and then her eyes start to water, and I feel like the worst person in the world.

"Jess—" I stop myself from reaching for her. I take a deep breath and force my lightning to die down first. I pull her close to me. She glomps onto my leg, and I put my hand on her head to comfort her. I try to speak calmly, so I don't go all electric again, but it's really hard when Gordon's giving me this confused look, like he has no idea what I'm getting so upset about. "Dad," I say through clenched teeth, "what the hell is wrong with you?"

"Well, son, I just thought—"

"You just thought what? That I'd be cool with you broadcasting my problems to the entire family? And as if that wasn't bad enough, then you want to tell freaking *Ted*?" Electricity burns beneath my skin as I try really, really hard not to let it spark again.

"Looking at flying schools is the next step, and we don't have a lot of time. Finding the right program for you is important. Ted might be able to help us narrow down our choices."

"*Don't* tell him about me! You do not have my permission to talk to him about me, *ever*. And if you think that telling him about my fear of heights is going to make him go easy on me or something, then..." I clench my free hand, then let it flop to my side. I just can't believe this.

"He's the one who decides whether you pass your test or not. It might help if he knew the whole story."

I feel like I'm going to throw up, and if Gordon tells

Ted about my fear of heights, I'm pretty sure I actually will. "How can you even suggest that? How can you even *think* about it?" My hands start to shake, and electricity runs up my spine, and I know if he says one more stupid word to me, I'm going to lose it.

I pick up Jess and set her on my chair. She doesn't want to let go of me, but I pull away, because I can't let her get hurt. At least she doesn't seem upset this time.

"Damien," Gordon says, "if you don't want to involve Ted—"

"Oh, *you think*?!"

"—then we'll leave him out of it. But just because I don't feel I should be the one to teach you doesn't mean I'm leaving you to do this all on your own. We'll go over the brochures together. We'll find the right program."

"*No.*" I hold up my hands for him to shut up, but they're covered in lightning. I put them down. "Dad, just... just *don't*. There is no *we* in this."

"But, Damien—"

"I don't want to look at brochures, I don't want recommendations, and I sure as hell don't want you talking to Ted about me. So if you're not going to help, then just stay out of it!"

Hurt flashes across his face.

I shouldn't have lashed out at him.

But how could he even *think* about talking to Ted about me? And how could he bring it up to me, in front of everyone, and think I'd be okay with that?

"I have to get to school," I tell him, even though everyone can see that I'm shaking and covered in electricity, and even though there's still another ten minutes before me and Amelia normally leave. "I'll walk," I add, so she doesn't think I'm taking Tom and leaving her behind. Then I storm out of there, grabbing my backpack on my way out the door.

So maybe Gordon was right about our relationship not being that stable.

Once I'm outside, I put my hands to my face and take a few deep breaths. I've just gotten my electricity to die down when the front door opens. A mixture of rage and dread and disappointment flares up in me, making more sparks race across my skin, because I assume it's Gordon.

"Damien, wait." It's Amelia. She's got her stuff for school with her. "I'll go with you. You don't have to walk."

"It's… it's too early." Melissa and Hil probably won't be ready yet, and there's not enough time for her to drop me off first. "It's fine."

"I'm still coming with you. I'll text Melissa and Hil. Hil's sister can give them a ride."

"You don't have to do this."

"But maybe I *want* to. You were really nice to me at Prom, and… I know you missed your weekend with Kat. Plus, I have something to say."

I start walking. Gordon's going to be leaving for work soon, and I don't want to be standing within lecture range when he does. "If this is about Zach—"

"It's not." Amelia hurries to catch up with me. "I mean, I think it's only fair that you tell me what he said about me, but— Do you have to walk so fast?"

I slow down a little, glancing over my shoulder toward the house. "I'm not telling either of you about the other one, okay? I'm staying out of it."

"We can discuss that later. Wait, does that mean he *did* say something about me?"

"I don't want to be in the middle of this. You're my sister, and he's my friend."

"But... is he upset at all?"

"Amelia, come on. Of course he is. I thought you had something to say? Something that *wasn't* about Zach."

"Right." She takes a few quick steps to catch up again. "Dad was being stupid back there."

"Thanks for your support. You didn't have to walk to school with me to tell me that."

"Will you shut up? I'm trying to say that... I'm trying to say I can teach you."

I stop walking. We're around the corner now, anyway. "You what?"

"I can teach you to fly. *Don't* laugh."

I'm trying not to. "You can't fly."

"I know that. Duh. But I thought I was going to be able to."

"So?" Last I checked, that wasn't even remotely the same thing.

"So, I spent my whole life preparing for it. I've read all the books on it, and I've watched tons of videos from the library and online. I know everything about it."

"Except how to actually do it."

"But I can help. And," she says, looking me over, "no offense, but there's no way you'd make it at flying school."

"Why's that? Other than the obvious."

"Dad doesn't see how people treat you at Heroesworth. The teachers and the students don't like you, and they wouldn't like you at flying school, either."

"I said *other than the obvious*."

"They're rigorous programs, and I've seen you on the stairs. You can't handle rigorous. You'd hate it there. And you already said you weren't going to one. So, I mean, it's not like you have anyone better to teach you."

"Wow, great. I feel so confident in letting you handle all of my flight-training needs."

"I know what the routine for the flying test is supposed to look like. I can help. And… I already know you're afraid of heights. I won't make fun of you or tell anybody or anything. And I helped you get up three sets of stairs to save Riley at the gala. So, you should give me a chance."

I consider that. "Why do you want to do this?"

"Because. I learned all this stuff for a power I didn't even get, and this way it won't go to waste."

"I'm not telling you about Zach."

"I *know*, okay? This isn't about that. But maybe it'll help take my mind off of him, and…" She glances up at me. "And maybe I just want to feel useful for once."

"Amelia—"

"*Really* useful. And not because somebody else told me to be. I want to do something only I can do. Something that matters."

"What you did at the gala did matter."

"I know, but I don't want it to be the only thing I ever do."

"And you think you're the only one who can teach me how to fly?"

"Yes. And it won't involve tall buildings or anything. You won't fall."

"You don't know that."

"You *won't*. And I'm not like Dad. I know how freaked out you get, plus *I* can't fly. So me training you means everything's going to be mostly at ground level."

I consider that. It certainly sounds better than working with Gordon, which isn't even an option, and it sounds way better than going to some flight school with yet another douchey teacher who doesn't want me there. Not that I was going to do that, either. So... "You really think that in two weeks, you can have me flying through hoops on the ceiling?"

She shrugs. "I don't know. But I know we can try."

CHAPTER 22

"I have information," I tell Kat on the phone that afternoon.

"Me, too. Your sister texted me to ask if I'd come watch movies with you guys again this weekend."

"No, I meant about our fieldwork assignment. Assignments. You know what I mean. And tell Amelia that if you come over this weekend, I've already called dibs."

"Damien, my time isn't something you can call dibs on. And I'm not telling her that, because you didn't."

"So, wait, we're watching movies with Amelia again this weekend?"

"Well…"

"Kat!"

"What? She said we could watch *Attack of the Killer Robot Zombie Slaves*."

I gasp, offended, and sit up on my bed. "How easily you've been lured to the dark side. Watching *Attack of the Killer Robot Zombie Slaves* was supposed to be *our* thing."

"Yeah, and we've been waiting to watch it for forever. This way we actually get to be in the same room. And hanging out with your sister is not 'the dark side.' She's actually not that—"

"You know, Kat, I can really only stay on the phone for a little bit longer, and I've got so much important information to tell you, so—"

"She's not that bad. There, I said it."

I cringe. "I think the line's cutting out. I'm going through a tunnel. We'd better restrict this conversation to only the essentials."

"A tunnel, Damien? You're in your room."

"You don't know that."

"Well, I know you're not going through a tunnel."

"Fine. I'm in my room. But I really do have important information to tell you."

"About our assignment?"

"Yeah. I've got a lead."

"Me, too." She sounds pretty excited about that, like she found out something big.

Maybe she found out where the painting is and we won't have to actually go through with staking out Frank's next robbery. I kind of hope that's the case, even if I was also kind of looking forward to impressing her with my info-gathering skills. Skills that involve just asking my grandpa, but whatever.

"I know when and where Frank's next robbery's going to be," she says.

"What?"

"Yeah, I know, I didn't think we'd be able to find any

info on Frank, either, because there, like, just *isn't* anything. But then I found out he was looking for people to work an upcoming job."

"Kat, you're totally stealing my thunder here. That's what I was going to say."

She laughs. "Great minds think alike. Or find information alike, I guess."

"I figured we'd sneak around the gallery and watch where Frank's goons take everything after the robbery."

"Long-distance high five. That's my plan, too. I just haven't told Tristan yet, because when I told him I couldn't find anything about Frank online, he made this big deal about how research is the cornerstone of fieldwork and how he has 'mad internet search skills.' But I don't see him coming up with anything better. So that means both our groups are going to be at the same place at the same time, doing the exact same thing."

"If you're saying it's going to be too crowded, you could always ditch Tristan."

"I'm saying we should work together."

Yes. Finally. We've only been waiting years for something like this. That's what I should say, anyway. It's what I *want* to say, except… "Kat, I don't know if we should. I mean, I want to, it's just—"

"Sarah will be butt hurt about it?"

"That's not how I was going to put it, but something like that."

"It's stupid not to work together on this. We're just going to get in each other's way if we don't. We already did get in your guys's way at the museum. And what are we supposed to do, follow the robbers to their stash in separate groups somehow? Just because Sarah, who's not even involved in this, might be upset that I got to work with you for once? That's ridiculous."

She has a point. Sort of. "I see what you're saying. I'm just not sure that Riley will be okay with pissing off his girlfriend like that. Or with teaming up with Tristan. Which makes two of us."

Kat sighs. "Tristan won't like it, either. But, honestly, I don't see how it makes sense for us to work alone on this."

"Well, all I really need is proof that Frank's the one who stole the painting. So, you guys just make sure to take a picture of it or something before you steal it back. Problem solved."

"Yeah, right. I'm not doing your assignment for you."

It was worth a shot. "Fine, Kat. If you won't do my homework for me, even though it's totally, like, not out of your way or anything, then I guess we'll just have to team up."

Kat squees in excitement. "This is going to be amazing."

"For you, maybe. You're not the one who has to tell Riley." And Sarah.

There's a knock on my door. Then Amelia calls out, "Damien?"

"I'm on the phone!" I shout back.

"It's time for flying lessons!"

"Um, *what*?" Kat says. "Did I hear that right?"

"No, you didn't," I tell her. "Everything's all muffled and echo-y up here."

"You don't even know what I think I heard. Did she really say *flying lessons*?"

I try to laugh it off, like that's completely ridiculous, which it sort of is, even if it's also true.

Amelia pounds on the door. "Damien!"

"I *said* I'm on the phone!" I get up and fling my door open, just as she's about to knock again. "I'm talking to Kat, okay? It's really important."

Amelia folds her arms. "More important than not flunking out of school?"

"You know," Kat says, "I have some homework I have to get to anyway, but you totally have to tell me what's going on later."

"Kat, do *not* hang up right now." I whisper that into the phone, turning away so maybe Amelia won't hear me.

Amelia uses her power to teleport my phone into her hand, except instead of hanging up, she actually starts talking to Kat. "Hey," she says, "this is Amelia."

I try to snatch my phone away from her, but she dodges out of reach, even though it means stomping on a really creaky floorboard in the hallway.

"Damien's going to have to call you back," she says. "If he really even does have something important to say, which I doubt. But you're coming over this weekend, right?"

Oh, my God. "*Amelia.* Give me my phone."

She holds up a finger, indicating I should be quiet. "Uh-huh. Yes! Bring it. And I've got this new movie I borrowed from my friend Tiffany that you're going to love. It's another rom-com, kind of like the one we watched last weekend, only this one's, like, really sad at the end. I just want you to be prepared, because I kind of cried a little last time I watched it. Maybe more like a lot. But it has a happy ending, so—"

"Amelia!"

"I have to go," she tells Kat. "See you on Saturday!" Then she hangs up—*finally*—and hands me my phone back.

"What happened to you not touching my phone anymore? Because of all the phone sex it's witnessed?"

She makes a face. "I know that isn't true."

"No, you really don't."

"Yes, I do. Kat already told me it was a lie, so don't even try to say it wasn't."

"*What?* Amelia, what do you mean Kat told you?"

"I asked her last weekend, when you went to the bathroom."

I can't believe this. "Why the hell would you ask somebody that? And don't tell me it just came up, because that's not a normal part of conversation."

"No, I didn't have time to work it into a conversation, so I just asked her. Because I believed you at first, but then I kind of suspected that maybe you just said that to gross me out. And I think Kat has a right to know what rumors you've been spreading about her."

"Seriously?"

"And she told me that it *wasn't* true, not even a little bit, and that you totally made it up to mess with me."

"How do you know she wasn't just being polite? And no more movie marathons if you guys are going to talk about me!"

Amelia just smirks, like she's finally gotten the upper hand on me, which she most certainly has not. "It's time for flying lessons."

"I'm kind of busy right now."

"Doing what? Talking to Kat? Because she said she had homework to do—I heard her."

"*I* have homework to do."

"You can do it later. This won't take that long."

"Amelia, I never said—"

She scowls at me. "You said you'd do it."

"But I didn't say I'd do it *today*."

"You have to do it *every* day. The test is in only ten days."

"Yeah, but—"

"No *buts*. Flying lessons start right now, or they don't start at all."

X·X·X

The video of what the flying test is *supposed* to look like ends, and Amelia clicks a button on her laptop to start it over again.

We're sitting on the edge of her bed. Amelia has the laptop balanced on her knees. She insisted that flying lessons needed to happen in her room, since my room was too associated with failure. I told her I didn't fail the flying test in my room, and she said it was at least associated with the *thought* of failure and that her room was failure free. Which I find extremely hard to believe, but whatever.

I turn away from the computer. "I've seen enough. There's no way I can do that. And if your whole plan was just to watch videos—"

"It's not. And if this is going to work, you have to actually give it a chance."

"Maybe starting with a reminder of how I'll never be good enough wasn't the best way to go."

"I showed it to you so you'd know what your goal is. And so you could see that there's really not that much to it."

I look at her like she's insane, which she obviously is. "Yeah, well, you're not the one who has to actually do it. Zigzagging through hoops on the ceiling isn't exactly my strong point."

"I *know*. That's why we're here. But I'm just trying to show you that it's not that bad. *Because*," she says, cutting me off before I can argue with her, "all you really have to learn is how to go up to the ceiling, how to go through hoops, and then how to come back down."

"Oh, is that *all*?" It still sounds pretty impossible to me.

"Yes. I just mean that you don't have to know everything about flying. You don't even have to be that good at it as long as you can do the test."

"I have to be good enough that Ted won't fail me."

"We'll work on that. But it's really only three moves."

"That involve being up high and me not freaking out the whole time."

"You can, though. You made it up all those stairs at the gala without freaking out. And you've flown before. Well." She hesitates. "I've never seen you, but you claim you have."

"Great lesson. I've learned *so* much."

"That wasn't the lesson. It was just part of it. You still have to fly."

I look up at the ceiling. My stomach twists. I feel dizzy, and we haven't even started yet. "Look, Amelia, I appreciate what you're trying to do here, but—"

"You flew for Zach," she says. "He told me about it. He asked to see you fly, and you did it."

"I... I mean, yeah, I did."

"He said you went up to the ceiling. I'm not even asking you to do that."

"You're not?"

"I just want you to get off the ground. For now, anyway. We won't get to the ceiling until next week. I made a chart," she adds.

"You didn't tell me that. About just getting off the ground." Not that it really matters, because this whole thing is still terrifying.

"I shouldn't have to. You need to trust me, and you're going to have to go up higher eventually. But this test is really important, and... why could you fly for Zach and not me? When it really matters?"

I swallow. "It's not like that. But Zach believed in me."

"I believe in you."

"And it was just once. It wasn't like this, where my whole future is riding on it."

"It's not your whole future. I told you, you could work at a gas station or at a superhero diner."

"Yeah, well, this might come as a surprise to you, but

neither of those career paths sounds particularly appealing." And whatever I end up doing, I want it to be my choice, and not because I flunked out of something else.

"It's still not your whole future."

"It feels like it. And even if it's not, it's still a lot of pressure."

"Stand up."

I get off the bed.

"Now fly."

I stare at her.

She makes a frustrated sound and waves her hand. "Just float above the floor a little bit."

"And then what?"

"And then stay that way. We're going for five minutes. But you won't fall, and even if you do, it'll be, like, an inch."

"Amelia—"

"Just do it, okay? It won't be that bad."

I want to keep arguing with her, because I *so* don't want to do this. We're already in the attic, which is *not* the ground floor, which means it won't really just be an inch. That's bad enough, and even if I don't have to fly any higher today, I will eventually. More like pretty soon. And then I'll have to do it in front of Ted, too, assuming I even get that far. All that feels way too big.

It would be so much easier to just quit now, before I humiliate myself. Before I make myself think there's even a chance in hell I can do this and then totally fail.

But I promised Kat I would at least try.

And Amelia's giving me this tentative, super hopeful look, like this really is her only chance to feel useful and she needs me to not just walk out of here.

And maybe it'll hurt more to try and still fail—to try *really hard* to only end up right where I started anyway—but Kat's right, I *do not* just give up. And maybe I don't know if I'm still the same person who loves fieldwork, the same person I was before everything that happened at the gala, but I know this one thing is still true about me. Or, at least, I can make it true.

So I take a deep breath and try not to think about how much is riding on this, and then I lift off the ground.

CHAPTER 23

"I just want to talk to you," Gordon says later that night.

"Can't. I'm busy." I gesture to all the worksheets and pieces of paper strewn around me on my bed. "Morality homework."

I wasn't actually doing homework—I dumped my backpack out to look for my phone charger right before he came in—but he doesn't have to know that.

I think I've made it pretty clear that I want him to go, short of actually telling him to get the hell out, but instead of leaving, he shuts the door and sighs. "You didn't say a word to me at dinner."

"Not true."

"Shrugging after I asked you how your day was doesn't count."

I almost shrug at him in reply, but I catch myself and pretend to be really interested in one of the pieces of paper instead.

"This... this isn't how I want things, Damien. Making the decision not to teach you how to fly wasn't easy for me, but I did it to help our relationship, not to make things worse."

"Great. Non-existent apology noted. You can cross it off your to-do list." I wave a hand toward the door without looking up from my piece of paper. It's actually my syllabus for Morality II and it turns out I have a paper due tomorrow, which I totally forgot about and haven't even started on. The topic is about when someone should or should not use their superpower in the field and the increased responsibility involved with having a dangerous power. A topic I have *a lot* to say about, but I already know my opinion on it is really unpopular and will just get me a *D* anyway. And it would only be a *D* instead of an *F* because my Morality teacher is really big on giving points for effort.

"I'm sorry for this morning." Gordon comes over to the bed and waits for me to move my stuff so he can sit down, but I don't. "I think some part of me knew you wouldn't be okay with getting Ted involved."

"Only *some* part?" Well, it's an improvement, at least.

"I should have known how you'd react. But I just felt..." He trails off and gestures to the papers on the bed. "Can I sit down?"

I shove just enough stuff over so part of the edge is free.

He sits. "I was just so frustrated that I couldn't help you. You came to me, and I had to turn you down. The one thing I really wanted us to do together, and I had to say no."

The one thing? What about teaching me how to drive? What about going out for ice cream? "It's fine. I don't need your help."

"Damien—"

"I *don't*." I look him over. "You were right. It wouldn't have worked out."

He looks hurt by that. "Every time you need me, I just... I can't find the right words to say."

"Take your time. It's not like I'm in the middle of a big assignment that's due tomorrow or anything."

"No, I meant that whenever you need me—"

"Dad, I don't—"

"—you come to me, and I say something that upsets you, or I say nothing at all."

"I was following you up until the saying nothing part. I'm going to need an example."

"At the restaurant. You came to me for help on whether or not you should stay in school."

"That's not how I remember it." *He's* the one who came to me, not the other way around. "And you didn't say nothing." But he didn't piss me off for once, either, which was refreshing.

"Helen could tell you were having a problem." He rubs his forehead. "A bigger problem than just dropping out of school, and she—"

"It wasn't her fault. And we really don't have to talk about it."

His face falls. "You heard us arguing."

I don't know how this is news to him. "She was trying

to help."

"She had something to say to you, and I had nothing. She's been retired from the League for twenty years, and I've only been out of it for a couple of months, and I've still got my job, and yet I've got nothing useful to say."

"That's not *completely* true. And I really do have to work on that homework assignment, so—"

"Everything I believed in turned out to be a lie."

I wince. I wrap my arms around myself.

"Finding out how Helen really felt about her statue, that she'd had mixed thoughts about her time in the League and never told me, only made things worse."

"It was my fault." I say that quickly, so that the words are almost unintelligible. "I broke the League."

"You helped expose them. You didn't make them what they were."

"But if you didn't know all that stuff they'd done, what they were doing, then you'd still be with them. And Helen's statue would still be in the Heroes' Walk, and none of this would have happened."

"Everything the League supposedly stood for was made up."

"But not to you. Not to everyone. You weren't doing anything wrong, and you would have been happier if you'd never found out. I did that. I messed things up."

"You did what you thought was right. And if I'd been paying more attention to what you had to say, about the League and about how other heroes treat villains, maybe it wouldn't have been such a shock to me."

I don't know about that. I knew how ashamed Mom

was of whoever she'd had a one-night stand with to end up with me, and I was still shocked when I found out it was the Crimson Flash. Probably not the best anecdote to tell Gordon, though, even if it really fits this situation.

"I've never believed in something as much as I believed in the League." He swallows, slowly, like he's tasting the words. Like he can't believe he said them and wishes he could take them back. "I'd been with them for my entire adult life, but I believed in them and knew I was going to join for as long as I can remember. It was what my father did, what Ted and Howard and I were going to do, and it was what we wanted for our kids, too. That was my entire life, spent believing in lies."

"Yeah, well, I spent my entire life thinking I was going to get a *V*. So, like, I know how it feels when your life doesn't turn out how you wanted."

"I'm over twice your age. You're supposed to feel lost at seventeen. I'm thirty-seven, and I thought I had everything together. And now... No wonder I can't help you figure out your life when I can't even figure out my own."

"I thought getting an *X* was the worst thing ever, and it totally ruined my life. At the time," I add, when he looks over at me. "But it turned out okay. Sort of. I mean, I thought I had my future planned out, too, and now I don't. But, like, it didn't actually change who I was. And the League rules might be really stupid, but you believed in them for the right reasons. So maybe the League turned out to be full of crap, but, I don't know, it doesn't mean your life was. And you still have your family and your job and stuff. You like those, right?"

"Of course I do. When I said I was lost, I didn't mean that—"

"I know."

"I love my family."

"And your job, right?"

He hesitates.

"Dad, come on. *The Crimson Flash and the Safety Kids* is a national treasure. And Sarah would *kill me* if she thought I'd said anything to jeopardize its continuation."

"I *do* love my job. I'm not leaving the show anytime soon. But all this with the League has made me realize that... I don't know. I just wish I was doing more, that's all." He suddenly glances around at all the papers on the bed and sits up, like he's finally realized he was interrupting. Then he looks at me all serious and says, "I probably shouldn't have told you all that. You're my son, and you're only seventeen, and I shouldn't be burdening you with my problems."

"Great way to ruin a conversation. It's not like I've been through stuff and *might* understand what you're going through. I liked that you were being honest with me for once, but if you didn't get anything out of this—"

"I didn't say that. And I'm always honest with you."

"Not like this." Not like he actually trusts me or cares what I think.

He gets up from the bed. "I'll let you get back to your homework. Though it's kind of late to still be working on something that's due tomorrow."

"I'm almost done."

"Okay, well, goodnight, Damien." He pauses before

opening the door to leave. "And... thanks."

"Don't mention it."

He laughs like he thinks I'm joking.

X·X·X

"Do you want my honest opinion?" Riley asks, wrinkling his nose at my notebook.

I snatch it back from him. "That depends."

"It reads like you wrote it in the car this morning."

"Well, the joke's on you, because I wrote it in first period."

He takes a sip of his milk. "It's not even typed. I could hardly read it."

"I didn't ask you to read it. I *asked* you if you thought it was long enough to bother turning in."

"It's not finished."

"It just needs a concluding paragraph."

"And an opening paragraph. And a point. And—"

"It has a point."

Riley raises his eyebrows, skeptical of that. "How long is it *supposed* to be?"

"Five pages. Double-spaced."

"So, five *typed* pages. You have one and a half pages of scribbling. And lunch is almost over. Isn't this for your next class?"

"I'm not going for *good* here, I'm going for *turn-in-able*. Enough for a *D*. Preferably a high *D*, but I'm not picky."

"Is there anything that's lower than an *F*? Because that's what I would give this paper."

"Are you saying I shouldn't even turn it in? Because that doesn't sound like something someone who cared about their grades would do."

"Someone who cared about their grades would have started at least the day before they had to turn in the assignment." He pauses, taking a bite of his peanut-butter-and-jelly sandwich. "Probably a lot sooner than that."

"They obviously wrote this prompt because of me."

"Yeah. Well, I guess I can see how that would make it hard to write about."

"It's not hard to write about."

"Then why did you wait so long?"

"Because. I totally forgot about it, okay? But, you know, I care about my grades so much that—"

"That you wrote it this morning?"

"That I wrote it *at all*. And we were supposed to be watching a movie in first period. So, like, I made a real sacrifice here."

"Well, my honest opinion is don't turn it in."

"Fine. Do you think she'd buy that I didn't understand the prompt?"

He rolls his eyes at me. "You could tell her you forgot, since that's what actually happened."

"Yeah, right. Like anyone at this school would believe that. Or care." Plus, if she gave me more time, I might have to actually write it. And, like, do a good job and stuff.

I close my notebook and cram it back into my bag, then scarf down part of my turkey sandwich to make up for the all the eating time I lost. "And one more thing, Perkins." I say that with my mouth full, so I'm kind of surprised that he actually understands me.

"You're going for the world championship of fastest sandwich eating?"

I swallow down my food. "It's about our assignment for Advanced Heroism."

"Oh."

"And you're not going to like it."

"I haven't liked anything about this assignment so far, so, yeah, probably not."

"We're working with Kat and Tristan." I hold my breath after saying that, waiting for his reaction.

He stares at me. He picks up the last bite of his sandwich, then sets it down again. He presses his hands against the table.

"Perkins—"

"You didn't even ask me."

Because if I asked, he might have said no. Or, like, thought he had a choice in this. "Kat figured out the same info we did, and she has the same plan. She and Tristan are going to be staking out the exact same robbery at the exact same time—"

"We can't work with them, X."

"If we don't work with them, we're competing against them. And…" And given our track record lately, I'm not so sure we'd come out on top. "I can't compete against Kat."

"She goes to Vilmore. You go to Heroesworth. You kind of already do."

"Not directly. Not like we would be with this." I look over at him. "Sarah will get over it."

He glares at me. "This isn't about Sarah."

I tilt my head.

"Okay. Maybe it's kind of about Sarah. But it's also about them going to Vilmore and about how their assignment involves *stealing* a painting."

"A painting someone else already stole."

"That doesn't make it better."

I shrug.

"X."

"What?"

"You're not really okay with that, are you?"

"I…" I pick part of the crust off of my sandwich, crumb by crumb. "I'm not *not* okay with it."

"We don't even know who they're stealing it for."

"We don't need to know." It's probably better if we don't. "And if they steal that painting back before we get a chance to prove who took it the first time—because, Perkins, we are *not* turning in Kat for this—"

He holds up his hands. "Of course not. I didn't say—"

"—then we'll be screwed. Plus, I mean… You know what happened at the train station."

"We wouldn't win if we had to compete against them, you mean." He sighs. "I still don't like it."

"It's the only way we're getting this done."

"We told Sarah we weren't working with them."

"We weren't. And look at it this way—it'll be way less dangerous than working on our own."

"You mean because there'll be four of us?"

"That and because if anything dangerous happens, we can just push Tristan in front of it."

Riley smirks at that, though then his face falls. "If we get caught—"

"We *won't*."

"But if the school found out we were working with *villains*, from *Vilmore*, there's no way we wouldn't fail the assignment. And I'd lose my scholarship, and you... well, you wouldn't have to worry about passing the flying test anymore."

"*If* we get caught, which we won't."

"I don't know. Helping them steal a painting..."

"We're not helping them steal anything. We're just finding it. Stealing it is their problem. And at least this way we have a chance of pulling this off. If we don't work with them, we might as well drop out now."

"And what about Sarah?"

"We'll simply explain to her that working with Kat is better than flunking out of school. And that it's totally my fault because I really, really miss Kat and I dragged you into it. And, I mean, that's not even a lie, so... so if she's mad at someone, it should be me."

"She'll be mad at both of us." He glances over at me. "You really miss Kat that much? I mean, is that was this is about?"

"It's about us not flunking out of school."

"You could tell me. If it was."

"It's *not* about Kat."

"But—"

"Geez, Perkins, how many times do I have to say it? It's about actually finishing our assignment. And figuring out if we still love fieldwork. And, like, not to put us down or anything, but right now, at this particular juncture in our academic careers, we could really use the help."

"*And?*"

"And yes, *fine*, I really do miss Kat that much. But that's not the reason we're doing this."

He studies my face for a second. "Okay."

"What, because I miss my girlfriend? That's a really stupid reason."

"Because you're right, this is kind of our only option. And Kat seemed pretty upset at Prom about the whole long-distance thing."

"We're fine. Don't do anything you don't want to do because of… because of whatever you think is going on."

"I'm not. Like I said, you're right, and I don't see any other way we're going to get through this assignment."

CHAPTER 24

"Hey, Zach," another birthday guest says when Zach goes to answer the door. "I— Oh, my God. Is that—"

"Yep," Zach says, sounding really proud of the fact that yes, I am at his birthday party. Something I guess none of his friends believed would happen, considering how almost this exact conversation has played out every time someone new shows up.

"Oh, my God, oh, my God!" the person at the door says. "I can't believe *Son of Flash* is here!"

Um, *what*? I glance up from my phone to glare at him.

The friend has thick glasses that make his eyes look extra big, and he gasps when we make eye contact.

I quickly look back down at my phone.

"Sorry, man," Zach's friend says. "I know what you said, but I didn't really think..."

"It's okay," Zach tells him. "Nobody else did, either."

They go join the rest of the guests, who are gathered

around the TV, trying to decide what video game to play first. Well, the rest of the guests except for me, Riley, and Sarah, since we're standing off by ourselves, against the far wall by the kitchen.

"I know you're mad," Riley tells Sarah, trying to keep his voice down.

"I'm *not* mad," Sarah says, though her teeth are clenched and she sounds pretty angry. Either because she really is mad at us, or because she's tired of him asking about it. My money's on both.

"Upset, then. Because—"

"Renegade," Sarah snaps, turning to me.

"Uh, secret identity anyone? Don't use our code names where just anyone could hear."

"They think your superhero name is Son of Flash—they've all said it, like, a million times. They're not going to be listening for another one."

Erg. "It's the principle of the thing."

"Anyway, tell him I'm not mad."

"Um."

"I'm *not*. I know what Kat said is true, about me not having a right to complain about you guys working with her. That means I can't be mad. So I'm not."

"Sarah," Riley says, "you can't just decide that."

"Yeah," I tell her, "and I'm sure 'not mad' is why you exploded that bag of chips earlier."

She glares at me. "Maybe I tore the bag with more enthusiasm than I should have, but it wasn't on purpose."

"Chips. Everywhere." I wriggle my fingers, acting out how they all fell to the floor. "And in my experience, telling people it wasn't on purpose when you explode something doesn't make it any better."

"And," Riley says, "if you *were* mad, we'd totally understand."

"But you'd still work with Kat," Sarah says. It's not exactly a statement, but not really a question, either.

He sighs. "See, that's not something someone who wasn't mad would say."

"Except that it is, because I'm *not* mad, therefore anything I say is something someone who's not mad would say!"

I pretend like I have a really important text so I don't have to be part of this conversation anymore. I really do have a text, only it's from Amelia, and it's not at all important. It says, *I know you're at Zach's party. Who else is there?*

I type back, *Lots of hot girls. In bikinis.*

She writes back instantly. *HA HA. That's SO not funny.* Then, two seconds later, *Megan's not there, is she? Or Krista?*

I scan the room. It's a mistake, because several of Zach's guests notice and rush over, like I invited them or something. I try to pretend I don't notice them, but they're standing right there, staring at me. And Riley and Sarah have moved to the kitchen and are arguing in hushed tones, so I can't use them as an escape.

One of the guys staring at me—because, despite Amelia's fears, there are *no girls* at this party; well, except for Sarah, I mean—is the one with the glasses who just got here, and the other has a T-shirt with stylized artwork of… of someone who looks a lot like me blowing up the roof of a school gym with their lightning power. Across the bottom, it says, *Be Truthful*, whatever that means, other than that I should probably be getting some kind of royalties.

"I can't believe you're *really* friends with Zach!" T-shirt Guy says, with this total look of awe on his face.

"He said you were," Glasses Kid says, "but we thought he was just exaggerating, because, like, you know. You're *you*."

"Yep, I'm me. I—"

"You're on my shirt!" the other one blurts out, like he just remembered he was wearing it. "Oh, my God, I've watched that video of you *so many times*."

I wince at that, though I try not to show it. "Great."

"Not that there's just one, 'cause there's, like, so many versions. But I've seen all of them, so it doesn't matter."

"*Matthew*," the one in the glasses says. "Seriously. You sound so dumb right now." He looks almost embarrassed for his friend, but then he turns to me and says, "Can we take a picture?"

I glance over at the kitchen. Riley and Sarah are still talking—though maybe not quite arguing now, it's hard to tell—and Sarah's eating one of the cupcakes I was told were off limits until after dinner. In the living room, Zach's playing video games with his friends. He looks happy—really happy—and not like his heart was recently smashed to pieces.

"Yeah, sure," I tell them. "Usually it's ten bucks, but since you're Zach's friends, I'll settle for royalty rights on any related merchandise."

They laugh—a little too hard—and take a selfie with me. Actually, three selfies, since everyone blinked in the first one and Matthew's T-shirt wasn't visible enough in the second one. Then they run back over to the group to show everybody.

My phone chimes.

Oh, my God, Amelia says. *I KNOW Megan's there! She's there, isn't she? Is she wearing her purple T-shirt that says I heart boys across the chest? Because she's SO OBVIOUS. Nobody even thinks she's cute when she does that.*

I write back, *She's not here.*

How do you know? You don't even know Zach's friends.

Because there are, like, no girls here?

There's a pause, then, *There's not? Then why didn't you text me back?!*

Because it doesn't matter who's at his party—you broke up with him.

Silence.

I probably shouldn't have said that, even though it's kind of true. I almost text her that I didn't mean it, but then she says, *I hate you,* and I shove my phone in my pocket instead.

"Do you really live with the Crimson Flash?" another overly eager party guest asks. I don't know where he came from, but he's standing *really* close. He seems to realize that and takes a step back, but only a tiny one, like he's afraid he might miss his chance to gawk at me if he gets too far away. "I mean, is he really your dad?"

"I'm not *Son of Flash*. But yeah, he's my dad."

"Can I get a picture? My girlfriend just *loves* that video of you."

"Blowing up the school?"

"No, the one you made after that. The What Heroism Means to Me video."

Great, my favorite. At least there isn't a T-shirt of that one. That I know about, anyway.

"She watches it literally every night. She even has a recording of that whole episode of The Crimson Flash and the Safety Kids, with your video interrupting part of it. Actually, could you record a message on my phone for her? She would *flip out*."

"Well—"

"Just say something like, *Hey, Bethany, this is Damien and you're really amazing and I love you.*"

"I'm not saying that."

"Whatever you *want* to say then." He presses record on his phone and holds it out to me.

I don't really *want* to say anything, since I don't know either of them or why anyone would want to watch that video of me more than once, if ever. "Hey, Bethany, um, be Truthful."

I know I've said the right thing because his eyes light up and he smiles at me and says, "Oh, my God, thank you so much!" Then he snaps a quick photo of me and runs off. A few seconds later, I hear him playing the recording for everyone.

Heads turn toward me. Matthew, the one with the Be Truthful T-shirt, looks almost disappointed when he hears the recording, like maybe he should have asked for that instead.

"How many times do I have to tell you?" Sarah says from the kitchen.

"Once, if you really meant it," Riley tells her.

Yep, friends still fighting. And Zach, a.k.a. the only other person I know at this party, seems pretty busy playing video games and having his friends hang on his every word, or at least every word that's about me.

"We hang out all the time," he says. "I don't know what's so hard to understand about that."

I'm, like, *this close* to texting Amelia and telling her Megan's here in her boy-catching T-shirt and that she should probably get over here as fast as possible. I figure her showing up would either end the party, or it would mean I'd have someone to hang out with. Er, not to hang out with, obviously, because it's *Amelia*. But she is good at getting in the way of people who want to take pictures of me and informing them that *she* happens to live with the Crimson Flash, too, and that I'm not as great as they think I am.

But it's Zach's party. So I probably shouldn't, like, purposely cause drama. Especially when I happen to know that no matter how happy he looks right now, he's been completely miserable all week.

The doorbell rings. Mrs. Perkins answers this time, since Zach's in the middle of his turn at *Aliens vs. Dinosaurs*.

"Hi, Mrs. Perkins," the new guest says. "Sorry I'm late. I forgot Zach's present and we had to go— Oh, my God. Is that him? Is that Damien Flash?!"

That is *so* not my name. Like, seriously.

Mrs. Perkins glances over at me with a slightly apologetic look, like she's pretty sure this is awkward for me. Or maybe she's just acknowledging how painful hearing *Damien Flash* was. "Yes, that's Damien," she says, only sort of correcting him.

"Can I talk to him?!"

"Well... I'm sure he wouldn't mind if you said hi."

What?

The kid runs to the gifts table to drop off the present he brought, then rushes over to Zach to say hello as fast as humanly possible—because, you know, manners—and then hurries over to me. He's actually so out of breath when he gets over here that he can hardly get the words out.

"You... Damien... Oh... My... God."

"Yeah, I can't believe I'm here, either."

"I've never seen a real supervillain before. Crap!" He claps his hands over his mouth. "I shouldn't have said that. That was stupid. It's true, though. And your girlfriend's a supervillain."

"Yep. Great fact spewing."

He blinks. "Can you do this?" He holds up his hands and flexes them.

I repeat the gesture.

"No, with lightning, duh."

At the word *lightning*, all of Zach's guests turn to stare at me, their eyes wide, like they've been waiting all night to hear that. There are only eight of them, but it feels more like a million.

"No lightning in the house!" Mrs. Perkins says, a horrified look on her face, like she thinks I might actually do it.

I mean, I *have* used my lightning in her house before, but only when she wasn't around, so it's not like she knows that. And I didn't break anything, so it shouldn't even count.

"We can go outside," the kid in front of me says.

"I don't really have lightning power," I tell him. "That's just something people add in on YouTube."

He doesn't buy it. "Come on, just do it a little bit."

All eight of them are hurrying over here now, the video game on pause. They all have their phones out, and I think a couple of them are already recording.

"I'm not doing it."

"Guys," Zach says, "let it go. Mom said no lightning."

Mom said? What about *Damien* said?

"That's right," Mrs. Perkins says in her sternest voice. "Absolutely no lightning."

"But he could fly, though," Zach adds absently, like he just thought of the solution to a problem instead of the worst idea ever. Then it dawns on him what he's said, and he looks pretty horrified. "I mean, he can't! I was just saying that!"

"Whoa, you can *fly*?" Matthew says.

"No," the kid who told me I'm a supervillain and have a supervillain girlfriend says. I guess he doesn't have *all* the facts. "That's a rumor. It's been disproven on three different conspiracy sites I follow."

"Well, they're wrong!" Zach tells him, defending me on autopilot. He immediately winces and says, "I mean, I guess they… they must know what they're talking about." He does *not* sound like he means it, though. He mouths *Sorry* at me.

"If you can fly, then do it," Facts Kid says. Only he doesn't just say it like a normal person, he says it with his phone already on record and this eagerness in his voice that kind of creeps me out, like either way, whether I prove I can fly or not, he's going to have the best video ever to post on all his conspiracy sites.

Conspiracy sites that are apparently about me being able to fly or not and apparently have no credibility whatsoever.

"Guys, come on," Zach says.

"Boys, that's enough!" Mrs. Perkins tells them.

But nobody moves. Actually, that's not true, because they all move *closer*.

Electricity runs up my spine. Sparks twitch across my arms. I feel like I can't breathe, and I have to get out of here.

"He can't do it," someone whispers. "I knew it."

Then somebody tries to move even closer, knocking into somebody else, who stumbles into me. Their hand touches my arm, and there's a zap. They cry out and back off, and then everybody moves the hell out of my way like I have a disease or something.

"I didn't mean—" I hold up my hands, trying to show that it was a mistake, but everyone just gasps and backs away in horror, like I'm about to fry them all.

I leave. Okay, I don't actually leave as in leave the house, because it's Zach's birthday and because I'm too freaked out and because I spend so much time here, I'm pretty sure I belong at this house more than any of these people do. If anyone should have to leave, it should be them. So I retreat to Riley's room instead.

Except I didn't expect it to be occupied.

Riley and Sarah are standing there, making out, but they jump apart when I barge in.

I guess I lost track of them after their argument in the kitchen.

Which explains why neither of them had anything to say about a mob of birthday guests wanting me to use my lightning and/or fly. And they were pretty quiet when I accidentally zapped someone from said mob, though obviously now I see that's because they weren't there.

Sarah adjusts her glasses. Riley's face turns bright red. He looks super embarrassed about me walking in on them, even though, as far as I can tell, it was just kissing. Really intimate kissing that I wish I could erase from my brain, but nothing that will scar me for life or anything.

Still, I feel *really* awkward. And like this is actually the last place I belong right now, probably because it is.

So even though Riley says, "X, wait," and even though I really don't want to risk the mob again, I turn and get the hell out of there.

CHAPTER 25

All I want to do is go up to my room and not have to see anybody, like, ever again. Except Kat, who I will of course invite to go live on a desert island with me. I think between my lightning power and her shapeshifting ability, we could survive pretty well. It would suck to not have internet, of course, but after what's probably already been posted about me tonight, I think I could go without it for a while.

But when I get home, Gordon's talking to *Ted* in the dining room. Ted is at our freaking house.

There's a moment where pure rage boils up inside me, because while part of me thinks Gordon definitely would *not* talk to him about me after I freaked out the other day, part of me also kind of thinks he would. Because I wasn't supposed to be home again tonight, so, like, what a perfect chance to go behind my back and invite Ted over so they can talk about me.

But Gordon doesn't seem alarmed that I'm here or

anything. In fact, he smiles like he's actually glad to see me and says, "Damien, you're home early."

Ted looks over at me, too. He looks as disdainful of me as ever, but... not like he recently learned my greatest weakness or anything. More like he was promised I wouldn't show up and is disappointed.

So, maybe Gordon *wasn't* talking to him about me.

"Is everything okay?" Gordon asks. "I thought you were staying over."

"Change of plans, that's all. Everything's fine." Or at least it will be, once they both stop staring at me, because there's *no way* I'm going up the stairs in front of Ted.

Gordon seems to take my lack of immediately leaving as an invitation to keep talking to me, mistakenly thinking I could possibly be interested in anything he and Ted are doing. "Ted and I were just discussing our glory days in the League."

Uh-oh. The League and Ted are pretty much my two least favorite subjects, and putting them together in the same sentence like that can't be good.

Ted kind of glares at Gordon, like he can't believe he's talking to me about this, either.

"I'm actually really tired," I say, trying to sound as uninterested as possible so maybe Gordon will take the hint and leave me alone.

He doesn't. In fact, he actually comes over instead, like he wasn't even listening. "Neither of us have been happy about leaving—"

"Dad, seriously, you don't—"

"—or about, well, about how things turned out in the

end."

"How you felt like your whole life was a big fat lie, you mean?"

Ted scowls at that. "Gordon, please. He couldn't possibly understand."

I search Gordon's face, wondering exactly what it is they've been talking about.

"We were discussing what I told you," Gordon says, "about upholding what I believed were the League's ideals and about wanting to do something more, and… Tell him." He nudges Ted with his elbow.

Ted kind of gapes at him, looking appropriately horrified with the situation.

Gordon ignores him and tells me himself. "Ted suggested we start our own superhero group. As soon as he said it, I couldn't believe I hadn't thought of it first. There were moments where I had glimpses of similar ideas, but they never fully formed into—"

"*Dad.*"

"What?"

"What the hell are you talking about?"

Ted rolls his eyes at my outburst, like this is proof I don't get it.

"Well, you see, neither of us have been very happy about having to leave the League. Of course, neither of us could *stay* after what happened—"

"Really?" I raise my eyebrows, because I seriously doubt Ted quit the League because heroes were shooting at me and my friends.

Gordon sounds a little annoyed. "Yes, of course."

I point at Ted. "He hates villains. He hates *me.*"

Ted glares at me.

"*Damien,*" Gordon scolds. "That's not... Well, you shouldn't..."

"I left the League because it was corrupt," Ted says, saving Gordon from trying to claim that me and Ted don't hate each other. "And hating someone and wanting to see them tortured are two very different things."

"Great, well, as long as we cleared *that* up. And seriously, Dad, I get that you miss the League, but do you really have to team up with *him*?"

"He's my brother, and of course I—"

"Oh, my God," Amelia calls from the stairs as she comes tromping down. "What did you *do*?!"

Crap. Crap crap crap.

She comes to a stop halfway down the staircase when she sees that Ted's here. "Oops," she says, clutching her phone. "I didn't realize we had company. I'll just go back to my room now—"

"Amelia," Gordon says, "what happened?"

"Nothing," we both say at the same time.

That only makes both of them more suspicious.

Amelia sighs, making it sound all dramatic, and says, "It's *personal*, okay? Damien, um, he talked to Zach about me when he wasn't supposed to."

"Oh." Gordon seems relieved. "Well, if that's all—"

"Gordon," Ted says, showing him his phone, "I think you need to see this."

Amelia bites her lip and shoots me an apologetic look.

I don't watch the video or anything, but I hear it. The

phone makes everything sound tinny and chaotic. Everyone wants me to fly, expressing various stages of disbelief, and then... then you can hear the crackle of electricity as someone gets zapped.

I cringe inwardly. My heart pounds during the moment of stunned silence as everyone's suddenly terrified of me, and then—

Ted pauses the video and shoves his phone in my face. It's frozen with me holding up my hands like I'm about to blast everyone with lightning. "What did you think you were doing?" He doesn't shout that, but says it quietly, with barely contained rage.

My voice comes out hoarse. I want to tell him to get the hell out of my face and leave me alone. But instead I look over at Gordon and say, "It's not what it looks like."

Gordon nods, and I know he believes me, but he looks kind of sad, too. Like maybe he feels sorry for me. Or maybe... maybe he wishes he didn't have a half-villain kid who made him look bad all the time in front of his stupid relatives.

Ted's obviously made up his mind about me, though. He holds his phone up at Gordon. "I don't know how you can just stand there after what you've witnessed. It's high time you faced the facts about him."

"Ted, he just told you, it wasn't what it looked like."

Ted scoffs. "And you *believed* that?"

"It *wasn't*," Amelia says. "Theo posted that, and he's way into conspiracy theories and stuff. He probably made it look way worse than it really was, because Damien wouldn't hurt anybody. Especially not at Zach's birthday party. And, like, you can see in the video they're all ganging up on him."

"So, all these innocent hero children are *ganging up* on a dangerous villain who could murder them all in one move?"

"Well, probably not *one* move," I tell him. "I mean, I could, but realistically I think it would be at least two or three."

Ted's eyes go wide and his face goes pale.

Gordon puts a hand to his temple. "*Damien.*" Then, to Ted, but sounding kind of worn out, "He's a good kid. I know it doesn't look like it in that video, but I promise you—"

"Honestly, Gordon, what would I have to show you about him for you to stop saying that? The evidence is everywhere. You have a dangerous villain living in your house."

"I'm *not*"—electricity crackles across my arms—"dangerous!"

"I just watched a video of you electrocuting a boy at a birthday party."

"I didn't—"

"Damien," Gordon says, "I think you should go to your room."

"What? Seriously?!"

"Everyone needs to calm down. So head up to your room and we'll talk about this in a bit."

I gape at him. I jerk my chin toward the stairs, hoping he gets the hint, but he doesn't. "Dad, I'm not doing that." Not with Ted here, anyway.

"Damien, you're not in trouble, but, please, just—"

"You let him talk back to you like that?" Ted asks, making it sound like that's the most shocking thing he's heard about me all night.

"He's not in trouble," Gordon says. "If he doesn't want to go to his room—"

"You're being a pushover. And I don't know how you can stand there and say he's not in trouble after what he did."

"He didn't do anything," Amelia says. "I just texted Zach, and everyone at the party's fine."

"He lucked out, then. But that doesn't mean he's innocent."

Gordon squeezes the bridge of his nose. "Ted, I'm handling it. And, Damien, I mean it, go to your room before I change my mind and you really are in trouble."

"Dad, *I told you*, I'm not doing that."

He gives me this pleading look, like he just can't understand why I'm being this way. Why I can't just behave for once when someone's actually watching. "Then I'll... I'll have no choice but to ground you."

"And, what, then you'll send me to my room?!"

"Don't make this harder than it is. I just need to talk to Ted about this situation, and that would be a whole lot easier without you around, making things worse!"

I swallow. "Well, if that's all you wanted, you should have said so." I move to leave. Not toward the stairs, of course, but toward the front door.

"Damien, I didn't mean—"

"Are you just going to let him walk out like that?" Ted

asks.

"*Ted.* I said I'm handling it!"

"Your dangerous and violent son who already electrocuted one person tonight is going off to do God knows what, and you're just letting him? You're not even going to ask where he's going?"

Gordon says something to that, but I don't hear it because I'm already out the door.

X·X·X

"The What Heroism Means to Me video?" Kat asks. "Seriously?"

I nod. "He said she watches it *every night*. And apparently he's okay with that."

We're sitting on her bed in her dorm later, eating leftover pizza and *not* looking at our phones. Or at least I'm not. Kat keeps getting texts from people asking her if she's seen the video, and she paused once to look up that T-shirt I told her about.

She grins at me. "Do you think that girl watches it so much because you're all sweet and vulnerable in it—"

"*Hey.*"

"—or because you're practically naked?"

"I'm practically naked in both videos, so… That first one. But, for the record, I'm not, nor have I ever, *ever* been 'sweet and vulnerable.'" I make a face.

Kat smirks. "Yeah, right."

"Shut up." I grab her pillow like I'm going to throw it at her.

She holds up her pizza and says, "Do *not* get sauce on anything!"

"Fine. But as soon as you finish eating that, you'd better watch out."

She takes a tiny bite of crust and chews slowly, making eye contact with me the whole time and trying to keep a straight face. Neither of us can, though, and we both burst out laughing. Then Kat accidentally sprays bits of chewed-up crust everywhere, which only makes us laugh harder.

When the laughter dies down, she pokes my leg. "Then what happened?"

"He wanted me to record a message for her—"

"He *what*?"

"—and to tell her she's amazing and that I *love* her."

"Oh, my God." Kat snorts with laughter and has to take a drink of her pop so she doesn't choke on her food, but she almost gets it up her nose instead. "He didn't."

"Yep. Like it wasn't even weird."

"What did you do?"

"Not *that*. I said, 'Be Truthful.'"

"Who knew Zach had such crazy friends?"

"It gets worse. One of them belongs to three separate conspiracy sites about me. Apparently they've proven I can't fly or something."

"Amateurs, obviously."

"And then he started demanding I show everyone my lightning—"

"I thought they wanted to see you fly?"

"Well, yeah, after Zach let it slip that I have two powers."

"Supposedly," Kat says. "I hear it's been disproven."

I grin at her. "That's when things really got out of hand."

"And then what? That's when you left? Poor Zach."

"Poor Zach? *Poor Zach?* What about me?"

"I mean, he's going to feel *so bad* about this. But I'm sure he understands why you left."

"Yeah, well, I didn't leave. I hadn't humiliated myself enough yet, so I walked in on Riley and Sarah."

"*What?!*"

"Making out. But, like, alone in his room, so… who knows?"

"With his little brother's birthday party going on? Scandalous!"

"I know, right? I mean, it was crazy awkward. I don't know how I'm going to face either of them ever again. And *then* I left."

"Wow."

"It gets worse."

"No, it does not."

"*Ted* was at our house when I got there. He had this brilliant idea that he and Gordon should start their own superhero group."

"Gross."

"I know. And then Amelia sort of spilled the beans about the video, which didn't go over too well."

She chews her lip. "So, your dad's mad at you?"

"I… I don't know. But I think if the word *disappointment* got thrown around, it wouldn't be unfair."

"Ouch." She winces.

I shrug. "It's okay. I mean, all things considered—"

"You're *not* a disappointment, Damien."

"Yeah, well, he didn't need another video of me losing control of my lightning."

"It's not that bad. The video, I mean."

"It looks like I'm about to obliterate an entire birthday party. And I did zap someone."

"Uh, no, someone *grabbed you* while you were covered in electricity."

"But nobody's going to be looking at it that way. And everybody knows I zapped that superhero last semester."

"Okay, but your dad knows you wouldn't do that on purpose, right?"

"Right, but..." I draw up my knees and rest my chin on top of them. "If I'm not a disappointment, I'm at least an embarrassment. He wants to start a superhero group with *Ted*. The guy who hates me. He cares what he thinks, and... He really didn't need to find out about this in front of him. Gordon said I wasn't in trouble, but Ted got all in his face about it, like Gordon should have been punishing me or something. Supposedly Ted doesn't believe in torturing villains, but I'm pretty sure he believes in torturing *me*."

"What did your dad say?"

"He got mad, and then... I don't know. I got out of there."

"It's nice having a car, isn't it?"

"I left Tom at home. I took the train."

"What? *Damien*." She reaches across the bed and swats my arm. "What's the point of having Tom if you never drive him?"

"I didn't want Gordon to think that getting me a car just gave me, like, the means to run away."

"Uh, I think you've proven you can run away on your own plenty of times."

"I didn't want Ted to use it against him. I didn't want him to be able to say that they shouldn't have given it to me."

"You could have taken the car."

"No, I couldn't."

"Have you ever even driven it?"

"You know I have. On Prom night, when I took Amelia home."

"That doesn't exactly count."

"It's her car. They only said it was for both of us because they didn't want me to feel left out."

"Which worked *so* well. And you know that's not true. That's not even what you told me when they gave it to you. You said—"

"They told me it was because they're proud of me, and because I wouldn't let Gordon get me anything big for my birthday. But let's face it, no matter how proud they are, I'm going to screw up again. I mean, I kind of already did. And I wouldn't let him get me anything big because I don't want it. Not from him."

"Damien—"

"He can't make up for sixteen years with… with *anything*. And I don't even want him to, but that's what he'd be doing."

"You kept the key. You said you changed your mind."

"But I can't bring myself to actually use it, so…" I take a deep breath. "He told me he didn't want me around tonight, that I was making things worse. He meant because Ted was there, screaming at him that I'm devil spawn or something, but there was this split second where that's not how I heard it."

"Wow. But, like, you know he didn't mean it that way."

"I know. But no matter what he says, I just can't stop feeling like it's only a matter of time before he really is done with me, just like my mom."

Kat points her pizza slice at me before taking another bite. "Your mom really messed you up."

"Thanks, Kat. You didn't tell me you were taking Psychology."

She rolls her eyes. "I just mean you know *why* you feel like that, and it has nothing to do with your dad or whether or not he wants to give you stuff."

"He wants to give me stuff *for now*. And if I accept the car, like, for reals, then it's like I'm saying I believe he actually wants me there. So then when one day he doesn't… It's just going to hurt that much worse."

"But maybe he's not going to do that, and you're missing out."

"On what? A car?"

"On letting him care about you. Not everyone's going to be like your mom."

"I trusted Grandpa, and you know how that turned out."

"Your grandparents think you're the best thing ever."

"And they still betrayed me. They've known me my

whole life. And I know they didn't kick me out or give up on me or anything, but they still ruined stuff between us. And Gordon can give me all the cars he wants, but I saw his face after he watched that video of me tonight. He didn't seem surprised or even mad or anything, just... *sad*. I'd rather he was pissed at me. And Ted—"

"Okay, I've never met Ted, but he's *so* not your dad."

"No, but Gordon doesn't see what a horrible douchebag he is. He's known him way longer than me, and now they're forming some superhero group together, which is a *terrible* idea, but Ted suggested it, so Gordon thinks it must be amazing. But I don't get how he can get along with someone like that and still care about someone like me."

"It doesn't mean he *doesn't* care about you, though. Or that he doesn't want you around. And... you can't just not trust anybody."

"I trust you. And I trust Riley. And Sarah if she's not holding explosives."

"That's a short list."

"It's been shorter." Way shorter.

"But—"

"I can't drive the car, Kat. I only kept the key to annoy Amelia."

"Okay," she says, not sounding like she believes me. "But, Damien, did you ever think that if you just push him away all the time, maybe *you're* the one who's going to end up ruining things between you?"

"Hey, as long as I screw things up before he does, then... then at least I never have to find out for sure that he would have let me down. Or how badly. I can always keep that tiny bit of hope that things would have turned out okay if only I hadn't screwed them up."

"That sounds like a great way to have a really crappy relationship with your dad. Gordon might do stupid stuff sometimes, but I can't see him letting you down on purpose. Not like your mom did. Or even like your grandpa did. And if you're just trying to prove you can mess things up before he can, well… I think you both deserve better than that."

CHAPTER 26

I get home around ten o'clock Sunday night, after spending two days with Kat in her dorm. And I was right, spending the whole weekend with her made it *so much worse* when I had to leave again. But I did, even though saying good-bye to her kind of destroyed me a little bit, and even though she was crying really hard, and even though it was pretty much the last thing in the world that I wanted to do.

I go up to my room when I get back and flop down on my bed. My eyes are watering, and there's a hollow ache in my chest and a tightness in my throat that won't go away. I feel empty, like I left part of myself back at Kat's and I don't remember how to function without it.

There's a knock on my door, and then Amelia calls out, "Damien?!"

I press my face harder into my pillow and don't say anything. I don't want to talk to anybody right now, and eventually she'll get the hint and leave.

"I know you're home! You missed your flying lesson yesterday! And knowing you, you didn't even practice on your own!"

I wipe my eyes real quick and get up to let her in, closing the door and hoping nobody heard her shouting about flying lessons. "Will you shut up? Not everyone needs to know about that."

"I—" She goes silent when she sees my face. "What happened?"

"*Nothing.*" But I can hear the thickness in my voice, and my eyes are still wet. I rub them with the back of my arm, as if that isn't super obvious. But it's better than actually crying in front of Amelia.

She doesn't look convinced, and I think she's going to demand a better answer than that, but then she just looks away and says, "I know it's kind of late, but we haven't done flying lessons today."

"Amelia—"

"And I bet you didn't practice on your own when you were at Kat's, so that means that if you don't do it tonight, you'll have missed two days of practice. You don't have that much longer before the test, so—"

"Are you insane? I'm not taking the test. You were here on Friday. You saw how Ted, like, completely hates me."

"Yeah, but—"

"He's going to fail me no matter what."

"He didn't *say* that."

"He didn't need to. And... come on, Amelia. I couldn't even go up the stairs in front of him—I'm not going to be able to fly in front of him, either."

"But you *can* fly."

"Barely."

"But you've been working really hard. You're getting better at it."

"Not better enough. And none of that matters if I can't fly in front of Ted."

She glares at me. "He thinks you can't fly. Like, not at all."

"I know. And if I show up to the test and can't even get off the ground again, it's just going to make him think he's right. I mean, he already thinks that."

She clenches her fists. "But he's *wrong*. And after what happened Friday night, it's more important than ever that you show him you can fly."

"I like where you're going with that, but there's a pretty big chance I'm just going to end up humiliating myself in front of him."

"He thinks he's right about you, but he's not. After you left, he said he *knows* you can't fly. He told Dad you need to stop telling people you can because it makes you sound crazy and it's besmirching the family name."

"I don't even have the family name."

"I know. And he said that the kids in that video wanted you to fly, but that of course you couldn't, and that's why you zapped somebody. He said your lies are dangerous and getting out of hand."

"Uh, if I didn't have flying power, I would just tell the school that and pass first year already." Actually, I wonder if it's too late for that. I could send them some links to the conspiracy sites as proof.

"Even if there's no way you can pass, you still have to show him you can do it. Because he thinks he knows everything about you, but he doesn't know *anything*, and you really, really need to throw that in his face."

I smirk at that a little, even though I still feel like crap.

"Even if you can't do the test right—which won't even be true because you will—and even if you kind of humiliate yourself, you'll humiliate Ted even worse when you show him you really can fly. Then he'll have to shut up about it, and—"

"Okay."

"Really? We can keep doing flying lessons?!"

"*Yes*. But keep your voice down."

"I *am*. Geez." She rolls her eyes at me. "And this is so exciting! Tonight you're going to hover for *twenty* minutes and then I think you're ready to go up to the ceiling."

"Tomorrow."

"But—"

"*Tomorrow*, and I'm not promising anything about the ceiling."

"Fine, but you have to hover for *thirty* minutes then to make up for it."

There's another knock at the door. It's Gordon this time, and I really, *really* hope he didn't hear Amelia practically shouting about flying lessons.

He must have at least heard that she was talking, though, so I probably can't get away with pretending I'm asleep. But it doesn't matter anyway because before I have a chance to decide anything, Amelia opens the door for him.

Gordon glances over at me. He does not look happy. Not mad, maybe, but *happy* is definitely not the word I'd use. "I need to talk to you," he says. Then, to Amelia, "It's late. You should be getting ready for bed."

"But it's not even ten thirty," Amelia says, glancing at her phone, which she must have just teleported to her hand.

"*Amelia.*"

"Fine." She makes a defiant huffing noise, in case he didn't know she was annoyed with him, and then mouths *Practice* at me before hurrying off down the stairs.

Gordon closes the door. He seems almost disappointed that she actually left, like he thought she'd put up more of a fight and he wasn't prepared to deal with me yet. "We need to talk."

"No, we don't." I wrap my arms around myself and sit down on my bed. I am *so* not in the mood for this right now. "I screwed up. You're mad. There's nothing more to say, so just tell me my punishment and be done with it."

"I'm not mad."

I glance up at him, not sure I believe that. "I embarrassed you in front of Ted, and you actually care what he thinks for some reason. So I get it if you're pissed at me. But just don't pretend it's okay when it's not."

He sits down next to me. "I'm not angry with you, alright? I just wish you hadn't run off like that. I wish you didn't feel like you *needed* to."

"I was at Kat's."

"I know."

"Amelia told you?" Not that I told her or anything, but

she must have figured it out, since I didn't go back to Riley's.

He tilts his head at me. "I'm not an idiot."

I raise my eyebrows at him, because this is news to me.

"When you don't come home, you're either at Riley's or at Kat's. And you don't come back from Riley's looking like... Well, like someone punched you in the stomach."

Great. "So, like, all those times I went to Kat's and didn't tell you, you've just been humoring me?"

"I thought you didn't want me to know."

"I thought you'd disapprove of me going out of town to spend the night with my girlfriend in her college dorm, completely alone and unsupervised." Or at least that Helen would. "I think they covered that in Parenting 101, but maybe you were absent that day."

"You want me to tell you not to go?"

"No, but I thought—"

"I trust you to make the right decisions for yourself. You're a good kid. And way more independent than I was at your age. I don't feel like I have to worry about you getting into situations you can't handle. And I know you miss Kat. I know you're going to go spend time with her. I just wish you didn't feel like you had to hide it from me. And that you didn't feel like you needed to run off." He hesitates, holding his breath for a second, then says, "I know why you didn't want to go upstairs on Friday."

"Too little too late. No gold star."

"I should have realized about the stairs. I... I shouldn't have asked you to do that in front of Ted, but I wasn't thinking."

"You were too busy wanting to form a superhero group with him." Which obviously involved no thinking whatsoever.

"It's just an idea."

A really bad one. "Dad, I know you're excited about it for some reason, but, like, how can you even think of working with that complete and total douche?"

Gordon winces a little. "He's my brother."

"Yeah, but he hates me. You saw how he was."

"I know, and I wish Ted would have shown more restraint Friday night and not overreacted."

"You wish he would have shut the hell up, you mean."

"He doesn't know you, Damien. We both know he's wrong about you."

"But I'm not wrong about *him*. He hates me and he hates villains. Just, like, as a general rule, just for existing."

"He quit the League, just like I did. He doesn't condone what they were doing, either."

"That doesn't make him a good person."

Gordon glances over at me. "I've always thought of him that way, though, as a good person. He's my older brother, and I've always looked up to him. Like how Alex and Jess look up to you."

"But, like, you know that he's *not*, right?"

Gordon sighs. "He'll come around."

"Yeah, sure, if he gets abducted by aliens and they give him a lobotomy, but that seems like kind of a long shot."

"He doesn't know you. If he did, he wouldn't have reacted that way to that video."

I find that really hard to believe, especially since it involved me zapping some superhero kid with my villain power. "It really wasn't what it looked like. I mean, it kind of was, but—"

"I know. And I know you wouldn't hurt anybody. I just wish you'd stuck around to tell me what did happen. I got a lot of phone calls this weekend."

"From your douchey family?"

"Well—"

"From *Helen's* douchey family?"

"From everyone. And I didn't know anything more about it than they did, because you'd run off without even telling me what happened."

I swallow and stare at my knees.

We're both quiet, an awkward silence building. Then he says, "When I said I didn't want you around—"

"That's not why I left." But I say that way too fast, and I can't bring myself to look at him.

"When I said that, I just... I wasn't thinking. Ted was yelling at me—"

"Then maybe you should have told *him* to leave."

"Damien, I wasn't telling anyone to leave. And I— " He tries to put his hand on my shoulder.

I jerk away from him.

He lets out a deep breath. "I know what I said hurt you, but I didn't mean I don't want you here."

I still don't look at him.

"Damien? I'm trying to say—"

"It's getting late. It's been a long weekend. So if I'm actually not in trouble, then... then I should really get some sleep."

"But I never meant—" He stops himself. "Yeah, you're right, it's... it's getting late. And it's a school night. I should let you get to bed. But if you want to talk about—"

"I'm *really* tired. Can you get the light on your way out?"

"I... Alright, Damien. I mean, of course." He goes to leave. His hand hovers over the light switch, and I think he's going to try and argue with me some more, but then he just says, "Goodnight," and flicks the switch, leaving me in the dark.

CHAPTER 27

Riley seems surprised to see me when I show up at his house Monday morning before school. Surprised, but also relieved. His hair's still wet from the shower and he's shoving the last bite of a piece of toast into his mouth when he opens the door. He looks me over, his eyes flicking to mine, and asks, "Are you okay?"

"Come on, Perkins, of course I—" I stop myself from lying to him. "No, not really."

"I can't believe what happened on Friday."

"I know. Like, what were you and Sarah *thinking*?"

He scowls at me. "*No*, I meant what happened with Zach's friends kind of mobbing you and making that video."

I follow him into the kitchen. He holds up a box of cereal, but I shake my head.

"I had no idea," he says. "About what was going on. Otherwise, I wouldn't have... I mean, me and Sarah wouldn't have—"

"Been about to do it in your room?"

He flinches. "We *weren't* doing that."

"Yet."

"Will you shut up? I'm trying to say—"

"I know what you're trying to say. You didn't know Zach's crazy friends were going to harass me or that I was going to end up zapping one of them."

He sighs. "You could have come back."

"I went to Kat's."

"You could have at least answered my texts."

"I had my phone off."

"Yeah, well, I didn't know what had happened to you." He sounds kind of pissed about that. And maybe kind of hurt.

"Perkins—"

"You ran out of here without even telling us what happened!"

"You were obviously busy!"

"And then Amelia said you got in a fight with your dad and *ran off*. Nobody knew where you were, X!"

I take a step back, running into the counter. "I was at Kat's. Everybody else figured it out."

"No, everybody else *hoped* you were at Kat's. You can't just disappear like that! You obviously weren't okay when you left here, and I didn't know if something had happened to you, or if you weren't speaking to me, or—"

"Geez, Perkins. Calm down. I'm okay."

"You just said you weren't."

"Yeah, but… it doesn't have anything to do with you. *We're* okay. You can stop freaking out."

"That's not—" He takes a deep breath. "Just answer my texts next time."

"Yeah, alright. If it's that important to you."

Zach comes running into the room. He doesn't have his shoes on, just socks, and almost slips and falls on the linoleum. He manages to catch himself and looks up at the microwave clock. "Crap! I'm going to be—" He stops mid-sentence when he realizes I'm there. Then he kind of gapes at me.

I hold up my thumb. "Let me see it."

He holds his up to show me his *H*. His eyes meet mine real quick, then dart away. "I'm *so sorry* about what happened on Friday!"

"It's okay."

"No, it's not. It's— *Crap*." He glances at the microwave again and then tears open the fridge.

"Dude," Riley says, "we can give you a ride."

"I'm already counting on you giving me a ride and I'm still going to be late! You better be ready to go." He looks over at Riley. "You don't even have your shoes on!"

"Neither do you."

"I'm getting them!" He pulls a handful of grapes, half a block of cheese, and a boiled egg out of the fridge, then stuffs them in a lunch bag. He grabs an apple off the counter and shoves that in on top. Then he turns back to me. "It's not okay, all the stuff that happened. Everybody thought it was so cool that you were here, and I thought it was so cool that they thought that."

"Zach," Riley says, "you can tell him in the car."

Zach doesn't budge, even though Riley's totally right. "I

have to say this now. Like, to your face."

"It's okay," I tell him. "You didn't mean for any of that to happen."

"But I should have known that it would! I just wanted everyone to know that we were friends, because they didn't believe me, and because you're famous."

"I'm *not*—"

"I exploited our friendship." He sucks in a breath. "I mean, if we even still have a friendship after what I did."

"It's going to be a really awkward car ride if we don't."

His mouth falls open and his forehead wrinkles up, worried.

"I'm kidding. We're still friends. Like, seriously."

He just looks more worried, though. "There's another video of you on the internet because of me. Now the whole world thinks you tried to hurt people at my birthday party. And I'm *so sorry*, and I know there's nothing I can do to take it back or make it up to you."

"I *said* it was fine."

"But it's *not*. And I'm—"

"Zach, if you say you're sorry *one more time*."

"But I am. I don't deserve to be your friend after what I did."

"Yeah, well, I didn't have to freak out and go all electric."

"Or run off," Riley mutters.

"Well, maybe I *wouldn't have* if you and Sarah hadn't been—"

"Oh, my God, X, will you shut up about that?! We were just kissing!"

255

"If that's what you want to call it."

"Whoa," Zach says. "At my *party*?"

"Shut up, both of you." Riley glares at us, but his face is turning kind of red. "It wasn't like that. And Zach? You did kind of a crappy thing, but you didn't mean for it to get out of hand, and it doesn't mean you don't deserve to be friends, okay? And *you*..." He points at me. "You can't help that stuff freaks you out sometimes. Or that you're full of lightning."

"I'm not 'full of lightning.' Are you full of invisibility?"

He rolls his eyes. "You know what I mean. And you still love Zach, so—"

"Okay, now you're just putting words in my mouth."

"—so of course you forgive him."

I glance over at Zach. "I'm sorry I kind of ruined your party."

He shakes his head. "You didn't. I mean, Quentin ended up going home, even though he was *fine*—he's the one you zapped—but that was only because his mom made him. And I made Theo leave because he was being a jerk to you, and because he posted that video. I thought he was my friend, but I don't know if I can be friends with someone who would treat you that way."

I smile at him. "That might be the best thing you've ever said to me."

"So, you're not mad?"

"Nope."

"But now everybody thinks you can't fly."

"That's okay, Zach. I don't care what they think. Besides, I'm going to pass that test, get my flying certificate—"

"There's no certificate," Riley says. "You know that."

"—and prove them wrong."

Zach nods. "Amelia told me. We ended up texting all weekend. She said she's giving you flying lessons and that you're—"

"Wow, look at the time!" I wave my hand at the microwave. And also, I'm going to *kill* Amelia.

Riley squints at me. "She's what?"

"We have to go. I don't know what time your school starts, but you're definitely going to be super late for it, and we need to leave *right now*."

"Did he just say Amelia was giving you *flying lessons*?"

"I can't hear you because you don't have your shoes on."

"But—"

"Don't just stand there, Perkins! Zach is going to be *late for school*. Seriously, get your act together. I'll meet you at the car."

CHAPTER 28

"So," Tristan says to Kat, "tell me the truth. Liv—cool or not cool with me bringing my new girlfriend to movie night tomorrow?"

It's Wednesday night, about one in the morning, and me, Kat, Riley, and Tristan are doing our assignments and staking out Frank's next robbery, which is taking place at an art gallery. We're all outside, hiding behind the side of the building and watching the robbers' van that's parked, like, right in front of the gallery. Just a white, nondescript van that might not look that suspicious if you didn't already know there was a robbery going on.

"Uh," Kat says, clearly not wanting to answer him, "didn't you already talk to Liv?"

"She *said* it was okay, but she didn't sound like it was. You're her roommate. What do you think?"

Kat stares really hard at a crack in the pavement. "Well..."

"Great. I knew it." Tristan folds his arms. "So, she's not

over me? We only went out for a month, and it was mostly just— It was just casual."

"I'm not saying she's not over you," Kat says, choosing her words carefully. "But I don't think she's ready to have your new girlfriend shoved in her face."

"Come on, Katie."

Erg. I cringe when he calls her that. Then I glare at him, but he's too busy discussing his love life to notice, so I exchange a look with Riley instead.

"I'm still part of the group," Tristan goes on. "You're saying I can't ever bring anybody?"

"I'm saying it's too soon. Give it another month."

"We'll be out of school in a month. Hey, who did we decide is having the end-of-year party?"

"Jordan. And... What's his new boyfriend's name?"

"Michael. Who *he's* bringing tomorrow, even though Lucas is totally going to be there."

"Okay, first of all, they've been broken up for way longer than you and Liv. And second of all, Lucas is bringing a date. And third of all, I thought you were asking because you didn't want to hurt Liv's feelings?"

"Why would her feelings be hurt unless she's not over me?"

Maybe because he's a horrible douche?

"*Because*," Kat says. "You guys used to make out on our couch"—gross—"and then end up in her room. But you're not going to do that now, and maybe she doesn't want to have to watch you make out with someone else like you used to with her, in, like, the exact same spot."

"Can we switch movie night over to me and Blake's?"

"*No.*"

"Fine, but next year, total reset button. New rooms, new couches, and I can bring whoever I want."

I roll my eyes at him.

"*What?*" he snaps. I guess he saw me that time. "You don't even know Liv."

"I know she can do better."

"Uh, are you serious right now?"

"Nobody's making you go to movie night. And obviously you already know she's not okay with you bringing your new make-out partner or you wouldn't be asking about it."

Tristan sort of half laughs, half scoffs. "Yeah, well, I don't see *you* at movie night. Speaking of people who can do better."

"What? What's that supposed to mean?"

"It means you're never around. We all bring dates when we go to the movies or to the waffle place, but Katie has to come alone. We're all going to go hang out, but she drops everything because you happen to call."

Kat scowls at him. "Don't act like everyone brings dates everywhere."

"Okay, but you *never* do. Some boyfriend you have."

Electricity runs up my back and across my arms. My sweatshirt hides the sparks, but Riley must hear it crackle—that or he knows me well enough to guess—because he suddenly takes a step away from me.

Kat folds her arms and gives Tristan a disgusted look. "Wow. I can't believe you think any of that is your business."

"I'm just saying that college is supposed to be *fun*. But you spend all your time waiting by the phone for some traitorous wannabe superhero who thinks he's too good for us and is never around. Everyone says these are the best years of our lives, but you're going to look back on yours and know you missed out."

Visible sparks run across my hands, and I know everyone sees. Maybe I should put them in my pockets, but I don't. Maybe I should also kill Tristan, but I don't, even though it's something I'm pretty sure *I'll* look back on with regret. And maybe my stomach also kind of clenches, because some of what he said might have a tiny bit of truth to it. Not like I think he's right or anything, but still.

He gets this smug look on his face, as if he thinks I won't electrocute him in front of witnesses.

But then I don't have to, because Kat takes an angry step toward him. A couple angry steps, actually. "Okay, you know what?" she says. "You don't get to tell me what I'm missing out on. You've never gone out with *anyone* for more than a month. You don't know what it's like to actually love somebody. And yeah, it sucks that me and Damien don't get to see each other all the time, but that doesn't change how I feel about him. I'm not going to throw away our future together—a future with the person I love more than anything—just because it doesn't fit *your* idea of what college should be. And if you think Damien is acting 'too good for you,' maybe that's just because you don't measure up!"

There's a moment of stunned silence as we all stare at her in awe. Well, as I stare at her in awe. I'm pretty sure

Tristan's just terrified.

Then Riley says, "Um, guys?" He points to the white van in front of the building.

There's a man walking toward it, except he's coming from the pizza place across the street and is carrying a toolbox and looks like he's soaking wet and kind of muddy. He's talking on his cell phone as he approaches the van. "Yeah, looks like it's all patched up. At least until they can get some of the pipes replaced. Didn't cause too much damage, so it could have been worse, but— Yeah, I'll be home soon. I'm getting in the truck right now."

He opens the back of the van, which we can now see from our hiding spot is full of tools and equipment, and adds his toolbox to the mix. Then he gets in the front and drives off.

So, not the nondescript-but-somewhat-suspiciously-parked van of Frank's team of robbers.

Damn it.

X·X·X

"They better still be here," Tristan whispers after we scramble—I mean, sneak—into the art gallery. He says it while glaring at me, as if this is my fault. "I am *not* failing this assignment because of you."

"You wouldn't even be here if it wasn't for me." Well, if it wasn't for Riley finding that writing on the wall at the museum that mentioned Frank, but I was the one who told Kat about it.

Kat motions for us to shut up. "We all assumed that was

their van. It's nobody's fault. Riley, you can turn invisible, so—"

"I'll go check out the rest of the gallery," he says, volunteering before she can finish asking him, though I can see on his face that wandering off into the dark to look for bad guys is *not* something he's looking forward to.

"I'll go with you," me and Kat both say at the same time.

She shakes her head at me. "I can shapeshift and stay hidden—I'll go."

"But, Kat—"

"It's recon. We just need to see if they're still here so we can follow them when they leave—we don't need to zap anybody. You two stay here." She points to me and Tristan. "And *don't*..." She pauses to think of the right way to put it.

"Don't kill each other," Riley says.

"Yeah, that. We'll be right back."

They head off into the gallery, turning right at the first hallway and disappearing from view.

Leaving me to stand here awkwardly with Tristan.

Great.

I glance over at him.

He looks away. Then, keeping his voice low, he says, "Hey, um, about what I said back there... about you and Katie..."

I glare at him. "What about me and Kat?" I think she made it pretty clear that it's none of his business, but if he *wants* to get electrocuted, I guess I can't stop him.

"I'm sorry, okay?"

That's *so* not what I expected to hear. "You're what?"

"I'm sorry. I shouldn't have said anything."

"You're apologizing to me?"

"Yeah, I guess I am. Don't get me wrong, I still think you're a stuck-up jerk, and I don't get what Katie sees in you, but... she's my friend, and I just shouldn't have said anything."

He goes silent and looks at me all expectantly, like I'm supposed to say something to that. I almost wish he'd said something to piss me off instead, because electrocuting him would be about a hundred times less awkward than this conversation. "Okay."

I think that's going to be it, because what else is there to say? But then he goes on. "It's just... What's your deal, anyway?"

"My deal?"

"Yeah, like, you're *not* a villain. You've made that pretty clear. But then you zap some hero kid at a birthday party—"

"That's *not* what happened."

"That's what it *looked* like happened. And I don't know much about what heroes do in their free time, but I know that's not it. So if you're not a villain, *and* you're not a hero, then, like, what are you?"

"None of your business." Just the person who's going to murder him if he doesn't shut up.

"Okay, but—"

"You've already decided I'm not a villain, so what do you care? And we shouldn't even be talking. Kat and Riley are trying to do recon, so—"

"*Okay.*" He holds up his hands. "I get it. No talking."

I watch him, thinking he's going to say something else, but he stays quiet. I feel my shoulders relax and my stomach unknot a little. Because not only do I not want to answer his stupid questions, but I'm not 100% sure that I could kill him silently and not, like, blow Kat and Riley's cover. Plus, Kat would have to explain to her teacher that her partner didn't make it back from their assignment, and that sounds like a lot of paperwork.

Then his phone rings. Really loudly. It blares through the hall, making us both jump.

Tristan swears and fishes his phone out of his pocket. It's way too late, though, because there are some clattering noises coming from an exhibit down the hall, and some guys—presumably the robbers—start shouting at each other to get out of there.

I glare at Tristan, but only for a split second, and then we're both running toward the exhibit. We sort of get there at the same time, except maybe he's slightly ahead of me and *maybe* I kind of elbow him and push my way into the room first. Because Kat and Riley could be in there, and what if they got caught when the robbers realized they weren't alone in this place? What if Riley turned visible or Kat got startled and they gave themselves away? Tristan doesn't care at all about Riley, and Kat's just his friend, and he was the one who was too stupid to remember to silence his phone, anyway.

Despite all that, he still calls me a jerk when I shove past him, but I don't care.

The room's a mess, like a group of robbers were in the

middle of stealing all the exhibit's jewelry from the cases when they got found out and had to make a run for it. A few precious stones and some broken bits of glass are on the floor.

"Kat?!"

"Right here," she says, peeling away from the shadows on the wall and shapeshifting into herself.

Riley turns visible—he was along the opposite wall—and comes over to join us.

"Nice going," Kat says, giving Tristan a look.

"Hey! It could have been him." He jerks his thumb toward me.

Kat just shakes her head. "It was *your* ringtone."

"I'm not saying it wasn't me," Tristan mutters. "I'm just saying it… it could have been anybody. It was a simple mistake."

"More like a stupid one," I tell him. "One you definitely made."

He scowls but doesn't say anything.

I make eye contact with Riley, then with Kat. "You guys okay?"

"Yeah," Riley says. "They didn't see us."

"We were sneaky," Kat adds. "They had no idea we were here. Then Tristan's phone went off and they took what they could and ran."

"I don't suppose they said where they were going?" I push some of the broken glass around on the floor with my shoe.

"Nope," Riley says. "We basically just watched them rob this place, and now we have no idea where they even took the jewelry they stole or how to get it back."

"Wonderful. What a successful mission." I glare at Tristan. Though, if our mission had to go bad, at least I'm not the one who screwed it up this time.

"Come on," Kat says, sounding a little defeated. "We should probably get out of here before anyone notices this place has been robbed and the police show up."

CHAPTER 29

"Come *on*," Amelia says, standing impatiently in our backyard. "You said you wouldn't do this unless it was dark out, which it is, and you said you didn't want to do it if Mom and Dad were home. Do you know how hard it was to get them to *both* leave the house at the same time? On a Thursday night?"

I shrug. "Not that hard?"

"*No.* I had to tell Dad that I needed him to get this one kind of ice cream he got me once, because I'm still getting over my breakup, but I had to pretend not to remember what flavor it was, even though I know it was mint walnut fudge chunk, and I said *he* had to go so he'd for sure get the right one."

"So?"

"And *then* I had to tell Mom that I needed, you know, *feminine products*. And she said Dad could get them, and then I had to make my eyes water and tell her that after suffering complete humiliation at Prom recently, I couldn't take even one more ounce of embarrassment, and could she please please *please* go with him and get them for me? Now Dad thinks I can't even remember what kind of ice cream I like, and Mom thinks I'm a complete mess! And I'm supposed to be watching Alex and Jess, but I left them *unattended* in the house, and if Mom and Dad find out, they'll think I'm a bad babysitter and I'll never live it down!"

"Jess is asleep and Alex is watching TV. What are they going to do, burn the house down?"

"Some babysitter you are. But I guess you're right—burning the house down sounds more like something *you'd* do. And that's not the point! The point is, I did all this work to get rid of Mom and Dad, and they'll only be gone for, like, twenty more minutes—"

"You could have sent them on a date night."

She glares at me. "I did all this because you said you'd practice the flying test routine for reals if it was dark out and Mom and Dad weren't home, and now all those things are true, so." She gestures to the open sky above us.

I look up and my stomach drops just thinking about it. I've been going up to the ceiling in her room all week now, but... Okay, even though her room's on the second floor and *technically* it's high up, and even though I've been super aware of that this whole time, it turns out it's not at all the same as, like, flying that high above the ground for real. In open space. And even though there's no way I'd do this during the day, it's still only eight o'clock at night, which means pretty much anyone could still look over here and see me practicing. And know what a loser I am. And that would kind of make me wish I was never born, so...

"Not happening."

Amelia makes an annoyed sound in her throat, but she doesn't seem too surprised. "You have to. You said—"

"I know what I said, but I... I have a lot of homework to get through."

"Yeah, right. And it's going to take longer for you to argue about this than it will to actually do it."

"We're really behind with our Advanced Heroism assignment. Riley's depending on me."

She snorts. "For what? I thought you guys already figured out that note you found."

"We— How do you know about the note?" We found it last night on the floor of the gallery, in the main hallway on our way back out. One of the robber's must have dropped it at some point, but I guess we were so panicked on our way in that we didn't notice it. It was a crumpled up scrap of paper that said, *The abandoned Heroes Hideout across from the tire factory.*

Which was obviously a location, but none of us knew what the hell Heroes Hideout meant, except for Riley, who explained that it was one of those pizza places you go to as a kid that has singing animatronic animals and games and stuff that you have to put tokens in to play and pizza that mostly tastes like cardboard. Then me and Kat—and, okay, also Tristan—said it sounded just like Villain Varmint's, which was the version we all went to as kids. Except Tristan claimed that Villain Varmint's actually had really *good* pizza, making it the superior franchise, which me and Kat quickly shot him down on, because "good" is not a word I'd use to describe any of the food in that place.

But pizza quality aside, going to an abandoned Heroes Hideout sounds pretty creepy. Creepy enough that maybe that note actually belonged to a serial killer or something and not one of Frank's goons. Which I would have said out loud, since I knew we were all thinking it, but then Tristan started whining about how there was no way we were going to this place, whatever it was, because we had no way of knowing if it actually had anything to do with Frank or not, and that even if it did, there was a pretty slim chance that it would have anything to do with the painting we're trying to find. I didn't want to sound like I was agreeing with him, plus it's not like we've got a lot of other leads to choose from—or, like, *any*—so I kept my mouth shut about the creepiness factor and said we were definitely going to check it out. This weekend, during broad daylight, when the chances of running into serial killers and/or deranged clowns will hopefully be as low as possible. And who knows? Maybe a creepy abandoned children's pizza place is Frank's idea of a free storage facility for stolen artwork.

"I know about the note," Amelia says, "because Riley told Zach, and Zach told me. Duh."

Riley better not have told Zach everything, like that we're working with Kat and Tristan. Not that I think Zach would tell on us, but apparently he *would* blab to Amelia, and she really doesn't need to know. "So, you and Zach are—"

"Still broken up, okay? And don't try to change the subject. This is about you, not me, and I *know* you don't have that much work to do, and I *know* you're just stalling because you're scared."

"What? I am *not*—" I choke down the denial. "Look, we've been over the routine in your room. I memorized all the moves. I've even been flying back and forth across the ceiling." A couple times. Badly. But it should still count for something. I'm sure I can wing it during the test, which is only two days away. Or possibly chicken out and flunk out of school and disappoint everyone I know. Either one.

"It's not the same. And I know this isn't the gym, and there aren't any hoops set up, but doing the test won't be like practicing in my room."

"I thought I could do this if we waited until after dark, but I can't. The neighbors might see."

"They probably won't, though. And if you can't do this when someone *might* see, then how are you going to do it in front of Uncle Ted?"

"I..."

"We've been working really hard at this. *You've* been working really hard. And if you can't do it now, then I don't see how you're going to do it on Saturday and prove him wrong. And Mom and Dad are going to be back soon, and I'm pretty sure they think I'm crazy now, and I won't be able to send them on another errand, so—"

"Fine, Amelia." I can't believe I just said that. But she's right. I know I have to do this.

She looks tentatively relieved, like she's still not sure I'll go through with it. Or maybe she's just scared of what the outcome will be—that I might totally screw up, proving I have no chance at this after all. "Okay, we'll pretend that the top of the house is where the ceiling is—"

"The ceiling in the gym is higher than that."

"I *know*. I was just trying to give us something to go on, but if you want to go higher—"

"I don't."

"Okay, then act like the top of the house is where the ceiling is. Go up, pretend to touch the ceiling, then zigzag through the hoops. The imaginary hoops that aren't really there."

I close my eyes real quick, then open them again and start floating upward, before I can give myself another chance to chicken out.

"Don't float!" Amelia says. "*Fly.*" She makes a zooming motion with her hand. "Actively. Like we practiced."

That's way easier to do with an actual ceiling, when I know how far I have to go, but I try anyway. I still hate the feeling of leaving the ground, even though it's gotten a little easier over the past week and a half, and I feel like a complete idiot doing this in the backyard. I imagine all the neighbors glued to their windows or on the verge of rushing outside to get a better look.

I go past the top of the house, then fumble to come back down to the right height, then reach up again and pretend to touch the ceiling. I make the mistake of glancing down at Amelia, to see her reaction to it, and then I feel like I'm going to throw up.

"You're doing great!" she shouts through cupped hands, even though I know it's not true.

And even though the last thing I want the neighbors to see—*if* they're watching—is Amelia telling me what a good job I'm doing, like I'm a little kid learning to ride their bike without training wheels for the first time who keeps crashing and burning and needs the encouragement.

I've been up higher than this—way higher. That's what I keep telling myself. We've practiced this enough in Amelia's room that I know the first hoop will be on the left. I go through the movements, which I've practiced a million times on the ground and in my head, if only a few times while flying. Left, right, left, right, left, right, then turn and do it all again. At one point the feeling that I'm going to fall overwhelms me, and I flail out my arms a little before I regain my bearings. Which would have meant touching one of the hoops, which would have lost me major points if this was the real test. My heart races, and I try not to think about it, or to hesitate too long. I pretend like I did it right and move on—another tip from Amelia, or more like from her third-grade drama teacher, who told it to the stars of the school play while Amelia and a couple of the other extras were eavesdropping.

"Oh, my God, you're doing it!" Amelia squeals.

She doesn't have to sound *that* shocked about it.

I screw up at the end and kind of fudge going through the last hoop, because I am *so* ready for this to be over. Then I move too slowly toward the ground, and Amelia motions for me to hurry it up and to keep my arms tucked in.

When I finally land again, I feel numb, like none of that could have just happened. Then it hits me, and I still can't believe it, but there's this moment where I feel like I could do *anything*. Like maybe, just maybe, I could even pass the flying test.

CHAPTER 30

All the superpower make-up tests are on Saturday. I can't decide if that's a good thing or a bad thing, because on the one hand, I have to go to stupid Heroesworth on *the weekend*, plus I'm super nervous and way stressed out, which isn't exactly how I like to spend my time off. But on the other hand, at least this means no one I know will be around to witness how freaked out I am.

Or to watch me completely fail. Not that I'm going to, I mean, because I'm totally going to pass this thing. Even if I feel like I might start hyperventilating.

Amelia actually wanted to come with me. She said that as my coach, it was not only her job but her "privilege" to see this through. And to be there for me and stuff. But I told her there was no way that was happening, because I really don't need witnesses. And she pointed out that if I do a really amazing job and totally show Ted, won't I want someone else to see that? And to maybe get a picture of the expression on his face?

She had a point, but I told her not to get ahead of herself and that if I actually manage to stick it to Ted, she'll just have to settle for my description of it.

Kat, Riley, Sarah, and Zach *all* texted to wish me luck. Which is cool of them, but also kind of just reminded me how my entire future depends on this. Riley also offered me a ride to Heroesworth, which I was *this close* to taking him up on, because unlike Amelia, I know he would wait outside if I asked him to, and because maybe it would mean feeling slightly less alone.

But in the end, I said no. I walked here, by myself, because I thought maybe it would help take my mind off things, or at least serve as some kind of warm up, but now that I'm here and still feel like I'm going to die, I can say with some confidence that it didn't work. Like, at all.

Before I head into the gym, where Ted is no doubt waiting to fail me if I'm even one second late—I double check the time on my phone first, just in case, but I still have a few minutes—I remind myself that I can do this. Ted's just some stupid douchebag who, through no fault of my own, I happen to be related to, and who happens to hate me. Well, that second one might be *a little bit* my fault, but he also hated me on principle, before we ever even met, so I don't think it counts. But he's just some idiot who doesn't matter, and it's just the school gym, which I have, like, blown up before, so *it* should be scared of *me*.

And maybe I didn't have a whole lot of time to prepare for this test, but like Amelia said, it's really only a couple of moves, and I've got them down. Well, pretty much, anyway. And I know what I'm supposed to do this time. Besides actually practicing it, I've gone over it in my head, we've gone over it out loud, and we've watched a million videos of other people successfully doing this routine. All I really have to do is be able to fly, follow the moves, and don't touch the hoops. And not touching the hoops is the only thing I really have to worry about, because that's the only part I haven't been able to practice in real life. But I've *watched* people do it—I've seen how they keep their arms and legs in close—and Amelia made me do a second run the other night, before Gordon and Helen got home, and she said I did way better that time and that I didn't even touch them. I mean, they were imaginary hoops and she was just guessing, but still.

Totally nothing to be worried about.

Then my phone chimes with another text. It's from my *mom*, and for a second I sort of stop breathing because I think she's texting me to wish me luck. But then I see that she's not. I mean, she *is* texting me, but it's not about the flying test. Because why would it be? She doesn't even know when it is, plus she's the last person who would wish me luck for something like that.

The text says, *Xavier's just dying for you to come over for dinner tonight! You can watch my little sweetiekins while me and Taylor slip out for a while.*

Little zaps of lightning run up and down my back. There's this moment where I'm so pissed at her, I want to throw my phone against the wall. But of course I don't. Though I do consider texting her back and telling her off for, well, *everything*, because how can she even ask me that? It's just one more drop in the gigantic bucket of her not caring about me.

I delete her text and turn my phone off. Then I take a deep breath and step into the gym.

Ted's just standing there, waiting for me, looking really bored. He glances up at the clock when he sees me. "You're my last make-up test. Five more minutes and I would have left."

"That's when my test is supposed to *start*."

"I don't tolerate tardiness. Especially when I didn't believe you'd show up."

Too bad *he* showed up. This would be so much easier if he'd, like, gotten sick and had to have someone else fill in for him—someone who doesn't have it in for me. But then I guess I also wouldn't get to see his face when I totally prove him wrong.

"Before you try and pull anything," he says, "let me just remind you that this is the only make-up test you'll be given, meaning it's the last chance you're going to get. So if you're going to pretend to have another emergency, be my guest, but know that that's it for you. Do you understand?"

Ugh. "Yeah, I get it."

"And?"

"And I'm ready to take the test."

He scoffs. "I'm trying to give you an opportunity here. Back out now and you don't have to humiliate yourself. Because I *will* tell Gordon when you fail to fly at all. My brother deserves to know the truth about you."

"Dad already knows I can fly." You know, from when he, like, pushed me off the tallest building in Golden City.

"We'll see." He gestures to the starting line that's taped on the floor. "Whenever you're ready."

I walk over to the line. My back's to him, so I can't see how badly he's judging me. The hoops look *really* high up, higher than I remembered, now that I'm standing directly beneath them.

But it doesn't matter. This is what I've been training for. And yeah, the idea of going up to the freaking ceiling and performing like some flying circus monkey for someone who hates me is still way terrifying. But not as much as it was three weeks ago, back when it felt completely impossible.

"Any second now," Ted mutters.

I want to tell him to shut up, but I won't give him the satisfaction. So instead I ignore him and make sure I get a good look at the ceiling. I note where all the hoops are. I imagine zigzagging through them, in order, then back again. My heart's racing and I feel dizzy, but I also *know* I can do this.

Everyone's counting on me. It feels like my whole life depends on this moment.

I lift off from the ground. And even though I can't see Ted, or the shocked expression that must be on his face, I hear him gasp. I make a point of flying *actively*, as Amelia calls it, instead of just floating. I'm slower than the people in the videos we watched, but I don't look down, just up toward my goal, and that helps.

I touch the ceiling. I ignore the urge to look at Ted.

My heart is beating super fast, and I can't believe I'm doing this. I move to the left, like I practiced, and go through my first actual hoop. It's big, but not as big as I was picturing, and I'm *so sure* I'm going to make a wrong move and hit the edges. But I don't.

I zigzag to the right, moving slowly but steadily through the next hoop. I keep it up, making my way through the routine. Sweat beads on my forehead and slides down my nose. I wipe it off with my hand and almost elbow one of the hoops. I freak out a little bit after that and accidentally look down, and then I kind of freak out *a lot*. I can't breathe. There's this moment where I panic, thinking my flying power isn't going to work and I'm going to fall and I'm going to die and this is all going to have been for nothing.

But Amelia's made me stay in the air way longer than this. Not this high up, but I didn't fall any of those times, and I'm not falling now. I try to just focus on the routine, like we practiced, and then I'm moving again. My breathing's still a little tight, but I'm moving through the rest of the hoops like nothing happened.

I get through all of them, and then I turn around and do it all again. The whole time, I pretty much feel like I'm going to die, but some part of me also feels like I've got this. And I'm *so* close to the end. All I have to do is make it through a few more excruciating moments, and then I'm home free and I never, ever have to fly again.

And okay, maybe I rush a teeny tiny bit through the last hoop, but just a little, and then I make myself slow down and do it right. And I'm extra careful not to touch the sides, because I think I pretty much *would* die if I made it this far and then screwed up on something so stupid. But I make it through the hoop, and then I tuck my arms in as I make my descent back to the floor. And even though this part was really hard to practice, since we didn't have the actual setup from the gym, I land exactly on the line of tape, right where I started from.

I take a moment to catch my breath and to bask in the fact that *I just did that*. This is the part where I should be taking a bow or something, but instead I look up at Ted. I expect him to be shocked and probably really pissed, because I just totally showed him up. But he doesn't seem like either of those things.

He's frowning at his clipboard, looking concerned. And maybe still kind of bored.

Like I didn't just do the most amazing thing I've ever done in my entire life. Like I didn't just prove that not only can I fly, but I can do his stupid routine, just like anybody else. Well, maybe not *just* like anybody else—I'm not going to win the Olympics anytime soon or be invited to compete in the Golden City Annual Flying Idiots Brigade or whatever—but he could at least admit that I nailed it.

I walk over to him. "Well? Were you even watching?"

He doesn't look up. "I was."

"And?"

"It was… not what I was expecting."

What? What does that mean? "I did the routine. What else did you expect?" Besides for me to totally fail.

"It seems that you *can* fly. You were better than I

imagined, I'll give you that."

I glare at him. "I did the routine."

"Yes, I'm aware of that. But the point wasn't to learn a routine. The point was to show that you have a handle on your ability and are ready to move on to the next level of coursework here at Heroesworth."

"I... I did that. I *do* have a handle on it."

He finally looks up from his clipboard. "I've seen students like you before, students who only study the test. It always shows in their performance. You did the routine in the most mechanical way possible."

"But..." He never said I had to do more than learn the routine. "You're just saying this because you hate me. You *want* me to fail, so you're making up an excuse!"

He sighs. "This is my job. I can't in good conscience pass someone who so obviously doesn't know how to actually use his superpower."

I clench my fists. Lightning burns a little beneath my skin. "I *can* use it. I just showed you I can!"

"Fly up to the ceiling and back as fast as you can."

"What?"

"Or spin in the air. If you can really fly, if you really deserve to pass this test, you should be able to do a few simple aerial tasks on command. Can you do that?"

I look up at the ceiling, at the hoops I trained so hard to be able to zigzag through. Moving sideways through the air was a big enough deal for me, and I had to practice a lot first. I thought I had this, but when I think about *spinning* in the air, my throat goes dry and my stomach twists up. I know I could fly up to the ceiling and back, but not fast, like he wants, and not with any more skill than I already did. The idea of doing crazy flying stuff I've never tried before, *on command,* makes me want to shrivel up into a little ball and never speak to anyone again.

"That's what I thought," Ted says when I don't answer him. And the worst part isn't even that he was right about me. It's the way he sounds like he actually *feels sorry for me,* like he could tell how much I really tried and is actually just doing his job.

CHAPTER 31

Me and Riley meet up with Kat and Tristan that afternoon, outside the abandoned Heroes Hideout across from the tire factory, which is in a semi-industrial section of Golden City. I'm not sure if the Heroes Hideout was abandoned *because* it was built so close to a tire factory, or if the tire factory came later, but neither one is really doing anything to relieve the creepiness factor of this whole area.

I was kind of hoping maybe Tristan wouldn't show up, since he made it clear he was against coming here. Not that he's not still whining about it, though. "Come on, Katie. Look at this place. It's..." He makes a face at the boarded-up windows and all the graffiti painted across the front of the building. "I don't know what we're even doing here. This is *not* the kind of place where someone hides priceless paintings."

He kind of has a point. I don't know what I was expecting, because *abandoned pizza place* doesn't really scream *great place to keep treasure*, but I thought when we got here it would make more sense. Like maybe it only *used* to be an abandoned Heroes Hideout but was now a swanky, state-of-the-art vault or something. Not that I know how we'd break into one of those, but it would at least mean we were on the right track.

Kat looks over at me. "Damien? What do you think? Because if you wanted to leave, and maybe do this another time—"

"Or not at all," Tristan says.

"—then we're all totally cool with that." Her eyes search mine as she says it, and I can tell she's thinking about how I failed my flying test.

I called and told her about it as soon as it was over. She said the important thing was that I'd tried really hard and that whatever the outcome, even attempting the test was a huge deal for me, let alone actually getting through it. And I know she's right, but I also know she was disappointed, or maybe just worried about me, and the whole situation still makes me feel like crap.

And then, after that, I had to call Riley and tell him the same thing. He said it wasn't my fault. He said he knew I'd tried really hard—that I *must have* if I was willing to work with Amelia—and that he wasn't upset. Or, at least, not upset at me, because it was super obvious he wasn't thrilled with the news.

He said he'd understand if I wanted to call off our mission today. He said maybe it doesn't even matter now if we find that painting or not, since I'm dropping out of school and he won't have a partner for Advanced Heroism anymore, which means he'll be back on the alternative assignment anyway.

When he mentioned me dropping out of school, I felt sick all over, because I guess now it's actually happening. I didn't want to think about it, so I said there was no way I wasn't finishing this assignment with him. Because all those things I said before about us needing to find out if this is still who we are haven't changed. And because I didn't want anyone to think I couldn't handle it, like that maybe I'm not hero material after all and the school is right to hold me back.

And now Kat's asking me if I want to leave, trying to give me a chance to back out without having to admit to everyone that today really, really sucked and I can't take it. Which is kind of cool of her, but I also hate thinking that she feels sorry for me.

"We're already here," I tell her. "And you guys had to come all the way from Vilmore."

"It's okay, though," she says. "We knew there was a chance this would be a bust, and I was going to come home this weekend, anyway."

"But we're here. Someone wrote that note for a reason."

"A reason that probably has nothing to do with Frank," Tristan says. "It could have been about *anything*."

"It's still the only lead we've got." And at least if I'm here, potentially dodging serial killers in an abandoned pizza place, I won't be at home, thinking about how my life is falling apart. "I say we at least check it out."

X·X·X

The inside of the abandoned Heroes Hideout looks, well, *abandoned*. There's dust on everything, and cobwebs, and the whole place smells kind of damp. The old animatronic animals—a horse in a cowboy hat with a big *H* on it and his two sidekicks, a dog and a cow wearing matching mini-capes, also with *H*s—aren't as creepy as I expected. I mean, they *are* creepy, don't get me wrong, but they also just seem really sad.

And that's *sad* as in, "Gee, it's really sad that people used to have fun here and now it's just empty and dirty," not *sad* as in, "Don't look now, but I think those animatronic animals have *feelings* and are going to murder us as soon as our backs are turned."

"Well, we've seen it," Tristan says. "Happy now? Can we go home already? Because some of us have homework to do."

"This *is* our homework," Kat says.

"Only if it has anything to do with that painting, and I don't see any paintings here, do you?"

There's totally a painting of a water barrel and some cowboy boots on the wall right in front of him. Not that that does anything to help us. "Maybe the note was talking about downstairs." I gesture to the super creepy opening in the floor where there's an even creepier-looking staircase descending into darkness.

Everyone looks at me like I've gone insane.

"Seriously?" Riley says. "*You* want to go down there?"

Want might be a strong word. But going down those

stairs into some terrifying basement full of who knows what still sounds less scary than going home and facing my future. "It could be a storage room. And if we don't at least check it out, we're going to always wonder if we missed out on something."

"Like, missed out on getting murdered?"

I make a couple of sparks twitch across my fingers. "We won't get murdered."

"So, *you're* going to murder somebody?"

"*No.* I'm just saying that we're not going in unarmed. Besides, we'll make Tristan go first."

Tristan glares at me.

"Wait," Kat says. "What if you're right and that really is where Frank's keeping the painting? Would he really leave it open like that? What if he's inside?"

"Well…"

"I'll go first," Tristan says. Not in a boastful way, like he's showing me up, but more like he thinks we really have to do this.

I consider the possibilities of what might be down there. Maybe old toys and games from when this place was running, or maybe rotten pizza toppings that never got used. Or deranged clowns who are also serial killers who are somehow immune to both lightning and fire and will actually succeed in murdering us all. Or, more likely —hopefully more likely, anyway—is that one of the robbers from the gallery had some business here. And since it doesn't seem like they'd be robbing this place, it was probably a meeting. Or the note really was related to the gallery job and was a reminder of where to take the goods they stole.

Which means the jewelry we sort of let them take might be down there. The painting that Riley, Kat, and Tristan's grades kind of depend on might be down there.

Frank might even be down there. And I know Grandpa said no one's ever seen him and lived, but...

But he's probably not here. Frank probably has better things to do on his Saturday afternoons than lurk in a basement, waiting to scare teenagers. Or murder them. Whatever.

And if we don't go down in that basement, we go home, which means facing everyone I've let down. It means answering a lot of questions I don't have the answers to, like if I'm really dropping out now, or what I'm going to do with my life, or what I could have done differently to make this not happen.

"*I'll* go first," I tell them. I hold up my hands, letting electricity wash over them—both for light and in case of bad guys—and make my way down the stairs.

CHAPTER 32

It turns out I don't need my lightning after all. There's a light switch in the basement that actually works, lighting up the whole hallway. I also figure that if there were bad guys down here, they would have had the lights on. I mean, unless they're asleep or psychotic and just pretending not to need light so we'd think no one was here and that it was safe and we'd let our guards down.

But either way, I can see that at least this hallway is clear. *And* that there are some really classy paintings on the wall, plus a fancy vase on a pedestal.

"Whoa," Kat says, gaping at one of the paintings.

It's not the one we've been looking for—unfortunately, because how cool would that be if we instantly found it based on my somewhat questionable decision to explore the creepy basement?—but it does look way too nice to have been part of the Heroes Hideout decor. Plus, all the Heroes Hideout stuff is cowboy themed, and this painting is of a sailboat, floating serenely in a patch of sunlight, while a bunch of sea monsters wait just beyond the shadows, churning up the water and showing their teeth.

But that's not the part Kat's looking at. She's pointing at the signature in the corner. *Harriet Hooper.*

"No way," Tristan says, even though I'm pretty sure Kat was talking to me.

"Who's Harriet Hooper?" Riley asks.

"The Director of Damage," I tell him. "She was a famous villain who died, like, ten years ago."

"Never heard of her."

Tristan snorts. "I bet you haven't. Typical letterist."

Me and Kat both glare at him.

"So," Riley says, looking a little confused, "she was a painter?"

Kat shakes her head. "No. Well, yes. She was an inventor *and* a painter. The League confiscated most of her inventions when she died, but there was some stuff that was never accounted for. Nobody ever knew what happened to it, or if it was even real, but..." She grins at the painting.

"But some people think there was a secret stash of her stuff," I add. "And I guess there is. I guess coming down to this basement was in fact a *great* idea. A great idea that happened to be mine, if anyone from the press asks or anything once we tell them we found this place and become, like, famous and stuff."

Riley looks unimpressed. "You're already famous."

Tristan snickers. "Not in a good way."

"We're not going to be famous," Kat says, though I can hear the excitement in her voice. "It's probably nothing. I mean, just because we found one of her works of art—"

"Two, no, at least three," Tristan says, moving down the hall to look at the other paintings.

"—in a really weird place that no one would have ever suspected was some secret villain lair—"

"A *villain's* hideout," I add.

"—doesn't mean we've found her long-lost stash that no one else in the world was ever able to find and that would totally be, like, really, really amazing."

"But someone else had to have found it first," Riley says, still not sounding that impressed. "I mean, the staircase was open."

"True," Kat admits.

I shrug. "Maybe Frank found it, or maybe he stole this stuff in the first place and has been keeping it here the whole time. And... and maybe the painting we're supposed to find really will be here."

"You're still going on about that painting?" Tristan says. "Who cares about our assignment when we've found *this*?"

Riley scowls. "And let me guess, now that you've found it, you're going to turn it in to Vilmore?"

"Only if we get extra credit." Tristan grins, way full of himself. "And what's your suggestion? Turn it in to the League?"

"*No.* I just don't think—"

Tristan ignores him and turns to Kat. "Do you think they'll let us keep something? I'm calling dibs on the bacon painting."

One of the paintings is two stylized strips of bacon

sizzling in a pan, only when you look closer, you realize the pan looks kind of like space, so I guess it's a statement about life or something. It's not the Director of Damage's best work, in my opinion.

"We're not keeping anything," I tell him, even though I kind of have my eye on the sea monsters painting. "We don't even know what we've found yet."

"Oh, right. We should wait until we've seen all of the goods before we start deciding who gets what."

"That's not what he meant," Kat says, giving Tristan a disgusted look.

"Whatever." Tristan rolls his eyes and wanders off down the hall.

Kat turns and whispers to me, "I really want that sea monsters painting, though, *if* it comes up."

"Me, too. Rock paper scissors?"

"Joint custody. But it stays at my place, because you have a tendency to…"

"Blast holes through the wall?"

"Yep. That."

Riley still looks confused. "Is this really a thing? I mean, I don't even get what we've found."

"Whoa!" Tristan calls from down the hall. "You have to see this!"

We hurry over and follow him through a doorway into a room full of what must be priceless artifacts that, like, totally puts the hallway to shame. There are shelves lining some of the walls, full of books and little gadgets. There are more paintings, too—a whole wall of paintings in intricately carved wooden frames—and a statue in one corner, and, in the middle of the room, sitting on a pedestal, is the coolest-looking raygun I've ever seen.

Except I don't even know if it's a raygun, but it looks kind of like one, only it's got weird blue tubes coming out of it, and a canister on the back full of some purple sludge.

I have no idea what it is.

I pick it up anyway, even though I have enough experience almost getting killed by Sarah's inventions that I should know better.

"Damien, wait!" Kat shouts, but it's too late, because I've already grabbed it.

It doesn't kill me. It doesn't even threaten to explode. But as soon as it's off the pedestal, there's this far-off clicking sound, and then the walls start to rumble.

"Oops." I set the weapon back in its place, but the rumbling doesn't stop.

There's a hissing noise, too, and a bad smell that makes us all start coughing.

Riley starts to shout, "We have to get—" but then there's a clanging sound, and a loud crash as something falls from the ceiling, and he screams.

"Perkins!" My blood runs cold as I turn around. In my mind I hear him screaming at the gala again. I feel the same fear I felt then.

There's a gash on his forehead and a metal vent lying on the floor that must have been what fell. Riley's shaking all over, and blood pours down his face. "I'm okay," he says, but he sounds like a robot, like he's not okay at all.

"Come on!" Kat cries. "It's a trap! We have to go!"

The doors are closing. Solid steel doors are sliding over

the entryways, trying to trap us here, because I am the biggest idiot in the world.

Someone sticks a metal bar in one of the doorways to keep it open—the same doorway we came in through. I think for just a second that someone saw us come down here and is going to rescue us. But the woman who ducks under the metal bar and waltzes into the room is carrying a raygun. And pointing it at us. And grinning.

"Nobody move! And no lightning—this whole room is filling with gas, and one spark will blow us all up!"

I lower my hand. I hadn't even realized I was getting ready to blast her. Tristan must have been doing the same thing, because out of the corner of my eye I see him put his hands down, too.

The other door to the room, the one without the metal bar holding it open, slams shut.

"Who are you?" Kat says. "And what the hell are you doing here?"

The woman looks like she's in her mid-twenties. She has strawberry-blond hair pulled into a ponytail, and I think she might be chewing gum. "The name's Frank."

"Yeah, right," Tristan says. "You're not Frank."

She blows a bubble with her gum and snaps it. "I think I know my own name."

"But Frank's a dude. He's, like, some middle-aged gangster."

She laughs. "Says who?"

Tristan starts to argue again, then doesn't. Kat's face falls.

We couldn't find any real info about Frank. So we just

assumed. Though, to be fair, she doesn't look old enough to have been the same Frank from ten years ago.

She makes a *hmph* noise. "You're thinking of my father. Guess you weren't as good as I thought. I knew you were onto me when I saw you at the gallery the other night. I was so surprised, because after that performance at the train station, well, I thought you were total amateurs. 'Long track record' my ass." She shakes her head at me and Riley. "But maybe your friends here did all the work. Too bad you couldn't have recruited them to get my ring back."

"*What?*" Maybe it's the gas filling the room, or maybe it's how frazzled my nerves are right now, but I don't know what she's talking about.

"Well, I shouldn't say *my* ring—it's my sister's, but our grandmother left it to both of us. I hired your little group to get it back from her dirtbag ex-husband."

"You hired us. That was you?"

She rolls her eyes. "Oh, my God, *yes*! Only you two botched it up. And I thought, 'Oh, well, that's what I get for trying to go cheap.' But *then* I saw you at the gallery. You thought you were being so sneaky. Well. I knew I must have underestimated you. You were onto me—"

"We weren't onto you! We were investigating that painting you stole from the museum!"

"What?" She blinks. "Why?"

"For *school*! It was just an assignment!" Electricity starts to burn beneath my skin. I take a deep breath. I can't let it spark, or we're all dead.

"The painting? I ripped it to shreds and burned it. It

had a map to this place on the back. Well, it was rumored to, and I figured if it didn't, I'd just sell it. But then I couldn't let it fall into the wrong hands. Just like I couldn't let *you* get ahead of me. The map said this room was trapped, but it didn't say what would happen. So I lured you here with that note, set up a camera out front to alert me when you showed up, and now, voila! Two birds with one stone! You know, I half thought this place would blow up the second you touched anything. Guess not, though. Aren't you all just *so lucky* today? Now." Any trace of a smile disappears from her face. She aims her gun at me. "You see that weapon on that pedestal next to you? Slide that over here *or else*."

"Or else what? You can't shoot us—this whole place will blow up!"

The metal bar that's holding the door open starts to creak.

Frank clenches her jaw. "Won't I? You sure about that? You *absolutely sure*?!" She takes a step forward, looking down the sights of her raygun like she's going to shoot.

I swallow. She won't do it. She *can't*.

"Damien!" Kat cries, and we all hear the fear in her voice.

The grin returns to Frank's face. She switches tactics and aims the gun at Kat instead of me. "Weapon. On the floor. *Now.*" Her finger moves. Just a tiny bit. Not enough to pull the trigger—just enough to scare the hell out of me.

"Kat!" Electricity runs up my spine.

"Don't give it to her!" Kat says.

But I do what Frank wants. I take the weird raygun-looking thing with the blue tubes sticking out of it from its pedestal again. I think about dropping it on the floor and breaking it, whatever it is, but my hands are shaking, and I'm trying so hard *not* to drop it, because I'm not certain Frank won't shoot Kat. I'm not certain she won't blow us all up, or at least take the risk. I wish I was, but I'm not. And I'm not sure how much longer I can keep my lightning under control, either.

I slide the weapon over to her.

Frank grabs it off the floor, still aiming at Kat. "Wish I could stay and chat," Frank says, heading for the door. "It was nice knowing you, or at least it was when I thought you were a match for me." She ducks through the door. Once she's on the other side, she puts her hand on the metal bar, the only thing that's keeping the door open.

And before I know what I'm doing, I'm running toward her. Because if she takes that bar, if she lets that door close, we're dead. And even if I can't use my lightning right now, I can still stop her from trapping us here.

Apparently Frank thinks so, too, because she pulls out a knife.

"Damien, no!" Kat screams.

It all happens really fast. Kat screaming, her footsteps behind me, and then Frank throwing the knife at my chest without even hesitating.

I have just enough time to register what's happening, to put the pieces together and realize I'm about to die.

And then Kat's hand is in front of me, and the knife is going *through her hand*, and she's screaming again, only this time in pain.

Frank yanks the metal bar out, and then the steel door slams shut, trapping us anyway.

Kat pulls the knife out of her hand. It clatters on the floor. She uses her shapeshifting power to heal the wound, though her face is still pale and she's gritting her teeth.

"You saved my life," I tell her, even though she knows that.

She nods, smiling at me. Then she coughs from the gas that's filling up the room. "You can thank me later."

"X," Riley says, coming over to us. "We have to get out of here." His face is still bloody, though he tried to wipe it off on his sleeve.

I start coughing. Now that the door's closed, the gas is definitely getting worse. "I..." I look around. Maybe Kat could shapeshift and squeeze through the vent on the ceiling, but that's also where the gas is coming from. The doors are shut tight. If I blast through them, the whole room explodes. "I don't know."

"X," Riley says.

"Just let me think!"

"*Move*," Tristan yells. "Get back, into the corner."

"What?"

"Now!" He holds up his hands, like he's going to use his fire power. In a room full of gas.

"Um—"

"Just do it!"

We all back up into the corner, like he says.

"Be ready."

"For what?"

But he doesn't say. He steels himself. Then flame bursts from his hands, and he creates a wall of fire around us. The gas at our feet ignites, just for a second, then gets sucked into the wall he's controlling, while the rest of the room turns into an inferno.

Tristan pushes the wall forward, just a little bit. Then a little more. His face is red, and he looks like this is taking a *lot* of energy.

"What are we supposed to do?!" I have to shout to be heard over the flames.

"Blast the door!" he says, straining to get the words out. He moves the wall a little farther, pushing the flames back, just past the door.

I nod, even though he can't see me. I look at Kat and Riley, and they move back into the corner, giving me some room. I've never had to blast through a solid steel door before, with no knob or anything, just a wall. But it only takes one try. I blast the hell out of it, making a hole big enough for us to squeeze through, and then all four of us get out of there as fast as we can.

CHAPTER 33

"Where were you?!" Amelia says when she bursts into my room Monday afternoon.

I'm lying on my bed, staring at the ceiling. I don't look up when she comes in. "You could have knocked."

"*You* could have been in the parking lot after school! I thought I was supposed to wait for you!" She marches over to the bed, stomping the whole way and making the walls shake.

"Why would you think that?"

"Uh, because I always do? But you didn't show up, and you wouldn't answer your phone, and Hil was going to be late for her piano lesson so she had to call her mom to come get her, and Melissa ended up leaving with her, because she wasn't sure what was going on. And I hated waiting by myself, but you still didn't show up, so I called Riley, and he said you went home early and that you decided to *drop out of school*."

I sit up, balling the ends of my sweatshirt sleeves

around my hands. "You knew I was going to." Not that I actually have, not officially as far as the school is concerned, but I don't see the point in going back. And I thought I could at least stick it out today, but it turns out I couldn't handle it. Not with the way everyone kept staring at me in horror, like I was a murderer they couldn't believe was allowed to walk free.

"No, I didn't. I knew you were thinking about it, but I didn't know if you'd really do it or not, or that you'd do it *today*. Especially since we only have a couple weeks left. And either way, you still could have told me I didn't need to wait for you!"

"Okay. I should have told you I wasn't going to be there. Obviously it won't be happening again. So, problem solved, you can go now."

She doesn't move to leave. Instead, she bites her lip and sits down on the bed. "But what are you going to do if you don't go to Heroesworth?"

"I don't know. It doesn't matter."

"Yes, it does. You can't just quit."

I look over at her, raising an eyebrow like she's insane. "Uh, yeah, I can. The Director of Damage's *fear ray* is loose in Golden City because of me. It's in the hands of some crazed criminal who's going to do who knows what with it, *because of me*." It's been all over the news ever since we described what we saw to the police on Saturday, after the stash of artifacts and the old Heroes Hideout burnt to the ground. Tristan managed to hold off the flames long enough for us to escape, but he couldn't actually stop it, and by the time we got out of there and called 911, there was no chance of saving it. Not that anyone was particularly attached to the old Heroes Hideout, but *not losing all the Director of Damage's long-lost gadgets and one-of-a-kind works of art we'd just discovered would have been nice.

The police matched up the info we gave them with what info they had on the Director of Damage, said it was her infamous fear ray that can terrorize someone into doing pretty much anything the wielder wants, and then they issued a statement to the press so they could warn everyone to be on the lookout.

They didn't exactly keep their mouths shut about my involvement, either. Especially when people started asking how this could have happened.

Damien Locke was involved, that's how. He teamed up with his girlfriend from Vilmore. He broke the rules, again, *and now no one can sleep safely in Golden City anymore.*

"You weren't the only one there," Amelia says. "Maybe they're blaming you on the news, but it wasn't your fault."

"My friends still got hurt because of me, and not for the first time. But that won't happen again if I quit. And I won't have to fly ever again, either." And I can finally stop worrying about whether or not I can survive Heroesworth, since, big surprise, it turns out I can't.

"Don't say that! You learned to fly really fast. You'd never even practiced before, and you're afraid of heights, but you still learned a lot in only a couple of weeks. If you take the test again next year—"

"That's *not* happening. I'm done with Heroesworth, just like I'm done with flying. I thought... Look, it doesn't matter what I thought, because I couldn't do it. I'm not a hero and I never will be."

"But you *are*. And I know you're not okay with just giving up."

"Trust me, Amelia, the world is better off without me interfering."

"That's stupid. You're better than this."

"No, I'm not. Whatever I thought—whatever *you* thought I could be, you were wrong, and you wouldn't have ever even thought that if you'd known the truth."

"What truth? You're being super dramatic right now. You always think you're—"

"The truth about you and Zach." I press my palms against my knees, bracing myself for this. Some part of me is telling me not to do it, to shut the hell up before it's too late, but I can't stop. The whole world hates me right now, and instead of being glad that Amelia doesn't, it's like I need her to hate me, too. "I know the real reason you guys broke up. It was because of something I said."

"What?" Confusion twists up her face. Confusion and disbelief. "You mean because you gave me bad advice? That was just a misunderstanding."

"No, because I gave *Zach* bad advice. We were talking about… about you and him, and I asked him if he loved you. And he said he didn't know, and I said…" I trail off, but I know it's too late.

"You said what?"

I shrug, like it's no big deal, like I don't even care. "I said he would *know* if he did. That really liking you and being *in love* with you weren't the same things."

She's just staring at me, horrified. "Why were you guys even *talking* about me?!"

"I'm the reason he was thinking about whether or not he loved you, okay? And you'd be better off if I'd just kept to myself and didn't interfere and just left everybody alone. Because if we hadn't had that conversation, he probably wouldn't have said all that stuff to you at Prom, about just liking you, and you guys would still be together."

"Is that why you came into the bathroom? Is that why you tried to comfort me?!"

Her eyes are wet. I look away and don't say anything, letting her think what she wants about me, even if it's not true.

"*Why?* Why would you do that?!"

"It wasn't on purpose. It's just what happens when I get involved in things. I ruin them, and people get hurt."

"You could have told me. *That* was on purpose!" She gasps and puts her hands to her mouth. "Oh, my God, I taught you to fly to distract myself from the breakup!"

"See, Amelia? It's like I said. I'm not a hero and I never will be. And everyone, including you, will be way better off if I just give up now and stop trying."

X·X·X

There's a knock on my door later. It's probably someone coming to tell me it's time for dinner, since it's a little after six and since I can smell food cooking, but I ignore them, even though I'm hungry, because there's no way I'm eating dinner with everybody.

I imagine Gordon and Helen sharing little looks about me. Maybe concerned looks. Maybe *What are we supposed to do with him now?* kind of looks. I mean, they don't seem mad about what happened, but Gordon's delinquent half-villain son unleashing some super weapon on the unsuspecting citizens of Golden City and then deciding to drop out of his alma mater can't be making them happy or anything.

And Amelia's pissed at me. Or maybe she really hates me now. And Alex is old enough to understand what a fear ray is and why it's crazy bad news that some criminal is running around with it, but from what he told me yesterday, he doesn't believe it was my fault. Not because he knows anything about what happened, but because he knows I wouldn't *let* that happen. Which is kind of worse than if he just blamed me like everybody else, because then at least I wouldn't have anything to lose. I haven't done anything to screw him over like I did Amelia, but I'm sure I'll still be able to think of something awful to say to make him stop believing in me—like that it really was my fault that weapon got taken—and the thought of that makes me sick.

Too sick to care about dinner. And it's not like I ate with them yesterday, and I hadn't even told them my decision to drop out of school yet then, so I wish they'd just take the hint and leave me alone.

Jess is the only one in this family I might want to talk to, and only because she's too young to understand *anything* about what happened, or about me and my non-existent future. But she's not the best dinner conversationalist, what with always having some sort of food in her mouth or getting way too focused on eating her peas individually, so I don't think her presence will, like, save me from dying of awkwardness.

Or from Amelia telling everyone what a complete and total jerk I am, which I would definitely deserve and which she will probably do anyway even if I don't show up.

And all of that isn't even taking into account the fact that I'm way too busy staring at my phone and reading all the stupid articles people are writing about me. I mean, I read the first couple, and now I'm mostly just skimming them, because you can only read about yourself dooming the entire world so many times before it gets repetitive.

Whoever's at the door knocks again.

"I'll eat later!" I shout.

"X? It's me," Riley says.

I tell him to come in.

He has his backpack with him. He drops it on the floor and then comes over. "You look like hell."

And he's the one with the stitched-up gash on his forehead. "Great, Perkins. Is that what you came to tell me?"

"No, I—" He notices what's on my phone and snatches it away from me. "Seriously? How can you read this stuff?!"

"They're all just saying what I already know."

"What, that you secretly conspired with Frank to steal that weapon? Or that you lied about there even being a weapon just for attention?"

"No, that I'm not hero material. That I was never cut out for this and had no business ever going to Heroesworth or endangering you guys—"

"You didn't endanger us."

"You wouldn't have gone down in that basement if I hadn't insisted. You and Kat got hurt, and we all almost died. If it wasn't for Tristan, we would have."

"*And you.* You blasted the door open."

"None of us would have been down there if it wasn't for me."

"But Frank would have figured out how to get the fear ray even if we didn't show up. And then we wouldn't have known about it at all, and nobody would have had any warning."

Nobody would be panicking about it, he means. "Look, Perkins, I know what you really came here for, and you don't need to say it."

"Yeah, I do. You didn't have to do that today."

He means when I told Mrs. Deeds and Dean Scott that *I* was the one who was working with students from Vilmore and that Riley didn't know anything about it until they showed up at the abandoned Heroes Hideout, and that he was against it, and that any involvement he had was only because he didn't want to abandon his partner in a dangerous situation.

"You would have failed Advanced Heroism and lost your scholarship." Because apparently that's the punishment for working with the enemy—automatic failure. Or at least it is at Heroesworth. Kat and Tristan have to do extra work to make up for not completing their assignment, but nobody even brought up the idea of failing them.

"I know, but—"

"There's no point in both of us going down for it. And I was the one who insisted we work with them, and that we wouldn't get caught. And I'd have had to repeat all of first year anyway, if I was going to stick around, so it doesn't matter if I failed the class."

"But I still went along with it. We were both guilty this time, and... you shouldn't have to take all the blame."

"It's done, Perkins. Just forget about it."

He takes a deep breath, not looking happy about that. "None of what they're saying about you is true, you know. You *are* hero material, and—"

"If you came here to convince me not to quit, you should probably just leave."

"Why, so you can go back to reading all that garbage people are posting? And I'm not going to tell you not to quit. I mean, I wish you weren't, and I'm really going to miss you next year, but I get why you're doing it."

"You do?"

"Yeah. It really sucks that this happened. And the stuff they're saying about you *isn't* true. But... what happened Saturday was awful. Between that and the gala, and what happened with your flying test, I get it."

"Okay. I mean, thanks."

"And I'm not going anywhere. I brought my stuff. I'm staying over."

"I didn't ask you to do that. You didn't even call first."

He gives me a look. "Like you ever call me first?"

"I could have had plans."

"Like staring at your phone all night?"

"I just... You don't need to be here. I already made Amelia cry, and I might say something stupid to you, too."

"She'll get over it."

"You don't know what I said."

"Well, whatever you say to me, I know *I'll* get over it. And I get it if you don't feel like hanging out, and we can just sit here silently if you want—I brought a book—but I'm not going anywhere. And I'm confiscating your phone."

"I'm supposed to call Kat later."

"Fine, but that's not the point and you know it."

"You really want to hang out with me right now? Even if I just want to sit here and think about how much my life sucks and not talk to you the whole night?"

"Yep. Even then. If that's what you want."

"It's not. I mean, the thinking about how much my life sucks part. And the not talking to you part. I don't really want to do either of those. So I guess you can stay."

"Good, because I already told you I was."

"Though maybe you could go downstairs and see if dinner's ready. And bring some back up here if it is."

"What, you can't just fly down there and see for yourself?"

"Shut up. I'm avoiding everyone. And I'm never flying again. So if you're staying, I'm appointing you to get dinner."

"Okay. I guess I can do that."

"What book did you bring?"

His face lights up. "*Scourge of the Elflands.* It's book four in the *Elf Plight* trilogy, which I know sounds wrong, because you can't have four books in a trilogy, but really there are *seven* books total now, they just didn't know it was going to have that many when it started."

"How many pages is it?"

"Er, around twelve hundred?"

"So you really thought I wasn't going to talk to you all night?"

"I thought it was a possibility. But also it's a really good book."

"I doubt that."

He scowls. "It *is*. I have the whole series. You can borrow the first one sometime."

"That's not going to happen. But... thanks, Perkins."

"It's fine. If you change your mind, let me know."

"No, I mean... thanks for coming over here. Even though you thought it might be so boring you'd be reduced to reading some lame fantasy novel all night."

He huffs at that. "It's *not* lame. And I'm your friend, X. *Of course* I came over."

CHAPTER 34

Kat doesn't pick up until after the tenth ring, and when she does, she sounds like she was asleep. "Damien?"

"Hey, Kat. Did I wake you up?" I know it's a weeknight, but it's only nine o'clock. Kat's usually up until at least midnight. "I was supposed to call, right?"

"What? Yes! Oh, my God, I can't believe I fell asleep! I was reading my Observing Heroes textbook for class tomorrow, and it's *so* boring."

"If you want to 'observe' a hero, I think that can be arranged. And you will *not* fall asleep." I say it out of habit, before I catch myself and remember I'm not a hero anymore.

"*Dude*," Riley says. He's sitting in the corner, reading the gigantic book he brought. "I'm right here."

"Riley says hi," I tell Kat.

"No, I didn't, I—"

"Oh, sorry, Kat, Riley specifically *isn't* saying hi to you, which is pretty rude."

Kat laughs. "Tell him I said hi back."

I shake my head at Riley. "She says she's never going to forgive you for your slight."

He rolls his eyes at me. "Whatever. And if you want me to leave the room, just say so."

"I don't know why you would think that." I haven't said anything I wouldn't have said if we were all here in person. I ignore him and go back to my phone conversation. "Anyway, I might have spoken too soon—or more like too late—about observing a hero, since there aren't any here."

"Hello?" Riley says. "Still in the room."

"You want my girlfriend to *observe* you? Inappropriate."

"What? No! I was just— You know what I meant!"

"Hey," Kat says, sounding really groggy, "if you guys are busy, maybe"—she yawns—"maybe we should just talk tomorrow."

"No, no, I'm not busy." I pause. "Are you okay? You sound a little off."

"Yeah. I don't know. I think I feel weird because I just woke up."

"If you want me to call you back in the morning—"

"No, it's alright. I need to wake up anyway, since I still have to get through the rest of my homework." She yawns again, which makes me yawn, too, even though I'm not that tired. "How was school today? Was it super weird?"

"Kind of."

"Were people jerks to you? Because I can come down there and beat them all up for you if you want. I don't go to your school, so I can't get in trouble."

I laugh. "You're going to beat up pretty much *everyone* at Heroesworth?"

"If I have to. But maybe... maybe next week."

"You don't have to do that. And I won't be there next week."

"Why? Did something happen?"

"I..." I turn away a little, so Riley can't see my face, even though he's pretending to read his book. And maybe I should have had him leave the room for this, but that would make it too real. That would mean that what I'm about to tell Kat is too horrible to have someone else in the room for, and I don't think I could handle that. "I'm dropping out of school."

She sucks in a breath. Then she's quiet for a second. "You're dropping out? Why? What happened?"

"You know what happened. I failed the flying test—"

"You could retake it!"

"In a *year*. That's... That would mean another whole year of Heroesworth." And I'd have to keep practicing my flying, probably that entire time. "And what if I still failed after all that?"

"You wouldn't!"

She doesn't know that, though. She didn't even see me do the routine. "It doesn't matter. I can't do it. I *shouldn't* be doing it. You've heard everything people are saying about me. There's no way you haven't."

Riley glances up from his book but doesn't say anything.

"None of it is true," Kat says, her voice pleading with

me. "You know that."

"Some of it is. And even if nobody said anything, I would still know."

"You'd know what?"

"That I'm not cut out for this. I got an X for my sixteenth birthday, and maybe I got it for a reason. I'm not enough of a villain or enough of a hero to be either one. I thought I could choose what I am, but it turns out I'm just nothing."

"That's stupid. That's the stupidest thing I've ever heard."

"I watched you get hurt! Because of me! A knife went *through your hand*. Right in front of me, because I was dumb enough to almost get myself killed."

"Everybody makes mistakes."

"I make too many."

"You didn't do anything wrong!"

"I watched Riley get hurt again, too, and..." I trail off, knowing he can hear me. "What happened at the gala really screwed me up. And if I was really meant to be a hero, it wouldn't have."

"That's not true," Kat says. "You know it's not."

"People keep getting hurt because of me, and I can't let that happen."

"You saved us, Damien. You blasted a hole through the door. And you saved everyone at the gala, too."

"Yeah, but nobody would have even needed saving if it wasn't for me. I can't pretend I'm a hero anymore. I get it if you're mad at me—"

"I'm not mad. I'm... I think you're making a mistake."

"I know this isn't what you wanted."

"It's not what you wanted, either. What are you going to do if you're not a hero or a villain?"

"I haven't figured that part out yet."

"Being a hero made you *happy*. How are you—"

"I don't know!" I swallow. "I'm sorry, Kat. I just... I don't know."

"The scandal will die down. People won't be talking about this forever."

"It's not about that, okay?"

"You're supposed to be somebody. We both are."

"But you'd still love me if I wasn't, right?"

"Of course." Her voice is kind of choked up, like nothing about this is actually alright. "I didn't mean that I wouldn't. But we both know you're making the wrong decision. You *are* meant to be a hero. It's who you are, even if you can't see it right now. Anything else you do is going to be settling. You get that, right?"

"This isn't about what I want. It's about what's right. Enough people I care about have gotten hurt because of me. I used to love fieldwork, but I don't anymore, and I don't know how to get that back. And... I tried really hard, but it wasn't enough."

"You mean for the flying test?"

"I mean for everything."

She's quiet. Except maybe I can hear her trying not to cry.

"Kat?"

"I have to go," she says. "I have all this reading to do."

"I love you," I tell her. "None of this changes that.

Nothing will *ever* change that."

"I love you, too," she says, definitely sounding like she's crying now, and then hangs up.

I stare blankly at my phone. My throat feels kind of tight.

Riley's watching me, not even pretending to read his book. "Me getting hurt wasn't your fault."

I shake my head. "You wouldn't have been in that basement or at the gala if it wasn't for me."

"I would have still been at the gala."

"But you wouldn't have been being chased by heroes from the League. The same organization you spent your whole life wanting to join."

"Don't remind me. But... I wanted to help you. And you're not the one who pushed me and left me for dead under a pile of rubble."

"But—"

"Mason's the one who did that, and if I'd just listened to you about him, I wouldn't have even been in that situation. I've thought about it a million times—all the things that could have gone differently—and there are *so many* different choices I could have made, and if I had, neither one of us would have ended up where we did."

"My grandpa was only able to attack the gala because I helped him build up the Truth."

"But that's on him, not you. You thought you were helping villains get more rights, which you were. And if I hadn't ditched you for Mason, I never would have won that award and I wouldn't have been at the gala. I mean, I would have, because I would have been helping you stop that massacre, but it would have gone differently. And Mason wouldn't have been there."

"It wasn't your fault," I tell him.

"Yeah, but it wasn't yours, either. There are a million different choices either of us could have made, but none of them make what happened our fault. And obsessing over those choices doesn't change anything. And... maybe what happened that night was already the best possible outcome. Maybe if we'd done even one thing differently, it all would have gone even worse. But we don't know. We *can't* know."

I think about that. "And what about now? How do I know if I'm making the right choices?"

"I don't think you can. I think we just have to do what seems right in the moment and hope for the best."

"So, it's hopeless?"

"I didn't say that."

"Kat was really upset. About me quitting."

"For the record? Everyone is. Well, everyone who matters."

"I thought you said you were okay with it?"

"I said I *get it*. I didn't say it's what I wanted to happen. You were supposed to be there next year. We were supposed to be partners. And maybe I don't know what I'm doing after I graduate, but I just assumed you'd be part of it."

"Yeah, me, too."

"But now you're not. Because you think you're not hero material. Which is stupid, because if *you're* not hero material, then I don't know who is."

"You think I'm making a mistake?"

"I think you have to do what's right for you, and I think you're the only person who can decide that. But everyone's going to miss you."

"Not everyone. Maybe you guys will miss me, but the rest of the world will be glad I'm getting out. They'll be relieved that I'm just going to live a normal life where I don't bother anyone or put anyone in danger."

"Yeah, well, screw the rest of the world," Riley says. "They don't know what they're missing."

CHAPTER 35

I'm supposed to be helping Helen move boxes around the back room of her antique shop, but I'm kind of distracted. I mean, I *am* helping—I'm just also checking my phone every five seconds. It's past noon, and Kat hasn't answered any of my texts.

I've sent seven of them. Okay, eight, but only because I accidentally hit send before I was done typing, which doesn't count. I've kind of been having a one-sided conversation with myself all day, getting more and more worried. She probably forgot to charge her phone. Or she put it on silent, because she's in class or at the library, trying to catch up on homework. She's not ignoring me, or thinking it's really pathetic that I've continued to text her all day when she hasn't answered.

Kat's not like that. *We're* not like that. Sometimes we end up sending each other way more texts than that before the other one ends up writing back. Usually about funny stuff that happens to us, though. Not about, like, how sorry one of us is that his life fell apart and that he's quitting school and is never going to live up to his potential.

But an uncharged phone is an uncharged phone, no matter what your messages are.

Or maybe she's still too upset to talk about it, and she's waiting until she knows what to say to me. Or until she's alone, in case I make her cry again.

Great.

"It's a good thing I'm not paying you," Helen says, grinning so I know she's joking. "Come on. One more, and then we'll stop for lunch."

Helen doesn't usually eat until around one, since sometimes she gets customers who come in during their lunch hour, but the shop's been pretty quiet today. Or at least that's what she told me—I wouldn't know because I make it a point not to hang out in places where I might get roped into random acts of manual labor.

I made an exception today because Helen didn't present it as a choice, and because I didn't think she'd buy any of my excuses, what with my friends all still being in school during the day and my homework load suddenly non-existent. Also, it felt good to be needed for something, even if I kind of suspect she did it just to get me out of the house for a while, and I didn't want to disappoint her.

She grabs one end of a heavy wooden trunk, and I grab the other. It was part of an auction lot she got for cheap a while back that she still needs to sort through. Actually, there might be several lots' worth of stuff here, since the back room is pretty full.

"Alright," Helen says, "we're just moving it across the room for now, to get it out of the way. You ready?"

I nod. We both start lifting. It's really heavy.

Then my phone chimes with a text. "Oh, wait!" I say, dropping my side without thinking about it.

"Ow!" The trunk slips, knocking into Helen's leg—the bad one she always limps on—and she and the trunk both end up on the floor.

I can't believe I just did that. I kind of stare at her in shock, dread and guilt slithering through my chest. "Are you okay?" I'm almost afraid to ask.

Helen can't talk at first. I think she got the wind knocked out of her somehow, even though she landed on her butt, or that maybe she's crying or panicking or something. Then I realize she's laughing too hard to get any words out. Finally, she nods. "I'm okay."

"I don't get what's so funny." And if she's really okay, then I want to check my phone. Which probably makes me a bad person, but it's like there's this itching in my brain because I *know* it's Kat, finally texting me back, and I have to see what she said.

Helen shakes her head, still laughing. "You're the worst help I've ever had."

I'm not sure how I'm supposed to take that, so I reach out a hand to help her up.

She takes it.

I feel a little better once she's standing again, proving that she isn't actually injured or anything. "I helped you move all of those," I tell her, gesturing toward the stack of boxes and crates along the far wall. We spent all morning moving them, and then prying them open so she could inspect their contents. None of them contained any cool treasure, much to my disappointment—though maybe that's for the best, since the last 'cool treasure' I came across got incinerated—and the whole thing was actually pretty boring.

I also spent a good hour coloring with Jess in Helen's office, which Helen has set up with a baby gate so she can leave the door open and keep an eye on her whenever she has to go deal with customers. Then one of Helen's friends I've never met, who apparently also has a three-year-old, came by and picked up Jess for some kind of play group. The friend obviously knew who I was and got super nervous, but maybe in a scared kind of way, not in a can-I-have-his-autograph sort of way. Then Helen sent me to go make a new pot of coffee, which I spilled all over, and then she didn't even drink what was left, so I know it was just to get rid of me.

"Last time I recruited Trudy's son to help, and he moved everything all by himself while me and Trudy were still chatting."

I scowl at that. "Great." I have no idea who Trudy is—one of Helen's friends, I guess. "So her perfect son didn't, like, drop anything on you."

"I didn't mean it like that. I just... There's a big contrast, that's all."

Uh-huh. Now that she's insulted me, I take out my phone.

The text is from Sarah. It says, *Emergency meeting at Secant's house this afternoon. That means YOU, Renegade!*

So, not from Kat. And Sarah wants to meet up, probably to chew me out for quitting. I haven't told her yet, but I'm sure Riley has. And if she somehow doesn't know and the meeting's *not* to chew me out, it will be.

"Hey," I say to Helen, "can I ask you something?"

"Me?" She puts a hand to her chest. She seems genuinely shocked. "After that bad advice I gave you before?"

"What? What bad advice?"

"When I told you it was okay to quit. I told you that as long as you were on that path, someone you cared about would always get hurt."

"Well, they did."

She shakes her head. "I thought quitting would protect *you* from getting hurt. But... I forgot how hard it is." She glances down at her leg. Getting injured and losing her superpower was why she had to quit the League. "I've had a lot of time to come to terms with it, and some days I think I have, and some days I don't think I ever will."

"So, you're mad at me for quitting?" And after she said she'd support me on that.

"What? No. I just wish I'd kept my mouth shut."

"I would have done it anyway. And... sorry," I tell her. "About, you know, blabbing everything to Gordon."

She looks like she has to think about that, like she isn't even sure what I'm talking about. Then understanding dawns on her. "Oh. It's okay. I should have told him a long time ago."

But she didn't. She told me, and I managed to keep it to myself for not even two whole days. "I didn't mean to tell everyone like that."

"I know."

"And if you want me to move all those boxes by myself, then I'll—"

"No, no, it's okay. How we've been doing it is fine."

Good, because I don't know who Trudy's son is, but either he's crazy strong, or his boxes were *way* lighter than mine.

Helen's laughing again.

"What?" I ask her.

"He has super strength. Trudy's son. I wasn't expecting you to do all that."

"Oh." She could have said that earlier. "Why didn't you get him to come in again?"

"He's got finals. *And*, believe it or not, I enjoy your company." She heads into her office, stepping over the baby gate, and grabs our lunches out of the fridge. She comes back and hands me an egg-salad sandwich and a bottle of water. "Now, what did you want to ask me? Keeping in mind that I'm the last person who should be giving anyone advice, if it's that kind of question."

I sit down on a nearby table. "I think… I don't know. Kat's not answering my texts."

"Ah." She leans against the wall, where she can still see if anyone comes into the shop. "Did you try calling her?"

I look at her like she's insane. "I sent her *eight* texts. Either her phone's off or she doesn't want to talk to me. But it's not like her to go radio silent." That's more like something I would do, which it turns out really sucks from the other side.

"But you think she's upset about something?"

"Uh, yeah. I'm dropping out of school."

"She's upset that you're dropping out of *hero* school?" I can hear the skepticism in her voice, and I know she's still thinking of Kat as Bart the Blacksmith's granddaughter.

Now I kind of wish I hadn't brought it up. "Never mind."

"No, I just... I told you I wasn't good at advice." She tries to smile, to pass it off. Then she says, "Eight texts is a lot."

"I know."

"But you said she's not the type to not answer. She probably just forgot her phone."

"She's worried we're moving in different directions. It was bad enough when I got an X instead of a V, but now I'm this loser who couldn't even cut it as a hero."

"And that's what she's upset about?"

"She doesn't like that I'm giving up on myself. She thinks I'm going to be miserable if I'm not a hero."

"She's worried that you're going to be miserable, so she's not answering your texts?"

Well, when she puts it like that, it does sound kind of ridiculous. "Okay, probably not."

"I'm sure she'll call you later. By tonight, you'll know you were worrying for nothing."

"Yeah, you're probably right." At least, I really hope so.

X·X·X

Riley picks me up from the antique shop after he gets out

of school, and then we go over to his house. I'm kind of nervous about this meeting Sarah called. Or at least about telling her how her dream of all three of us becoming some amazing superhero team is never going to happen. And I still haven't heard from Kat, which is starting to really freak me out. And even though all that stuff Helen said makes perfect sense and I'm sure there's a good reason Kat hasn't answered me that doesn't involve her hating me or being dead in a ditch somewhere, I still can't help worrying.

"So," I ask Riley as we cross the yard to his front door, "did Sarah say what she wanted to talk about?"

"She didn't tell me any more than she told you."

Which sounds suspiciously like he *does* know something but doesn't want to tell me. "This isn't, like, some kind of intervention, is it? To get me to not give up on being a hero?"

"No. I mean, if it is, she didn't tell me. Why? Do you want it to—"

He shuts up as we walk into the house and gasps in shock. Zach and Amelia are on the couch, making out. Except 'making out' doesn't quite cover it, since they're practically horizontal and there are shirts out of place. Not off, just not all the way *on*. Thankfully I don't actually see anything, or at least nothing that will give me nightmares for the rest of my life.

Zach and Amelia pull away from each other, but they're both breathing kind of hard, and it's not like we don't know what we just walked in on.

"What the hell was that?" Riley says, glaring at Zach.

"What were you— What if Mom came in?!"

Zach swallows. His eyes dart over to mine, like he's not sure if I'm going to zap him or not.

"We were just going to your room," Amelia says. "Right, Zach?"

"Uh-huh." He takes her hand as they get up from the couch.

"*Zach*," Riley says. "Wait."

But I guess running off with Amelia overrides listening to his brother lecture him, because Zach acts like he doesn't hear. He and Amelia disappear into his room and close the door.

Riley still looks shocked. "That was weird, right?"

"Yep." I follow him into the kitchen.

"I thought they were broken up. And even when they were together, I've never seen them act like *that* before. Have you?"

"Other than finding condoms in your brother's room?"

"You know what I mean. And where were *you* back there? I thought you were against this."

I hold up my hands. "I said I was staying out of it."

"Two seconds ago they were broken up, and now they're practically having sex on the living room couch. But you're staying out of it."

"It's none of my business. That's what everybody kept saying."

"No, that's what *Zach* kept saying, because he didn't want you to be right."

"Yeah, well, maybe I wasn't right. And you can stop worrying about why they're back together. I fixed them."

He pauses in the middle of opening the fridge and stares at me in disbelief. "You fixed them."

"Don't say it like that. Look, Perkins, the only reason they broke up was because I interfered."

"You don't know that."

"So I told Amelia the truth. Sort of."

"Because you're 'staying out of it.'" He closes the fridge without taking anything out.

I sit down at the kitchen table. "I said it was my fault Zach was thinking about whether or not he loved her. I told her he wouldn't have said he only liked her at Prom if it wasn't for me."

Riley gapes at me. "But you don't know that, X!"

"I kind of do. He would have said *something* different."

He sits down across from me. "So now they're back together because Amelia thinks Zach might love her after all?"

"What happened was my fault. They never should have broken up in the first place. Does it really matter how they get back together?"

"*Yes!* She's going to find out he doesn't feel that way."

"Maybe he does."

Riley snorts. "If he loved her, he wouldn't have had to think about it."

"I'm not all that convinced she loves him, either. She just likes the idea of it."

"So, nothing's actually changed between them, but now they're back together under false pretenses. And because of that they're probably going to sleep together."

"Come on, Perkins. We don't know—"

He silences me with a look. Then he lets out a deep breath. "Zach's going to be heartbroken. And I know it's probably really not any of our business, but I don't think he's ready."

"To make use of the condoms? Or to have his heart ripped out again?"

"Both. Either one."

"Well, that's just great. Where were you a month ago when I was saying that?"

"I agreed with you! I don't know why you think I didn't. But I figured things would work themselves out. Which they kind of did, until you started meddling again."

"I was trying to fix what I broke. Actually, no, that's not true. I was trying to make Amelia hate me, which I guess I succeeded at."

CHAPTER 36

"We need a plan," Sarah says after she shows up for our meeting at Riley's house. She takes out a piece of blank paper from her notebook and puts it in the middle of the kitchen table. "That's for ideas."

"Ideas on what?" Riley asks.

"On how we're going to track down that fear ray and get it back." Sarah fishes a pen out of her backpack and sets it on top of the paper. "I can't believe that was *Frank* who hired us to get that ring for her. And I can't believe she called us *amateurs*."

"*Total amateurs*," I correct her.

"I know we failed to get the ring, but it's not like we still demanded payment. Which was very professional of us, so I don't know why she has to call us names. Well, she doesn't know who she's up against."

Except I kind of think she does. I glance over at Riley. "Didn't you tell her?" I whisper.

"I thought *you* should tell her," Riley says. "You're the

one who's dropping out."

Sarah wrinkles her forehead. "What?"

"I'm dropping out of Heroesworth." I say it fast, then brace myself for her reaction.

"Oh." She frowns a little, then goes back to what she was talking about before. "Frank's going to find out that we're more than a match for her. The job at the train station went south because of unforeseen circumstances, not because we're unqualified."

"Sarah? Didn't you hear me? I said I'm *dropping out*. I'm not going to go to hero school anymore."

"I heard you."

"You're not going to say anything?" I share a surprised look with Riley. Sarah's probably the last person who I thought would be understanding about this.

She sighs and pushes her glasses up the bridge of her nose. "We can discuss it later. Right now, finding the fear ray has to be our number-one goal. And this way you'll have more time for freelancing."

"Seriously? You're not, like, going to flip out and ask me what I'm going to do instead?"

"Okay," she says, sounding kind of annoyed, "what are you going to do instead?"

"No, that's— I wasn't trying to get you to ask. I just thought it was weird that you didn't."

"You can still be a hero. I don't go to Heroesworth and *I'm* still part of this group."

"I know, but—"

"You were really inconsistent about your time there, so I already resigned myself to the fact that you might not end up fully trained. At least, not formally, because we can all learn in the field. And you can still apply for colleges. Now, if we're going to find this fear ray, we're going to have to find Frank. And before you say it, that's not the name she told me when we were working for her, and I already tried calling the contact number she gave me, but it's disconnected."

"Sarah, wait. When I said I was dropping out of school, I meant I wasn't going to be a hero anymore."

"What?" She blinks at me. "That's ridiculous. Of course you're still going to be a hero. You have an *X*."

"Yeah, I have an *X*, not an *H*. I'm quitting."

"So, what, you're trying to be a villain again?"

"No. I'm just *out*. Of everything. No heroism, no villainy. I'm just going to be a normal person with a normal life and a... a normal job, who doesn't put his friends in danger or go looking for fear rays."

Sarah wrinkles her nose at that. "That doesn't sound like you."

"Well, it is me. Maybe it wasn't in the past, but this is how it has to be from now on."

She looks at Riley. "And you couldn't talk some sense into him?"

"It's his choice. If he wants to quit—"

"He *doesn't*." She turns to me. "And even if you misguidedly *think* you want to quit, you still have to find the fear ray first. You're the one who lost it into enemy hands, so it's your responsibility to get it back."

"Hey," Riley says. "I was there, too. It wasn't all Damien's fault."

"But he's supposed to be a hero. We were supposed to be a team. He can't just stop. Maybe you can drop out of school, but you can't drop out of your destiny."

Ouch. "If my destiny is to screw up over and over again while my friends keep getting hurt," I tell her, "then I don't want it. And yeah, I *can* just stop. The whole city's freaking out about this fear ray. That means *real* heroes are working on finding it and getting it back. I've caused enough damage, and they don't need me getting in the way and making things worse. Because that's what I do—I make things worse. And the city's made it pretty clear that they've had enough of me. So I'm sorry if it doesn't fit into your plan, but I'm quitting school, I'm quitting being a hero, and I'm quitting this group."

X·X·X

Me and Alex are sitting on the couch, playing a racing game he got for Christmas. It's about seven o'clock, and I still haven't heard from Kat. Which is freaking me out so much that I actually ate dinner with everyone instead of hiding in my room, since I needed the distraction. Even though it meant putting up with Amelia telling everyone how amazing it was to be back with Zach, and how in a few years from now they won't even remember this little blip on the road map of their relationship. And about how she can't wait until next fall, when they'll both be going to Heroesworth.

When she mentioned Heroesworth, Gordon looked over at me with this really hurt look on his face, like he was a puppy I'd just kicked, and all my insides kind of shriveled up. I pretended to be real interested in my phone, which I had out next to my plate so I wouldn't miss it if Kat texted me back. Gordon hasn't said anything to me about deciding to quit school, or about how badly I screwed up on Saturday, but I figure it's only a matter of time. Not that he seems mad or anything, since he would have yelled at me by now if he was, but he definitely seems sad. And disappointed. And I don't really know what to do with that.

"Yes!" Alex shouts as he narrowly avoids a giant cake that rolls across the screen. The racing game is dessert themed, and this is the baked-goods level, which is his favorite. I know that not only because he told me, but because he's had us play it, like, five times in a row. "Did you see that? That's the first time I— *Hey!*"

He's mad because I just hit pause. Because I'm pretty sure my phone just chimed. I grab it from the arm of the couch.

"It's no fun if you keep pausing all the time," he says.

"It's important." Except it's not, because it's not from Kat, and it's not even a text. Just an email from Sarah detailing all the reasons why she thinks I'm screwing up my life, as if she hadn't made it clear earlier. Oh, except her email includes a list of colleges she's thinking of applying to next year, along with some programs she thinks I might be interested in that would help facilitate a career in superheroing. Because even if I'm "taking a break," it doesn't mean I won't still need some skills when I come to my senses.

Which is *so* wrong because, for one thing, I already have skills. And for another, the programs she listed are things like robotics and chemistry and astrophysics. Which sound more like programs *she* would be interested in, not me. As if I could even get into a program like that, let alone actually finish it. I'm not even sure I could get into any of the schools she mentioned, especially since I don't plan to go back to regular school with her next year. I mean, I thought about it, but it turns out that a year of Heroesworth isn't exactly transferable, on account of us studying completely different things. So I'd be held back a year there, too. Figures.

Her email is at least a page long, but I only write back two words: *Not happening.*

"Okay, ready," I tell Alex as I hit the start button to unpause the game. Jumping back in where we left off is kind of disorienting, and we both end up swerving around and almost missing the next checkpoint.

Alex's car looks like an ice-cream sundae. Mine is a piece of tiramisu, which is one of the fastest cars in the game, even though it doesn't look very aerodynamic. The steering is horrible, though, which Alex warned me about when we started. Now he keeps tutting and shaking his head whenever my tiramisu careens off the road, like I really should have listened to him.

"Come on!" Alex screams at the TV. He leans forward as his sundae is just about to cross the finish line.

My phone chimes again. I press pause.

Alex groans. "This is your last pause. I mean it! After this, you can't do it anymore." He hesitates. "Unless it's a real emergency, like if the house is on fire or if you're about to throw up."

"I told you, it's... important." It's just another email from Sarah.

It says, *You could go to GCU. They'll take almost anybody, even someone with your reputation. It's my safety school, but I'd be willing to go there with you if you got in.*

Wow, so inspiring. I'm so glad there's a school out there with low enough standards that they'd still take a total loser like me.

When I don't answer right away, she adds, *You could study something besides science. Riley just pointed out that it's not your strong point.*

I write back, *Tell Perkins that subtlety isn't his strong point.* Then I set my phone down. If she emails again, I'll ignore it. I don't want her getting her hopes up because she thinks that me responding means I'm actually considering this.

"Please tell me you're ready," Alex says.

"Yeah, sure."

"That doesn't sound ready."

"I—" I shut up as Gordon wanders in from the kitchen. I say *wanders*, but maybe it's more like he's deliberately coming over here. To talk to me.

He sighs and rubs one side of his face. "Damien, I need to talk to you."

"I'm busy." I nudge Alex. "Tell him."

"He's busy, Dad," Alex says. "We're about to start playing again, and I told him he can't pause anymore. We have to do at least one whole round without stopping, and *then* you can talk to him."

What? Who told him he could say that? "Actually, I have, um, something I have to do after this."

"We need to discuss what happened," Gordon says. "I know I should have said something sooner, but I just couldn't—"

I press the start button. "Can't talk. Seriously. This game is really intense." Well, it is for about one second, and then Alex's car crosses the finish line. "I need total silence for this next round."

"After this round, then."

"I told you, I have something to do. I'm, uh, going over college programs with Sarah."

"Oh." He sounds dejected. And hurt. He's doing that whole kicked puppy thing again. "You know, son, you don't have to decide your future right away."

"But I'm really excited to major in business. Or maybe film studies."

"Is that where you get to watch movies?" Alex asks.

"Yes. Definitely." I have no idea what people in film studies do. I'm not 100% sure it's even a real major. "I can't wait."

"That's... that's great," Gordon says, sounding like it's anything but great. And like he might cry or something.

I pretend I don't notice and focus on the game.

"Okay," Alex says, "we're playing this level *one more time*, and there can't be *any* interruptions." He turns and gives Gordon a stern look, apparently not picking up on how upset Gordon is.

"Yeah," I add. "Whoever wins this round gets a

fabulous trip to the park tomorrow *and* one of the cookies I know Amelia has hidden in the cupboard."

Alex perks up at that. "I'm *so* going to win."

The race starts up. Gordon's still standing behind us, sighing and just generally looming, like he can't take the hint that I don't want to talk to him. What's the point? I screwed up. I made choices he doesn't like. He's upset about it. The end.

"Oh, yes!" Alex cries. "I hit the first check point already! I can practically taste victory!"

My phone rings. My heart pretty much stops beating when I see that it's Kat calling.

Alex shakes his head. "*No.* Do *not* pause the game! You promised."

I hit pause and drop my controller. "I forfeit. You win." I'm already grabbing my phone and swiping to answer it. "Kat?"

"Damien," she says, "I'm *so sorry*."

"Forfeiting is lame," Alex mutters. "You're no fun."

I ignore him. "Sorry for what? Are you okay?"

"Yeah. I overslept this morning—like, *way* overslept—and then I rushed out of here so fast that I forgot my phone. And when I came back this afternoon, my battery was dead, and then Tasha and Liv wanted to go meet up with everyone for pizza. And I was so tired, I almost didn't go with them, but Liv said Tristan's new girlfriend was going to be there and that she needed both of us for support. We only just got back a few minutes ago, and I turned on my phone, and, Damien, I had *no idea* you'd been texting me."

"I thought maybe... After last night, I thought maybe you just didn't want to talk to me."

Alex looks over, even though he's playing another round of the game on his own. Gordon's still sort of hovering behind us. I motion for him to go away, and he sighs and goes back into the kitchen.

"Of course I want to talk to you," Kat says. "Even if I'm upset, I never don't want to talk to you."

"I was getting really worried. About you. I thought you were either avoiding me or that something horrible had happened."

"You mean like when you disappeared and ran away to live with your grandparents without telling anyone?"

Hot guilt slithers through my chest. "Yeah, like that. But I'm kind of irresponsible and inconsiderate. You're not."

"I'm okay. I just haven't been sleeping well the past few days."

I can't help but notice that *the past few days* is basically the same amount of time that Frank's been on the loose with the fear ray, no thanks to me. Not that I think Kat's stressing that hard over the fear ray in particular, but getting stabbed through the hand and then almost dying in a fire and then being questioned by the police for hours wasn't exactly a relaxing day off. "Are people being weird to you? About me?" Because it was already public knowledge that me and Kat are a thing, and now the fact that I was illicitly working with my supervillain girlfriend on a Heroesworth assignment is in pretty much every news segment and article being written about me.

"No," Kat says. "I mean, kind of. Not my friends or anything, but a couple of people have given me dirty looks or come up to me and asked why I let you give that fear ray to Frank on Saturday. Which isn't what happened, and I told them that."

"So, people are harassing you at school. Because of me."

Alex looks over again at that, then quickly back at his game.

"Just a few people," Kat says. "It's not a big deal. It's not anything like what you have to deal with."

"But—"

"It's not your fault. And there's only a few more weeks of school, and by next year everyone will have forgotten about it."

True. Hopefully, anyway, because by then I will have spent a whole summer being a non-hero and not getting into trouble or causing any scandals. "Listen, Kat, about last night." I take a deep breath. This isn't really a conversation I want to have in the living room, with Alex totally listening in and Gordon and Helen probably able to hear me, too. I should go up to my room, but I don't think I can talk on the phone and go up the stairs at the same time, or at least I don't think I can do it while talking about anything important. And after not hearing from Kat all day, I'm afraid to hang up, even if it's just to call her back in a few minutes.

"I overreacted," Kat says.

"No, you didn't. I'm sorry for all the stupid things I said, and I'm sorry for not being who either of us wanted me to be."

"Damien. That's not—"

"Maybe this was always going to happen, and that night at the gala just made it happen that much sooner. Or maybe it screwed everything up to begin with. I don't know. And I know you think I'm making a mistake, but this is what I have to do."

"I want you to be happy," Kat says, her voice quiet. "I don't want you to throw everything away."

"I know. And I don't want you to be disappointed in me."

"I'm not. I'm just worried about you. You wanted to be a hero so bad. Enough to put up with going to Heroesworth for *an entire year*."

"I wouldn't say an *entire* year. Just most of one."

"It's still a big deal. And I was so excited to get to work with you. It made it seem like maybe me being a villain and you being a hero was actually going to work. Like maybe it took a long time to get there, but our original plans we had before you got an *X* might not have been so crazy. But then one stupid mission with me goes wrong and you want to quit."

I wince. "It's not like that. It's not because of you."

"You said you didn't want your friends to get hurt. Well, I didn't want *you* to get hurt. Because that knife was aimed right at you, and it... it would have killed you. You think that doesn't bother me?"

"Of course it does," I tell her, though the truth is I hadn't really thought about it.

"Because I don't know what I would do without you.

And if that knife had gotten to you when I could have stopped it... I don't even want to think about it. And yeah, it hurt like hell when it went through my hand, but I can heal. And even if I couldn't, I still would have done it, if it meant saving your life."

"I don't want you to have to get hurt because of me. Not you, not Riley, not anyone."

"It's fieldwork, Damien. Sometimes it's dangerous. Sometimes people get hurt. That's just the job. It's not because of you."

"We were there because of me. Tristan wanted to leave, and nobody wanted to go down those stairs."

"You didn't force us to be there. And Tristan was just whining because it wasn't his idea. He *always* does that."

"He does?" I mean, I can totally see that.

"Yeah. I've gone on enough missions with him to know how he is. It didn't help that it was *your* idea, either. And not because there's something wrong with you, but because he's jealous of you."

"Well... *obviously*."

"Even if you weren't there, we still would have gone in, because I didn't come all that way just to be scared off by some boarded-up windows."

"But you wouldn't have gone down those creepy stairs."

"Probably not," she admits. "But that doesn't mean Frank still wouldn't have come after us or gotten the fear ray."

"I set off the trap. I thought the fear ray looked cool, and I grabbed it without thinking."

Kat scoffs. "There was no way you could have known it was trapped."

"No, but I just... Maybe I didn't mean for any of that to happen, but bad things still happened to you guys because of me."

"First of all, no they didn't. But second of all, so what if they did? Because guess what? Making sure nothing bad ever happens to anyone isn't your responsibility."

"Kat—"

"And if it *is* your responsibility to make sure that everything goes absolutely perfectly, why even have a team, huh? I mean, you're the only one who's allowed to ever be in any kind of danger, right? So why not leave everyone else at home and just go by yourself."

"Because the school wouldn't let me?" I say that to lighten the mood, because I hate that she sounds mad at me, but she doesn't laugh.

"The school wouldn't let you work with us, either, but you still did it. But you don't choose to go on missions by yourself. And if you tried, I'm betting Riley wouldn't let you. *I* wouldn't let you. And neither would Sarah."

"I... I didn't say I wanted to do it alone."

"No, but you can't handle working with anybody, so you've just decided to sit everything out. That's the real reason you're quitting, isn't it?"

"I told you. My friends keep getting hurt because of me."

"No, not because of you. Your friends *choose* to take that risk all on their own. And all you see is that you put them in danger, when really you do everything you can to protect them. You put everything on yourself, and that's not fair."

"Everything that happened at the gala was my fault." I hate how tight my voice sounds when I say that. How anyone listening couldn't help but hear how much it messed me up. "I know Grandpa was responsible for most of it. I *know* that, but it still feels like... I should have been there."

"You *were* there. You did everything you could to—"

"I should have been there when Riley got hurt!" I clench my fist. "He was trying to distract the League, so they'd leave me alone."

"So you could save everyone. Damien, you needed him to do that. Everyone at the gala would have died if he hadn't done that for you."

"I know." My voice sounds really tight now, and I know Alex notices, because he glances over again, a worried, kind of scared look on his face. "But I still hate that I wasn't there."

"He was with Mason. You didn't know—"

"I knew Mason was a douchebag."

"But you still didn't know he would do *that*. Nobody did. Mason probably didn't even know."

"I could have stopped it. I could have—"

"No, you couldn't. You can't control everything. You can't control other people. They get to make their own choices, the same as you."

"But if I'd been there—"

"Then everyone at the gala would have died, including Riley. Including *you*. We all took risks. Your arm got burned pretty bad when you came to help me and Sarah. You always downplay it, because of what happened to Riley, but someone from the League *shot you* with a raygun. I hate that that happened to you. But it did, and it happened because you were trying to save me, and that really scares me sometimes. But that doesn't mean it was my fault or that we didn't need your help, just like how you needed Riley's help and how what happened to him wasn't your fault. And if something had happened to me, then—"

"Don't even say that, Kat."

"But if it had, that wouldn't have been your fault, either."

"I... I don't know how to feel that way. I don't know how to let go of all this. And if I'd just stayed away from Grandpa and the Truth, then all that stuff at the gala wouldn't have happened. Riley wouldn't have gotten hurt, and we'd still like fieldwork, and I wouldn't be... you know."

"You were like this before the gala, though. You've never been a team player."

"What does that mean?" And why does she say that like it's a bad thing?

"You always call all the shots. Like when you got in trouble for zapping that superhero last semester."

"I thought he was a murderer."

"I know, and I get why you zapped him, but when you told me about it, you said Riley told you not to do it. But you didn't listen to him."

"So?"

"So, you probably didn't even think about listening to him. You always have to be in control."

"I don't... I don't *always*."

"Damien, I *know* you, and yes, you do. You know you do. You and Riley were supposed to be partners, but you didn't let him have a say in anything."

"Well, I mean, when he agreed with me I did."

"Uh-huh. You made yourself in charge of everything, just like you're making yourself in charge of whether or not anybody else gets hurt. But none of that is your job. You're not supposed to call all the shots, and you're not supposed to take all of the risks. We all have different skills and abilities, and we all have to look out for each other and share the danger. That's what makes us a team. But you taking everything on yourself and thinking you'd somehow rather take a *knife* to the chest than let me get hurt at all isn't helping anyone. It's just driving you crazy. You can't control everything."

"I can try."

"But you shouldn't. And even if you quit being a hero, it's not going to solve anything, because you'll still be making the same mistakes."

"But at least no one else will get hurt."

"That's not true. You can't control what happens to everyone, and either way, *you'll* get hurt. And I don't want that for you. Nobody does."

CHAPTER 37

It's the middle of the afternoon the next day, and I'm sitting on my bed, staring at my phone. Specifically at the GCU website, because maybe after another five emails Sarah kind of got to me. Or at least made me curious, because I still don't think I would get in or that going there really sounds like me. But maybe it wouldn't be so bad, as far as settling goes, because at least then I wouldn't be alone. Not that me and Sarah would end up having a lot of the same classes, but still. And if I'm going to have a normal job, maybe I should aim slightly higher than gas-station attendant or waiter in a polyester cape.

Actually, when I mentioned that to Sarah, she pointed out that I'm probably the last person anyone would want working at a gas station, what with my tendency to go all electric, and that I'd probably end up blowing the whole place up. So I guess that just leaves the diner option.

The website shows lots of pictures of really happy students smiling into the camera while looking up from their textbooks or lounging on the grass with their friends. The sun is shining and the lighting is perfect and everybody looks like they're having fun and not worrying about what they're going to do with their lives.

I hate to admit it, but it looks kind of nice. I try to picture myself there, meeting up with Sarah to do homework and inviting everyone over for movie nights. *Everyone* probably meaning Kat and Riley, who will most likely be too busy with their villain and hero careers, two things I really, *really* wanted to have at some point but gave up on. Not that I'll resent them for it or anything, but I'm pretty sure that when they talk about moving on with their lives and getting cool jobs and stuff that I will feel left out.

But that's going to happen anyway, so wouldn't I at least like to be able to pretend I've got something figured out when it does? Wouldn't I like to be able to say, "Hey, will you guys shut up about all the exciting missions you've been going on, because I have all this Business Finance homework to do?"

Ugh. On second thought, I'm pretty sure I *wouldn't* want to be able to say that.

And I can't really picture myself doing homework with Sarah, since hers will probably involve building robots and doing lots of crazy math or something, and mine will involve... Well, *not* that. And it's one thing for all these students in the photos to look so happy—besides probably being models who are getting paid for it—because they're not the Crimson Flash's delinquent half-villain son the whole city knows about. Nobody's seen videos of them blowing up the gym at Heroesworth, and nobody blames them for letting some criminal wreak havoc on the city with that fear ray. Not that Frank's actually wreaking havoc with it yet, or at least not that anybody knows about, but it's only a matter of time. And either way, everyone's terrified at just the idea, which is bad enough. And if I went to that school, everyone would know who I was, and they'd know that once upon a time I was trying to be a hero but couldn't cut it. They'd look at me with contempt or at best feel sorry for me, which isn't really any better.

I mean, that would still be a step above how people treat me at Heroesworth, so that's something, I guess.

And maybe it wouldn't go that way at all. Maybe nobody would care who I was or how many videos of me they'd seen on YouTube. And maybe my friends wouldn't be too busy for me, and I wouldn't even care if they were moving forward with their lives because I would be, too. *Maybe.*

But then I scroll through the list of majors, and I get this horrible sinking feeling, because I know my heart wouldn't be in any of these.

A knock on my door startles me. I didn't realize anybody was home, since Amelia's over at Zach's and it's too early for anybody else. Then Gordon says, "Damien?"

I could pretend I'm not here. I could tell him to go away and hope he actually listens. But instead I put my phone away and tell him to come in, because we might as well get this over with.

"We need to talk," Gordon says. He paces across the

room a couple times, not even watching out for the creaky boards, which makes my stomach lurch a little bit. He runs a hand through his hair and lets out a deep breath. Then he sits down next to me on the bed, resting his elbows on his knees and his chin in his hands.

He doesn't say anything right away, and every second of silence makes me feel more and more like I can't breathe. I sit up, bracing myself. "Dad, just say it already."

He shakes his head. "I don't know what to say."

Seriously? He must have come home early from work just so he could corner me, and now he *doesn't know what to say*? "Let me make it easy for you. I screwed up, the whole city hates me, and on top of that you're disappointed in me for deciding to quit. And you're going to say you're—"

"Damien, I'm not disappointed in you."

"—not disappointed in me, but we both know you are, so. I was going to say don't bother, but you already did."

"I'm not disappointed in you."

I raise an eyebrow at him. His shoulders are hunched, his mouth is turned down, and if I had to suggest a photo definition for the word *disappointed*, this would be it. "You don't exactly look happy or anything."

"Of course I'm not happy. All of this, everything that's been going on, it's just so..." He trails off, apparently still not able to say it. Then he changes his mind and adds, "It's just so hard to deal with."

I swallow. *I'm hard to deal with.* That's what he just said, or it's what he meant, at least. "Okay. Great."

"Damien—"

"No, I get it. I screwed up, and I deserve whatever you're about to say to me. And it's obvious that you *are* disappointed—we both know you are—so just admit it."

"I am," he says, his voice quiet and full of shame.

And now that he's said it, I wish he hadn't. I wish I hadn't just made him do that, because knowing it was one thing, but hearing it is so much worse. I pull my knees up, hugging them to my chest and wishing I could disappear.

"But not with you," Gordon says. "I'm disappointed in myself."

"What?"

He spreads his hands out. "I feel like I've failed you as a father."

"Um, *what*?"

"I wanted you to follow in my footsteps. I hoped, anyway. And I know that's part of why you went to Heroesworth in the first place."

"It was my choice. I wanted to go. And I told you before, that wasn't why."

He gives me a side look, like he doesn't quite buy that. "I wanted you to do the same things I did. I wanted us to share those experiences, and… for you to be like me."

"Dad—"

"But you're not. And your life isn't like mine. And I should have realized that sooner." He scratches the side of his face, looking kind of guilty. "We're different people, and that's okay. But I wanted certain things for you, and they didn't work out. I watched how hard you struggled with going to Heroesworth and how hard you tried to keep up with everything that was happening to you, and I didn't do anything about it."

"There wasn't anything you could have done. And none of it had anything to do with you."

"I could have been there for you."

"You *were*." Mostly.

"I hate that there's nothing I can say to help you. You've been going through something awful, and I wish I could fix it, but I can't. I don't even know what to say."

"So?" It's my problem, and I don't remember asking him to fix it, whatever that even means.

"My father always used to know what to say."

I scoff and lean back against my pillows. "Your dad's a douchebag. I bet he said stupid crap to you like *buck up* and *win one for the team*."

One side of Gordon's mouth turns up in a smile. "You're too young to realize I don't have all the answers."

Is he serious right now? "I hate to break this to you, but I've known that since the moment we met. I never expected anything like that from you, so don't worry about it."

He winces. He looks like he's about to say something to that, then hesitates.

I decide to change the subject. "I've been looking at GCU. Sarah thinks I can get in." I say that too fast, like I'm not that comfortable with the idea, which is true, and like I'm terrified of what he might say next if left to his own devices, which is also true.

Gordon nods. There's a pained expression on his face, as if someone just kicked him in the shins and he's trying not to show it. "So. Business, huh?"

"I prefer film studies."

"That's... great. I'm happy for you, that you have something to work towards." But he says that like he's eating sawdust and telling me how wonderful it tastes.

"I lied." Maybe it's because I feel sorry for him, or maybe it's because the words felt wrong coming out of my mouth, but I suddenly really need him to know the truth.

"What?"

"I'm not thinking about film studies. Or business or whatever. I... I'm not going to college."

"You could," he says. "You're a smart kid. If you want to go—"

"I don't. It's just something that Sarah said, and I thought..." I shrug. "It doesn't matter, because I looked at the list of majors and I thought about the careers I could have, and I'm not interested in any of them." None of them feel even remotely right. I know deep down that they don't. "But the one thing I was interested in stopped being fun for me, like, months ago. And then I failed the flying test, and I failed Advanced Heroism, and the whole city hates me, and on top of that, my friends are disappointed in me. Kat and Sarah are, anyway. And Amelia. I mean, Kat says she's not, but I feel like she is." And like even if she really isn't, she probably should be. "And me and Riley were supposed to be partners, and now we're not. I'm not going to work with him and Sarah, and everything's falling apart. Maybe I'm making a stupid decision, but I just couldn't do it anymore. And giving up all of that isn't easy. Quitting Heroesworth—really quitting—is hard. When I was going there, I had no idea what my future would be, and it was kind of terrifying, but at least I had a *direction*. I was aiming toward something, even if I didn't know what it was. Now I just have nothing."

Gordon takes a deep breath, then lets it out slowly. Finally, he says, "You don't have to have anything figured out. Actually, I'm kind of glad you don't."

"What if I never figure it out, though? What if I never find anything that makes me happy like fieldwork did?"

"I don't know."

"You don't know? What kind of stupid answer is that? You're supposed to say that *of course* I'll find something else."

"I can't promise you that, because I really don't know. But you'll be okay." He clears his throat real quick, then says, "Ted told me about the flying test."

My whole body tenses up when he mentions Ted's name. I kind of hoped we wouldn't have to talk about this. "He was lying. Whatever he told you, it wasn't true."

"Damien, he said you weren't nearly as bad as he thought you would be. I know how that sounds, but it's high praise coming from him. Especially given... the situation."

The situation being that Ted hates me, he means. "But I still failed."

"But I'm still really proud of you."

"For flying?" Hopefully he won't ask how I learned. I think he's the one person on the planet Amelia hasn't blabbed to.

"For trying so hard at something that was so difficult

for you. If you can do that, then you can do anything, and I know I don't need to worry about you. Things might be hard now, but you'll figure it out. You always do."

"Everything's falling apart."

"Not everything. You still have your family and your friends. Everyone cares about you because of who you are, not because of what you're doing with your life."

But I thought being a hero, or even being a villain, was a big *part* of who I was. I glance down at the *X* on my thumb, wishing it could tell me what to do.

Then Gordon says, "Listen, Damien, about what you were saying earlier… about not expecting things like that from me—"

"It's fine. I wasn't trying to get at anything."

"You're my son. I want you to expect things from me. Even if it's unreasonable, like that I have all the answers."

"I think I made it clear that I know that you *don't*. Besides, I'm not a little kid. I don't need that."

"When you said you didn't expect *anything like that* from me, you meant you don't expect me to be your father."

He looks me in the eyes as he says that, and I feel sick. I look away. At the bedspread, at the ceiling, at my Superstar poster on the wall. My mind races, trying to come up with excuses for why I can't be here right now or for why he needs to leave, but I can't think of anything. "I didn't… I told you, don't worry about it."

"I know I missed out on most of your life, and that means there are some things we can't get back. I never tucked you in at night or taught you to ride a bike. I don't know what your favorite bedtime stories were or when you lost your first tooth. I don't even know what you looked like."

"Mom has pictures," I mumble. If she hasn't gotten rid of them to make room for ones of Xavier. My grandparents would still have some, though.

"That's not my point. I never got to protect you from the monsters under your bed."

"I didn't need protection from them. I set up traps." At least until Mom stepped on one. Then I never heard the end of it. "And just because you weren't there doesn't mean I was alone. I had Mom. I had Grandma and Grandpa. I didn't *need* anyone else." And now that they've all betrayed me, I don't need them, either. "I wasn't sitting around wondering where you were, and you didn't even know I existed. You don't owe me anything. You don't have to try and fix my problems or say stuff to make me feel better."

"Yes, I do. You're my son."

"Yeah, but… I can take care of myself."

"I wish you felt like you could rely on me."

"I don't know why you want that." I don't know why he can't just be happy with how things are. He gets to buy me food and clothes and stuff and feel like he's taking care of me, and I don't ask for anything difficult or complicated. Most of the time, anyway. Unless I screw up. And even then, I try to keep it to the minimum.

"You don't know why I want that," he repeats, sounding numb.

I don't say anything.

"Okay," Gordon says. "Obviously you have a lot to think about. With everything that's going on. I'll just... I'll leave you alone." He gets up to go, then hesitates.

I hold my breath, afraid he's going to change his mind and stay. Afraid he's going to say something he can't take back. Or worse, that I will.

But then his shoulders deflate, and if he was considering saying something else, he doesn't. He just leaves.

CHAPTER 38

"I don't want to talk to you," Amelia says. At least I think that's what she says—it's kind of hard to understand her, since she's crying so hard. She also kind of says it into her pillow, which she's currently squeezing the life out of.

I'm standing in her doorway. She just got home from hanging out with Zach, and I heard her stomp her way up the stairs like she couldn't get to her room fast enough. Then she sent me a text that said, *I hope you're happy. Me and Zach broke up again, just like you wanted.* "If you didn't want to talk to me, why did you text me?"

"Because. You didn't want us to be together, and now you got your wish. So just close the door and go away."

I close the door, but I don't go away. "Amelia—"

"I figured you'd hear it from Zach soon anyway, and I didn't want him to be the one to tell you."

"I didn't want you guys to break up. I never said that I did." I move closer to the bed, but I don't sit down. I just stand there awkwardly, imagining all the possible reasons they could have broken up after what me and Riley walked in on yesterday. "What happened?"

"None of your business. It's private." She stares down into her pillow, not looking at me.

My blood suddenly runs cold. I think of what Riley said yesterday, about how Amelia and Zach were going to end up sleeping together under false pretenses. Because of me. "Amelia... what happened?"

She sniffs really big and shakes her head. "I don't want to tell you. Can't Kat come over again?"

"She's at Vilmore. And she'd tell me anything you told her."

"No, she wouldn't."

"Yes, she would. And whatever it is... you can tell me."

"I can't." She sniffs again as more tears slide down her face. "You're my brother. And you're Zach's friend."

"I was both of those things last time and you still told me."

"But you only pretended to comfort me, because you felt guilty, so I don't know how I'm supposed to trust you, even if I did want to talk about it with you, which I *don't*."

"I wasn't pretending to comfort you. I meant it. And it wasn't because I felt guilty." Well, not *only* because of that.

She gives me a mean look, her voice bitter. "You sat here that whole night with me, trying to make me feel better, but you knew what really happened. You knew it was because of *you* that my heart got broken, and you didn't even care."

"That's not true." I glance down at the floor, then back up at her. "Did you sleep with Zach?"

"*What? No.* No way. I told you I wasn't going to do that." But she says it to her pillow, not me, and her face turns kind of red. Well, it was already kind of red from crying, but now it's even worse.

Okay, great. This would be an excellent time to get Kat on the phone. Except maybe I don't want my girlfriend and my sister discussing their sex lives—one of which involves me—especially while I'm in the room. I mean, there's no way I'd leave the room, either, so it's kind of a non-option. "So. It, um, didn't go so well?"

"Oh, my God! I just told you I didn't sleep with him! I'm not *like that*."

"Uh-huh. Just like you weren't 'like that' on the couch with him yesterday."

"Shut up."

"Are you okay?"

"I *didn't* do it!"

"If you say so. But it's still a valid question."

"I..." Her face falls, and her shoulders sort of deflate. "I was thinking about it. I mean, we almost... we *almost* did it."

I'm not sure I want to know what that means. "Okay. Great talk. I think we're done here."

"I know what I said, about waiting, but I also really wanted to do it. But it was weird because we went to his room, and he already had condoms."

"Well, yeah. You weren't going to do it if he *didn't*, right?"

"No, but... it just seemed weird. Like, he said he got them a while ago for just in case, but that means he was thinking about it."

I give her a look like *duh*. Even though I was shocked to find them, too. But I'm not, like, going out with him.

"But I wasn't thinking about it. Not like *that*, like it was really going to happen. It all felt scary and real all of a sudden. And it wasn't anything he did, so don't get mad at him or anything. At least, not about that part. You can get mad at him in a minute. But I was really..." She glances up at me, like she's weighing whether or not to finish that sentence. "I was really overwhelmed. Were you overwhelmed? Your first time?"

"Um. I thought you didn't want to hear about that. I'm your brother."

"I know, but none of my friends have ever done it. Only your friends, and they're not here. So were you overwhelmed?"

"No."

"Is that just a boy thing? Was *Kat* overwhelmed?"

"*No*. I mean, I don't think so." I sit down on the bed.

"So, there's something wrong with me."

"Maybe you're just not ready. And it still felt like a big deal, even if I wasn't overwhelmed."

"Did you plan it out?"

"Look, Amelia, maybe you should just finish your story. Tell me why I should be mad at Zach."

"If you won't tell me, I'll just ask Kat, and she'll tell me everything, even the parts you don't want me to know."

Erg. "She won't."

"She already told me you lied about having phone sex. I'll just ask her if you made it special and had, like, rose petals all over the bed and stuff."

"No rose petals. Geez. Who does that?"

"I saw it in a movie. So, did you plan it out? Or was it spontaneous?"

"Both? I don't know. It's not like either of us said, 'Hey, I have five minutes free at exactly seven p.m. tomorrow. You want to lose our virginities?'"

Amelia wrinkles her nose. "Five minutes?"

"Half an hour. Whatever. It wasn't planned out, but it wasn't like we didn't know we were going to."

"Did you take her to dinner first?"

"What, like, *ever*?"

"No, that night."

"It wasn't at night. It was during the day, on one of those prospective student tours at Vilmore. Kat had gotten her acceptance letter and wanted to see the campus again. I went with her, even though I didn't get in. Spring semester was over and summer classes hadn't started yet, so the dorms were mostly empty. We ended up breaking off from the tour, and Kat pulled me into a room nobody was living in, and then it just sort of happened."

"*She* pulled you into the room? So, you weren't thinking about it?"

"Of course I was thinking about it. We both were. Kat just acted on it first."

"And then what happened?"

"I don't know. Then we went and had lunch in the cafeteria."

"Like it was nothing?"

"No, like it was time for lunch. What else would we do?"

"It's supposed to change your life. You even said it was a big deal. So it seems weird to just go have lunch afterward, especially in a cafeteria. That doesn't sound very romantic."

I shrug. "It was the next part of the tour."

"Did you at least pay for hers?"

"No. And what's your obsession with me buying her food? You make it sound like I owed her something."

"That's what guys are supposed to do. To show their appreciation, I guess."

"That's creepy. And Kat paid for lunch. For both of us. Well, technically her dad paid for it, since he gave her the money for the trip, but whatever."

"So, it didn't change your life?" She wrinkles her forehead in disbelief.

"I don't know. Not that much. Can we get back to what happened with you and Zach already?"

"In a minute. So, you didn't do anything to make it special for her?"

I sigh. "It *was* special. And I don't know why you think that's my responsibility."

"Because. Girls aren't supposed to... you know."

I raise an eyebrow at her. "Aren't supposed to what?"

"Have sex. Because their lives might get ruined and then the boys just get to walk away. That's what Tiffany's grandma told us. She's really old, and out of nowhere one day she said, 'Don't you girls ever let any boys into your hen house, because they're all foxes who will leave you high and dry.' We were trying not to laugh when she said it, but it was also really scary."

"That's not going to happen."

"How do you know?"

"Because me and Kat are careful."

"But it could still happen. That's what they taught us in school. No matter what you do, it could still happen, and every time a girl has sex, it's like playing Russian roulette with your future."

"Seriously? They told you that in school?"

"Only this one teacher. She was kind of crazy, though. I think mostly she was trying to scare us."

"We're not playing Russian roulette, okay? It's not like that."

"But—"

"We're not. And if Kat got pregnant, the last thing I would do is walk away."

"You say that now, but you don't really know."

"*Yes*, I do, Amelia. My mom raised me by herself. She had sex with some random guy in a dirty subway bathroom—*without* a condom or anything—and she got pregnant with me and never saw him again. Well, until I tracked him down."

Amelia looks kind of sick. "Okay, we can talk about me now."

"She didn't tell Gordon about me. He probably would have been there if she did. But he wasn't, and she was alone, and I would *never* do that to Kat. So don't tell me I don't know."

Amelia nods, not saying anything at first. Then she whispers, "Did you... did you miss him?"

"No." I stare down at my knees. "There was nothing to miss."

"But you said you tracked him down. So—"

"I was curious, after I got my *X*. I didn't know Mom had slept with a superhero until then, and I wanted to know how bad the damage was."

"But didn't you want—"

"*No.*"

"You don't even know what I was going to say."

"It doesn't matter, because I didn't want anything from him." I still don't. "Just tell me about what happened with Zach."

"But—"

"Amelia."

"Okay, okay." She takes a deep breath and props her hands behind her on the bed, steadying herself. "We went to his room, and things happened really fast. I kind of wanted them to, and I know Zach did, too, because he showed me the condoms. And then I felt kind of freaked out, because it meant it could really happen. But I didn't say anything, because we'd just gotten back together, and I didn't want anything to go wrong between us. I didn't want him to think I didn't want to, even though I wasn't sure. And then..." She glances over at me, then down at the bed. "Things went really far. I mean, we went farther than we had before. And Zach was really into it, but I couldn't stop thinking about how he'd been kind of planning this and I hadn't, and how it might actually happen and what that would mean and how I couldn't picture myself as someone who'd had sex. And there was also this fear building up in me, because of the whole Russian roulette thing."

"The teacher that told you that was messed up. Just for the record."

"In my mind, I was like, 'What would Mom and Dad say if I got pregnant?' So suddenly I was picturing myself having to tell them, and how ashamed I would be. And Zach was taking his clothes off, and I didn't think he was thinking about that, about what he would have to tell his mom if something happened. And that made me feel really alone, even though he was right there. So I told him I loved him again. And he said"—she sucks in a breath, her voice getting high-pitched and new tears springing to her eyes—"he said, 'I really like you, Amelia.' That's it. That he *likes* me. And he said it like he thought it was okay for him to say that back to me after I told him I loved him. Like this is how it was going to be between us. And I realized even though we were back together, and even though you said you were the reason he said all that at Prom, that nothing had changed. I broke up with him because he didn't love me, and that was still true."

"I'm sorry I interfered. And I'm sorry I told you all that, about it being my fault."

"Well, it *was*."

"I know. But… I made it sound like something happened that didn't. I should have stayed out of it."

"Well, then I kind of freaked out. Because he was opening one of the condoms, like this was *really* going to happen, and he had no idea how upset I was. I told him I made a mistake, that I couldn't do it. I started getting dressed really fast, so he would know what I meant. And he asked me what was wrong, because I guess he really didn't know, and I said getting back together with him was a huge mistake. That we shouldn't have been doing what we were doing, because that was a huge mistake, too. I was kind of mean, because I was so freaked out, and he started crying when he realized I was breaking up with him again. He said we didn't have to sleep together, that he wasn't trying to pressure me. And I know he wasn't, but it wasn't just about that. He doesn't care about me the way I care about him. So it's over, for reals this time. And I don't know what he's going to tell you, but that's how it happened for me."

"At least you guys were honest with each other. It could have gone a lot worse."

"But now I know Zach's never going to love me, and he's not going to be my first, and I don't know what I'm going to do."

"You want to watch the sad movie?"

"The movie's not sad—it's *happy*. I just watch it when I'm sad. You'd know that if you'd paid attention when we watched it."

"I *was* paying attention. That lady's boyfriend left her for another woman, and then she got fired from her job, and then her dog got sick. You don't call that sad?"

"That was only the beginning part. Her dog got better, and she met that veterinarian guy who was a way better boyfriend, *and* if she hadn't gotten fired, she wouldn't have decided to start her own clothing line, and she wouldn't have been so successful. So it was happy. And yes, I want to watch it."

"You want me to call Kat? We can put her on speaker phone."

"No. I don't want to have to tell anyone else what happened yet. So that means it's just you, and you have to pay attention this time. And no texting with Riley while we watch, because I'll know you guys are talking about me."

I put my phone on silent. "There. Happy now?"

"No," she says, her mouth turning down, and I know she's not talking about my movie-watching habits.

"It's his loss, Amelia."

She nods, but her eyes are full of tears, and she's too choked up to say anything.

CHAPTER 39

"That's what you called me over here for?" I ask Grandpa. I'm over at his house, because he called and said he had something urgent to discuss. I wasn't really planning on getting out of bed before ten, what with having nothing to get up for, but he made it sound important.

"The auction's tonight," he says. "I thought you'd want to know."

"You could have told me over the phone. Or in a text." And then I could have told him exactly what I'm going to tell him now. "I'm not going."

"I'm not telling you this because I think you've got money to burn, kid. I'm telling you because Frank's auctioning off that fear ray you let him—er, *her*—get a hold of."

"Don't say it like that." I rub my finger across a stain on the table. "I was protecting Kat. And Frank would have taken it anyway." I know I said it was my fault, but hearing Grandpa blame me just feels wrong. Like maybe it really *wasn't* all on me.

"However you want to look at it, Frank still took that fear ray on your watch. Getting it back sounds like the kind of thing you'd want to do."

"Well, I don't."

"It's going to be a big auction. More weapons than just that fear ray are going to be up for grabs. It's the big-ticket item, so they won't put it up first. Maybe not until the end."

"Great. I still don't see why you couldn't have told me over the phone."

"I wanted to make sure and go over the details with you. I don't like the idea of my grandson hanging out at a place like that, especially with the intent to steal the best item at the auction. The best I can do is make sure you're well informed."

"It's not going to happen."

"I didn't think you could face off against Frank and live to tell about it, and I was wrong. And… I know how much something like this must be weighing on you."

"You're not listening to me. I said I'm *not* going."

He gives me a stern look. "I don't want to sound like one of those idiots on the news, but I don't like the idea of that fear ray being on the loose out there, either."

"So *you* steal it."

"I'm the leader of the Truth. I can't be caught doing something like that. And I'm not the one who lost it in the first place."

"I can't get it back, okay? We can tell some real heroes,

and they'll—"

He scoffs. "*No*. No way in hell is my grandson telling the League about this."

"Come on, Grandpa. I wouldn't tell the *League*. But... someone." I drum my fingers on the table. There have to be other superhero groups out there now. If Gordon and his stupid brother Ted are thinking of starting one, then tons of other people must be doing it. "We could tell Heroesworth."

He raises an eyebrow. "I kind of thought I was. Wouldn't they send you?"

"I'm quitting."

"What do you mean, you're quitting?"

I hold up my hands, then let them fall back down. "I mean I'm dropping out. I'm not going back. I thought everyone knew that already."

"And where would I have heard it? All I know about my grandson these days is what I see on the news, and they didn't mention you were a quitter."

I swallow. "I'm not a quitter. But I can't be a hero anymore."

"Why? Because one mission didn't go your way?"

"I thought you didn't want me to be a hero. Or to go to Heroesworth. You should be relieved."

"If you told me you were quitting to go to Vilmore, maybe I would be. But I look at you, at that sullen expression on your face, and I don't see someone whose life choices I should be relieved about. *You* wanted to be a hero. You went to that damned school, even though they didn't know what they were doing. And even though they treated you like dirt. I know they did, so don't try to deny it. And if you put up with all that for so long, you don't just drop out because you suddenly changed your mind."

"Fine, I'm a quitter. I failed as a villain, so I stopped trying. Now I failed as a hero, so I'm giving up on that, too. Is that what you want to hear?"

"The way I remember it, Vilmore offered you a full-ride scholarship and you turned it down."

"That doesn't count. They rejected my application, because I wasn't villainous enough, and they only offered me admission and the scholarship after I saved everyone at Homecoming. Which was more heroic than villainous."

"You were looking out for villains. Most heroes wouldn't do that. And what they liked about you was your bravery and your willingness to act."

"You don't know that."

"Yes, I do. I met a member of the admissions board through the Truth. He complimented me on having such an amazing grandson."

Fine, so maybe he does know. "It doesn't matter. Because I'm not any of those things anymore."

"I don't buy that. And my point was that you didn't fail as a villain. You could have gone to Vilmore. You could have had a place with me, too, but you turned it all down. To be a hero. To be around people who don't understand you. Who are always going to see you as some kind of wild card because of where you come from."

"And because I blew up part of the gym." Among other things.

"You chose to be a hero. You chose to go to that school.

And you put up with a hell of a lot to make that happen. But now you're out."

"Yep."

"And you don't care if the whole city's terrified of that fear ray. Villains, heroes, and everyone else alike—they're all scared out of their minds that Frank's going to use it. And maybe Frank hasn't, but I can guarantee you that whoever buys it at that auction tonight *will*. They'll pay a lot of money for it, and they'll make good use of it, and there won't be a damn thing anyone else can do about it."

"That's not true. Someone will stop them." Somebody else, who knows what they're doing.

"Maybe. But probably not before a lot of damage gets done."

"This city is crawling with heroes, Grandpa. It doesn't need me screwing everything up. If you're really worried about the fear ray getting into the wrong hands, then tell someone else."

"I'm not going running to some hero. And I'm sure as hell not telling them about a secret villain auction."

"But you're telling me about it. Obviously you *don't* see me as a hero. And you've got plenty of people who work for you. You could get someone you trust to do this."

"I trust *you*, Damien. And the point wasn't that I'm scared of what might happen after this auction takes place. The point was that I thought you'd want to finish what you started."

"I am finishing it. By doing what I should have done in the first place and staying the hell out of it."

X·X·X

Mom looks really surprised to see me when she answers her door.

Which is understandable, since I'm kind of surprised to be here. I'd planned on going home after I left Grandma and Grandpa's house. To go home and maybe listen to loud music and hide under my covers so I could try and forget how disappointed in me Grandpa sounded.

Grandpa, who hated that I was a hero and that I went to Heroesworth, was actually *disappointed in me* for quitting. Of everyone in, like, the entire universe, I would have thought he'd be the last person to feel that way. Okay, second to last, since I'm sure Mom really doesn't care that I quit. Actually, she's probably happy about it, or she will be when I tell her, and I can just picture the smug I-told-you-so look on her face.

"Damien," Mom says, "what are you doing here?"

"Can't I just stop by?"

She sighs, sounding annoyed, and moves out of the way so I can follow her inside. "I wish you'd called first. The house is a mess."

The house was *always* a mess when I lived here. Way worse than it looks now. Except now she doesn't want me to see it, like I'm a stranger instead of her own kid. The thought leaves a bitter taste in the back of my mouth.

"Taylor took Xavier to the park, and I only have a few minutes to myself. *Minutes*. You can't believe what it's like! So you're going to have to make this quick. And if this is about what I saw on the news, you should know there's nothing I can do about that fear ray. I didn't invent it—I don't know how to stop it."

"It's not about that."

She looks me over. "You're not going to do anything stupid, like try to get it back, are you?"

"No, I'm not."

She closes her eyes for a second and lets out a deep breath, relieved. "Good."

"Like you care." The words just come out, bitter and angry, even though I didn't mean to say them.

Her mouth twists into a scowl. "Damien, of course I care."

"You could have fooled me."

"I don't know what you came here for, but I don't have time for this."

"You made me afraid to fly."

She rolls her eyes. "Oh, not this again."

"You ruined my life!"

"Damien, don't be so dramatic. I did *not* ruin your life. This is why I'm glad my little Xavier sweetiekins isn't a teenager yet. You have no control over your emotions."

"*Seriously?!* I'm not the one with no control!"

"See, there you go again, having some kind of outburst." She waves her hand.

"He's not even here—you don't have to suck up to him. And if he's not a teenager now, he will be in, what, a few days? Because you won't stop messing him up, just like you did with me!"

"I'm not messing him up. I'm only doing what's in his best interest."

"In *your* best interest, you mean."

"And you should thank me, for what I did for you."

I clench my fists. Little sparks of lightning run down my arms. "You made me afraid of heights."

"I made sure you wouldn't turn out like *him*."

"You didn't even ask me what I wanted!"

"You were too young to know what was good for you." She gives me a look that says *Not much has changed.* "And what was I supposed to do, tell you that someday you might grow up and be able to fly? Because your father was a *superhero*? I couldn't do that to you."

"No, instead you let me find out on my sixteenth birthday, in front of hundreds of people. And now I failed the flying test because of you!"

"Well, you still have your lightning."

"You don't understand."

"I understand that I only have a few minutes of time to myself, and I don't want to spend them arguing with you. So if you're done making your little accusations—"

"You're not listening to me!" She tries to turn away, like she can just dismiss me. I get in front of her. And then I lift off the ground, so that I'm actually *flying*. Well, hovering a few inches above the floor, but whatever. It still counts.

Especially when she gasps, and her eyes go wide. She's never seen me fly before. Revulsion flicks across her face, and I don't like seeing it—it kind of really hurts—but it's still worth it, to know how much she hates this. That I can fly.

"I could have been a real hero," I tell her, "if it wasn't

for you. If you hadn't made me afraid of heights, I would have passed that flying test. I wouldn't be dropping out of school!" And if I'd passed the test, maybe I wouldn't have insisted we go inside the abandoned Heroes Hideout on Saturday. Or I at least wouldn't have insisted we go down those creepy stairs. Maybe Frank still would have stolen the fear ray—she would have found some other way to get to it—but it wouldn't have been my fault. Or felt like it was, anyway. And Kat and Riley wouldn't have gotten hurt, and Tristan wouldn't have had to save us, and the whole city wouldn't hate me. And… "If it wasn't for you, I wouldn't have had to quit being a hero!"

"Damien," Mom says, her voice seething, "feet on the floor while you're in my house." The lasers in her eyes flash, she's so mad.

I land. I keep glaring at her, though, and I don't look away. "You ruined my life. Everything would have gone completely differently if you hadn't done that!"

"I did what I had to in order to protect you. To make sure you grew up right. It's not my fault you decided you wanted to become some *hero*." Her mouth twists on the word. "I'm not the one who put the idea in your head for you to become something you're not. If you want to blame someone, you can blame your father."

"But *you*—"

"And of course you failed as a hero. You can only play make believe for so long." She shrugs.

I feel worse than if she'd slapped me. My hands start shaking, and lightning burns beneath my skin. "You don't even know what a hero is."

"I know I'm not looking at one now. You just told me you're dropping out. It's about time, if you ask me. I don't know *what* you were even doing at that school. Lying to yourself, I suppose. And if you went to spite me—"

"I went because *I* wanted to! *Me.* And you don't get to tell me that I'm not a hero, because maybe I dropped out, but I still had potential. I could have been one, and you don't get to tell me who I am! *Nobody* does, but especially not you!"

She stares at me in shock.

I'm shaking all over, now that I've said all that, and I should probably just leave. Because there's no way she's going to say anything I want to hear. I'm not even sure what that would be. That she's sorry? That of course I have hero potential—even she can see it now—and I never should have quit? I just told her she can't tell me who I am, which is true, so why am I waiting for her to? Especially since we both know the next words that come out of her mouth aren't going to be anything good.

She starts to say something right as I start to say that I should go. We both stop, then just stand there in awkward silence again. My heart's pounding, and I want to know what she was going to say. I need to know, even though the chances of it not making everything worse are pretty slim. But she doesn't look angry right now, and she's not yelling at me, so *maybe*—

She opens her mouth again, to say something.

Right as my phone rings.

I think maybe I should just ignore it, like I don't even hear it, so maybe she'll go on. But the moment's ruined, and anyway I'm already reaching for my phone on autopilot.

The screen says Kat's mom is calling. I was already shaking, but now I feel like I'm going to be sick. Like there's ice water running down my back. I tell myself it's probably nothing—Kat probably forgot to charge her phone again and her mom's just trying to get a hold of her. But as soon as I hear her mom speak, I know that's not true.

"Hello? Damien?" Kat's mom says, a tremor of fear in her voice, which is also thick from crying.

"Where's Kat?" I ask, and I don't sound anything like myself. I sound like someone who's terrified to hear the answer to that question.

"She's in the hospital. We don't know—" She chokes up, and it's another agonizing couple of seconds before she can speak again. "We just don't know what's going to happen. But you should get down here. And you should hurry."

CHAPTER 40

It turns out Kat's been so tired all week because the knife Frank threw at her was coated in poison. The same one that was meant for me. The doctors figured out that it must have been the knife, and that it should have been fatal, except that her shapeshifting ability's been keeping her alive. It's been healing her fast enough to keep up with the poison, or at least it was, because now she's really sick. And the doctors don't know what the poison was, and they don't have the antidote, and they have no idea how long she can keep fighting it, since it's a miracle she's been able to fight it at all.

Mrs. Wilson tells me all that on the phone as I make my way to the hospital. She says it like she's had it explained to her a million times, or like she's had to explain it to other people over and over, until she knows it by heart.

I feel numb. I feel sick and shaky all over. Like my body understands what's happening, even as my brain keeps going over it, replaying Mrs. Wilson's words until they don't mean anything, unable to comprehend the facts.

Kat got poisoned.

Kat's in the hospital.

Something really bad is happening to her, and she might not make it.

None of that sounds like it can be true. Except when I finally get to the hospital—it only takes me twenty minutes, but it feels like a lifetime—Kat's really there. She's lying in a hospital bed, her skin a sickly pale that looks almost green.

Her mom is sitting in the room with her. I don't see her dad anywhere, but there's no way he's not around somewhere.

"Damien's here," her mom whispers, squeezing Kat's hand.

Kat looks over at me. A smile twitches at the edges of her mouth, then fades when she sees the devastation on my face.

Her mom gets up and goes into the hallway, muttering about leaving us alone for a minute and getting a cup of coffee.

"Kat?" She was fine the other day. She was tired, but she was *fine*. Or at least I thought she was. But I didn't actually see her. Did she look this pale when I was talking to her on the phone? Did her friends notice?

"It's going to be okay," she says, but she sounds weak and tired and not at all like herself, and I'm not sure I believe her.

"They said it was the knife."

"It's not your fault."

There's a chair on her other side, where her mom was sitting. I should take it, but instead I stay standing, afraid to take my eyes off of her. "It was meant for me."

She tries to shake her head but stops partway through the movement. "Not your fault," she mumbles.

I lean in close and take both of her hands in mine. "Kat..." She can't really be this sick. This can't really be happening. It feels like it's happening to somebody else, and at the same time it feels like my heart's being ripped out, real and painful. Because Kat doesn't look like someone who's going to be okay, and the doctors think she shouldn't have even made it this long. And I can't imagine losing her. I can't imagine living the rest of my life without her in it.

I can't imagine it, but I start to anyway, and then my eyes water, even though I'm trying not to cry. Because crying makes this real, and I don't want Kat to think I'm giving up on her, like I think she really won't make it.

But it's too late, and Kat's face crumples as she starts crying, too. "I thought I was okay. If I'd gone in sooner—"

"You couldn't know. It's okay, Kat."

"I'm sorry. I'm so sorry, Damien."

"It wasn't your fault." Hot tears slide down my face, but I'd have to let go of her to wipe them off, so I don't. "I love you."

"I love you, too. No matter what happens."

"Don't say that. You're going to get better. The doctors are going to figure something out. Just keep fighting it, okay?"

"I'm so tired," she mutters, her voice barely audible.

"Kat? Did you hear me? You're going to be okay. I'm... I'm not going to let this happen to you!"

She makes a *mmm* sound of agreement, but her eyes are closed, and I don't know if she really heard me.

"Kat?"

But she's asleep, her breathing deep and even.

There's a commotion outside the room, and then I hear her dad's voice. "What the hell is *he* doing here?! I told you I didn't want him anywhere near her!"

"He deserves to know what's going on," her mom says. "And Kat was asking for him."

Her dad marches into the room, glaring at me. "Get out. Now."

"I—"

"She's here because of you!"

"Tom!" Kat's mom scolds. "It's not his fault. And keep your voice down—Kat's asleep again."

"*Out.*" Her dad grabs my arm and drags me into the hall. "You're the last thing Kat needs right now. You're not allowed to see her—do you understand me?"

No, I don't. I don't understand any of this. It feels like the whole world's turning upside down, or maybe like I'm turning inside out. "I... I didn't mean for this to happen. I didn't— I wouldn't—" I swallow. "She wasn't supposed to get hurt."

"But she did."

I nod, because it's true, and because my throat is really tight and there are already tears in my eyes and I don't trust myself to speak.

"You're a danger to everyone around you—you always

have been—and now we might lose her because of you. So just get the hell out of my sight and don't come back."

X·X·X

I call Gordon. Because I'm too freaked out to take the bus. And because I really don't need people taking pictures of me right now. And if even one person says one word to me about losing that fear ray, I'll probably end up blasting a hole through the roof. Or worse.

So now I'm in the passenger seat of Gordon's car. We're just sitting in the parking lot at the hospital. I tried to explain to him what was going on over the phone, but I'm not sure I even formed full sentences. I think he got the gist of it, though. Kat. Hospital. Me freaking out.

I run my hands through my hair. "I have to go back in. I should go back in."

"Damien—"

"They didn't let me ask anything. I hardly got to see her. I can't just leave. They can't—"

"They're not going to let you back in. Her parents don't want you there."

"Not her parents, just her dad. And I don't care what he says because he doesn't understand. He thinks it's my fault, and it kind of was, but—" I choke up, pressing my hands to my face as new tears form so Gordon doesn't see. Not that he can't already tell. "I didn't mean for this to happen."

"I know." He tries to put a hand on my shoulder, but I pull away.

"I never mean for *anything* to happen, but it still does. First Riley got hurt, and now Kat, and she was protecting *me*. Because I did something stupid, and she said she can heal, she said it was okay, but it's *not*, because she isn't. I can't... She's going to die, and it's all my fault."

"It's not your fault."

"You don't know. You weren't there."

"I know you would never do anything to hurt her. And you don't know that she's going to... that she's not going to be okay."

"She's going to die. Just *say it*." I suck in a breath. I feel like I can't get enough air. And like I'm going to throw up.

"You don't know that."

"She is. She is, and you can say it's not my fault, and that's what she said, too, before she fell asleep. Because she can't even stay awake for very long. But it is, and she doesn't know, because she just said that, because she doesn't want me to... to spend the rest of my life blaming myself. Because she's not going to be there. And I'll always know that I—" A sob interrupts me. I try to stop it, but I can't.

"Damien, you can't blame yourself for this."

I shake my head. "She wouldn't have been there if it wasn't for me. And now she's in there, and I'm out here, and I have to go back. I shouldn't... I shouldn't have come out here." I try to move, to get out, but something's stopping me. I realize it's my seatbelt and scramble to unbuckle it, but my hands are shaking and my eyes are blurry and everything just feels so *wrong*.

"They won't let you back in. We can try again later,

after her father's had a chance to cool down."

"No. He won't. He hates me, and he doesn't think I deserve to see her, and he's right, but I can't—"

"He's not right."

"But he is, because if I'd stayed away from her—"

"Damien." Gordon grabs my shoulders. He makes me look at him. "Listen to me. He's not right about you. You and Kat really care about each other, and she's lucky to have you in her life. And... you can't stay away from the people you love just because they might get hurt."

"She might *die*."

"But not because of you."

"She never got hurt when she was out with Tristan. Only when she was with *me*."

"Because she loves you. Because she wanted to protect you."

"We were supposed to... The rest of our lives—we were supposed to spend them together. Now she's not. I don't—I have to go back—"

"Later. We'll come back later."

"There might not *be* a later!"

"You need to calm down first. It's not going to help anything for you to go see her like this. And you said she's asleep. Let her rest for a while, and then we'll come back. I'll talk to her parents."

"Her dad won't listen to you."

"I'll talk to her mother, then. We'll figure this out. But right now, there's nothing you can do here."

CHAPTER 41

Riley has a worried look on his face when I show up at his door later that afternoon. I told him what was going on with Kat. Well, I texted him, because I didn't think I could say it out loud without freaking out again. And maybe it's because of that, or maybe it's because when he sees me he can tell I've been crying, but his forehead wrinkles up with concern, and he lets out a deep breath and says, "You look like hell, X. Like absolute hell."

"Great. Thanks, Perkins. Kick me while I'm down why don't you."

"I just mean that you don't have to be here right now."

"Yes, I do, because we have to find Frank." Because she's the only one who might have the antidote.

Riley looks me over again, like he's not sure I'm really up for that, but then he says, "Okay," and I follow him inside.

Sarah's sitting on the couch. She gets up when I come in. Her sleeves are balled around her hands, and she's biting her lip, looking at me like I might break. Like she thinks I shouldn't be here, either. "It's really short notice," she says, "for finding Frank, but I'm up for the challenge. I've been thinking about it since you texted earlier, and, well, I haven't figured out a way to find her *yet*, but I'm working on it."

"It's okay, Sarah. I know where she's going to be. My grandpa told me about a secret villain auction that's happening tonight, and Frank's going to be there, auctioning off the fear ray she stole. So that's where we need to be, too."

Sarah nods, though she doesn't say anything.

Riley still looks worried. "X... Are you sure you're up for this?"

"I'm okay, Perkins."

"No, you're not. Your girlfriend's in the *hospital*. And even if you hadn't told me how sick she was, I'd have known as soon as I saw your face. You're obviously not okay, and... you don't have to be."

I take a shaky breath, hating that he's right. "Fine, I'm not okay, but it doesn't matter, because Kat doesn't have a lot of time, and—" I swallow. "I have to do this."

"Yeah, but we can give the info to someone else. There are tons of capable heroes in Golden City. We just need to find one and tell them about the auction. We could even call the police, and they'll find someone to handle it. It doesn't have to be *us*."

That's basically what I said, when I was trying to convince Grandpa this wasn't my problem. I shake my head. I pace back and forth in front of the couch. "It has to be me, it has to be us. I can't trust Kat's life to anyone else, and I... I know I said this was my fault." My voice gets tight, and my eyes sting, and I have to focus on breathing in and out so I don't lose it in front of Riley and Sarah. Because I don't want them to see me cry, but even more than that, it might make them decide I'm really *not* up for this, and I don't want them doubting me. "And maybe it is. And maybe it's hypocritical for me to say I don't trust her life to anyone else, after what I did—"

"You didn't *do* anything."

"—but I just can't. My grandpa trusted me with this information about the auction, not somebody else. And I trust *you guys*, not some random heroes we don't even know. I *can't* let Kat... I can't let her die. And if I don't do everything I can to save her, I won't be able to live with myself. What happened with Frank is personal, and I have to fix it. The poison, the fear ray—all of it."

"Okay," Riley says, "but it's not all on you. It *wasn't* your fault. And either way, you don't have to do this alone."

"Right," Sarah says. "We're a team, and we'll figure this out together."

There's a knock on the front door.

Riley rolls his eyes. "Zach must have forgotten his keys again."

"It's Tristan." At least, I think it is, because this is when I told him to show up here when I messaged him on Facebook.

Riley gapes at me. "What do you mean it's Tristan?"

"I invited him."

"To my *house*?"

"He's not my favorite person, either, but we need everyone we can get, and he was part of this. He screwed up at the gallery when he left his phone on, but we'd all be dead if it wasn't for what he did on Saturday."

"See," Riley says, "now I know you're not okay." But he goes and answers the door anyway, and then Tristan joins us in the living room.

"Hey." Tristan nods, acknowledging us and letting his backpack slide to the floor. "Is she… How is she?"

I shrug and look away. Her parents haven't called to update me, and the only way I can keep it together is to assume that means nothing's changed.

Sarah steps forward and holds out her hand to him. "Hi, I'm Sarah Kink, and we're going to be working together on this. Kat might have mentioned me, since she was considering bringing me in on your last mission."

Tristan raises his eyebrows at her—because of course Kat *wasn't* considering bringing her in on that and it's probably the first he's hearing about it—and just sort of stares at her hand for a second before finally shaking it.

"Great," Sarah says. "We're glad to have you on board. When you get a chance, can you write down your blood type for me?"

"*Sarah.*" Riley nudges her.

"What? I said when he gets a chance. It doesn't have to be right now."

Tristan turns to me. "You mentioned a plan?"

"Frank's going to be auctioning off the fear ray tonight," I tell him. "The plan is we sneak into the auction, find her, and hope she has the antidote."

"That's your plan? Sneak in and *hope*?"

"She'll have the antidote," Sarah says. "If she uses poisoned knives, she'll need to have it on her in case of emergencies."

"But what if she doesn't bring her knives to this thing and leaves the antidote at home?"

Sarah shakes her head. "She'll have it. Or she can at least tell us what the poison is."

"You think Frank's going to tell us anything?" Tristan takes a step back, like he's repelled by how wrong he thinks Sarah is. "We almost didn't survive last time. We're lucky to even be alive. And if it had just been me and Katie..." He shudders. "We wouldn't have gotten out."

Or if it had just been me and Riley. I hadn't thought of it that way until now. "I'm not saying this isn't going to be dangerous, because it is, and I get it if anybody wants to back out. Things might end badly tonight, and especially after what happened last time, I understand if anybody doesn't want to confront Frank again."

"X, come on," Riley says.

"I mean it. If anybody wants to leave—"

"We don't," Sarah says. "We're coming with you."

I nod.

Tristan stays quiet.

Sarah clears her throat really loudly and gives him a pointed look.

I kind of thought he'd be on board with this, especially since he came all the way over here from Vilmore, but maybe he was only on board when he didn't know we'd be facing Frank. Or maybe when he thought I actually had a plan that was at least somewhat thought out, and now that he knows that I don't, maybe he doesn't think it's worth risking his life over. And maybe I shouldn't have even brought Riley and Sarah into this, because I might just be leading them into danger, too. And even though I was relieved when they said they were coming with me, part of me also kind of hoped they wouldn't. Because I have to do this, but they don't, and if my plan's going to get anybody killed, well, it should just be me.

But I need this to work—*Kat* needs it to—and I don't like my chances of going in alone.

"It's cool," I tell Tristan. "You don't have to do this."

"No, I..." He takes a deep breath. "Confronting Frank is stupid. It's crazy and reckless. Even for Katie, this is... it's kind of insane."

Riley glares at him. "Nobody asked your opinion. If you're not going to be part of this—"

"I didn't say that." He scowls at Riley, then turns to me. "For the record, your plan is stupid. But I don't have a better one, and Katie's life is on the line, and..." He shoves his hands in his pockets and shrugs. "You're going to need my fire power. So I'm in."

He says it like he's doing me this big favor. Like I'm not possibly going to survive without his stupid fire power, even though I have lightning. And would win in a fight. Just, like, if anybody's keeping track. And yeah, I know I asked him here because he saved our lives with said fire power, but I didn't *beg* him. I didn't say that we'd all be totally lost without him or not be able to pull this off. I just thought that maybe he cared about Kat enough to do this and that *maybe* he'd be useful.

But even though all those thoughts are kind of making one of my eyelids twitch—well, those thoughts along with the slightly condescending look he's giving me—I restrain myself from telling him to get out of here. And from pointing out that all he can really do is start fires and that he's basically just a walking book of matches and not to get too ahead of himself, even if he did save our lives or whatever.

So instead, somewhat grudgingly, I say, "Welcome to the group."

"On a temporary basis," Riley adds.

"Remember to silence your cell phone. And Sarah wasn't kidding about needing your blood type."

"A sample would really be best," Sarah says. "Though since we're in a time crunch, I guess I can get it from you later."

CHAPTER 42

The auction is at an all-villain nightclub downtown. The kind of place where a bunch of villains could all gather for the evening and nobody would think anything of it. Plus, it's a really high-end, fancy sort of place, or at least that's what Grandpa told me, since I'm not actually in it yet. I am, however, wearing a nice jacket and pants that aren't jeans in the hopes that I won't stand out too much once we do get in, even though the whole city pretty much knows who I am and that I don't belong here.

For now, though, I'm standing by the back door with Sarah and Tristan, waiting for Riley to come let us in. When we got here, it was obvious we wouldn't be able to use the front entrance, and not just because there was a line running all the way from the door down the side of the building, which we really didn't have time for. But none of us is eighteen, let alone twenty-one, and even though Sarah has a fake I.D., she doesn't have a *V* on her thumb, which is mandatory at a place like this.

Tristan keeps jiggling his leg and sighing really loudly, like he just can't wait to get out of here. "This sucks."

Sarah purses her lips, making a sour face at him, and picks a piece of lint off her dress. I think maybe she's regretting being so welcoming. "It's just a few more minutes."

He loosens the tie around his neck and scratches underneath the collar of his shirt. "*If* he shows up. And did I really have to wear this?"

I roll my eyes at him. "I said to bring something to dress up in—I didn't say you had to wear a tie. And Riley *will* be here, so shut up about it."

"I had to wear it to hide a tomato-sauce stain. And I give him two more minutes before we move on to plan *B*."

Sarah pushes her glasses farther up the bridge of her nose. "We didn't discuss any other plans."

"We don't need to discuss it." Tristan jerks his thumb at me. "Use your celebrity status, man. All you have to do is go up to the front entrance and they'll let you in."

"Or ban me from the event. The whole city knows I'm underage. And that I don't have a *V*."

"I bet they'd still let you in, though. After all that sucking up you did with the Truth."

I glare at him. Lightning prickles up and down my back. "If I go through the front entrance, Frank's going to know I'm here. *If* they'd even let me in." Which I'm not so sure about, and the last thing I need when we do get in is for security to be on the lookout for me. Er, I mean, that's the second-to-last thing I need, since the first one is Frank, like, knowing we're here and trying to kill us. But it's still pretty high up on my list of things to avoid. "And if you're going to whine all night, you can just go."

"I wasn't— I'm just saying, is all. Katie's really sick, and we don't have time for this. And your friend should have been here by now to let us in, so either he got caught or he decided to bail and we're standing out here for nothing."

"Maybe that's something *you* would do," Sarah says, sounding really pissed at him now, "but Riley wouldn't. Not ever."

"If you say so. I mean, hero type like him suddenly finds himself in a nightclub full of villains? Maybe he couldn't take it."

Sarah narrows her eyes at him. She puts a hand in her purse and digs around for something—probably something to murder him with.

"Dude," I tell him. "*Shut up.* I didn't bring you here so you could be a letterist douchebag and make tonight even worse than it already is."

"I'm just saying that—" He stops himself. He takes a deep breath, then tries again. "It's just hard standing around here when Katie's in the hospital and it feels like we're running out of time."

I want to scream at him that her name is Kat—*Kat*, not Katie—and that he has *no idea* how freaked out I am or how hard this all is. But if I do that, I'm going to lose it and possibly end up attracting attention to us—either from shouting or by accidentally blowing a hole through the wall, which I guess is plan *C*—and I can't afford that. So I push down the nerves and the feeling that if we don't get that antidote in the next five seconds I'm going to throw up, and I tell him through clenched teeth, "Riley will be here."

"He could have gotten caught." Tristan keeps his voice low when he says that, like he really means it and isn't just trying to cause trouble. "He can turn invisible, but it must be pretty crowded in there. Maybe he bumped into somebody, and they noticed, and—"

All three of us jump as the door beside us clicks open. It moves slowly at first, and even though this is what we've been waiting for, I have this moment where I worry it's not Riley and that we've just been found out by the staff or something. But then Riley turns visible and motions for us to follow him inside.

"Took you long enough," Tristan mutters.

Me and Sarah both glare at him.

"I got a little lost," Riley says. "It's really crowded in there, and the door I was going to use to get over here was locked, so I had to find another way around."

I think Tristan's going to say something snarky to that —he certainly *looks* like he is—and I'm ready to admit I made a mistake and tell him that he really should just get out of here. But then all he says is, "Are you guys coming or what?" as he follows Riley inside.

X·X·X

I was hoping it would be dark inside the nightclub, so there'd be less chance of anybody noticing us, or, more specifically, of recognizing me, but unfortunately the lights are all on, on account of the auction. Right now people are bidding on some supercharged raygun.

There are signs up everywhere that say all weapons are to be picked up *after* the auction, and only after full payment has been made. Sarah frowns at one of them, like she's thinking what I'm thinking—what we're all probably thinking—that the fear ray needs to not be on that list.

Tristan folds his arms and tilts his head at me. "Okay, now what?"

"Now we find Frank." Obviously. I'm just not sure how we're going to do that. I glance around the room, but there are a ton of people here, and I don't see anyone who looks like her.

"We should split up," Riley says, and my stomach kind of twists, because this is starting to feel a little too much like the gala.

Me, him, and Sarah, all dressed up, going our separate ways and trying to find a weapon, trying to stop something really bad from happening. But I tell myself tonight is completely different. The gala's long over. Kat's not here, and neither is Amelia, and Tristan isn't Mason. And splitting up to cover more ground doesn't mean we're all going to end up in danger, or that I won't be there to stop people from attacking my friends.

But that doesn't mean it's the right thing to do, either.

"X—"

I shake my head. "We're sticking together. Frank's going to be with the fear ray. She's not going to be out here, in the crowd." At least, I don't think. "We need to look for her backstage, and... she needs to not find any of us alone."

Sarah nods. "Good thinking, Renegade."

"Renegade?" Tristan looks confused for a second, and then he smirks at me. "You're Renegade? That's your superhero code name or whatever?"

"Renegade X," Sarah corrects him. "I'm the Cosine Kid, and Riley's Secant."

"Sarah." I grit my teeth. "Don't tell him our code names."

"But he's part of the group."

"*Temporarily*," Riley reminds her. "And it's not funny." He says that last part to Tristan, who's really obviously trying not to laugh.

Tristan holds up his hands, like he wasn't doing anything, but then he says, "Do all heroes have stupid names, or is it just you guys?"

I kind of wish it wasn't so crowded in here, so I could at least act like I was going to zap him. "We don't have time for this."

"I didn't think you could get any lamer than *Son of Flash*, but you guys sound like a math club, not a superhero team. What do you guys do, terrorize villains who suck at algebra?"

I ignore him and make my way through the crowd, to a door that leads backstage.

"We don't *terrorize* anyone," Sarah says. "That's not what heroes do."

Tristan snorts at that.

"We're not the League," Riley adds, sounding annoyed.

"Whatever, man. Just as long as kids keep doing their

math homework, right?"

I clench my fists, really not sure why I invited him. And then I have this thought about how hilarious Kat's going to think all this is when I tell her, and it totally guts me. Like I just found out about her being sick all over again. I take a deep breath, trying to steady myself.

"You okay?" Riley whispers.

I nod, just once.

He nods back, though I'm pretty sure he knows it's a lie. Then I try the knob, but it's locked.

I mean, of course it is. They've got all the valuable items from the auction somewhere back there—they're not just going to leave everything open to the public.

"Stand back," Tristan says, elbowing his way past me. "I'll take care of this." He puts his hand on the knob, and I watch it turn red as it heats up and starts to melt.

"I could have done that," I mutter, though not without, like, having to blast it for a while and attracting a lot of attention.

Tristan just gives me a smug look, like we both know he's better at this than me. Then he has to jump back a step as some molten metal almost lands on his shoes.

Once the knob's gone, the door swings open, and all four of us slip backstage.

I don't know what I expected to find, but this is just an empty hallway, with no big signs pointing in the right direction that say, *Fear ray over here!* or *Big-ticket items from the auction we don't want anyone to steal, right this way!*

"Maybe we should split up," Sarah says. "Unless

anyone knows which direction we should go?"

"We're not—"

Tristan interrupts me. "She's right. We don't know where they're keeping the fear ray *or* if that's where we'll even find Frank. Frank might not even be here, and the sooner we know that, the sooner we can figure out where she really is."

I hate that he's making sense right now, even if I don't agree with him. "She's here. I know she—" My phone buzzes, since I have it on vibrate. My heart lurches into my throat as I grab my phone, afraid that it's about Kat. But it's just a text from Gordon.

It says, *Where are you?*

I consider writing him back, but only for a second, and then I decide against it. I can't tell him where I really am, because he wouldn't approve. Or at the least he'd worry about me, and probably for good reason. And while my first instinct is to lie to him and say that I'm at Riley's, I decide against that, too.

And then I notice that I do have a missed call, after all. It must have gone off while we were in the crowd, and even though I had it on vibrate, I guess I didn't feel it.

It's from Kat's mom. My hands start shaking and I feel like I can't breathe.

Everyone's staring at me now.

"What happened?" Riley asks, his voice almost a whisper.

"Kat's mom called. I don't... I don't know." She didn't leave a voicemail. She didn't text. Maybe she didn't even mean to call me. Or maybe what she had to tell me was too horrible to say to a machine.

Tristan takes out his phone and checks it, like maybe he would have gotten a call, too, which kind of really pisses me off. But it's still a disappointment when he says, "Nothing here."

Maybe Kat's mom called the house when she couldn't get a hold of me. She could have gotten the number from Kat's phone. Maybe that's why Gordon texted, wondering where I was. I hit the button to call her back, but it just rings and rings. Then I try calling their house, just in case, but nobody picks up.

Panic claws through my chest, and my throat feels tight, and I *hate* this. There are a million different reasons why that missed call might not mean anything, but I can't bring myself to believe any of them, and instead the worst scenarios run through my mind.

"X," Riley says.

I shake my head. "I'm okay."

He opens his mouth, then doesn't say anything.

"We have to focus on finding Frank," Sarah says. "That means splitting up."

Riley glances over at me, then at the others. "We'll go in teams of two. That way no one will be alone. I'll... I'll take Tristan."

Tristan folds his arms. "Don't do me any favors. There's no way I'm partnering up with some letterist douchebag."

Sarah glares at him. "He's not letterist. Or a douchebag." She looks Tristan up and down, then adds, "That sounds more like *you*."

Riley takes a step forward, so he's between them. "I'll

go with Damien. Sarah, try not to kill Tristan, okay?"

"I can't make any promises."

"Kill me?" Tristan laughs a little. "I'd like to see you try."

Sarah reaches a hand into her purse.

"Look," Riley says to Tristan, "if you're not going to add anything to the group—"

"I got us through that door, didn't I?

"—then maybe you should just leave. You're slowing us down."

"Me? *I'm* slowing us down? How long did it take you to let us in? This could have all been over by now if you hadn't—"

"Nobody's leaving," I tell them. "And nobody's splitting up, even if—"

"Hey! What are you kids doing back here?!"

We turn to see a security guard running toward us from down the hall.

Crap. My mind races, trying to think of something to say—a lie that explains why we're here, why we shouldn't get kicked out—but it just goes blank. I tell myself I have to think of *something*, because if we have to leave right now, before we get that antidote, then Kat's not going to make it. But that thought only makes it worse, and I freeze up, my mouth slightly open, not saying anything.

The security guard does *not* look happy to find four teenagers wandering around backstage. "How'd you even get in the club?"

"We're testing your security," Sarah says. "What you should really be asking yourself is—"

"Don't listen to her." Tristan steps forward, shaking his head at Sarah and smiling like this whole situation is hilarious. "She's kidding. We're here because my uncle's the caterer, and he said it would be cool if me and my friends hung out for a while. We've never been to a nightclub before, and we just wanted to say we came to the auction, because our friends are *never* going to believe we were here."

The security guard takes that in. "Your uncle should know better. You all look underage to me, and it is not 'cool' for you to be here, and especially not backstage."

"We're not drinking, and we're not getting in the way of the auction," Tristan tells him, keeping his voice calm, like we really are just here for some bragging rights and aren't causing trouble. "I swear."

"You're still going to have to vacate the premises, and I'm going to have to—" He stops in mid-sentence as he looks over at me, recognition suddenly flashing in his eyes. "Aren't you Alistair Locke's grandson? From the Truth commercials?"

Tristan scowls.

"Yep," I tell the security guard.

"I can't... That's..." He shakes his head and wipes his palms on his thighs. "Please tell your grandfather, and yourself— Please tell yourself how much I—" He winces. "Let me start again. What you did, it was just... It's hard to put into words how much it means to me. What you and your grandfather did for villains. And I can't thank you guys enough."

I feel sick, and I don't know what to say. He just told

me how much what I supposedly did means to him, when really he should be kicking us out, and now he's standing there with this big, hopeful grin on his face, waiting for me to acknowledge him.

All I have to do is say, *Thanks, I'll tell him.* All I have to do is smile back. But I can't bring myself to do either of those things. And maybe I was frozen before, but now I can't stop the words from coming, even if they're the wrong ones. "You shouldn't be thanking me. All I did with those commercials was *lie* to the people who believed in me. The biggest thing I did for the Truth was almost get a bunch of people killed. So don't"—I swallow—"don't thank me."

Beside me, Riley cringes. Tristan looks like he just ate something really sour. Sarah bites her lip and stares at her shoes.

I watch the security guard's smile fade. He looks me over again, like he's seeing me for the first time and not sure he recognizes me anymore.

I lean back against the wall and rub my hands across my eyes. I wish I hadn't said any of that. I wish I hadn't *meant* it. But I did, on both counts, and I can't take it back now.

"Look," the security guard finally says, "all I know is that we got my niece back from the League because of the Truth. Because of those commercials, and people believing in you, we got her back. She's only sixteen. She'd never hurt anybody, but they took her, and—" He chokes up, just a little, and shakes his head. "That's all I know, that we got her back, and that's all I care about."

I feel like a jerk for the things I just said, even if they were true, and for not being who he wanted me to be. "Okay," I tell him. And then, because that doesn't feel like enough, I add, "Thanks."

He nods. "But you kids really shouldn't be here. I'm going to have to— What's that?" He squints at the door behind us, the one with the missing knob.

We all turn to look at where he's pointing, as if it's news to us and we had no idea.

"That was like that when we got here," Sarah says. "That was a while ago. There might be someone lurking backstage—they could be anywhere by now."

The security guard's eyes go wide. He swears under his breath, then says, "You kids need to leave," before grabbing his walkie-talkie and running off down the hall.

At least now we know which direction to go. Once he's gone, we take the security guard's lead and head down the hall, because I figure he wouldn't have run *away* from the items he was trying to protect if he thought there was an intruder on the loose. I'm just not sure what we're going to do when we run into him and possibly all the other security guards he's called for backup. Saying we got lost probably won't cut it, especially not if Frank's there.

If she's there. Because there's still the possibility that I was wrong, and she didn't come here tonight, and all of this is for nothing because Kat's still going to—

An announcement from the loudspeakers interrupts my thoughts as someone says, "Ladies and gentlemen, please return to your seats for our next item, the Director of Damage's fear ray. Up until recently, the fear ray was believed in some circles to only be a myth, but we have the real thing here today. And to prove it, there'll be a short demo before the bidding starts, performed by none other than its finder, Frank herself."

All four of us stop moving. We look at each other.

"Where's the stage?" I glance around, looking for the quickest way up there.

"Wait," Riley says. "What are we going to do? We can't just—"

"I can't let her get away!"

"I know, but we need a plan! We can't just run in!"

There's the muffled sound of applause, probably as Frank takes the stage.

She's there, right now, with the antidote on her. And the fear ray. And who knows what other weapons.

And Riley's right—rushing in without a plan is probably a stupid idea. I have no idea how I'm going to get Frank to give me that antidote, let alone how I'm going to keep her from killing me. But it doesn't matter, because I'm out of time. This is it.

"I have my lightning," I tell him. Then, to everyone, "Stay here."

But none of them do. All three of them follow me as I race toward the door marked *Stage*.

CHAPTER 43

We hear Frank's voice through the loudspeakers. "Good evening, ladies and gents! Do I have a volunteer from the audience? One lucky person is going to get *terrified* out of their mind—who's it going to be?" There's a pause, then, "No one? No one's going to take this once-in-a-lifetime opportunity?" She makes a *tsk* sound. "Such a shame. Then I guess it's going to have to be *all of you*."

The whole audience starts screaming.

We arrive onstage a second later. Frank's wearing a pair of purple-tinted safety goggles and holding a remote control in one hand. Besides what look like a couple rayguns in holsters around her waist, she's also got the fear ray hanging from a strap across her chest, except it becomes obvious as we get closer that it's *not* the fear ray. It's a plastic replica.

"Quiet!" Frank yells. "Or you'll get another dose!" She waves the remote at the audience, threatening them, and they all go silent. She turns to us. "And you. Get out of here."

Lightning's already running down my arms. I hold up my hands. "We're not going anywhere."

Frank smirks at that. At us. "If I push this button again, the fear ray gets you, too. And then you'll do whatever I say. So you might as well do it now."

Tristan's got flames in his hands. Sarah's holding a tiny raygun. Riley's invisible. Frank could push the button, but could she do it before one of us attacked?

"I don't have time for this," Frank says. Then, to the audience, "Will Bernard Hargrove *please* come to the stage so I can give that bastard what he deserves?"

There's a murmur in the audience. A man stands up and starts making his way over.

Frank addresses us again. "Well, you're still here, so I guess we do this the hard way."

"We just need the antidote!" I shout.

"The antidote?" She frowns, like she's confused and doesn't know what I'm talking about, and for a second I think it actually doesn't exist. And that I'm going to throw up. "*Oh.*" She waves her free hand in our direction. "That's right, your little girlfriend's not here this time, is she?" She tilts her head and pouts her lips in mock sympathy. "Though it's kind of late to be asking for the antidote, since she should be dead by now." She shrugs, as if it's no big deal. "Well, just remember, you brought this on yourselves."

Frank holds out the remote, pointing it toward the disco ball on the ceiling. Her thumb twitches on the button.

But not before I zap the remote.

The audience shrieks in terror.

Frank swears and grabs the rayguns from the holsters around her waist. She doesn't hesitate—she aims and fires. Except, not at me.

Riley cries out and turns visible, holding his shoulder.

My blood runs cold. I feel like someone just poured ice water down my back. Electricity crackles across my skin, making my hair stand on end.

"Did you think I didn't know where he was?" Frank shakes her head at me. "You underestimated me, just like Bernard here. Are you there, Bernard?" she asks, not turning to look.

Bernard's standing on the floor just in front of the stage. He's middle-aged and old enough to be her dad—so, probably not an ex-boyfriend. He hauls himself up onto the stage, shaking all over and watching Frank with a horrified look on his face. "I'm here," he says quietly, just loud enough to be heard.

"You see," Frank says, "Bernard thought he could kidnap me and get away with it, because I was just some weak, scared little girl. He thought he could use me to lure my father to him. Isn't that what you did, Bernard?"

"Yes," he admits, not looking at her.

"Tell them what you did."

He swallows. "I... I never laid a hand on you. I didn't hurt you. I didn't—"

"You kidnapped me when I was fifteen!" Frank says, keeping her rayguns trained on us and not looking back at him. "You kept me locked in a room in your basement for two weeks. You *terrified* me. And when my father came to pay your ransom—"

"Francis, please."

"It's *Frank*! Just like my father, the one you killed. He brought you the money, and—"

"And I let you go. The money was to let you go."

"—you *killed* him. Right in front of me. And the thing is, Bernard, you terrorized me, and terror never lets you go. It's been with me all these years. And now you're going to feel the same terror, over and over again."

"Please, Francis—*Frank*—please, I—"

"*Stop arguing.*"

He shuts up, his next words dying in his throat with a little whimper.

"You're going to be afraid, as afraid as I was, and you're going to do it in front of all these people. And then I'm going to kill you. You understand?"

He nods.

Frank doesn't see, because she's still watching us. "I said, *you understand*?!"

"Yes!" Bernard says, his voice coming out a squeak.

"And as for you." Frank aims one of her rayguns right at my chest.

Lightning surges in my hands. "We just need the antidote."

Riley's face is pale. He's biting his lip, still holding his shoulder.

Out of the corner of my eye, I see Sarah's hand shaking, the one holding her raygun.

Frank looks like she's actually considering giving me the antidote. Just for a split second. And then she says, "Nah, let's just end this."

She fires her raygun.

Both of them.

But not before I dive out of the way, the rays just barely missing me. I land hard on the floor of the stage and try to zap Frank, but I miss.

Tristan throws a fireball at her. It hits her forearm, and she screams and drops one of the rayguns. She fires the other one at him.

Frank starts to say something to the audience, something that sounds like, "Get them!" but Sarah has the same idea, and her voice drowns out Frank's as she screams, "The League is here! Everybody run for your lives!"

The whole audience erupts in pure chaos as everyone starts freaking out and running in all directions, including toward the stage.

Bernard takes off.

Frank shouts at the crowd to go back to their seats, but they're too panicked to listen now, and she has to run to avoid getting crushed by the stampede.

In all the commotion, the four of us slip off stage.

"Let's go!" Sarah shouts.

"Not yet!" I tell her, looking up at the disco ball in the ceiling. "There's something we have to do first."

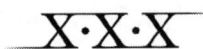

We stuff the fear ray into the trunk of Riley's car, then pile in.

With all the chaos in the nightclub, nobody noticed us go upstairs to the rafters. Or they didn't care, because everyone was under the influence of the fear ray and running for their lives. Everyone except us and Frank. I kept expecting her to show up and murder us the whole time, but we didn't see her.

The fear ray was positioned in the ceiling, with the end stuck into the disco ball. Frank had it set up to amplify the signal, so she could get the whole room at once. And while the rafters weren't exposed to the rest of the club, there wasn't exactly a real floor, either. Just some paneling in between the boards to make it look nice.

Riley tried to volunteer to go get it, even though he was injured. Before I could tell him that was ridiculous, Sarah insisted she was going to go instead, and Tristan gave them both weird looks, like he didn't get why either of them would be so eager to do this.

But I told them I would do it, because it didn't make sense for anyone else to take the risk. Not when I can fly. Sarah pointed out that people who can't fly take that risk all the time to work on ceilings, and I said we didn't have time to argue and that it would be faster this way. And then I proceeded to practically crawl across the beam, inching my way along and taking forever, while Tristan tried to ask Sarah and Riley what the hell was going on. He said if he'd known it was going to take this long, *he* would have done it.

He also told me he always knew I was a loser, but not

until I was safely back on solid flooring with the fear ray in hand.

I handed it to Riley, who turned invisible—turning the fear ray invisible with him—and then we hurried back to the car, which was only a couple blocks away but felt like miles.

Now the fear ray's safely hidden in the trunk, just a few feet away from where I'm sitting in the backseat. A dangerous weapon the whole city hates me for losing, that Frank just used to terrify and control a whole bunch of people, and we've got it in the trunk.

I look out the windows, trying to see if Frank followed us and is coming to kill us or something. I don't see anything, but it's also kind of too dark out to tell.

Sarah's in the driver's seat. She adjusts it, moving it way forward in order to reach the pedals, since Riley's a lot taller than her. She turns the key in the ignition, and there's a collective feeling of relief, as if the car being on means we're safe.

I look at Riley, in the front seat. He's still got his hand over his shoulder. "Perkins. Are you—"

"I'm okay," he says. "It's not that bad."

But he cringes a little as he turns to tell me that—plus I still remember what it felt like when I took a raygun beam to the arm at the gala—and I know it's worse than he's making it out to be.

"What about everyone else?" I ask. "You guys okay?"

Tristan fidgets in the seat next to me. He doesn't say anything right away, then nods.

Sarah takes a deep breath. She catches my eyes in the

rear-view mirror. "Ready," she says, though her hands are shaking on the steering wheel. "What next?"

Riley turns to me again, the pain on his face turning into a scowl. "And don't you dare tell me to go home."

"I'm not." Though I hate that he got hurt again, and that it was because of me. If I hadn't blasted that remote, Frank wouldn't have shot him. But I didn't know she was going to do that, and either way, I can't afford to worry about it right now. "I mean, if you wanted to leave—"

"I *don't.*"

"—then I would get it. But I'm going to need your help. All of you. Because we've got only one more shot to get that antidote from Frank, and I… I can't do it alone."

"Well," Tristan says, "I know I'm not going anywhere. The mission's not done, and you're right"—he looks me over, clearly not liking what he sees—"you can't do it alone."

Sarah nods. "Me, too. I mean, *me too* as in I'm not going anywhere. Not *me too* as in you can't do it alone. Though, if I'm being realistic, you probably can't, so I'm not *not* saying that. I just would never actually say that, because it's kind of rude and I'm your friend. I mean—"

"Thanks, Sarah."

"You're welcome."

"And… thanks," I tell Tristan, not quite looking at him.

"No worries," he mumbles, not really looking at me, either.

"It's the four of us against Frank," Riley says.

Sarah grins. "So she'd better watch out."

I can't help grinning back at her, even though Frank

pretty much just kicked our asses. Tonight hasn't really gone as planned, since the plan was to, like, actually get the antidote. But we faced Frank again, and we're still here. All of us. And we have the fear ray.

And even though Riley got hurt, and even though we're all kind of shaken up after that fight, it doesn't feel like the end of the world. Not like I expected it to—not like it would have even just a week ago. And maybe it's because of all the adrenaline, or because I can't think about anything except getting Kat that antidote, but it feels good to have challenged Frank and still come back alive. It feels *really good*, like maybe we can do anything—or at least that we can do *this*—and like maybe it's all going to turn out okay.

"So," Tristan says, "what's the plan?"

"We'll do whatever you need us to," Riley says.

"And I've gotten a lot better at driving downtown," Sarah adds. "And my night vision has improved. So we can go pretty much anywhere. Though we might have to get gas first if it's very far." She purses her lips at Riley, as if he should have been prepared for that.

"We don't need to go far," I tell them, "though we will be downtown. We've got the fear ray, and Frank still needs it to get her revenge, so—"

My phone buzzes. It sounds extra loud in the car, especially since everyone seems to hold their breath, or maybe that's just me.

It's Kat's mom again. I answer it, barely able to get out the words, "Hello? Mrs. Wilson?"

I can hear her crying on the other end of the line.

"Damien, honey, it's Kat. She's—" She chokes on a sob, unable to go on for a second.

And in that second, I feel like the whole world gets sucked into a black hole. Like nothing else exists except this conversation. My body is numb, my breathing slow and shallow, afraid that if I breathe too hard, I'll miss something.

"She's fading fast," Mrs. Wilson finally goes on. "The doctors think that she— They don't think she has much longer. You should come. To say good-bye."

My heart stops beating. Time slows down. And I think if I can just stay in this moment forever, if I can just will time to completely stop, then this won't be happening. Or it will, but Kat will never actually be gone.

But my heart doesn't actually stop—it thuds in my chest, beating too fast, if anything. And time doesn't actually freeze, because then Mrs. Wilson says, "Damien, did you hear me?"

"Yes." I feel my mouth move, but it's like someone else is controlling it. I know I should say something else, but that's all that comes out. Just *Yes*.

"I'll talk to Tom. I'll make sure you get in to see her."

"Okay."

"Where are you?"

"Downtown," I tell her. "Not far."

There's relief in her voice when says, "*Good.*" Like even though I'm close, I might not make it.

"Tell Kat to hold on. Tell her I'll be there as soon as I can."

"I will," Mrs. Wilson says, then hangs up.

I stare at my phone, still in shock. There are tears in my eyes. They slide down my face, and more replace them, and even though I tell myself I'm not crying—that I *can't*, because I don't have time and because this can't really be happening—I know it's not true.

Everyone's staring at me. There's a heavy feeling in the car, the air full of tension. I don't know if they heard the whole conversation or just my side of it, but it must be pretty obvious that the news wasn't good.

Riley asks what they all must be wondering. "Is she—"

"Her mom says there's no time." I sniff and rub my face with my hands. "That I should get down there right now to say good-bye."

Tristan's mouth hangs open. He looks kind of sick, then quickly turns away, toward the window.

"Which hospital?" Sarah asks, checking her mirrors as she prepares to pull out of the parking space.

"Golden City General, but we're not going. Not yet."

"Don't be stupid," Tristan says.

Riley gives me a worried look. "X..."

"I can't say good-bye to her. Not when there's still a chance we could get the antidote."

"You might never see her again. Even if we do manage to get the antidote, it might be too late."

"I... I know." I grip my knees with my hands, my fingers digging in too hard. I know what he's saying, that missing out on the chance to see Kat one last time, to say good-bye to her, is something I'll regret for the rest of my life. But I could never forgive myself for giving up when there was still even a chance of saving her. And yeah, if I don't get to say good-bye, I'll spend the rest of my life hating myself. But not as much as I'll hate myself if I don't even try to stop this, if I don't take that risk. So there's no question. "We still have to find Frank."

"Dude," Tristan says.

"I know what I'm doing."

He gives me a really skeptical look. "*Do you?*"

"I'm totally on board," Sarah says. "But maybe you should text Kat your good-bye, just in case."

"We'll make it," I tell her, even though I'm not so sure. Even though, if I'm being completely honest, it feels kind of unlikely. But I push that thought down. I rub my hands over my eyes again and hand Tristan my phone. "Start recording."

He raises his eyebrows, like he still thinks I'm being crazy, but he pushes the button and motions for me to start talking.

"This message is for Frank. I have what you want, and you have what I want. Meet me in the park by the place where you first saw us—you know where I'm talking about. Be there at ten o'clock."

I nod at Tristan. He hits the button to stop recording, then hands me my phone.

"That's only ten minutes from now," he says. "It'll take us at least fifteen to get to the gallery from here."

"And there's no park by the gallery," Riley adds.

I shake my head. "We're not going to the gallery. Frank was there that night, at the train station, when we went on that mission. She said she was watching us."

Riley frowns. "But... what if she doesn't realize you

remember her saying that? Or what if she was watching us *before* that?"

"She'll figure it out."

"In ten minutes?"

I post the video to YouTube. Then I send a link to Sarah. "Send that to the email address you had for Frank."

"Okay, but it might not work. I mean, she might not check it. I don't think it's her real email."

"Doesn't matter. It's still a start." I cross post the link on Facebook, then send it to a couple of news sites—well, gossip sites—that like to talk about me, even though it makes me kind of sick. But I don't even know if Frank's going to see this message, and the more people posting it, the higher the chance it will get back to her.

I just have to hope she's watching.

CHAPTER 44

It's ten after ten, and Frank hasn't shown up yet, and every second that ticks by makes me feel like I'm going to explode. She has to show up. She *has* to. Maybe I overestimated how much she still wants the fear ray. Or maybe she figured this was a trap and decided not to bother. Except she's bested us twice now, and I really doubt the thought of us lying in wait for her is going to scare her off.

It occurs to me that even though it's a relatively small park that maybe I should have been more specific about where to go, but that might also have, like, tipped off the police or the League or something about where this meeting was taking place. I'm standing by the lamppost near the main entrance by the road, just far enough back that no random passersby should be able to see me, especially since I'm holding the fear ray. Riley's invisible, waiting by the bench across the clearing, on the other side of the trail. And Sarah and Tristan are hiding off in the trees to my left, in case—well, *when*—we need backup. But even though I know they're there, I still feel really alone as I wait, not knowing if Frank is even going to come, my thoughts about what happens if she doesn't all piling up.

Or if she does show up, but I don't get the antidote.

Or if I do, but it doesn't matter because it's too late. Because this has already taken longer than it was supposed to, and I don't know if there was ever any time for it in the first place. And Kat might be lying in her hospital bed right now, in pain, wondering why I didn't come to see her. This was the last chance for the person who loved her most in the world to tell her that, and I didn't show up. Assuming it's not already too late. Because maybe she already thought all that stuff, and I never came, and now she's...

I slide a hand across my face, even though I'm supposed to be watching for Frank. I can't afford to think that way. My throat feels thick, and my eyes are starting to water again, and part of me just wants to call it and say this isn't working. Frank's not coming, and I'm wasting the time I should be spending with Kat.

But I can't give up on this.

And Frank's going to be here. There's no way she's not.

And Kat knows that I love her, and that I'd never just ditch her. That if I'm not there right now, it's not because I don't care.

A stick breaks somewhere to my right. I jump and whirl toward it, gripping the fear ray. I don't see anything. But it's dark, the light from the lamppost not reaching that far.

"Frank?" My voice is hoarse. I hate how unsure I sound, like someone scared and alone, waiting for some crazed murderer to sneak up on him in the park, not at all in control of the situation. I clear my throat.

There's silence. I strain to hear something, anything.

And then Frank struts into the clearing like she owns the place, a raygun in her hand, trained right on me. She's got on the same purple-tinted safety goggles as before, and she taps them with one finger and nods at the fear ray, saying, "That thing won't work on me, but this raygun will work just fine on you."

"Yeah, well, those goggles don't make you immune to lightning." I keep the fear ray pointed at her anyway, though, as she walks across the clearing and faces me. "All I want is the antidote."

Frank laughs. She pulls a tiny bottle of green liquid out of her pocket and holds it up. "You mean *this*?" She makes like she's going to drop it on the paved trail.

I jump, startled, and lurch forward a little, holding out my hand like I have any chance of saving it from where I'm standing.

But she doesn't drop it. She gets this satisfied smirk on her face and tucks the bottle back into her pocket. "I could trade you, I suppose. Or I could just take what I want."

I clutch the fear ray, holding it close. "You're not *taking* anything. Just give me the antidote, and—"

She reaches for one of her holsters and pulls out another remote, like the one she had at the nightclub. The one that she had the fear ray hooked up to.

"Guys!" I shout. "*Now!*" It's not the most subtle signal—

Sarah wanted me to make the sound of an owl hooting, but we all agreed that would still be super obvious—but at least there's no way to misinterpret it.

I expect Sarah and Tristan to come rushing out of the bushes, as planned. But instead, nothing happens.

"Oh, are you calling for backup to deal with me?" Frank says. "How cute. But I already took them out. Did you really think I showed up late?"

My whole body goes tense and my blood suddenly runs cold. I glance over to the left, where Sarah and Tristan should be. Frank *took them out*, and whatever that means —that they're hurt, or something much worse—it's clear they're not coming.

My stomach twists. *My friends got hurt again, because of me.*

But she couldn't have gotten to Riley, because I would have seen. At least, I think I would. If he was standing where he was supposed to. If it wasn't too dark over there, so that Frank could have done something from the shadows.

All those thoughts race through my head as Frank holds up the remote. She pushes the button. There's a blast of purple light. Right as someone invisible tackles her, knocking her to the ground, the remote skidding out of her hand.

But it's too late.

The light flashes and the fear hits me in a heavy, dizzying wave. In an instant, the world is closing in on me, suffocating me, until I can hardly breathe. The ground feels unstable, and I'm going to fall—I *know* I'm going to fall. It's that feeling of standing on the edge of a cliff with no railing, of being thrown off a building, of the ground lurching out from under me.

I'm on my hands and knees, the fear ray pinned between me and the ground. I try to stay in one spot, so I won't fall. And even though I can see that the ground is still there, that there's nowhere to fall *from*, I can't make myself believe it. Because seeing the truth doesn't outweigh the feeling that something terrible is going to happen.

It already did happen. Frank *took out* my friends, and I can want that to mean they're just hurt, that they'll be okay somehow, but I know that it must have been something worse. Something they won't recover from.

And Kat. How did I ever think there would be time for this? How did I think I could save her? *I'm* the reason she got hurt—and now it must be too late. She might be dead. Sarah and Tristan might be dead.

All because they tried to help me.

Riley cries out, and I look up to see him turn visible as Frank pulls him up by his injured shoulder and presses her raygun to his temple.

He holds his head up, wincing from the pain, and I think the fear ray must not have gotten him. Maybe the light didn't affect him while he was invisible. But it doesn't matter, because either way he's her hostage.

"Perkins!" I reach a hand toward him, but other than that I don't move. I can't. I'm shaking all over. The ground is two seconds away from falling out from under me, and if I move, I'll die.

There's still some part of me, in the back of my mind, telling me that that's not true. That the ground is solid, that I can move. But I can't bring myself to believe it.

I'm going to fall. Even though I can fly, it's not going to matter, and I'm going to fall, and it's not going to be okay. And Kat's not going to make it, and Frank's already done something terrible to Sarah and Tristan, and now she has Riley, too, and I can guess how that's going to end. Someone's pointing a raygun at my best friend again—my best friend who already got shot once tonight—and she's going to kill him.

It's like the gala all over again, except this time I'm not going to be able to save anybody.

"Hand over the fear ray," Frank says, her voice cocky and sure, expecting me to do what she says.

And I'm terrified of what will happen if I don't, but I've already lost everything else. The fear ray's the only thing I have left, and despite my terror, I can't bring myself to give it up.

Frank scowls. "Do it or I kill him." She jabs the raygun harder into the side of Riley's head.

"X, don't give it to her!"

"Shut up!" Frank jams her thumb into the wound on Riley's shoulder, and he screams.

The same way he did at the gala, when his leg was broken. It's the same scream I haven't been able to get out of my head the past few months. Everything that happened that night is happening again. All the things I've been dreading are *happening again*, and it's almost like I knew they would, like this whole time I've just been waiting for everything to come crashing down.

There are tears in my eyes, and my mouth waters like I'm going to throw up, but nothing happens. And everything going wrong tonight—everything I've been dreading blowing up all at once—is the worst thing that could have happened. But it also feels kind of freeing, not having to dread it anymore.

"Give me the fear ray!" Frank shouts. She clenches her teeth and says, "I won't ask again."

Riley winces, either because he expects her to hurt him again or because he expects her to pull the trigger, but she doesn't.

A new wave of terror washes over me. Riley can't die. I can't *let him* die. But I can't give her the fear ray, either, because if I do, I'm pretty sure she'll kill him anyway. I'm afraid I'll lose my best friend, and that I won't get the antidote, if there's even still a chance of saving Kat. And those fears are worse than the other one, the one telling me to give it to her. Because as long as I have the fear ray and she doesn't, then I still have something to leverage.

"Let him go." My voice shakes, even though I sound like I mean it. "And give me the antidote. You can still help me save Kat."

Frank scoffs.

"And if you don't, then you're just as bad as that guy who kidnapped you."

Frank's lip curls at that and her eyes narrow. "You have five seconds before I shoot him."

"X," Riley says, his voice so quiet I'm not sure if he really says it or just mouths it. "*Run.*"

But I can't. Even if I wanted to, I can hardly move. Not that it matters, because either way, I'm not going anywhere. I ignore him, focusing on Frank. "And you have five seconds before I zap this thing." I hold out the fear ray. I make electricity run along my free hand.

Frank gasps. She tries to stop herself, but not before it's too late. "You won't," she says. "You're too afraid of what I'll do, of what will happen to you and your friend." She says it like a suggestion, like if she puts the thought in my mind, it'll take over me.

And she's right, I am afraid of what she'll do. But I've been afraid for so long, it hardly has any meaning anymore. And I'm *so tired of it*. Still, my heart races, and I feel like the world is spinning out of control. Like I'm going to fall. Like everything in my life is going to fall apart. And part of me just wants to curl up in a ball, clutching the ground for dear life, and wait for all of this to be over, no matter what the outcome. But if I do, everything really will fall apart.

I make myself look at Frank. "You're using fear on us the same way Bernard used it on you and your dad. And if you kill Riley, or if Kat dies because of you, then you're the same as him!"

"You don't know what you're talking about!" Frank screams. "I'm *nothing* like him! *Nothing!*"

My free hand shakes as more electricity gathers in it, sparking and crackling. I hold it closer to the fear ray, ready to destroy it.

Frank licks her lips. She's not shaking, like me, but there's still a slight tremor in her voice. "You're not going to do that. We'll both lose."

"Yeah? *Try me.*" My whole arm glows with electricity, and all the hairs on the back of my neck stand on end. "I've been so afraid of everything for months, ever since the gala! I've let down everybody I care about! I've let down the entire city. And I've let down myself. And I'm pretty sure you're going to kill Riley either way. It's probably too late for Kat. So don't tell me what I will or won't do, because I've got *nothing left to lose*! But you still do. So you either give me the antidote and let Riley go, or I end this now and obliterate this thing."

Frank sucks in a breath. "You wouldn't," she says, but she's already easing her grip on Riley, pulling the raygun away from his head.

Right then Sarah and Tristan come tearing through the bushes, shouting and rushing into the clearing. Tristan's got flames in his hands, and Sarah's got her raygun out. She fires it as soon as she sees Frank, hitting her hand and making her drop her weapon.

"Get away from him!" Sarah shouts, aiming again.

"The police are on their way!" Tristan says. He doesn't shoot flames at her, possibly because Riley's still too close, or possibly because there are a lot of trees and bushes around here and he might accidentally burn down the whole park, but he looks like he would if he had to.

Frank's outnumbered, and she's dropped her raygun. And there are sirens in the distance. She swears under her breath, then takes one last look at me and the fear ray before taking off.

As soon as Frank's gone, Sarah lowers her weapon and

runs over to hug Riley. "I'm sorry it took us so long—she surprised us and knocked us out before we could warn you guys."

"That was a crazy good shot," Riley says, impressed. "I didn't know you had that kind of aim."

"Yeah, I didn't either. I was just trying to fire a warning shot, but I guess I got lucky."

"You... *what*? You could have killed me!"

Sarah says something to that, but I don't hear. I feel hollow inside, and not just because I'm still under the effects of the fear ray. "She was going to give me the antidote."

"It didn't look like it," Tristan says. "Sorry," he adds.

"She was going to... I got through to her, and she was going to give me the antidote." My mind races, trying to figure out a way to make it still happen. I could make another video, set up another meeting. But there's no time, and even if there was, I know deep down it's over.

I saved Riley, but I didn't save Kat. Or maybe Sarah and Tristan saved Riley—maybe I didn't even do that much. Maybe I was wrong about getting through to Frank, and she was just going to take the fear ray and kill us both anyway. And now the police are almost here, and I'm going to miss my chance to see Kat. If there even still is a chance. But I can't not show up, I can't not even *try* to be there.

"I have to go." I scramble to my feet, even though the ground still feels like it's going to crumble beneath me, like maybe I'm already falling. I shut my eyes, steadying myself.

"I'll drive you," Riley says. He doesn't have to ask where I need to go.

"Your shoulder's still injured," Sarah says. "I can—"

Tristan cuts her off. "I'll do it. You guys wait here for the police."

Riley hesitates, but only for a split second, before tossing him his keys.

"Come on." Tristan jerks his head toward the road, in the direction of the car.

I'm so desperate to get out of here, and every second we're not on our way might mean we're too late. Or that the police will get here and not let us leave. But I have to do this first.

I hold the fear ray in both hands and zap the hell out of it, until it's black and charred. I toss it on the ground.

"That was like that when we got here," Sarah says, to no one in particular. "I don't know what happened."

The sirens are getting louder.

"Let's go," Tristan says.

He takes off for the car, and I take off after him. Every footstep feels unsteady, my stomach lurching with the anticipation of falling. But I keep moving, because I have to, and because I'm too numb to care anymore.

Kat's not going to make it. I *almost* saved her, but I didn't, and now the rest of my life will be without her.

"It's not your fault," Tristan says when we get to the car. He's fumbling with the keys, trying to find the one that unlocks the door.

"I know." My shoulders start to shake.

"Hey, um, don't... You did everything you could. You

know that, right?"

But I'm not crying—or at least I'm not *only* crying—I'm laughing, too. Because it's not fair. Because I *did* do everything I could, and it still didn't work out. And it really wasn't my fault. But it wasn't Tristan and Sarah's fault, either, because there was no way they could have known Frank was about to cave.

If she even was. I guess there's no real way of knowing.

And I know that by tomorrow, and probably every day after that, I will blame myself for this. Because it's not as easy as knowing I did everything I could or that it wasn't technically my fault. But right now, the whole situation seems completely ridiculous. And I wonder why I've felt so horrible the past few months, because it suddenly hits me that I *didn't* screw up at the gala. I saved everyone that night. Riley got hurt, but me and Amelia got to him in time. And even if he's messed up—even if we both are—it won't be forever. Well, maybe not for him. After all this, I'm not sure what will happen to me. And maybe that night didn't feel like a victory at the time, but it does now. All of a sudden, it does. I didn't fail. I didn't let anyone down. It was all just my perception—it was never what really happened.

Maybe victory is as much of a perception as failure is. Maybe neither one of them is ever real, and it's all just how we see them.

And maybe someday, probably a long, long time from now, I'll look back on tonight and see it completely differently. Maybe I'll even be able to forgive myself.

"Damn it," Tristan mutters. He's still fumbling with the

keys, his nerves making his hands too unsteady. They make a jangling noise as he accidentally drops them.

It's then that I glance down and notice that my door is unlocked already. Riley must have forgotten to lock it when he got out earlier. Which isn't like him, but we were all in a pretty big hurry, plus he'd been shot recently, so, like, maybe he wasn't at his best.

I open the car door.

And I realize Riley didn't forget to lock it.

Because sitting on the seat is a tiny bottle full of green liquid.

CHAPTER 45

Tristan drops me off at the entrance to the hospital, because it's faster than parking first, and I make it all the way to the floor Kat's on before anybody tries to stop me. Kat's dad stands there in the hallway, his arms folded across his chest, his eyes red and tired.

He just says one word to me. "*No.*"

So I guess her mom didn't get through to him. "I have to see her. You have to let me see her!" I have the little bottle of green liquid Frank left for me clutched in my fist, afraid to loosen my grip on it and accidentally let go. "I have the antidote!"

"I don't have to let you do anything! You're the reason she's in there, and you're the reason we"—there's a hitch in his voice as he chokes up—"have to watch our daughter go through that. To see her dying."

"You're not listening!"

"I don't care what Mary told you. You're not getting in there!"

"But I have the *antidote*!" I force my fingers to uncurl around the bottle enough to show him.

He blinks at it. There's a flicker of hope in his eyes, but then it disappears, and he gives me an exasperated look. "All you do is cause problems for everyone around you. Why should I believe you about anything? I can't believe I'm standing here, wasting time arguing with you, when Kat could be gone any second."

"I would *never* hurt her." Not on purpose. "I know things went wrong, and Kat got hurt protecting me, but... but I'd be dead if she hadn't."

He scowls, like that wouldn't be such a bad thing.

"And I'd do the same for her. I'd take her place if I could, but I can't, and she's *dying*, right now, and this can fix her! And even if you don't believe me, it's not like it can make things any worse!"

He hesitates, like he's thinking it over. I see the thoughts play out on his face—the hope that I'm right and the fear that I'm wrong.

Three hospital security guards come running toward us from the elevator. One of them tries to grab my shoulder, but I twist away from him. Electricity runs up my spine, and I have to keep myself from going all electric, so I don't damage the bottle and lose the antidote.

As if this decides something for him, Kat's dad gets this disgusted look on his face and says, "Stay away from our family." He nods at the guards. "Make sure he—"

But he doesn't get to finish that sentence, because I zap him—I actually *zap* Kat's dad—and run past him.

Someone screams—a nurse, or maybe the receptionist

—but I don't turn to look. The guards run after me, shouting for everyone to stay back and muttering things into their walkie-talkies as they chase me down the hall.

I guess they don't like that I used lightning in the hospital. Or that I used it *on* someone, even if I didn't actually hurt him, and even if he kind of had it coming.

I race around the corner, toward Kat's room. The security guards are right behind me. Adrenaline spikes through my veins, along with a surge of electricity. The fear ray hasn't completely worn off yet, making everything worse, and it's all I can do to keep my lightning from running across my skin and endangering the antidote.

Kat's mom is on her feet, peering into the hall, probably wondering what the hell is going on. She moves out of the way when she sees me come running.

There are two doctors in the room, looking bewildered. Kat's lying in the bed, her eyes closed, not moving. Her skin looks wrong—waxy and almost gray.

"Kat!"

"She can't hear you, honey," her mom says. There are tears in her eyes, and she doesn't say it's because Kat's asleep, but she doesn't say it's because it's too late, either. But the machine hooked up to Kat says she still has a heartbeat, and I know there's still time.

"Give this to her. You have to—" I shove the antidote into Mrs. Wilson's hands right as the security guards burst in behind me and electricity washes over me.

"Get him out of here!" one of the doctors says.

The security guards don't grab me—they can't—but they all point weapons at me.

"Come on," one of them says, trying to make his voice soothing, like nothing bad is actually happening here. "This isn't going to help anything. You don't want to hurt anybody."

Kat's dad pushes his way into the room. "Get him away from my daughter!"

I ignore all of them. I look only at Mrs. Wilson. "It's the antidote," I tell her. "We can still save Kat."

Her eyes widen. She glances down at the bottle in her hands, stunned. Then she turns to the doctor beside her and says, "Give this to her. *Now*."

The doctor glances over at me, skeptical, but the other one's already grabbing a syringe. He takes the antidote from the first doctor and injects Kat with it.

"Okay," one of the security guards says, "that's enough. Come quietly, or we'll be forced to take drastic measures."

I'm pretty sure he's bluffing about the drastic measures, but I nod anyway. Now that I've done what I came here to do, the fight goes out of me, and my electricity disappears, leaving me feeling exhausted and empty. But despite what he said, nobody moves to haul me out. Everyone in the room seems to be holding their breath, waiting for something to happen.

Kat's parents squeeze each other's hands, their faces pale.

I don't know how fast the antidote was supposed to work, or if it worked at all. It might have been too late.

We all stand there for what feels like forever.

Then Kat's dad, sounding completely broken, says, "Get him out of here."

One of the security guards takes a risk, now that I'm not covered in lightning anymore, and grabs my arm.

"*Tom*," Kat's mom says. She jerks his hand, trying to point at Kat, and gasps.

Kat's eyelids are twitching. Her face maybe doesn't look so ashen and gray anymore. And then, slowly, she opens her eyes.

"Kat?!" I tear away from the security guard and practically throw myself at the bed.

"Damien," she says, her voice quiet and hoarse, like she hasn't spoken in too long. The corners of her mouth turn up in a smile. "You made it."

X·X·X

The rest of the night is kind of a blur. Given the circumstances, both the hospital and Kat's dad decided not to kick me out, even though I used my lightning and resisted security. I stayed with Kat as long as I could, until the hospital insisted that I had to leave because I'm not related to her. I tried telling them I was actually her cousin and that we didn't like to tell people because it's so taboo and that's why none of us had mentioned it before, but they didn't believe me.

Actually, they said that only *immediate* family members were allowed to stay, anyway, so it didn't matter if I was her cousin or not, though the nurse who told me that was smirking the whole time, so I'm pretty sure she didn't believe me. Especially when Kat's dad rolled his eyes.

Tristan came in a while before that, after he managed

to find a parking space, and he was obviously relieved to find Kat still alive. He called her *Katie* about five billion times, and I was the only one who seemed to notice. Or to be angrily clenching my fists until my nails dug into my skin and left little marks. I mean, it wasn't that bad, because Tristan really came through for us, and I couldn't have saved Kat without him. Probably. So, like, if he wants to call her Katie...

Nope, still not cool with it. But I didn't say anything, which only goes to show how magnanimous I am.

Then Tristan had to leave, to go give Riley his car back so they could all go home. I stayed with Kat, even though I knew they were going to kick me out soon. When they finally did, Kat's dad offered me a ride home, though he said it like he was asking if I wanted him to eat a plate of steaming dog poop. Which kind of really made me want to take him up on it, even though it would be just as uncomfortable for both of us. But maybe just a tiny bit more uncomfortable for him, since he's the one who was wrong about me.

But in the end, I decided it wasn't worth it—not after the night I'd had—and I just called Gordon, even though it was late. I'd texted him after I knew Kat was okay, to tell him where I was. He must have heard about the video by then—he must have seen it—because instead of just texting back he called to ask if I was alright. He didn't ask for details, just if I was okay, and he sounded really relieved when I said that I was.

Now it's the next day, and I'm over at Riley's house. It's Friday, but he didn't go to school, for obvious reasons.

Though Zach apparently didn't, either, because he jumps up from the couch when I come in, says he has homework to do, and then runs off to his room.

Riley sighs. "I told him you weren't mad." He hesitates. "You're not mad, are you?"

"That he and Amelia broke up? Or that he wanted to have sex and she didn't?" I shake my head, because it doesn't matter. "Actually, I feel kind of bad for him. For both of them. How's your shoulder?"

Riley ended up at the hospital last night, too, though it was after I'd left. He makes a face. "Not great, but it'll heal. And at least they didn't have to screw anything back together this time. How's Kat?"

"Good. I mean, she's going to be okay. She texted me earlier to say she's hopefully coming home tomorrow and that she never realized just how much she hates Jell-O."

Riley smirks at that. Then he gets this serious look on his face. "And what about you, X? You got hit with that fear ray last night."

"It wore off *hours* ago. I'm fine."

"Yeah, but... are you? I mean, I didn't get hit with it, and I was still terrified that Frank was going to kill us. And I didn't know what she'd done to Sarah. I can't imagine what it was like for you."

"Well, Perkins, to be honest, it really sucked."

"No kidding."

"But..." I take a deep breath and lift up my shoulders in a sort of shrug, because I'm not sure how to put this. "It also kind of didn't. I mean, everything was horrible, and I thought the worst had happened to everybody, and that it was going to happen to you, and to Kat, and I..." I swallow. "I hated it, but I also felt kind of relieved. Because I didn't have to worry about it happening anymore. I know that's stupid, but—"

"No," Riley says, "it's not stupid. I get it."

"We were really badass at the gala. Both of us."

He smiles a little, but he shakes his head. "Maybe when I wasn't buried under a pile of rubble, or hiding in a hotel room, delirious with pain."

"No, even then. Because... Okay, look, Perkins, the thing is, you didn't give up."

"Uh, I'm pretty sure I begged you to leave me there."

"Yeah, but you didn't mean it."

He gives me a skeptical look.

"The *point* is that you wouldn't have even gotten hurt if you weren't so badass. We both saved a lot of people that night. We took risks, and some of them didn't pan out, but everything turned out okay. Well, mostly. And last night... we were pretty badass last night, too."

"I was *so* scared that Frank was going to kill you."

"Yeah, me, too. I mean, that she was going to kill *you*. And you'd already been shot, and it was kind of like the gala all over again, except this time it was worse somehow."

"But it didn't feel as bad as I remembered it."

"Me, neither. And I've never been more scared in my entire life, thanks to the fear ray, but it turned out alright. And I don't like that Kat was sick, or that you guys were in danger, or that Frank was maybe going to kill me, but for the first time in a long time I felt like I could actually handle it. Like whatever happened, I could trust myself to get out of it, instead of just screwing everything up. That's what I mean about us being badass last night, and at the gala. It's not just the times when we had to, like, stay alive in an actual fight, you know? Because these past few months, I haven't felt like I could trust myself. And maybe that's the thing I missed most about fieldwork, that feeling that *anything* could happen, but that I'd be ready for it."

Riley nods. "Things got bad last night. Really bad."

"Yeah."

"I thought if I got hurt again..." He lets out a deep breath. "I don't know what I thought. That that would be it for me, I guess. Like even thinking about doing fieldwork anymore was hard enough, but if I got hurt, I figured I really would be done with it. Whether it's what I really wanted or not."

"So did I. I thought if all that happened again, if it even came close to happening again, that I'd be done."

"But we're not done," Riley says.

"Nope. Not even close."

"So I guess you're right. We must be really badass, because after all that, I still want to do fieldwork."

"Of course you do, Perkins. Because it turns out that, even after a few months off, we're still really good at it."

He grins. "We're going to ace next year. Well..." His face falls. "We would have. If you were going to be there."

"Don't worry, I'm not dropping out." I never officially filled out any paperwork, so as far as the school's concerned, I'm just a delinquent loser who didn't show up for a week. And even if my grades don't end up perfect or anything, I should still be able to pass most of my classes."

"X." He tilts his head. "You're still being held back a year. And I'm still going to get stuck working with someone else."

"Maybe Mason is available."

He shudders. "Don't even joke about that."

"Relax. You're not going to get stuck with somebody else. I'm going to be there."

"You failed your flying test."

"I know."

"And you failed Advanced Heroism."

"Yes, I *know*. You don't have to look at me like that." Like he thinks I've completely lost it.

"Okay, but if you know all that, then you know you're not going to be in second year with me."

I roll my eyes at him. "If I said I'm going to be there, then I am."

"Really? So, you talked to the school?"

"No."

"Oh. Did they talk to you? Did your dad—"

"No, and no. I haven't done anything yet."

"So, you're just hoping, you mean."

"I have a plan."

He gives me a really skeptical look. "Well, Zach will be happy that you'll be in his classes next year. Maybe you guys can partner up. Once he knows you don't hate him."

"I just said I'm going to be there next year. What part of that didn't you understand?"

"Pretty much all of it."

"My plan will work." I think.

Riley conveniently glances away and doesn't say anything.

"It *will*." I look at my wrist, even though I'm not wearing a watch. "In fact, I should go soon. I have somewhere I need to be. But first..." I head over to Zach's room and knock on his door.

Silence. Almost like he's avoiding me, even though we both saw him go in here and it's not like he can pretend he's not home.

"Come on, Zach!" Riley shouts.

I'm just about to knock again when Zach opens the door. His shoulders are slumped, and he looks miserable.

"Hey," I tell him.

He stares at the floor, only acknowledging me with a slight movement of his head that might be a nod.

"We're cool, okay?"

He wraps his arms around himself, obviously not believing me. "So, Amelia didn't tell you?"

"She's Amelia. Of course she told me."

He winces. "How much?"

Like, all of it? But I can't tell him that. "Enough."

"So, you know that we... That I wanted..."

"Yeah."

He looks like he might be sick. "I couldn't say it. I know she wanted me to, and I thought I could, but as soon as she said she loved me again, I just... couldn't."

Me and Riley exchange a look. Then I tell Zach what I pretty much told Amelia. "At least you were honest. It could have been worse."

"No, it couldn't. It was the worst moment in my whole

life. And Amelia hates me now, and so do you—"

"I *don't*."

"I told you he's not mad," Riley says.

Zach scowls, not buying that. "You said we weren't ready. And I guess you were right."

"Yeah, I was, wasn't I?"

Riley glares at me.

"Er, what I mean is, I *was* right, but I could have been wrong."

"You didn't want Amelia to get hurt, but she did. She said she loved me, and I just said I liked her, and I saw the look on her face. And I thought maybe we could pretend that hadn't happened and just... *you know*." His face turns kind of red, and he doesn't look at either of us. "She was freaking out, and then I was freaking out, and now it's really over."

"I already told you, I didn't want *either* of you to get hurt. But I should have stayed out of it. And... I shouldn't have worried about Amelia getting hurt, because obviously she can take care of herself."

"Yeah," Zach says, his voice kind of a squeak. "She was really mean."

"She was just—"

"I know. She was upset, because I couldn't say I loved her, because I guess I don't. And she didn't want to sleep with me, either, so she was upset about that, too."

"That's not..." That's not completely true, but I stop myself from finishing that thought, because I figure maybe Amelia doesn't want me telling him. Plus, no matter what her reasoning, he'll still be hurt by it.

"Everything you didn't want to happen did," Zach says. "Because of me. And I know what you said before, about not wanting either of us to get hurt, and about me and you being like brothers. But that was before I... before me and Amelia... A lot has happened since then, so—"

"Zach. Nothing's changed." Well, besides his and Amelia's relationship totally exploding. "Between us, I mean. You're still my friend. You're still like a brother to me."

He looks up, surprised. "Really? But—"

"But nothing. We're cool, okay?"

Zach gives me a tentative nod. "Okay."

I pretend to look at my non-existent watch again, then grab my phone to check the time for reals. Crap. It's almost eleven. "And now I really have to go."

"Because of your so-called plan?" Riley asks.

"*Yes*. Just trust me, Perkins. I've got this." At least, I hope I do. I'm going to feel really stupid about all this if I don't.

"You need a ride? Since you're in such a hurry."

"Normally I would take you up on that, despite the skeptical attitude you're giving me, but I'm afraid you're out of luck, because I drove here."

Riley takes a step back. "You drove here?"

"You don't have to sound so shocked."

"Like, by yourself?"

"Yes. You know I have my license."

"Yeah, but... It's not that I think you can't drive."

"Uh-huh."

"It's just that you don't."

"I do. Sometimes. I drove Amelia home from Prom."

"Only because you had to. That was a special situation. It doesn't really count."

"Okay, but I *can* drive. And I have a car."

"That you don't use."

"Well, I'm using it now."

Riley doesn't look convinced. "You sure you don't want me to drive you? Because you can leave your car here, and we can—"

"I'm fine, Perkins. I'll be okay. And now I really do have to go."

"You're sure about this?"

"Yep. My plan will work."

"I meant your driving. But now that you mention it, I'm not so sure about this plan, either, whatever it is."

"It'll work." It has to. "And either way, you'll know in about half an hour. Just turn to Channel Five. Or hang out on YouTube."

Riley squints at me. "Just do *what*? X, what are you—"

I wave him off, indicating there's no time to explain—which is true, even if it's also convenient—and then hurry out of there before I miss my chance.

CHAPTER 46

The Golden City Annual Flying Competition is taking place in an arena downtown. A really big arena, it turns out. Kind of more like a stadium. And the stands are pretty much *full*. Like people actually care about this for some reason. I figured there'd be a few hundred people here, max. I wasn't counting on doing this in front of thousands. At least, not right away—not until they watched it on TV or on the internet.

I hesitate when I get down to the floor, where Ted and the other flying coaches are, because I could still turn around and go home.

But then I'd for sure have to repeat first year, and me and Riley wouldn't get to do fieldwork together. And all my friends would graduate a year ahead of me—well, except for Zach—and I'd be left behind. Plus, I told Riley I'd fix this, that I'd be there next year, and I meant it.

So. I guess I'm really doing this.

The stage area of the arena's set up with all sorts of

hoops and bars, both vertical and horizontal, and there's even a vault, except it's, like, ten feet off the ground. There's a girl about my age doing her routine right now, and I can't help watching as she leaps up to the vault, does a handstand, propels herself into the air, does about a million flips, and then flies backwards through one of the hoops. I also can't help thinking I'm totally screwed.

Ted's standing off to the side, watching the girl's routine. He has a really serious look on his face as he scribbles down notes. I wonder if she's one of the people he coaches, or if she's the competition.

I clear my throat. "Ted."

He jumps and then visibly cringes when he sees me. "What are you— You know what? It doesn't matter what you're doing here—you need to leave."

"You have to give me another chance to pass the flying test."

He laughs. "*No.*"

"But—"

The audience makes an *ooh* sound, and Ted glances over at the girl doing her routine. Whatever cool thing she just did, I guess he missed it, because he turns and scowls at me. "You had your chance. You can retake the test *next year.*"

"Next year's too late. Look, I know why you failed me, but you can give me any flying tasks you want, and I'll do them this time."

"You think the rules don't apply to you. You think you should get a *third* chance, because what? Because we're related?" He makes a disgusted face when he says that last part.

"I only *need* a third chance because we're related."

He scoffs. "I did my job, plain and simple."

Maybe, and it's possible that he would have failed me anyway, because he was right when he said I just learned the routine. But him hating my guts and wanting me to fail didn't exactly make him unbiased. "We both know you don't like me. I mean, I don't like you, either. This is your chance to humiliate me in front of all these people on live TV, and on about a billion videos on YouTube. You know flying's not my best skill or anything. I'm probably going to screw up and look stupid, and the whole world's going to be watching." If not right now, then later, over and over again. The thought actually makes me kind of sick, but I keep going. "I'll never live it down."

"You want to do it here? Now?" Ted glances over at the stage area, where the current competitor is just finishing up her routine.

"The competition's ending soon. I wouldn't be taking up anybody else's time slot or anything. I'm not competing. I just want the chance to prove to you that I can do this. You give me as many flying tasks as you want, and I'll do them. The competition will officially be over, and if the audience wants to leave, they can, but you know that they won't. They'll stay, and they'll watch me make an idiot out of myself."

Ted taps the end of his pencil on his clipboard, considering it. "I can't just take over this arena for my own private use."

"I bet you know someone who can, though. Call in a

favor."

He clenches his jaw and glances over at someone near the judges' stand.

"And," I add, "if at the end of all this I still haven't proven to you that I have a handle on my flying power, then I guess that's that. I'll fail for reals and have to retake the test next year."

"No," Ted says. "If you fail this, you drop out of Heroesworth. You don't belong there—I don't know why Gordon can't see it."

I hesitate. I know I was considering dropping out, but I changed my mind, plus it was different when it was my idea. Dropping out because douchebag Ted wants me to, because he doesn't think I should be there in the first place, kind of makes my skin crawl.

"I…"

"If you want to do this, that's the rule. You make a fool of yourself in front of all these people, so they see what side of your family you really take after. And when you fail, you drop out of Heroesworth, and you never look back."

"*If* I fail," I correct him.

He kind of chuckles at that. "We'll see. Do we have a deal?"

I nod. We don't shake hands on it, though there's an awkward moment where I think we're both considering it. He goes over to talk to somebody official about this, and I just stand there, wondering if maybe I've just made a huge mistake.

I haven't even practiced since I took the test. Other

than lifting off the ground a little at Mom's house, I haven't flown *at all*, and that wasn't exactly some acrobatic feat or anything. It barely counts. And now my whole future's depending on this. I'm going to have to actually fly in front of a live audience of thousands of strangers. Who theoretically aren't even sure that I can fly, since there are conspiracy sites dedicated to arguing about it, and they sure as hell don't know I'm afraid of heights. But they might find out in a few minutes. The whole world might know my worst secret.

This was a bad idea. And now I can't stop imagining some awful video of me falling or even just looking freaked out while I'm high up, and thinking about how many people will watch it, criticizing every frame. Discussing my every move and what each facial expression might mean. All the gossip sites will post clips and make outlandish assumptions. New message-board threads will pop up where people will argue about every aspect of it. And they won't just argue about whatever videos come from this, but about *me*. As if they know me, when really they don't.

The whole idea creeps me out. But there's no way in hell I'm walking away now. If I do, Ted will think he's better than me and that I wasn't up to his challenge. That I can't really do what I just said I was going to do. But I can—or, at least, I really hope I can—and after everything that happened last night with Frank and the fear ray and almost losing Kat, not to mention Riley and Sarah and even Tristan, I kind of don't care. Everyone's going to be scrutinizing the videos of me whether I fail or not, so…

whatever. And humiliating myself in the arena is better than humiliating myself by not even trying.

Ted comes back with a grim look on his face, but he's nodding, meaning he got permission for us to do this, I guess.

I wait through one more competitor, and then while they announce the winners. There's a huge round of applause from the audience when the winners come to collect their medals. Then, just as everyone starts to get up from their seats, the announcer says, "Wait a minute, folks. We have a special bonus performance from, uh, Damien Locke? *Oh*, I mean Son of Flash!"

Me and Ted both cringe when he calls me that. Ugh.

"Yes, we have Golden City's own Son of Flash here today to perform a short flying routine that's sure to be one for the history books!"

There's a lot of chatter coming from the audience. Some people leave, in a hurry to beat traffic, or maybe because they don't care. But most of the audience sits back down. A charge of excitement and anticipation spreads through the stands. A *lot* of phones come out.

Ted gives me a really self-satisfied look as we head into the stage area, like he already thinks he's won. He stays off to the side, but he gestures for me to go stand in the middle. A spotlight follows me, and there's some random, tentative clapping from the audience. The hoops hanging from the ceiling look *way* higher up now that I'm standing right beneath them and have to crane my neck back really far to even see them.

Someone from the audience shouts something that

sounds like an insult, only I can't actually make out the words. It could have been anything, like, *You don't belong here*, or, *Who are you kidding?* or, *You can't do this.*

I force myself to keep my head up and face the audience, even though I can't really see them, because of all the bright lights surrounding me. My hands are already shaking, but I hope nobody notices. I don't have a microphone, so I just wave to everyone as a way of introduction.

Ted doesn't ask me if I'm ready, he just starts barking orders. And he *does* have a microphone, so the whole arena can hear him, so if I screw up, they'll know. "Up to the ceiling and back as fast as you can."

I look up. All the way up to the ceiling, which is so far. My stomach twists and I wish I was anywhere else right now. Terror claws at me, telling me I can't do this. I can't even do the first task, and everyone is waiting for me to move, for me to screw up. But I remember how I felt last night, when the fear ray made me think the ground was going to fall out from under me. I could hardly move, because I thought I was going to fall and that I wouldn't be able to catch myself.

This can't be worse than that. Even with the audience tense and silent, wondering why I'm just standing here, flying up to that ceiling can't be worse than how I felt last night. And it can't be worse than falling off a building, which I've survived more than once.

Ted starts to say something, either repeating his directions or telling me I've already failed, but I take off and he doesn't finish.

I fly up to the ceiling, actively, like Amelia taught me. And even though my speed probably wouldn't be considered "fast" by anybody in this competition—or possibly anyone who's ever been able to fly—it's the fastest I've ever flown. I want to close my eyes, but I keep them open, focused on my goal. I don't look out at the audience, or down at Ted. *Especially* not down or at Ted. And then I touch the ceiling, and I think, *I can't wait until Amelia sees this*, and I smile and stupidly glance around me.

My stomach drops. I feel like I'm going to fall, like maybe I already am, and there's a moment before I get a hold of myself where I'm flailing and I know I must look terrified.

The whole world just saw me freak out.

I force the thought away, because if I stop to worry about it, I'll fail. So I pretend all the muttering running through the crowd has nothing to do with me. Besides, even if people are wondering what the hell just happened or what the hell is wrong with me, it's not like they know the truth. Not yet and not for sure.

My way down is slower than my way up, but I still push myself to go as fast as I can. When I get back to the ground, I'm so sure Ted's going to tell me that's it, that I've already lost, but instead he's ready with another command. I don't even have a chance to catch my breath before he says, "Up through that hoop, then down a little and spin through the air."

This time I don't hesitate. I fly up to the hoop he pointed at and move through it, though maybe not the most gracefully. I descend a little until I'm a safe distance from it and then...

And then I do just about the lamest air spin ever. I twist sideways, super awkwardly and clumsily at first. Then I pick up speed, and I'm pretty sure I'm still doing it wrong, but I'm doing *something*, and that has to count, right? I try to remember if I saw someone doing this in any of the videos me and Amelia watched, but they were mostly of just the routine for the test, and I have no idea what this is supposed to look like. But I'm spinning, and I'm in the air. And maybe the audience isn't awed by my performance, but I seriously can't believe I'm doing this.

"Around the bars!" Ted shouts.

I don't know what that means, either, and I think he's gesturing something, but I'm too dizzy to look down at him and see. I fly over to the bars, but really it's more of a *swoop*. I, Damien Locke, actually *swoop* over to the bars.

There are vertical and horizontal bars set up back and forth like an obstacle course, all at different heights. I have to go around a vertical one, then over a horizontal one, about five times. And I assume that, like with the hoops, I'm not supposed to touch them. Going around the first vertical one is easy, but the horizontal bar after it is a lot higher up. I've never seen this setup before, let alone practiced it, so I know my performance here isn't, like, the best or anything, but slowly and carefully I make my way through it.

Then Ted has me zigzag through the air. Then go through all the hoops, but in a different order than the flying test, so I can't just count on muscle memory. He has me race up to the top of the ceiling again—as if once wasn't enough—only this time he tells me not to come back down.

"Hold it!" he shouts.

I'm hovering inches from the ceiling, at the very top of the arena. With everyone watching. I'm glad Amelia made me practice being in the air for prolonged amounts of time, but my nerves are still getting to me. Because the longer Ted makes me stay here, the more I realize just how high up I am. Way higher than the gym at school. Not nearly as high as the top of the Golden City Banking and Finances building, but still. All I did there was fall—I didn't have to hover and do tricks while the whole world watched.

I can't help thinking about how the videos of all this are going to look. How Damien Locke, a.k.a. Son of Flash, put on this really awkward, pretty terrible performance, like what everybody needed after watching all the perfect competitors was to see someone who was the complete opposite of that. And I wonder how long Ted's going to make me hover here. Probably until I crack, or until the audience gets bored and starts to leave—whichever happens first.

I don't know how much time goes by with me hovering there. It's probably only a minute or two, but it feels like a lot longer with so much riding on this and the whole world watching. Then Ted's voice booms out across the stage area. "Backflip. Right there, where you are."

Yep, right here, where I am, hovering only a million feet above the ground. Just do a backflip, like it's no big deal. Like I've ever even thought about doing a backflip in my entire life, in the air or on land. I don't move. Can't I just hover here for another couple minutes and call it good? Staying in one place isn't so bad. I might actually be kind of good at it. They should have a separate category in the competition just for people who fly in place for extended periods of time. Actually, they could already have a category like that, for all I know. But I doubt it.

"We're waiting," Ted says. He keeps his tone professional and polite, like he's talking to one of his flying students and not to the nephew he hates.

A backflip. Just move backwards, so that I can't see bazillions of feet of nothingness between me and the floor, until I'm upside down. No problem. Nothing difficult or terrifying about that. It's not an insane thing to do when you're this high up, and especially not if you're also terrified of heights.

The camera's probably doing a closeup right now. The official camera broadcasting this to Channel Five. Not to mention all the people recording this with their phones, though at least they probably can't see my face or how scared I am. They'll have to see it later, on the official video, along with everybody else who wasn't here today.

I can't do a backflip. If Riley's watching right now, he probably knows this is it, that I'm not really going to make it to second year with him. I don't know if Kat's watching or not, because I made her promise she wouldn't if her dad was in the room, plus she might be asleep, since she's still recovering from the poison. But if she is watching, she probably knows I can't do this, either. That everything else

I did just now was pretty spectacular, relatively speaking, but that this is asking too much.

But then I think, *What do I have to lose?* And before I can answer that question—because the answer is *a lot of things*, like my dignity and possibly my breakfast—I go for it. I actually do a backwards flip in the air.

Well, okay, not *actually*. But I try to. I arch my back and try to make myself turn over backwards in midair. It does not go well. Because, like, as soon as I'm not in a normal, upright position, I kind of freak out. Panic spreads through my chest and makes me feel way too warm. There's a moment where all I can see is the ceiling, and I can't stand the idea of not being able to look down and see how far away the ground is. Not that I make a habit of looking at the ground from this high up, but knowing that I *can't* just look over and see it really freaks me out.

I twist and flail my arms in the air until I'm right-side up again. I cry out, and even without a microphone, I don't think it goes unnoticed. My face feels hot, and I'm breathing too hard, and my nerves are racing. And I don't fall or anything, even though I feel like I'm going to, but I know I can't stay up here anymore. I have to get down, *now*.

I land—too quickly, and I kind of stumble as I do it—and the arena is silent. I shut my eyes, but then I make myself open them again, even if it's just to stare at my shoes.

When Ted doesn't ask me to do anything else, the announcer says, "Son of Flash, everybody!"

There's some polite applause from the audience, but

nothing like the roar when they were clapping for the actual winners of the competition. Not that I expected it or anything, and not that I care, because right now I just need to get out of here.

Ted stops me when I try to walk past him. "Hold on," he says.

"Save it. The last thing I need right now is a lecture."

He scowls at that, and electricity burns a little beneath my skin. My face feels hot with shame, and I don't need Ted rubbing it in that I couldn't cut it. That now I have to drop out of Heroesworth. I don't know how I'm going to tell Riley, or Kat, or my dad.

"I wish I didn't have to do this," Ted says.

"Then don't." I start to walk away again.

He holds out a hand to stop me. "You did... okay." He says that so grudgingly, I'm not sure if it's supposed to be a compliment or an insult. "Much better than during your test."

"I failed. I couldn't do everything you asked. So—"

"You didn't fail."

"I what?"

"You didn't fail," he repeats, looking like it's physically painful for him to have to say that to me. "You were right, I may have been biased during your previous test, though I still stand by my decision—the same decision I think any good flying coach would have made. I didn't believe you had control over your flight. But after your performance here, even if it was a bit crude, it's clear to me that that's not the case. Even if your control is at the most elementary of levels."

"You mean, I passed?"

"Don't get me wrong, I'd really like to fail you. I still have strong misgivings about you going to Heroesworth. But any flying coach could watch the video of everything you did just now, and… I don't doubt that they would pass you."

"I couldn't do the backflip." I feel stupid as soon as I say that. I shouldn't be offering him reasons to fail me.

"It's an advanced move. I didn't expect you to be able to do it."

"So, wait, that's it? I really passed?!"

He looks away and nods. "I'll inform the school I made a mistake."

CHAPTER 47

I'm sitting on the couch later that afternoon, trying to watch TV, except that every time the commercials come on, there's one about how "Son of Flash" pulled some strange aerial stunt today at the Annual Golden City Flying Competition, with more to come on the five o'clock news. And there are closeups of my face, but only while I was freaking out and looking crazy.

Then the front door opens and Gordon comes in, even though it's a little early for him to be home from work, and I turn it off.

"I've been calling you all afternoon." He stares at me like he's never seen me before. "I saw the video."

Which is exactly why I didn't answer his calls, so he'd hopefully have time to get whatever crazy, misguided excitement he has over me following in his footsteps out of his system before talking to me about it. "It's not what you think," I tell him, even though I have no idea what he thinks. "I'm not... I don't care about flying. I just needed to pass the flying test, so I can move on to second year."

His smile falters, but then he nods, as if he knew that all along. "Second year. But how did you... You learned to fly without me."

I raise an eyebrow at him. "Uh, yeah, you refused to help, remember?"

He winces. "I know, but... I'm so proud of you. The whole time I was watching that video, I held my breath, unable to believe what I was seeing. Someone at work showed it to me. Everyone was talking about it."

"Great."

"And with your... issues... with heights, I just couldn't believe it. You really flew. Like a pro."

I slide farther down into the couch. "More like someone who could barely fly at all, you mean. But I passed. Ted changed his mind, and I made him call the school before I left." He said he was busy and would do it later, and I think he actually meant it, but I couldn't take the chance. I got out my phone and started making a video of us, explaining to the world that he was my uncle, Ted Tines, and that we were super close and I just had to thank him for this chance to fly in front of everyone. A video I would *never* have posted—and in fact I deleted it from my phone as soon as I got out of there—but Ted didn't know that, and he decided maybe he did have time to put in a quick call to Heroesworth after all.

"That's great." Gordon comes and sits down next to me. He starts to get out his phone. "Do you want me to call the school? To talk to them about your Advanced Heroism class? There might be something you can do to—"

"I already talked to them."

"You did?"

"After the whole flying thing"—I wave my hand around in a circle, like it wasn't a big deal—"I went down there and talked to somebody in the office. They said I can retake it over the summer and still start second year with everybody else."

"Oh." From the tone of his voice, you'd think that was a bad thing. He puts his phone away. "Summer school, huh?"

"Yeah, so if you had plans for some kind of family vacation, especially one that involves sleeping outdoors and hunting and gathering our own food, I'm *so* sorry to inform you that I'll have to stay home."

He laughs a little, but he still sounds upset about something. "I wasn't planning anything."

Good, because there's no way in hell I'm missing out on three whole months of hanging out with Kat. "Then why do you seem disappointed? I know I screwed up by failing the test in the first place, and for failing Advanced Heroism—"

"Damien, you didn't screw up."

"I kind of did, though. And I get that this isn't the ideal setup, but I figure one summer-school class is way better than dropping out or having to repeat first year." Even if Riley won't be there and I'll theoretically have to work with someone else. Though I don't think anyone else failed this class—just me, everyone's favorite half villain who can't cut it at hero school—so I'll probably spend all summer working on the alternative assignment. But at least in September I'll be back where I should be. "I'm not leaving Heroesworth, and I'm not falling behind. I thought you'd be proud of me."

"I am."

"You don't sound like it."

"Damien, I'm really proud of you for staying in school. For handling all of this. And for what you did today, with your flying. It was really something. You should be happy."

"But you shouldn't?"

"That's not what I meant. I just... I wish I could have helped you. You needed me to teach you how to fly, but I turned you down."

"You made the right call. It wouldn't have worked out."

"And obviously you didn't really *need* me to, since you figured it out on your own. You didn't need me for anything." His shoulders slump.

I squirm in my seat. I pick up the remote, like I might turn the TV back on. Why is he saying this to me? Doesn't he know it's super awkward? "Dad... that's not..."

"You're so grown up," he says. "You're independent. You can take care of your own problems. It's what every parent wants for their kids. I just wish I hadn't missed out on the part where you actually needed me."

He takes a deep breath, or maybe he just sniffled a little bit. Is he going to cry? I suddenly feel sick and like I really need to get out of here.

And I never thought I'd say this, but *thankfully* just then Amelia barges in. She flings open the front door, shouting, "Oh, my freaking God!" Then she drops her backpack on the floor and hurries over to me. "I saw the video. It's all *anyone* was talking about today!"

That's kind of terrible news, but I can't help grinning at her. "I still can't believe I did all that."

"Your backflip could use some real work, and that's *not* what the spinning part was supposed to look like, but *oh, my God*. You really did it!" She jumps up and down, squealing.

"Yep, and I passed the test this time."

"I told everyone how I was your flying coach and how you couldn't have done it without me."

The smile on my face disappears. I clench my teeth. "You *what*?"

"Don't worry, I only told Melissa and Hil. And Kim and Meghan—that's Meghan-with-an-*h*, not the annoying one with the shirt who thinks she's way cuter than she is—and Kylie and Chris and Mark and T.J. and Lucy."

"I've never even heard you talk about most of those people."

"And everyone in my Female Heroes of History class, because that was right after lunch, when everybody was watching it. And of course I showed it to Mrs. Cunningham, because she was really impressed with my superpower test, and I wanted to ask her if she thought I should start a portfolio for my work as a flying coach, because it's never too early to start a portfolio. I think I read that somewhere. And then during Costume Design, a bunch of people came up to ask me about it—the video, not my portfolio, because I haven't made it yet—and they wanted to know if it was true, if I'd really coached you, and I said—"

"You told the whole school!"

She shrugs. "They were going to see it anyway."

"But they didn't know I had to get flying lessons from my *little sister*. Who can't even fly."

"You taught him to fly?" Gordon asks, because he really was the one person on the planet who still didn't know, apparently.

"We spent weeks training," Amelia says. "We both worked really hard."

"Seriously? *I* worked really hard. You just stood there and told me what to do."

She sniffs in outrage. "Uh, that's what coaches *do*. Supervising is hard work. It's very mentally taxing, and I had to put together lesson plans and draw on my vast knowledge of flying videos. Plus, you weren't the best student ever or anything. Maybe if you'd been more cooperative I would have had an easier time, instead of having to wrangle you into doing your lessons."

"Wrangle me?! Amelia, you did not have to *wrangle* me. And I was the one risking my life and actually doing the flying."

"You weren't risking your life."

"It felt like I was!"

Gordon gets up from the couch, still looking really down. "I'll leave you two to figure this out."

"Dad, wait." I can't let him go like this.

"It's okay, Damien. I'm really proud of you. For all you've done." He starts to leave again.

"Dad, I…" I ball up my hands and slide them under my

legs. I can't believe I'm saying this, especially with Amelia here. "I *do* need you, okay? Maybe I didn't in the past, but that doesn't mean I don't now. You were really there for me, when Kat was sick. And when I didn't know what I was going to do about school. You could have told me what to do, but you didn't, because you trusted me to make my own decisions. And when you knew I was going to Kat's, but you didn't say anything, because… because you thought I didn't want you to know. Maybe you don't think those things are that important, but they are to me. My mom kicked me out, and my grandparents betrayed me, and everybody like that that I trusted let me down. I don't need you to solve my problems for me, but I do need you to be there. To not do what they did. Because I"—I swallow—"I couldn't take that."

"Damien, I'm not going anywhere."

I nod, even though I can't quite bring myself to believe him.

He comes around to face me. "I mean it. Look at me, okay?"

I don't. I can't. I stare down at a worn spot on the arm of the couch.

"I'm not going anywhere," Gordon says again. "No matter what happens. And neither are you."

"Until you change your mind."

Amelia sits down on the couch like nothing's going on. Like I'm not freaking out. "You can't leave," she says. "I already invested way too much time into you."

I *think* she's trying to cheer me up. She might actually be serious, though. I smile a little anyway.

"I'm not going to change my mind," Gordon says. "I know it's hard for you to trust that, and just saying it isn't enough. I can't prove it to you in a day, or even a year. Maybe, after what happened with your mother, I won't ever be able to prove it to you. But I promise you, Damien, I'm always going to be here for you."

I still don't look up from the couch, but I nod again in acknowledgment. Because even if I can't make myself believe him, I really, really want to.

CHAPTER 48

It's Saturday afternoon, and Kat's home from the hospital, and I'm lying on her bed with her in her room. She still seems really tired, but at least her skin doesn't look gray anymore, and she can stay awake for hours at a time now. The doctors said she should make a full recovery, but that after having to use her shapeshifting power that much for that long to fight off the poison, it's going to take a little while for her to get her energy back. Which might only mean taking it easy for a few days, or it might mean more like a week, but either way, I figure we've at least got the weekend together.

Kat squeezes my hand. "Look, a giraffe."

I squint up at the purple canopy over her bed. We're cloud watching, or pretending to, anyway, since we're indoors. "Where?"

"See?" She points at the fabric. "Right there. That piece of fuzz is its eye, and that swirl is part of its neck."

"So, wait, it's just a giraffe head? Not a whole giraffe?"

"The head and the neck. And that twirly bit—"

"It's a hair."

"Yeah, that piece of hair is one of its front legs. Your turn."

"Dog in the corner pocket." I point to the far end of the canopy. "It's a German Shepard. A police dog, and it's only one day away from retirement."

Kat laughs. "I *almost* see it, but its head isn't shaped right."

"No, it's just wearing a hat. One of those flat ones."

"Ahem." Kat's dad clears his throat from the open doorway—because apparently we can't be trusted, even though I spend plenty of time with Kat, alone, behind closed doors at her dorm—startling us both.

The bed squeaks as we sit up.

He looks us over, his eyes narrowing, like he thinks we might have been getting away with something somehow. "Can I get you anything?"

"Thanks," I tell him, "but Mrs. Wilson's already got my cookies-and-lemonade order covered. If I think of anything else, I'll let you know."

He glares at me, and I can practically see a vein popping on his forehead. "I was talking to *Kat*." He looks at her. "And I still think you'd recover better alone."

Which is his way of saying he wishes I wasn't here.

"*Dad*," Kat scolds.

"The doctors said—"

"The doctors said I shouldn't get stressed out, but *Damien's* not the one stressing me out."

Her dad stands there, quietly seething.

"Here we are!" Kat's mom says, sounding super cheerful, especially in contrast. "Fresh chocolate-chip cookies and homemade lemonade. Where do you want these?"

I gesture to the nightstand. "Just set them there for now. Did you bring four cups?"

"We only had three that matched the pitcher, but I can go grab another glass for you."

"Nah, that's okay. Me and Kat can share."

"Are you sure?"

"*Mary*," Kat's dad says. "Don't cater to him."

"It's no trouble." Then, lowering her voice, "Leave them be, Tom."

He looks away. "What do they need four cups for, anyway?"

As if answering his question, the doorbell rings downstairs.

"I'll get it," Kat's mom says, giving her husband a stern look before hurrying out the door.

He tilts his head at Kat. "You already have one visitor."

"Oh, my God," Kat says, "how many times do I have to tell you? Damien's *not* a visitor!"

"And now you have more? You're not supposed to have people over."

"No, I'm not supposed to tire myself out. Which I wouldn't be if you'd stop arguing with me about everything! And Damien's my *boyfriend*, and he saved my life. So stop trying to say he shouldn't be here."

"I wasn't—"

"And you know what? Since you offered, there *is*

something you can get me."

"Really?" He sounds relieved to have an actual task to do. That or he wasn't looking forward to finding a way to justify why he still doesn't want me here even after I saved her life and he didn't.

"I could really go for some hot-fudge waffles."

"Hot-fudge waffles?"

"From the waffle place at school. You know, the one we went to when you guys came up for brunch?"

"That's at Vilmore," he says, stunned. "That's a long drive."

"But it would *really* make me feel better."

"They'd be cold before I got back."

"That's okay—they're good cold, too. Can you make sure we have some ice cream to go with them? And while you're at Vilmore, can you stop by my dorm and get First Mate Suckers?"

First Mate Suckers is the stuffed pirate octopus I gave Kat for her birthday, back in November.

"I don't know... It's awfully far."

Yeah, almost like she wants him to leave her alone for a couple hours.

"Please?" Kat says. "You said you wanted to do something for me."

Riley and Sarah appear in the doorway. Sarah's beaming at Kat's room, but Riley looks super nervous, especially when he notices Kat's dad.

"We'll see about the waffles," Kat's dad says. Then he gives Riley and Sarah a really serious look and tells them, "Do *not* wear her out," before finally leaving.

As soon as he's gone, I feel Kat relax beside me.

Riley's standing with his arms at his sides, like he's afraid to touch anything. "Are you sure it's okay for us to be here? Because it didn't really sound like—"

"It's fine, Perkins. And you can shut the door." I figure since Kat's not alone with me, the open-door rule doesn't apply. Though for all I know it'll just make her dad suspicious that we're having a foursome.

Riley closes the door, then stands there in the middle of the room, like he's still not sure if he's allowed to be here.

Sarah, on the other hand, can't stop smiling. "It's so great to finally come over. Seeing each other's rooms is an important step in building a friendship."

"Right," Kat says, not sounding nearly as enthusiastic. "It doesn't really feel like my room anymore, though. Not after being at school for so long. It's going to be weird being back here this summer."

"You can always come over to experience the familiar comforts of my room," I tell her. Then, to Riley, I say, "Did you bring it?"

He nods.

Sarah grabs her backpack and pulls out two DVDs. One of them is *Attack of the Killer Robot Zombie Slaves*, which me and Kat have been trying to watch together for weeks, if not months. We were going to stream it, but we took so long getting around to watching it that it's no longer available. So yesterday I was going to rent it, but I found a used copy in a bargain bin for three dollars instead. And I'm sure that it being in the bargain bin, or the fact that there were about five copies of it in there, had nothing whatsoever to do with its quality. The other people who got rid of it must not have been true connoisseurs of low-budget horror films and didn't understand what they were passing up.

But anyway, I bought it super cheap yesterday so I could watch it with Kat, then forgot to bring it with me when I came over here. And there was no way I was going to leave and give Kat's dad the chance to not let me back in. So since Riley and Sarah were coming over anyway, I asked them to pick it up. I did *not* ask them to pick up the other DVD they brought, which is the romantic comedy Amelia made us watch with her.

"Uh, I didn't ask for that," I tell them.

"Amelia forced it on us," Riley says. "She wouldn't let us leave without it."

"Yeah," Sarah adds. "She said it would make Kat feel better. We had to swear on our lives we wouldn't lose it, though."

Riley points at me. "So that means don't lose it, X."

I put a hand to my chest. "What? Me? We're at Kat's house—clearly she's the one responsible for it. And what, you think Amelia's going to come after you if something happens to it?"

"Yes, I do. She was really serious." He looks around and lets his shoulders relax a little. "So, you wanted to show us something?"

I gesture to the cookies and lemonade.

"You wanted to show us some snacks?"

"*Homemade* snacks that I happen to know are delicious."

He scrunches up his forehead. "That's why you invited us over?"

"No, I invited you over because I knew it would piss off Kat's dad."

"You *what*?!" Riley's nostrils flare and his eyes go wide. He glances behind him at the door, like Kat's dad's going to bust in and tell him off for being here.

"And because I knew he wouldn't be able to complain about the door being closed if you guys were here." Or at least I was betting on it.

"You had us come over here to annoy her dad?!" His eyes flick over to Kat's. "I didn't— We wouldn't have come over if—"

"You're my friends," Kat says. "You're allowed to be here."

Sarah smiles at that. "This is great."

Riley still looks worried. "I can't believe you, X. You invited us over here just for that."

"*And* for cookies and lemonade," I tell him. "Geez, Perkins. It's like you don't hear anything I say."

"And to watch your flying video," Kat says.

"*What?*" I force a laugh. "Kat, you're hilarious. We're so not watching that. Everyone's already seen it. Nobody wants to watch it again." Especially not me.

"Yes, we do," Riley says. "We can watch it while we have our cookies and lemonade you're so enthusiastic about."

Sarah nods. "I thought that's why we came over, for the viewing party."

"Viewing party?!" This is getting out of hand.

"Besides," Kat says, "we haven't all watched it together. Or with you." She gestures for Riley and Sarah to sit on the floor while she grabs her laptop and sets it up at the end of the bed where we can all see.

I pretend to laugh again, though it sounds even more forced this time. "It's going to be the same video everyone watched yesterday. You don't need to watch it with me—that's ridiculous. And you know who has a car and a license and who could totally go get you those waffles you wanted?"

"No way, Damien. You're staying."

"It's not that bad, X," Riley says. "I was really amazed. I mean, you were actually *flying*."

"Whatever. It wasn't that great." I fold my arms across my chest.

Sarah scoots closer to Riley as they both try to get comfortable on the floor. "You showed remarkable skills for someone who's afraid of heights and hates flying."

"And you really passed the flying test?" Riley asks.

"Yep, and I'm retaking Advanced Heroism this summer. I'm not going to miss anything, and we can still work together."

He exhales, looking relieved.

Sarah reaches up and grabs a cookie from the nightstand. "Okay, I'm ready. Let's watch it."

Kat's already got the video—the official one from Channel Five that has all the closeups—ready to go. She leans forward to hit the space bar.

"*Wait.*"

She sighs. "Damien, we're watching it."

"But before we watch anything, we should probably, um, make some plans. Just, like, before we get distracted."

Kat squints at me. "Plans? For what?"

"Uh, fieldwork plans! For this summer. Right, Sarah?" I look over at her, hoping she'll back me up on this. "You're back from hiatus, and me and Riley are ready to get back to going on missions again."

"Summer vacation isn't for a few more weeks," Sarah says, even though I thought she would have jumped at the chance to make fieldwork plans. She must really want to watch this stupid video. "And besides, you already said you were spending all your time with Kat."

"Well, yeah, but maybe not *all* my time—"

"You said every second. You said you were going to set your phone to send out an automatic *Do Not Disturb* text anytime anyone tried to contact you this summer, because the two of you were going to be—"

"Sarah, Sarah, Sarah. Obviously that was before we decided to do fieldwork again."

"It was this morning. It was only three hours ago. Do you want to see the email?"

"Ha ha ha, no. That won't be necessary. And what I meant was that, um, that Kat's joining our group, too!"

"Wait, I'm *what*?" Kat says.

"Really?!" Sarah says at the same time, sounding way more excited about it than Kat.

"Uh, yeah, so we should probably spend whatever time we have before we get kicked out of here going over the ground rules. Or maybe inventing some. Kat, tell Sarah your blood type."

"I don't know my blood type. And nice try, Damien, but we're watching the video."

"But you are joining the group, right?" Sarah asks.

"Yeah," I tell Kat. "You don't want your fieldwork skills to get rusty. Not everyone can come back from more than three months off and still be as good at it as we are."

Riley grins at that, but then he says, "We could still probably use some practice."

"You failed your fieldwork class," Kat tells me.

"Gee, thanks. Way to rub it in."

"So maybe *you're* the one who needs me to help you with your fieldwork, not the other way around."

"I failed on a technicality. I also saved your life. I mean, we all did."

"I saved yours, too," Kat points out.

"Okay, okay, you're hired already. You can stop begging to join our group now."

She rolls her eyes at me. "I didn't say I'd join."

"You didn't have to. That muscle in your cheek twitched that means you're excited about something, and if you really didn't want to do this, you would have said so by now."

"Shut up. It did not."

"It did. Face it, Kat, I know you too well."

"And I know *you* too well. You're not getting out of watching that video."

"If I watch it, will you join our group?"

"If you're good, then… then I'll think about it." But she's smiling as she says it, and her cheek twitches again, and I know what her answer will be.

SPECIAL THANKS TO THE FOLLOWING CITIZENS OF GOLDEN CITY

Name and Alignment	Power
Badass, V	Being a badass
Tasha "Explaitten" Turner, H	Explaining things
Jynx, V	Pyrokineses
Captain Chaos, H	Makes people's voices high and squeaky
Wynter, V	Can control cutlery with his mind
Accelerator Ray, H	Kinetic manipulation
Biblio, H	Can pull artifacts from books to use them. Unfortunately, for every minute the item is held in this world, Biblio must interact and be in the world he pulled the item from, so since usually the most exciting and best items come from adventure or fantasy novels, those scenes are the most dangerous
Kravix, V	Able to make multiple copies of himself and all gear he is wearing

Terra Firma, H	Heavily armed dragon-cyborg
Ion, H	Controls and manipulates electrons
Lamp, H	Glows
The Fangirl, H	No superpowers, just gadgets
The Shadow, V	Information manipulation
The Zapper, V	Can kill flies with the blink of one eye
Mighty Ebonstar, H	Badassery
JW, H	No power
Novastorm, V	Pyrotelekinesis
Badonkadonk, H	Levels her foes with a single clap
Pix, H	Superspeed
Alpha Dominus, V	Super strength
Astra, H	Healing light
The Clever One, H	The ability to put something clever here
SilensVigilo, H	Flight

Bookdragon, H	Hoarding ALL the books and protecting them
The Deaf Lemon, V	Can communicate with citrus fruit
Bibliotheca, H	Literary teleportation
Daimadoshi, H	Absorbs powers
The Professor, V	Can teach someone a superpower with the aid of a person with said superpower
Big Rig, H	Telekinesis
Oceanus, H	Able to manipulate and transform into water and water-like substances
Misspook, H	Time traveling trickster ghost. Low-level royalty, serving her Queen in the intelligence game, before passing away, with a skewed sense of right and wrong (perhaps an accidental villain in doing what she believes is right). Favorite course of action is to travel back in time and create a sort of butterfly effect to produce what she wants, when she wants
Arcade, V	The ability to play video games
Ponzi, V	Luck manipulation

Nature Woman, H	Able to communicate with, and control the actions of, animals
Sight, V	Laser vision
Xndria, V	Empathic manipulation
Techmage, V	Technology manipulation
Mr. Notorious, V	Evil genius
Mizumi, V	Controls water in all its states
Antifreeze, V	Complete immunity to brain freeze
Colby Holland, H	Creates an impenetrable shield around himself and one or two other people
Seraph, H	Pyrokinesis
Destructor, V	Super strength
Nagginator, V	Finely honed talent for ruining everyone's good time of laying around, video-gaming and TV-watching 24 hours a day by butting in with ridiculous exclamations like, "We need to get something done around here!" or "Have you finished your homework / piano practice / chores?!" or "My living room carpet is not your personal garbage /

laundry basket!!"

Zephyr, H	Aerokinesis
Sugar Devil, V	Convincing everyone to eat more sweets!
Wacky Woodsman, V	Tree control
The Naked Mole Rat™, V	Invisibility
Captain Megaphone, H	Sonic boom ray
Kaz, H	Power nullifier
Crisco, V	Capable of deep frying anything with his mind
Secrets, V	Knowing the secrets of those around them
Pyro Hazards, V	Pyrokinesis
Obscure Tobin, V	Everyone recognizes her but can't remember from where. Even if they've never met her in the first place. It comes in handy when a server doesn't pay close attention to their customer and hands her food that was paid for. Since she seems so familiar
Gygax the Destroyer, V	Growing to a giant size and

	trampling things
The Leviathen Prince, V	Being super edgy all the time
irisheyz_5@yahoo.com, V	Stops time
Nayorth, H	Technopathy
Kesal Exuo, V	Technopath
Ghost Girl, H	Intangibility
Sumasuun, V	Can sleep anywhere
SuperGertjan, H	Super zijn
Mistress of Time, H	Stops time by snapping her fingers
Scantrontb, V	Teleportation
Xenocide, V	Electricity manipulation
Syncarida, V	Ability to make random objects look like spiders
The Whisper, V	The ability to control the density of matter
Moonsget, H	Shapeshifts into a wolf
Scapamouche, V	Phasing

The Stenographer, V	Supersonic hearing. Stenographs compromising conversations for blackmail
Dark Thea, H	Turning into any animal
Hot Dog Bangarang, H	Teleportation
Force, H	Gravity manipulation
Circe, V	Charmspeak
Silver Tongue, H	Omnilingual
SwordFire, H	Moves at high speed
Dark Banshee, H	Sonic scream

ABOUT THE AUTHOR

CHELSEA M. CAMPBELL grew up in the Pacific Northwest, where it rains a lot. And then rains some more. She finished her first novel when she was twelve, sent it out, and promptly got rejected. Since then, she's earned a degree in Latin and Ancient Greek, become an obsessive knitter and fiber artist, and started a collection of glass grapes.

Besides writing, studying ancient languages, and collecting useless objects, Chelsea is a pop-culture fangirl at heart and can often be found rewatching episodes of *Buffy the Vampire Slayer*, *Parks and Recreation*, or dying a lot in *Dark Souls*. You can visit her online and sign up for her newsletter to get a free copy of *Damien Locke's Guide to Golden City* at www.chelseamcampbell.com.

3 1125 01044 2455

Made in the USA
Middletown, DE
19 November 2017